The Pact

Book II

Battle Hymn of the Republic

Robert Patrick Lewis

ISBN-13: 978-0-9859404-4-7
ISBN-10: 0-9859404-4-1

For Natalia,

My friends, family, Brothers and Horsemen have saved my life, kept me alive and convinced me to keep going.

It was you who taught me to embrace, love and cherish my life with those around me.

Without the second, there is no point to the first.

Thank you, I love you.

Table of Contents

Acknowledgements

Editing: Page by Page Editing

Cover Design: Bryan Dolch

Beta Readers: John Donoho

Ryan Mercer

Frances Marmon

Bob Lewis

Brian Schimian

Shobin Paulson

Introduction

Truth can be stranger than fiction.

While at some points in the following book things may seem hard to believe, I assure you that every part is based in truth and reality.

The story that unfolds in *The Pact Book I* was based on conversations with my former ODA and news stories in 2013 covering events happening around the world.

Since 2016, we have found that much of the premise from Book I was accurate: our enemies around the world becoming close allies, with corrupt politicians in our own nation attempting to weaken our military, disarm our populace and selling state secrets to our enemies.

Beyond an invasion of the United States of America by her adversaries (Russia, China, Iran, Hezbollah) there are other parts of this book that may delve into aspects of the world which you find incredible and unbelievable.

As this is a work of fiction, there are surely some literary liberties that I took to blend certain parts into the story and this world that I am creating. I will be adding content to ThePactBook.com in order to share with you some of the nuggets of truth which formed the basis for this book. If you come across something that you feel is too far a stretch of reality, please check out the "Truth is Stranger" page on ThePactBook.com website.

Whether it be open-source intelligence regarding the enemies who play a role in this book, quantum physics, futuristic weaponry or declassified CIA memos reporting new ways to gain military

advantages, I hope that you are inclined to take that journey with me and learn about some of the things that created the ideas which formed this story.

To those of you who reached out to me since *The Pact Book I* was published, I thank you for your patience. There have been some twists and turns since 2014 regarding this trilogy, and I'm grateful to those of you who prodded me to push forward with Book II.

Writing is my passion, and as some of you may know from my interviews, I have over two dozen other books already outlined. There are two distinct series and many one-offs whose characters and storylines are fighting to move from my head to fully-formed books, and screenwriters have already reached out to me with their attempts to bring these stories to the screen.

And if you haven't gathered yet, there is a common thread starting with my first book and moving through the storyline, which will continue beyond Book III.

As some of you may also know, my former publisher and I split ways before this book was published. I spent six months after our split querying nearly every agent representing military & espionage authors and many literary fiction agents. Only one asked to see this manuscript.

It seems literary agents don't think people want to read about combat stories from an actual combat veteran without a ghostwriter. Who would have thought?

So I must ask for your help.

While I love writing more than anything and plan to be doing so for the rest of my life, it does not seem that agents, publishers or book buyers see this genre as commercially feasible (with some even responding that people don't want to read about or buy books on these topics anymore).

When I left my former publisher, they removed *The Pact* from Amazon and I lost several hundred reviews (and as some of you have seen, the book went up to $1500 per copy until I corrected the problem). If you have read the first book and have the time, please leave a review on Amazon (now listed under *The Pact Book I (The Pact Trilogy)*).

I cannot overstate how much it would help.

Potential readers trust what you have to say about a book much more than what I say about it on the back cover, so it would be a great help and a favor to me if you could at the very least leave a rating and/or a short written review.

And if you really enjoy this book, please share it with your friends, share it on social media, leave a review on Goodreads. Your enjoyment of and comments about these books are the fire that burns my desire to continue writing, and as I'm building this momentum without an agent or publisher, I need your help to keep it going.

If you do not enjoy this book, please reach out via my social media profiles and tell me why.

I've already begun writing *The Pact Book III* and part of *The Patriot* series. Those of you who have reached out know that I am very attentive to messages via Twitter and Facebook, and appreciate both compliments and constructive criticism.

Thank you for coming along with me on this wild ride.

Prologue

"SUKEN SINS *(sons of bitches)!!!"* The Russian Major screamed and slammed his meaty cannonball-sized fists down on the expensive boardroom table so hard a crack erupted clear across to the other side.

His comrades shot furtive glances to each other around the multi-million-dollar conference room that overlooked Sunset Boulevard and trembled slightly.

They knew how Dmitri got when he was angry. And none of them wanted to be the object of the famed rage of this Spetsnaz war hero, the one known as "Creeping Death" from the stories of his "techniques."

One story told that he once flayed an Ossetian war prisoner alive during interrogation because his blood spilled on Dmitri's boots while beating a confession out of him. Forcing a team of prisoners to gang rape the man's wife and daughter in front of him was just Dmitri's way of getting warmed up.

Then there were the stories of Afghan children used as target practice, and of course the scores of women whose screams permeated the dead of night from his penthouse apartment in the recently commandeered Chateau Marmont nestled above the Hollywood Hills.

Once a playground for the rich and famous, the thousand dollar a night luxury hotel was now a barracks for Russian officers. They had declared open season on the California girls they had heard so much about while growing up in the cold and lonely Russian nights.

Everyone in the room had dreamt at some point of bedding a beautiful Hollywood starlet...but as with everything else in his life Dmitri chose to accomplish that dream by sheer force and infliction of massive amounts of pain if he didn't get his way.

The Lieutenant at the front of the room's knees began to shake as Dmitri moved his view from the table back to him, squared his gaze like that of a wolf visually locking down his prey and adjusted the full force of his venomous hatred square into the center of the Lieutenant's chest.

"What do you mean we can't get any planes in without a runway, and can't get equipment to fix it in without planes?" Dmitri snarled at the poor Lieutenant.

"It is our duty to push and secure everything from here to the East coast, while the Chinese move from the South up to Canada."

The Russian Major, looking to the casual observer to be more of a bear than a man, stood upright and pulled the bottom of his uniform blouse tight as he craned and cracked his thick, muscular neck first on the left side, then the right. The entire room jumped with each loud and resounding "crack" of the vertebrae.

He began to walk slowly to the front of the room, towards the trembling Lieutenant and his map complete with troop levels and movements across North America.

"Do you know what it means, comrade, if the Chinese take Denver before we do?" Dmitri didn't shift his burning stare by even a millimeter as he walked.

"It means, comrade, that I will have failed my mission. Do I look like the type of person who fails his missions to you, Lieutenant? "

Standing face-to-face at the front of the room, so close the Lieutenant could smell the morning cigarette still lingering in Dmitri's breath, the Lieutenant's hands started to shake so violently he dropped his telescopic pointer.

He was locked so deeply in Dmitri's hateful gaze that he seemed to be entranced in a snake charmer's spell, waiting for a snap of the fingers or a secret word to wake. But there were no fingers snapping and no waking from the nightmare in front of him.

"WELL???" Dmitri screamed with a rage that would frighten Satan himself, so close the spittle from his mouth covered the Lieutenant's face and the sheer force of Dmitri's hot and angry breath moved his frightfully rigid body back a step.

He put his hands squarely on the Lieutenant's shoulders, and the room of comrades couldn't tell if he was about to console or crush the soul of his prey.

The Lieutenant began to move his lips but found even sound too frightened to attempt an escape.

"I cannot hear you," Dmitri bellowed into the young officer's face as the man's bottom lip began to quiver, shoulders hunched like a mouse who knows he is about to be devoured and has no hope left for escape.

"Nyet," the Lieutenant managed to eek out as Dmitri stared intently into his eyes, burning a hole so deeply into his psyche that the man would never be able to walk fully upright with self-pride again, no matter what level of accolades or heraldry he accomplished.

"Precisely," Dmitri responded and reduced the volume of his voice but not the veracity of his message nor intensity of his hate and stare.

"There is a reason that I am here, and a reason that you are here comrades."

Dmitri spoke to the entire room of Russian military officers now.

He pulled his face back from its attack on the Lieutenant, motioned for the young officer to pick up his telescopic pointer from the floor and began to walk the room from corner to corner, behind the seated officers.

Had they been grizzled war veterans like Dmitri, they would have noticed him walking the same path as a combatant taking down the room in Close Quarters Battle (CQB), squaring each corner and sticking rigidly to his path, moving quickly but calculated and carefully with each step towards his objective, never deviating, never looking away from his target, never considering the possibility of anything but mission success.

"I know the stories about me comrades. I know what you say in the light of day behind my back but would be terrified to say in the black of night or close enough for me to hear. You call me a monster for the things I've done, and the things that I can do and the things that I will do."

He brought his icy cold stare back to the Lieutenant, who was still standing frozen at the front of the room.

"And I am a monster. This much is true," Dmitri said with a chuckle, a sign of pride that he could very well be one of the most feared weapons in the arsenal of Mother Russia.

"But what we need here, now, are monsters."

Dmitri looked around the room as he walked, at each of the officers placed in command of various parts of the invasion and plans to take over the United States of America.

"You logisticians and strategists have done a superb job of bringing us to this point, but now it is time to let the monsters loose."

Back at the front of the room, having made a complete circumambulation, Dmitri looked back upon his comrades, the seated Russian military officers, and stated his purpose for being there.

"My original mission was to advise you, based on my experience, to accomplish your mission. But above all, my instructions were to accomplish the mission at all costs, to take the United States from West coast to East. If you were unable to accomplish the mission your way, my role is to change from advisory to command."

He let the last sentence linger in the air along with the scent of cigarettes and coffee for just a moment.

"From what this man has just told us, you are currently unable to accomplish your mission."

Looking around the room for objections and finding none, Dmitri changed the game.

"So now comrades, it is time for the monsters to show you how war is meant to be waged."

CHAPTER 1

MOVEMENT TO CONTACT

The familiar stench of acrid black smoke was the first sensation to let me know we had arrived.

Our fighting had been the small-unit tactic, house-to-house urban warfare in Iraq and Afghanistan, and what I had seen in documentaries and read in books about large-scale world wars hadn't prepared me for what we encountered.

When our Black Hawk helicopter suddenly changed course and began a rapid descent to the landing pad, I saw the Houston ship channel on my starboard side. This was the largest port in the largest city in Texas, so it was a position of immense strategic importance.

My fellow Texans had made it clear they wouldn't go down without a fight, and the port which was once teamed with commercial liners moving goods back and forth for sale was now clogged with the smoke-filled wreckage of foreign battleships and transport ships, erupting with a dingy smoke which permeated the air and filled my nostrils with the ever-familiar scents of a warzone.

This was our first leg of the trip with Jim, from the resistance headquarters in Austin to the front lines; we would land in Houston to see where the enemy had been stopped cold, refuel and then make our way up and down the coast to view the other areas where they had attempted to put troops on our soil.

After we exited the helicopter so the crew could refuel, Jim led us to a small building just off the tarmac as the thick Houston humidity caused each of our skin to emit beads of perspiration.

He sauntered to the front of the room and started to speak the moment we were all seated (after a brief stretch to work the ride and soreness out of our bodies), the fast wetness of sweat rings readily apparent on the backs of our shirts and now sweat-soaked hair & beards.

"So, what do you boys think?" Jim asked the room in his characteristic southern drawl, as he rested his hands on the hips of his tall, wiry frame and spread his legs in a stance that resembled a cowboy sizing up a wild horse in preparation for breaking its will in a battle of wits and perseverance.

The silence was deafening with our team still in shock from the trip and events over the past few days.

None of us knew what to say, or even where to begin if he had the right words. Jim, being the wise sage of wisdom that he was, sensed the teeming questions in our heads and broke the silence.

"Rob, I know this must be difficult for you, being from Houston and all, but you'll be glad to know the enemy never made it off a single ship. We knew they'd attempt to land here, but unlike the allied landing at Normandy during World War II they didn't have the forethought to emplace spies to try and fool us into thinking the primary effort would be somewhere else. This was their main effort for the third coast, and it became their graveyard."

After he scanned the room for questions and found none, Jim moved on to the agenda.

With a telescopic pointer he motioned to an oversized map of Texas with various battle indicators of red arrows which indicated enemy movement and icons that denoted troop size & unit type, concentrating on Houston first.

"We're right about here, in the Houston ship channel at the Port of Houston. After the helo is filled up we'll be traveling northeast to Port Arthur, where you'll find much of the same situation, then making our way south along the coastline."

He stopped to ensure sure we were paying attention, indicating this wasn't going to be a sunshiny accidental tourist type of trip, and his warnings came next.

"Once we get southwest of Galveston it gets a little hairy," he stated and paused, moving his telescopic pointer further west.

"We stopped them coming up the ship channel, but they brought everything in here to try and land. Our troops gave them such a fight that the channel is still clogged with the wreckage, but they have a massive amount of ships in the water outside of

Galveston trying to make landing. We're keeping an eye on them and using our air force to blow their landing vehicles to hell as soon as they leave the carriers, but be sure you're strapped in when we take off from here, because we'll probably take hostile fire."

He moved the telescopic pointer south to Corpus Christi and Brownsville, taking a moment to gather his thoughts before he continued.

"If we have to land the bird and move by ground vehicles it will most likely come from one of these locations. As it turns out the drug cartels from Mexico, Central and South America not only took money to sneak the initial fighters across the border, but are now using their legions of soldiers as mercenaries. They were well armed to begin with, but have now been outfitted with proper surface-to-air offensive and defensive capabilities, and they're putting up a nasty fight on the Mexican border along with the Chinese."

He pointed to the familiar red rectangles with an "X" inside them which denoted infantry, and as he smacked several which included a gull wing symbol above the X, Jim glanced back to us.

"And yes, there are airborne units in place as well. Even after we destroy the enemy and this thing is over, these cartels are going to be a force to be reckoned with for a very long time. The Chinese haven't been in a major war since the 1950s, but the veracity of the drug-fueled cartel foot soldiers has made up for any lack of experience."

Underneath the infantry icons we discovered for the first time the magnitude of what we were involved in. Being isolated in Colorado we had been forced to go off of what we knew, never really being sure of the scope of this invasion.

But as Jim stood at the front of the room it hit us with full force.

The map showed us that lines and battlefield "fronts" were well established, with infantry falling behind the armored units, artillery, air assets, field hospitals and headquarters elements. To the lay person it would have just been a sheet full of gibberish, but it let us know that our greatest fears had been realized: this wasn't going to end anytime soon.

As I tried to formulate a question in my head about their logistics and our ability to get behind their lines to disrupt operations, a skinny man in an air force uniform poked his head in the door to give Jim a nod.

"Ok boys, if you need to use the facilities, this is your last chance for a while. I'd suggest loading your pockets with some of the snacks from the back of the room; if this gets hairy we may not be eating for quite some time," he said as he pointed to a counter lined with packages of various treats meant for long term sustainment and meal replacement.

"We lift off in ten minutes, they're spinning up the rotors now. Latrines are down the hallway, I'll meet you boys on the bird."

Jim turned to the door and followed the Airman out to the tarmac. As soon as the door was closed the room became dreadfully silent, and we heard the helicopter begin its loud startup.

"Well, you heard the man," announced The Major, moving to the front of the room.

"Load up on snacks and hit the head. Come back in here before you go out to the bird, Josh and I will come up with a "go to hell plan" and linkup location should the helo go down."

He looked around the room at all our eyes tracking him but not moving and slammed his palm on the desk, emphasizing his point by yelling, "***NOW***!"

This was our cue to move, and it became a race to see who could get to either the snacks or latrines first, before a line started or the best choices were stuffed into someone's pocket.

During lift off I strained my eyes to take in as much of the surroundings as possible, and to get a look at where I grew up. I spent almost my entire youth in Texas, and everything before college in Houston.

As we sped on a northeasterly azimuth and zipped to and fro over the I-10 highway I craned my neck to try and sneak a glimpse of my childhood. I was raised in a suburb north of the city, and the direction we were currently moving would take us even further from any fond memories.

With the cruising speed of our Black Hawk the trip would take less than a half hour, and as the familiar hot and humid air of Texas rushed past my face in the open bay of the helo, a montage of childhood friends and events filled my mind.

We had been moving so fast since the day of the invasion that I had never stopped to think about so many details.

Where are my childhood and college friends? are they ok? Where is my family?

After my little sister and I each got into college my parents opted to leave Texas for the Georgia coast. They figured that if you're going to be hot and humid, you may as well live on the water.

When my team and I began devising our pact, I knew that my parents owned a much better asset right in their backyard to utilize in this event, which would prove much easier and safer for them than it would have been to link up with us in Colorado.

Being an avid sailor while he was in the Navy, my dad purchased a sailboat to tinker with in his retirement years which was docked in the water behind their house.

With a list I provided of what food & medications to always keep stocked in case of the unthinkable, all they needed to do was go into their backyard, board the boat and take an extended vacation should they see the signals which led our group into action.

But I hadn't heard anything from them yet. I had been so busy watching after my kids and running missions that I never realized their call to let me know they were ok hadn't come.

As the Black Hawk pilot's voice came over the intercom to tell us we were ten minutes away, I knew I had to stop feeling sorry for myself and get my head back in the game. I wasn't the only one who wondered where their friends and family were, and I had to keep my mind focused on the present - not the what-ifs.

The Black Hawk began to slow and we watched urban sprawl creep into the terrain below, which let us know we were close to our first stop in Port Arthur. After we crossed over the city and then Sabine Lake, we made a right turn to head southward along a canal which fed out into the ocean.

Jim, sitting in the first row of webbed seating, turned to the rest of our crew and spoke into his microphone forcefully.

"We're now flying along the Texas-Louisiana border, which cuts this ship channel in half. To the right, or out the starboard side you'll begin to see oil platforms in the Louisiana water surrounded by ships. The enemy couldn't get into the channel as we bombed the hell out of them when they tried, but they succeeded in taking over all these platforms. We think they're using them for headquarters, but we know they'll eventually start commandeering as much oil as possible. Some of these rigs have underground pipelines directly to the refineries in Port Arthur, but some use tankers to transport. We gathered intel they are working on stopping the pipelines, and let's just say the tankers aren't coming to US refineries anymore."

As the Black Hawk made a sharp right turn to move back in the direction from which we started in Houston, I craned my neck to get a view of the carnage. Smoke-filled ship hulls and wreckage lined the entrance to the channel and packs of ships which bore the flags of several different nations surrounded the oil rigs that dotted the horizon.

I had never found an interest in joining the Navy for that reason exactly. A few members of my family made it their service of choice, but I always thought that if someone was going to be shooting at me, I wanted my feet on terra firma.

As I looked out upon the smoking hulls and sinking wreckage I silently wondered how many enemy sailors had been asleep in their bunks, writing letters to loved ones or looking at pictures of their families when our bombers sent them to an ocean grave.

But the warrior inside of me told the loving father to take a backseat; war is hell, and many a family has been torn apart throughout the history of man when their fathers, brothers, mothers and sisters fell in combat.

After the last oil rig was out of sight, the Black Hawk altered its course to take us back over land until our next destination.

Being on the port side of the helicopter, I still had an ocean view for the remainder of the flight. I couldn't help but wonder as I gazed out into the seemingly endless span of blue which filled my horizon.

The ocean intrigued me, but also terrified me in the same respect. It's human nature to be afraid of what one can't see, like a child afraid of the dark, and the black depths of the deep water were something that made my spine tingle with trepidation.

I thought back to sailing trips with my family as a kid and how my dad, a well-traveled and experienced sailor would try to get the sailboat tilted so far to one side that the railing went underwater.

My mom, the consummate daredevil with a strong southern backbone would smile with excitement, but I couldn't help but contemplate what dangers lurked beneath the water, waiting for one large errant wave to knock us over and provide dinner to a silently lurking predator.

But while the sharks, eels and Navy SEALs where the carnivores of the ocean, I had been quite happy in my military life as a carnivore of the land.

I wouldn't bat an eye to scale the side of a sheer cliff up a mountain in Afghanistan with a sniper rifle or mortar strapped to my back, fly head first into a room full of gunfire with my Brothers to take down a target, or jump out of a C-130 high above the ground, praying that my parachute would remember to open.

But the ocean, that deep, dark, cold and cavernous ocean always gave me goosebumps.

I was jolted out of my thoughts when the pilot's voice came back over the radio to announce that we would be over Galveston in five minutes.

Galveston was a city on the coast just southeast of Houston and was the point of entry into the Houston ship channel. I remembered the expression on Jim's face and inflection in his tone when he told us it may get a little hairy south of Galveston, so I gave myself another once over to ensure my straps were tight and ammo was where it needed to be.

I was observing the armada of ships adorning the water out of the open door of the Black Hawk when Jim came over the radio once again.

"Remember, this was the primary invasion point for the enemy on the southern coast. We took out every one of them who got into the ship channel and it pissed them off something fierce. They're still pretty testy, so we're going to move back over land to maintain a decent chance of making it home in one piece."

With timing that made it seem as if they were listening to Jim speak, I heard the eruption of heavy machine guns and saw a flurry of red tracers flying in our direction from several of the Russian destroyers which dotted the horizon.

The Black Hawk made a fast bank maneuver to the right to ascend rapidly as the red flashes fell into the ocean, far from their mark.

"Yeah, they're too far out to effectively hit us at this distance, but like I said, they're still pissed," Jim chimed in over the radio.

The Black Hawk transitioned its path to fly over the Galveston Bay and I saw scores of military ships, burned out and annihilated in various stages of sinking from the ocean to the channel and into the bay. A few had succeeded all the way through the bay to the Houston ship channel, but most ended their journey right below us.

I watched Jim speak into his microphone but couldn't hear him, which told me that he was on another net speaking with someone outside of the bird. Being an extrovert he was still gesturing with his hands as he spoke. Seeing him nod his head up and down let me know he was finished with that conversation, and I listened as he chirped our internal net to life.

"The men on the ground in Corpus Christi are telling me it's too hot to land there right now. They're engaged with enemy forces as we speak, so we'll be heading up to San Antonio and taking ground vehicles from there. The front lines are very active here, and we can't risk flying around just to be tourists when we know they have anti-aircraft assets down there."

I felt the helicopter make a slight turn to the right. As it began moving farther inland, I watched the pilot's body jolt upright in the front seat and slam the controls forward.

"BRACE FOR IMPACT!" he screamed into the microphone as an orange flash flew past the open bay of the Black Hawk.

I felt a concussion behind me and the helo began to spin around uncontrollably. Another orange streak of fire flew by the window as I grasped for something to hold and steady myself.

The earth raced towards us at lightning speed as the pilot continued to talk, loudly but eerily calmly for what was in store.

"WE'RE GOING DOWN. BRACE FOR IMPACT. WATCH OUT FOR THE ROTORS WHEN WE HIT THE GROUND AND RUN AS FAR AWAY FROM THE BIRD AS POSSIBLE. THIS AIN'T GONNA BE PRETTY!"

My forehead smacked my knees as we made violent contact with the earth, and in my daze everything went silent and started to move in slow motion.

Did I black out? Am I awake? Is this a dream?

My ears were ringing like a prizefighter who just had his bell rung in a title fight, and my vision was too fuzzy to make out anything other than shadows and figures as I looked around the cabin to assess the situation.

The Black Hawk must have hit the ground, bounced and landed on its side, because out of the bay I saw grass stuffed into the door on my side and I was hanging from my seat straps.

As my vision tightened I looked around the cabin and saw the other men cutting themselves out of their straps and climbing out on the open side.

It took a little work to reach around to the knife latched to my right pocket, but as soon as I flipped it open and cut myself free I heard the sound of incoming rounds.

First it was just the crack of a rifle several hundred meters away, but I began to hear the whiz of bullets flying closely past the open bay door, followed by more striking the skin of the helicopter.

Thankfully were each wearing our body armor on the flight so I had my ammo and pistol with me, but it took a few moments to fish around in the cabin to find my rifle before I climbed towards the sunlight.

I took a brief pause with my head still inside the helo and gave myself several pumps before jumping off the webbed seating and out of the aircraft.

I fell roughly to the ground and felt two hands grab the straps of my body armor and pull me to safety in front of the downed aircraft. I opened my eyes to see Josh and Dave smiling at me, with Josh the first to speak.

"Hey Rob, you gonna lay down all day or are you gonna fight?"

Dave chuckled and pointed past the tail of the helo.

"Bad guys that way."

I rolled over to my side, did a combat pushup to get myself off the ground and low crawled to the side of the helo with my rifle aimed past the helicopter's tail.

I looked through my ACOG [Advanced Combat Optical Gunsight] and found several civilian jeeps lined up with men in various stages of uniform jumping out of them and running towards us.

Not having to question whether they were friend or foe, I began to pick out the men already firing at us and take them down one by one.

By the time my first magazine was dry on ammo the rest of the team had exited the aircraft, taken up defensive positions and begun firing back.

A few rounds from the M203 grenade launcher affixed to the bottom of my rifle took out the jeeps (and men still in them), and I transitioned back to target practice.

One of the men picked up a long tube, put it over his shoulder and took a knee as Klint yelled to the rest of the group.

"RPG... INCOMING!"

Josh searched for any cover away from the downed helicopter, and finding a patch of trees about a hundred meters away he shouted his instructions to all of us.

"LEAPFROG, 100 METERS RIGHT!"

Our training instantly kicked in, and we picked up and made a run for it. The entire group ran far enough to get away from the blast, and as the RPG exploded near the helicopter we hit the ground and began our tactical movement.

With half of our team running ten meters at a time, the others would lay down suppressive fire, and when the lead element stopped they would fire while the first element ran past them to continue the forward momentum.

When the entire team made it to the woodline there were only a handful of enemy fighters remaining, but with their jeeps turned into smoking wreckage from my M203 rounds they didn't have any escape plan.

While they began to shoot and frantically look for somewhere to hide, Ray rested his rifle on a low-hanging tree branch to brace himself and steady his aim.

Each time one of the fighters would pop up to fire his head would instantly turn into a violent explosion of pink mist, and Ray would hold out his hand for a fist bump as he took aim on the next one.

Josh directed the element that had been trailing in the leapfrog to move around in a flanking position. As they took off further into the treeline, we started to each lay down a heavy base of fire to keep the enemy focused on us rather than our team who was moving to deal them their final blow.

Tony shot a pin flare high into the sky over the enemy's heads a few minutes later to let us know they were in place. The flank maneuver worked perfectly. Our heavy base of fire kept the attention solely on us, and the fighters never even thought to guard their flanks as our second element moved into position to finish them off.

Their lack of military knowledge to watch their flank, the most basic maneuver taught in the Ranger handbook that all US military (and many of our enemies) studied for elementary warfare tactics told us these were not trained soldiers or even hardcore terrorists.

These poor devils were likely cartel members, merely handed a gun, paid a little bit of money and told to go fight without training, much like many of the foot soldiers we had encountered in Afghanistan.

They didn't have a bone to pick with us or hatred in their hearts, but had families to feed and picked a fight with the wrong hombres.

As the pin flare reached the top of its crest and started a flaming descent towards the ground we lifted our base of fire and began to shoot high over their heads.

The untrained cartel members would most likely not even know the difference, not having the presence of mind to realize the effective fire that had been whizzing past them was gone, replaced only by the crack of our rifles.

By raising our field of fire it allowed the second element to complete their job. As we fired over the enemy's heads, kept their attention on us and heads down, that element formed a line and walked directly through the enemy ranks.

They became executioners, putting rounds into motionless bodies and kicking weapons away from lifeless hands as they stepped over corpses, not stopping until they cleared the entire line.

Once Tony and his team cleared the objective and stopped to take a knee it was our turn to get on line and walk through.

We moved north-south intersecting their east-west, doing a second sweep to ensure that none of the enemy soldiers were still clinging to life with a hidden weapon to retaliate.

Once we finished our sweep, Tony and Josh took assessments of men, weapons and equipment on the limit of advance.

After they confirmed none of our guys were hurt and everyone had ammo left, he split his element into two and sent the men as a scout party to ensure there weren't any more enemy hidden in the treelines, waiting to shoot when we dropped our guard.

Only after both teams returned with the "all clear" were we able to let out a sigh of relief and begin to focus on what came next.

And, of course, return to making fun of each other as we usually did.

"Damn Tony, that took you guys long enough, I think those Twinkies in your pockets might have slowed you down a bit. We need to put you on a diet," joked J-Lo.

"Nah, I stuffed your mother in my rucksack last night. I'll make sure to drop her off before we start moving again, she's just dead weight anyway," Tony shot back without missing a beat.

As we continued to make each other the butt of numerous tasteless jokes, Jim walked to a tree stump in the middle of our group where we now rested on a knee, forming a circle of soldiers facing outwards to maintain a security perimeter.

He pulled a map out of his pocket and sat down with an audible groan, laughing to himself as he unfolded it.

"Well boys, I'd like to say thank you for that," he chuckled dryly.

"Keeping you alive is extremely high on our priority list sir," answered Josh.

"I don't think they'd let us stick around if we showed back up without you, so consider it an act of selfishness."

"I don't mean just keeping me alive," Jim replied.

"They don't really let me out much. It's been years since I've been in a firefight that wasn't training, I forgot how much..."

He paused to look around at us and continued with the smile of a deviant five-year-old boy.

"...fun it is."

Each of us, on a knee in our security perimeter, nodded our heads in affirmation. You gotta love what you do, whether it's fixing cars, flying airplanes or fighting wars.

Jim may have been locked in an office and chained to a desk for the past decade as a staff officer, but deep down inside the warrior soul still burned in him, and I could tell from the fire in his eyes that it was fully awake again.

Sitting on the stump with the map unfolded in his hands, Jim glanced up at Josh, The Major and Tony, who were huddled around him, and laughed.

He paused for a moment and continued.

"Well boys, it looks like we're flying to the front lines on this trip after all. We're a helluvalot closer to our men there than we are to San Antonio. The enemy pushed their lines up all the way east of Nuevo Laredo to the coast just south of Kingsville, meaning it's a relatively short ride. I started sending distress calls once we hit the ground and there's a bird en route to pick us up."

"I thought it was too dangerous to fly there," added JLo.

"Well they seem to think it's a little more dangerous for me to be here on foot. So this little incident earned us a first class ticket," Jim laughed.

As the three leaders around him nodded in accordance, he began to show them on the map where we needed to go.

Listening with one ear and planning with the other, Josh directed a few of the guys to salvage any ammo and weapons from the corpses on the objective and do a final sweep to ensure there weren't any enemy left in hiding to start shooting when we had our guard down.

The Major ordered Klint and I to check on the Black Hawk pilots; they hadn't made it out of the cockpit yet.

Due to the effective fire we started receiving as soon as we hit the ground our first priority had been fighting before we could transition to our jobs as medics.

We kept our rifles at the low-ready as we crept along the side of the Black Hawk, moving slowly and cautiously. Combat rarely held any similarities to what you would see in the movies, but I had still half expected the helo to have erupted in massive explosion shortly after it crashed.

As we reached the front of the downed helicopter I motioned for Klint to take a knee and pull security while I checked the pilots.

I knew that we had a bad situation, as I saw blood pooling in the section of the windshield that was buried in the earth, along with blood splatter in other sections of the cockpit.

My expectations of finding anyone alive plummeted as I walked around the front of the aircraft to search for a way in and assess the situation inside.

I found the pilot, somehow ejected from his seat and crumpled against the ground, with the upper part of his torso buried under the front console and only his legs visible, dangling lifelessly in the air.

The co-pilot was still strapped into his seat, raised in the air as the force of gravity pulled his body down against his seat straps. His head was rolled to one side weighed down by his helmet, but I didn't see any blood or obvious injury.

Putting my face to the windshield to have a better view I noted his chest rising and falling ever so slightly, drastically increasing my desire to get inside quickly.

Taking a quick glance around the only available entrances I found were the doors on the side of the Black Hawk sticking out of the ground, which would require me to climb and then find my way around inside. I looked at the windshield, already spiderwebbed from the impact, and decided to take the path of least resistance.

A few quick blows from the butt of my rifle cleared the rest of the windshield out of my way and I climbed inside to reach my new patient.

Once inside the cabin I tried to find a place to brace myself; the co-pilot seemed to be about 150 pounds and was hanging from his seat straps about six inches from my head as I stood on the crushed hull of the cockpit, lodged in the cold earth.

The pilot's body was mangled and twisted between my feet, but just to be sure I removed my shooting gloves to check him for any signs of life. Crouching down and moving my hand to his neck to search for a pulse, his head rolled to one side and revealed that the entire left side of his skull had been caved in, with part of his brain exposed.

Not finding any signs of life I moved my focus entirely on keeping the co-pilot alive, which meant figuring out a way to bring him down from his seat and out of the cockpit without killing him in the process.

Being a soldier meant you often saw gruesome things, as war is anything but a clean act or process.

Being an orthopedic surgeon had its share of blood and gore as well, but there was something different about being able to prepare for it, and of course being in a sterile hospital with scrubs, nurses, music playing and clean instruments which made it all quite palatable.

But being a combat medic, seeing multi-system trauma everywhere, finding bodies burned and mangled, never knowing what to expect or if you had the supplies to handle it, took its toll.

The most important lesson an 18D [Special Forces Medic] could ever learn was a strong ability to compartmentalize; it would take a lot for the average person to straddle the corpse of a comrade, hoping not to slip in his blood while you cut his living partner out of a seat to save his life.

For an 18D, it was just another day and I couldn't spare the time to dwell on it.

Taking a moment to size up the situation I knew I couldn't do it on my own safely. I peeked my head out of the cockpit and directed Klint to bring Dave to me. By far the tallest and the largest of the group, I thought the task I had in mind would be a piece of cake for him.

I kept my sights on the woodline as I waited inside the cockpit, feeling like the proverbial fish in a barrel. If there were a sniper in the woods somewhere he could easily put a few rounds in me before I could manage my way back out to find safety or cover.

The cabin was packed so tightly and opening to escape so small that I began to ponder how many rounds he would pump into my body while I tried to squirrel my way back into the concealment of the wreckage.

While I waited for Klint and Dave to return, the medic part of my brain contemplated which sniper rounds would do me in.

Would it be those rounds finding their way through the exposed armpit of my body armor, ripping through my abdomen and tearing apart my lungs, possibly hitting my inferior vena cava along their path?

Or those shredding the backs of my legs, rupturing the femoral artery and leaving me to die in a pool of several people's blood, unable to even stand up, helpless in the back of this downed helicopter?

Perhaps it would find its mark just below the back of my body armor, entering and slicing my lumbar spine above the sciatic nerve, rendering my legs and vital organs below the wound completely useless and irreparable in these circumstances, leaving me to pull myself along the ground without use of my legs as they walked rounds further in to decimate the rest of my being.

Morbidly and methodically playing the different scenarios of my own death sentence over and over in my head, I began to hear the soft banter of several men as they moved along the skin of the aircraft, which alerted me they had arrived to help.

Klint walked around to the front of the cabin to take a look. Seeing a few other men on a knee to pull security around the downed helo, I stepped back out to apprise he and Dave of the situation.

After pointing out the corpse, the living, the space and the height problems, we began to formulate a plan.

Klint handed me a neck brace for the co-pilot. Standing on the pilot's chair I could raise it just high enough to emplace it on him. Wiggling my way back to the cabin, I moved the litter [military tactical medical stretcher] out of the front window to Klint, after which Dave took his place in the cockpit.

It was poor medical practice to have a knife near an unconscious patient dangling in the air, but we couldn't think of any other way to get him out aside from cutting him down. As Dave braced his massive legs and put his hands on the pilot's shoulders, I crawled up to cut him loose.

Removing one strap at a time was enough for Dave to rebalance himself as the co-pilot was freed, and after the final one he was able to ease the co-pilot down and out to Klint, who transferred the patient to the litter.

While Klint performed his medical assessment once the co-pilot was on the ground, I began to move around the cabin to search for any supplies that would be useful. I found several small first aid kits, some stashed MRE's [Meals Ready to Eat] from the crew and a few thermite grenades.

Throwing the first aid kits and MRE's up and out of the elevated cabin door, I cradled the thermite grenades and crawled back out of the windshield to give Klint a hand. He had already completed his initial physical assessment and was now listening to the co-pilot's lungs as he breathed.

Still unconscious, I saw massive bruises beginning to form as Klint moved the stethoscope around his exposed chest. Looking up at me and shrugging, he gave his diagnosis.

"Aside from the bruises and being unconscious, I can't find any severe issues," he reported.

"The impact must have knocked him out, and I'm assuming the position he was in when we hit reduced the oxygen and blood flow to his brain, keeping him asleep. He's gonna wake up with one hell of a headache, but he'll live. I checked his neck; no breaks or injury, but it'll be sore."

Josh, who was listening in from a few feet away, interjected.

"When do you guys think he'll be awake?"

"No way of knowing," I responded.

"Serious trauma like that, it all depends on the person. We don't know how reduced his oxygen and blood flow to the brain has been. It may be minutes, it may be days."

"Well the vehicles are all destroyed, you did a bang-up job with those 203 rounds Rob," Josh said with a "you're not gonna like what comes next" tone of voice.

"So I guess since you're the medic, and the one who destroyed the vehicles, you get to carry the co-pilot until he wakes up. The helos won't land next to the wreckage of another that just got shot down, so we'll have to move this guy. Move him over to the group so we can figure out where the new birds are landing."

"Awesome," was the only sarcastic reply I could muster.

It was never well received for a soldier to ask how far a march would be or how much weight he'd have to carry, so I shrugged my shoulders and prepared myself mentally for the pain I was about to endure.

"At least we have the litter," Dave chimed in.

"I missed my workouts the last few weeks, so I'll help you carry him if you don't mind."

I smiled and turned to Dave to shake my head affirmative.

"You're alright big guy, you really are. I don't care what they say about you."

Not getting the joke, he shot me a puzzled look as the other guys laughed.

"Better get saddled up and ready to go," ordered Tony.

"We've got about ten clicks [kilometers] to move, and this guy is going to make it rather slow."

By that time the entire team had migrated to the downed Black Hawk and Josh called us into a circle to brief our route of travel. Using a pine needle from the ground he showed our location on the map, and where Jim indicated we needed to go in order to link up with the helos coming for us.

If we were an infantry company we would have at least 120 men with heavy weapons, vehicles and air support, and could easily walk along the nearest road to make a beeline to our link up point.

But with only twelve fighters from our team, Jim, an unconscious co-pilot, no heavy weapons, no vehicles, and no way to call in air support we'd have to go the sneaky route and choose to move cautiously through cover whenever we could find it.

Unfortunately, the part of Texas we were in and would be traveling through consisted mainly of open fields. That meant that not only would we be moving slowly, carrying a patient on a litter and outgunned by almost any force we would possibly encounter, but the cover we had to move through would be spotty at best.

I tossed the thermite grenades to J-Lo and nodded to the Black Hawk as I moved into my position at the rear of the litter.

From that position I could watch and assess the co-pilot as we moved. I wanted to have him out of the way before J-Lo used the thermite grenades to both destroy any chances of the enemy getting their hands on our equipment or intelligence, and as a fiery Valhalla-style funeral pyre for our comrade the pilot, so we started moving.

We were several hundred meters away from the Black Hawk when I heard the explosion, felt the wave of heat against my back and said a silent prayer for the soul of the pilot.

Thank you for getting us this far, Brother. May your soul find peace now that your mission on this earth is complete. Via con dios.

CHAPTER 2

THE FRONT LINES

I could tell we were drawing near the front lines by the smoking wreckage and acrid black stench that comprise the distinct smells and scenery of war.

Out of my open door in the helicopter I could see the skeletons of Russian fighter planes & bombers one minute, followed by the carnage and piles of bodies in uniforms and then the gutted-out carcasses of Chinese tanks next to bomb craters that had brought their inhabitants to meet their maker.

It felt like ages since I had last landed on a base in a combat zone, and the pilot's warning didn't give me much time to prepare.

"Strap yourselves in boys, we're coming in hot," I could hear him smiling on the other end of his microphone as he gave us his warning.

Four loud and rapid "whooshes" filled the air as the countermeasures deployed from behind the open doors and screamed through the sky. As I turned my head to watch their trajectory, my stomach suddenly felt as if it were in my throat when we went completely weightless.

The pilot steered the helicopter sharply down and to the right, and I could see the childishly evil grin on some of our men's faces as if we were on the scariest part of the rollercoaster that only the bravest kids would ride.

Our body weight was pushed completely against our harnesses, as for a moment the only thing I could see out of our open doors was the ground that we were parallel to. It only lasted for a moment, and I had a brief instant of terror as I faced ahead and wondered if the pilots were going to drive us head-first into the earth as they pushed their joysticks straight down.

I was relieved yet still queasy when the pilot completed his 180 degree downward corkscrew maneuver and began pulling up on the joystick, this time trying to bring our nose back up to level off for a rapid landing.

The Black Hawk's landing gear bounced off the ground when we touched down forcefully. I smiled half-heartedly as I unbuckled my restraints, glad we hadn't ended up on our side again.

We were situated on a helipad in what looked like the middle of every Forward Operating Base [FOB] I had ever been on in Iraq or Afghanistan, tasting the slight tinge of *deja vu* and flashbacks.

In the distance ahead I could see a wall that rose high in the air complete with guard towers, parapets and machine gun emplacements at regular intervals which encircled the entire perimeter of the base.

Are we still in America?

As we ran to escape the beating turbulence of the helo's rotors I observed our surroundings of dreary one-story plywood huts surrounded by impromptu concrete barriers and lined with sandbags on every side, leaving just enough room for an entry door.

I wondered which direction led to the action as I jogged off the helipad. I soon found my answer as I reached the edge and my senses were able to take in the surroundings.

Once I escaped the whir of the rotors, I saw a series of zig-zagging and double-stacked ten-foot high concrete barriers, what we called T-barriers, forming a hallway.

On the first wall was a humorous and cryptic message in black spray paint, meant to invoke a last bit of humor but instill the seriousness of the situation in anyone walking along that path on their way to war.

"*No respawns beyond this point.*"

Jim noticed me looking at the wall and smiling wryly.

"We're not exactly sure who put that up there, but the young guys seem to get a hell of a kick out of it. They've taken to kissing their hands and slapping it on their way out."

"It's referring to video games," I chuckled to Jim.

"What do you mean video games? Is there a video game named respawn or something?"

"No. A respawn is when a character dies in a multi-player video game, and they're allowed to come back to life and into the fight after waiting a few minutes. It's called a respawn."

Jim contemplated the new meaning of this message, laughed to himself and spoke as he turned to walk.

"Thanks Rob, you've successfully depressed me for the day."

"Glad to help Colonel," I smiled cheerfully.

As we gathered on a plywood sidewalk away from the backwash of the rotors, Jim grinned and contemplated his new understanding as we formed in a group around him.

"Well boys, I promised you a view of the front lines of World War III and that right there is as close as I'm allowed to get," he said, pointing to the closest guard tower.

"Who wants to see?"

Our team looked at each other, still queasy from the helicopter landing and having a hard time believing we were actually there.

As if to snap us back to reality, we heard the whistle of an incoming mortar and a loud barrage of high-caliber automatic weapons fire ending with an explosion in mid-air.

Jim smiled and pointed.

"They're still having a hard time understanding that our Phalanx system can blow most of anything they lob at us out of the air. And every time they do, we can triangulate its point of origin and shoot whatever launched it to kingdom come."

In response to his words, we heard the loud but unmistakable eruption of a Howitzer field artillery cannon from the other side of the base.

"It's not quite as busy here as it used to be, but it's definitely not over," Jim continued.

"I can't let you boys walk through the front gates as there are currently ground troops in contact beyond the perimeter, and you're not a part of the roster here so it would just confuse everyone. I can, however, take you up in the guard towers and let you get a lay of the land. Sound good?"

Seeing our heads nodding in accordance, Jim led us to a nearby building which had several HUMVEEs parked in front of it. Stepping in the doorway just enough to show his rank, we heard him ask the occupants for keys and he strode back outside once he acquired the two needed sets.

After loading into two of the HUMVEEs and following Jim as he drove the lead vehicle, we began to hear small arms fire and explosions as we neared the perimeter wall.

Parking next to a locked door at the bottom of one of the guard towers, he instructed us that there would only enough room in the tower for half of our team at a time.

I was chosen to go in the first group, and after climbing a set of stairs that were high enough to make me feel out of shape we reached the top. Stepping off the last stair and into the room, I found a pair of young soldiers watching carefully behind thick bulletproof windows surrounded by several feet of heavily reinforced concrete.

There were black marks on various parts of the windows and small-arms projectiles dangling haphazardly into the glass on the other side from a failed enemy attempt at taking out the tower.

But the soldiers weren't focused on the window; their attention was on a display screen overlayed with green target sights which they were moving around the battlefield before them.

"I recognize those from the MRAP [Mine Resistant Ambush Protected] trucks. Does that have a .50 cal turret attached to it somewhere?" JLo asked the young soldier.

"Hell yeah it does," he replied.

"Well it's not exactly the same thing, but it's the same technology," added Jim.

"They use the joystick to move a camera around the battlefield and can zoom in on anything that interests them or acquire targets. We have FLIR [Forward Looking Infrared Radar] cameras all over the place, so these boys can get imaging in thermal, night vision or just about anything they need to see what's going on."

The window ahead of us lit up as we felt an explosion, reminding us that we weren't there for the technology. Taking a step forward and looking out at the terrain I couldn't believe what I was seeing.

The horizon was nothing more than carnage for as far as I could see, entranced in a dark and hazy smoke that seemed to be the epitome of the fear and fog of war.

In the distance I saw the view change from dirt and tumbleweeds to the outline of wreckage scattered across the landscape, and beyond that I could just make out a large mass of something that definitely was not natural.

A terror began to eat into my soul as I realized that we were looking out at our enemy: foreign troops who had come to take our country and freedom from us.

One of young soldiers zoomed the camera out farther and focused on the bodies of Chinese tank crews lying lifelessly about their destroyed vehicles, now stained haphazardly with their demise.

Beyond those we observed piles of dead bodies strewn across the battlefield, with impact craters surrounded by dirt painted red from blood and body parts randomly scattered about their wake.

Straining the camera to the extent of its range, the soldier began to zoom in on the fuzzy outlines of what we could tell was the enemy camp just beyond our view.

As JLo and I pressed our faces closer to try and make out the details, Jim spoke from behind us.

"Ok boys, time for someone else to get a turn. We have things to do."

A hand on my shoulder from Jim told me it was time to move, and as I made my way back down the long staircase I heard him tell the young soldiers that another group would be up to have a look.

When Americans had watched the coverage of the wars in Iraq and Afghanistan, the general populace didn't understand that most of the footage shown on the nine o'clock news was from reporters who were actually in the Green Zones, safe establishments well inside the largest cities.

Those Green Zones were stocked with dining halls operating twenty-four hours a day, cafes where high echelon ISAF [International Security Assistance Force] officers would leisurely sip their iced espressos to lament the heat and drink vintage wine with dinner while they sat behind thick walls with masses of guards and private security details to keep them safe from the wars ravaging the rest of the country.

But when you got outside of the Green Zones, and especially beyond the major cities like Baghdad, Kabul, Kandahar or Basra it was a completely different story.

Outside of the wire the safety, luxury and respite from the heat offered by palaces with marble floors were replaced by tents with intermittent air conditioning and zero protection from incoming rounds or the shrapnel flung in all directions from exploding mortars.

But, for those of us who cared about actually winning the war that was where you really got to know the people, their country and customs, which was the only way to truly win the hearts and minds needed in the types of wars we had fought.

This was different.

After the initial invasion and outside of the Green Zones those wars in Iraq and Afghanistan had been mostly urban fighting with smaller units going about their battles in the streets, never truly having a front line.

This was something that none of us had ever seen up close, and had only learned about from history books and archival footage from past wars. This was a true world war, complete with battle lines and massive units vying for a strategic move that could gain the slightest of advantages to turn the tide.

"How was it?" The Major asked as I stepped back onto the ground at the bottom of the tower.

"See for yourself," was the only response that I could muster, still coming to terms with the reality of what I had just seen.

"This is bigger than I think we ever imagined."

After the last group was back from the top of the tower, Jim informed us that our briefing had only just begun and led us to a building deep inside the heart of the base.

It was a dizzying reality to look at the maps adorning the TOC [Tactical Operations Center] as I followed him through a final plywood door, still having a hard time grasping that this fortress was on American soil.

A tall and robust clean-shaven man with a slight gut and salt-and-pepper hair in desert camouflage was tapped on the shoulder as soon as we walked in, and an enormous smile hijacked his face when he saw Jim.

As the man barreled across the room Jim snapped to attention and rendered a salute, to which the hefty man laughed and gave a quick and nonchalant return gesture, then stuck out his hand for Jim to shake as he came within distance.

As he neared us, I could see the two subdued brown stars adorning his lapels denoting that he was running the show.

"General," Jim greeted him.

"Jim," the General returned.

"These the boys from Colorado?"

"Yes sir," Jim responded after a quick glance at us.
The General took a step back and gave each of us a once over before he addressed us.

"Well men, I've heard an awful lot about you, but I imagine you've been kept in the dark for the most part about what exactly is going on here. Jim told me that he filled you in with whatever he could, but as the ground truth has been changing every few hours he knew we'd have to get you out here to see what was going on up close and personal. Now if there aren't any questions, I'd like to get right into it so we can get to work."

The General took a step back and prepared to move across the TOC as The Major raised his hand.

"Well I take that back, it looks like we do have a question. How can I help you Major?"

"General, I thought this was the front line. What in the world is a two-star General doing this close to the action? Shouldn't you be in Austin at the resistance headquarters?"

"That's a good question son," he responded in an authoritative but charming tone.

"It seems technology has become both our best friend and our worst enemy. We became so dependent on high tech and wireless communication that we forgot just how easily it could be lost. The primary reason we had so much trouble with Al Qaeda and the Taliban in the desert wars was that they went old school and used word of mouth, drop letters and runners rather than the cell phones and emails our intelligence units had been so focused on being able to hack."

He observed us for a moment to ensure we were following, and pointed to the sky with one finger as he continued.

"The Russians and Chinese knew how dependent we had become on technology, so once they hacked all of our power stations and intel networks, they focused on finding the orbits of our military satellites and where our network hubs were. Once the invasion kicked off they started blowing those satellites out of the sky, and communications between here and Austin became so unreliable that we couldn't coordinate our battle plans."

The General pointed to Jim and winked at us.

"I'm sure you've figured out that Jim here is a rather smart and stand-up guy, so it was just easier for me to be here coordinating with runners sending our intel back to him, than vice versa."

He looked up and down our line for any more raised hands, and seeing none he continued.

"So if there aren't any more questions, we can give you an update on what we have going on here and where we could use your help."

"Our help?" Josh questioned.

"We came here because we heard a radio transmission and thought you were other freedom fighters, but we have to get back to our families in Colorado. All due respect General, but this is a traditional blue-on-red operation you have going on here. That's more of an infantry, armor and artillery scenario than anything the twelve of us could help with."

"Well you're right on one part. This has become the typical world war scenario, complete with no-man's land and entrenched front lines, much different from the small unit tactics you used in Iraq, Africa and Afghanistan. But make no mistake, we need people with your particular skill sets now more than ever."

The Major, seeming to already know what was in store, gave us the sign to "zip it" and nodded for The General to continue.

"Right. Up to this point in the battle it's been continuous chaos, with everyone doing their best to survive and keep the enemy off our shores wherever possible. But now that the lines have been pretty much drawn, it's time to start working on Phase II of our operation."

"Phase II?" Asked The Major.

"The Battle Hymn of the Republic, son. It's time for us to go on the offensive."

Josh, having too much respect for The General's rank to speak out of turn but not understanding where this was going, stepped up.

"Wait a minute sir," he started as he moved forward and stood at full parade rest, as if he were front and center in a command inspection.

"We're outnumbered. We're surrounded on all sides and are fighting not only China and Russia but also the drug cartels, Al Quds and Hezbollah. I'm all about taking it to the enemy and coming home with heads on stakes, but that seems like a tall order."

"Right you are Sergeant. But that's where the situation has changed significantly."

Walking to a map of the United States laid out on a desk in the back of the room, The General waited for us to gather around him. As we each drew closer and saw the military icons adorning the map, we knew exactly where he was heading.

"We're not alone in this fight, and we have more help than you might think."

He pointed to red lines forming a corridor, moving from the southern coast of Texas, north through most of Arizona and Nevada on the western side and following the southern border of Georgia up the east coast to West Virginia, where it cut sharply back to the midwest and rose again through Iowa, ending at the Canadian border with Minnesota.

"The lines in the sand have been drawn and contact has been established with other teams around the country. It goes a long way to show what happens when people give up their right to defend themselves, as the entire west coast has fallen due to an unarmed citizenry in Southern California and Washington. We held them on the southern part of the east coast where we had expansive military bases and an armed populace, but the enemy rolled right on into the states in the northeast whose politicians enforced gun confiscation, paving the way for them to take over."

"So you're saying we're going in there to take the entire east and west coast?" asked The Major incredulously.

"Yes, but not on your own," chimed in Jim.

"We've been in contact with SEALs and Marines in San Diego as well as Rangers from the 75th and operators from 1st Group up in Washington. For the east coast we still have active infantry, Marines, Special Forces, Rangers, OGA [Other Governmental Organizations] and combat units out of Forts Bragg, Benning, Camp Lejeune and in Virginia, as well as several militias we've been in contact with out there. Those boys have been keeping their skills sharp, and while they may not be uniformed military they're a huge asset as they know the terrain better than anyone."

The General stood, broad shouldered, taking turns looking each of us directly in the eye as he spoke.

"You boys have been through a world of trouble, and have dealt some serious damage to the enemy. For that your country thanks you. But we need you to get out and reinforce those teams, show them that we have a unified, national resistance with a battle plan and whip those invaders so bad they run home with their tails between their legs."

"What about our families?" I asked.

"We can't just leave them in Colorado, they'll be sitting ducks once the enemy fixes their location.

"We can't afford any airframes to go pick them all up, but we can give you extra trucks and security to form a convoy to get them. You're welcome to bring them back to stay in Austin, which is the safest place in the nation at this point. We'll make sure they're taken care of while you continue to serve your country."

"Can we have a few minutes to talk about this amongst ourselves General?" The Major asked.

"Of course you can. I'd say you can have all the time in the world, but time isn't exactly a luxury we're full on right now." The General and Jim turned and began to walk towards the front of the room.

The Major looked to each of us in the circle and met affirmative head nods all around.

"Sir," he called out before the two were halfway across the room.

"We're in."

"Excellent," The General replied as he walked back towards our group.

"Then let's get to it. Jim will muster up a security detail to go with you back to Colorado. I'm sure you guys are starving...we don't have much to offer, but I'd suggest grabbing some hot food before you get on your way."

"Roger that sir," Josh agreed.

The General took pause for a moment, holding our attention before any of us dared start moving.

"Please don't take my briefness for carelessness about the situation. I understand exactly what I'm asking of you, and each of your families. But make no mistake, men. This is the most pivotal moment in our nation's history since her formation and she needs you now more than ever."

From the back of the circle, Ray piped in.

"If not me, then who. If not now, then when."

The General grinned from ear to ear and nodded in approval.

"Give em' hell, boys."

Josh slapped Ray on the back as our group began to move in search of our first hot meal in several days.

"You know Ray, it's few and far between that anything serious comes out of your mouth, but when it does it's downright poetic."

"What can I say Josh?" Ray smirked.

"I just get all hot and bothered in the presence of flag officers."

"That's more like it!" Josh laughed as we made our way out of the room.

After grabbing our lunch and taking a few minutes to change our socks and wash our faces Jim returned with an amused smirk on his face.

"Boys, I know it must be dizzying with all of the information I've thrown at you since you've met me, but we have to go a little further down the rabbit hole before you depart."

"Ok sir, I don't see how anything short of proving the existence of aliens could really shock us at this point, so give it your best shot," smirked Josh.

"Roger that," he replied with a knowing grin.

"Follow me boys."

Jim turned and walked out of a door at the back of the room and we proceeded to follow him through a maze of hallways and side doors that required ever-increasing and heightened security procedures to open. He finally stopped and waited for us at an elevator that had no buttons to summon it and was housed in the only reinforced concrete room we had seen since our arrival.

Once all of our group was inside the cramped elevator lobby with the door closed behind us, Jim nodded and began.

"We've got a team to go back with you to Colorado to get your families. This is a pretty important mission for us, and I can't explain exactly why at this juncture but it will become readily apparent when the time is right. So please hold off on the questions that I'm sure you'll have until you return with your families. Perhaps they will get answered on the road."

Seeing the whole of our group nodding in accordance, Jim turned to the elevator door and stuck out his hand, palm facing up, fingers extended and touching the door.

A blue laser-light immediately shone down from the top of the elevator door and we each shifted around to watch the laser light scan Jim's entire palm, from fingertips to wrist.

After an audible beep Jim stepped to the left where a hidden compartment door lifted up, which he moved his face directly in front of, keeping his eyes open as a green beam shone, scanning his face from forehead to chin, resulting in another beep of the same tone.

As Jim pulled his face back and stood upright the elevator doors opened.

"Whoa," said Ray.

"Are we going to Area 51 or something?"

Jim turned his head to look at him, smiled and shot him a wink, then turned back around to walk into the elevator, take his place at the back and motioned us to follow.

When the last of the team was cramped in the elevator, shoulder to shoulder and nuts to butts, Tony remarked from the front of the pack.

"There aren't any buttons. What do I do?

"Patience," Jim whispered with a smirk.

As Jim's loud whisper faded from our ears the doors silently closed and the elevator began to rocket straight down at a speed so quickly it lifted all of our boots off the ground.

The looks of amazement and wonder were impossible to hide from our faces, but as we were beginning to learn it was best to just go along for the ride and trust that Jim would explain everything.

After ten seconds of downward travel, the elevator came smoothly to a stop and a robotic female voice sounded from somewhere above our heads.

"Restricted area. Authorization code, please."

"Juliet Six, Bravo One, Hotel Niner, Five Tree Alpha."

"Number of pax for admission and destination, please," the detached voice requested.

"Thirteen pax to staging area Charlie," Jim answered to the ceiling.

"Roger that Sir. Thirteen pax, cleared for entry."

The doors rushed open with an audible "whoosh" of air, and as Tony turned to look to Jim for confirmation he signalled to exit the elevator and turn left.

As we filed out of the door, I could feel a pressure change in the hallway and marvelled at the long and sterile-white corridor, lined for several hundred meters in each direction with large steel doors lining its entirety.

Once we were out of the elevator Jim began walking past us, turned once he was at the front of the group, smirked and motioned for us to follow him.

We passed the first door about ten meters from the elevator, a door that seemed identical to the elevator bay we had just exited with an A at its top, and moved another hundred meters down the hallway to the next, again identical to the elevator door aside from a single letter C.

Jim stopped in front and waited for the entire group to join him. As the last of our team was massed behind him, he repeated the procedure with his palm and face, this time turning to shoot us another wink before the doors whooshed open.

He disappeared through the doorway and everyone began to follow. As I walked through the door I was absolutely awestruck at what I was seeing.

Being the last one through the door, it immediately closed as soon as my boots were through the doorway and I stopped in my tracks behind the rest of the group, all standing in amazement with their eyes scanning the enormity of what we were encountering.

"Well, whaddya think?" asked Jim with an amused tone to his voice.

"I know you boys didn't get to see our base at DIA, and while this isn't exactly the same it's a close second."

Our group was silent, still staring in amazement at what appeared to be an airplane hangar converted into a planning and loading bay.

By my estimates the ceiling, full of reinforced steel, was at least twenty meters high with the room fifty meters across and one hundred long, all made of institutional grey concrete.

At the far end of the cavernous room I could see various ground vehicles, from HUMVEES and MRAPs to ATVs, motorcycles and Toyota Hilux trucks. While most were black, we could see that a few were in different stages of being painted with our enemy's colors and flags on the side.

Between us and the vehicles were a few planning areas, set up exactly as we had done while serving in Special Forces, preparing for quick-action missions in airplane hangars while waiting for the order to go, complete with standing whiteboards, sand tables and maps.

Closest to us, just a few meters from where we stood, were our favorite part of any military base: the weapons, situated in metal cages that were approximately four feet tall and three feet across each, stacked two high and painted in the typical military OD green color.

There were five rows on either side of us, lining the room starting about a meter in from the doorway and stretching all the way to the walls on both sides.

Squinting my eyes I could begin to make out the organization, although my mind couldn't fathom the numbers and sheer firepower that existed within them.

Closest to us were pistols, hanging neatly in each cage, characterized against the rear of each with racks of identical types, ranging from the standard military-issue M9s, 1911s, Glock 17s, Glock 19s, MEUs, Sig Sauer P226s, Sig Sauer M11s and an entire line of cages that my eyes weren't keen enough to make out.

The next row farther from us was full of submachine guns, from MP5s, Uzis, Calicos, Scorpions, Daewoos and cages upon cages of various other models.

Following in suit came the rifles, and I spied the obligatory M4s, AKs, HK416s, SCARs, MK 18s and many others.

Further down the same row I could see the size of the cages change, and moving a step to my right I could see the reason: those cages were full of long-range and sniper rifles, from the .300 Winmag that we all loved to the Barrett .50 cals, M40s, M21s, M110s, M210s and even a few Dragunov Russian sniper systems.

Fourth came the meat of the room: the cages of crew-served and fully automatic weapons. Again in the larger ones I spied cages full of M249s, M240s, some old M60s, mini-guns, Russian RPDs and RPKs.

Finally we came to the cages that I knew would make the 18C's feel like kids coming downstairs at first light on Christmas: explosives.

First the rows were filled with the anti-tank weapons from LAWs, AT4s, Russian RPGs, M79s, M72s and detached M203s.

Halfway down the row came a new type of cage designed specifically to house what could be both the most dangerous and beneficial for our current use: the demolitions.

First came the carefully housed blasting caps, det cord, explosive breacher's tape, canisters of explosive foam, concussion/stun grenades, frag grenades and finally wide OD green tough boxes full of what I knew must be C4 and other types of explosives.

After giving us a few moments to stand in awe and drool all over ourselves at the sheer firepower, Jim turned and once again addressed the group.

"Ok boys, I know you're a little light-handed after losing the compound, so we're gonna let you take whatever you need for the trip back to Colorado to get your families. We'll have to take an inventory before you leave and please don't take anything you don't need nor expect to use. We are at war after all and have quite a few freedom fighters to outfit. But before we do that, I need to introduce you guys to the team who will be coming with you. Rob, can you come here?"

I shot a glance to Josh who I could see was already compiling scenarios in his head and lists of what exactly would be best suited for each scenario. He snapped out of his mental accounting long enough to give me a slight head nod that I could go, so I left the guys and walked to stand with him.

Arriving next to him he put his hand on my shoulder and leveled his eyes with me.

"I have a feeling you may catch on to what's going on here before the rest of the group, so I want you to have a look over at the team in the planning bay and tell me what you see."

We were still a good distance away from their team, all but one seated in school-style desks with attached chairs, listening and watching the man at the front who seemed to be briefing an operations order for our upcoming movement.

I couldn't quite make anything out aside from basic military uniforms, dark tanned skin and bearded facial features, so not knowing exactly what Jim was referring to I began to move closer to their group.

I was still a few meters from them when I saw it. The recognition shot through my mind but was immediately put to rest by the logical part of my brain.

But that can't be...

From that distance I could see that while the men were all in the same US military uniform the only markings they had were a single patch on each shoulder, emblazoned with a crimson Maltese cross.

"Templars?" I asked.

"Templars," Jim repeated.

"You mean like the Templar Knights?"

"Not like. The Templar Knights."

"How can that be?" I asked in disbelief.

"Think about it Rob," Jim replied with a matter-of-fact tone.

As the rest of the team circled around us, he raised his hands to let us know he was about to teach another invaluable lesson.

"The Templars were originally a band of chivalric Knights whose charge was to protect Christian pilgrims en route to Jerusalem. At first sworn to vows of piety and chastity, they invented the first banking system so those very pilgrims wouldn't have to carry money and risk the chance of being robbed and losing everything. This made the Knights Templar very wealthy, and caused them to acquire great sums of riches and favor with much of European aristocracy, both for their chivalric duties to the Christians and alignment with The Vatican. But of course also for their money."

He smiled and winked at me, allowing the last word to hang in the air for a moment and sink in before continuing.

"But with great wealth comes jealousy, and it wasn't long before King Philip the Fair of France found himself in debt. Rather than doing the responsible thing and acting as a true leader, he chose to steal himself out of trouble. He and Pope Clement conspired to destroy the Knights Templar and take their wealth for himself."

Again Jim paused to ensure the group was paying attention to this important history lesson, which had been stricken and purposely left out of all but the most sacred of texts.

"Pope Clement gave a Papal edict forbidding the Knights Templar, and on Friday the 13th all Templars in France, the nation which they called home, were ordered to be rounded up and put to death. Jacques DeMolay, head of the Templars, was burned alive at the stake for heresy along with countless other members of the Order because they wouldn't divulge their comrades location. Since approval of the Church was the only way for the King to get away with such a travesty, it was quickly swept under the rug and kept out of most history books at the direction of the Pope."

Looking around the group Jim could see that we were hanging on every word, soaking in the knowledge we had only been told as rumors and conspiracy theories.

He continued.

"King Philip and Pope Clement's plan was to execute and obliterate the entire Order, but by the hand of God several Knights escaped with their lives. They found their way to a few different locations, some to Malta, many to Scotland, where they were welcomed by true Christians who knew the dark secrets of the conspiracy enacted by the King and Pope. The Knights Templar had a new charge and purpose from that point forward: to fight royal despotism and feudal oppression wherever it may be. It was in Scotland that the Templars joined Robert the Bruce and were largely responsible for his victory over King Edward II of England who was trying to invade Scotland."

Josh interjected from the back of the room.

"But we're not in Scotland, what are these guys doing here?"

"Well," Jim answered, "think about it. The Templars took on the charge of fighting the tyranny of dictators and the church. The pilgrims who came to America were seeking to escape religious persecution from an English King who started his own religion and made it one with the state. Does that sound aligned to their mission?"

All heads nodded in accordance, and he continued.

"As I've told you before, this nation was started with Masonic ideals, which the founders, who were Masons, never tried to hide. Christian pilgrims were setting off on a journey for which they needed protection, escaping religious persecution from a royal despot who combined church and state for his own best interests. I have to ask you, where else do you think they'd be but here? Someone had to be there to protect the very first Travelers, and that task fell to men, Knights and Masons who had been doing just that for hundreds of years."

"But how is that possible? How in the world could they have been here for so long and we've never heard of this? You're saying that everything we've been taught about history was wrong?" Dave asked incredulously.

"Not wrong," Jim stopped to contemplate for a moment.

"Just incomplete. Remember, the Templars started as a very overt Order, having no need to hide their actions and purpose. The very legend of them protecting Christians on their pilgrimages helped to keep more Christian pilgrims safe. But they learned in a very vicious way that the world is full of evil men, some much more powerful than mere mortals through politics and money, who would seek to harm those swearing to uphold virtue, values and an oath to protect the good and innocent."

Josh nodded in agreement.

"I can follow that, but the military? These guys were in the United States military and we never knew it or even heard of them?"

Jim chuckled.

"You never heard of the underground bases either, did you? It was of the utmost importance that their existence not be discovered, or the insiders responsible for this very invasion would have followed the examples of King Philip and Pope Clement. The knowledge of their presence was well above Top Secret, information only shared through whispers among those who we knew could be trusted with this truth."

"And these guys are our convoy security? Isn't that a little bit of overkill?" asked Ray.

"Besides the task of protecting Christians, The Templars had another, covert mission that superseded everything else, a treasure to protect that was worth more than life itself. I'm not going to get into what that is at this juncture, but these men have a vested interest to ensure everyone on your compound gets here safely."

"What?" questioned The Major.

"What do these guys have to do with our families?"

"Not your families. You picked up some additional people after your mission at DIA...the Lodge was in contact with us the moment they left with you. All I can tell you is that losing Jacob in the attack on your compound dealt a brutal blow to these men's mission, making the mission to get his family back here something that each of them will die or suffer the worst pain imaginable to ensure happens. Now, clearance or no clearance that's as far as I can go on the subject with you at this time, so let's move on."

"Ok, let's redirect. How do you have this facility on the front lines? You can't tell me that you built all of this, without the enemy knowing, while you were engaged in head-to-head war?" I asked Jim.

"Not at all Rob. And I know you're a smart guy so I'm not insulting your intelligence or military prowess here, but..."

He trailed off for a moment, contemplating the best way to explain without sounding condescending.

"The most important part of war for its designers is to choose the location of each battle. If you can select the battlefield and ensure it's to your advantage, you can control and win the fight," he said, squinting his eyes and watching my face carefully to check that I was picking up the message he was putting out.

"You didn't just build this, did you?" I asked, feeling like an idiot the instant the words came out of my mouth.

"Of course not. When we began war gaming all possible scenarios, enemy coming across the Mexican border was the most obvious. They have a major highway pipeline for logistics, we have way too much territory to effectively cover everything and they could have easily been amassing troops in the deserts of the

Baja, southern Mexico, Central or South America for a long time before we would even know what was happening. There are still a lot of generals down there who aren't too happy with our actions in the 1980's, who wouldn't take much convincing to help our enemies give us a healthy dose of payback for sticking our nose in their countries between the Sandinistas, Contra's and any other number of parties. A battle may be short-lived, but a war can burn for ages as some people can be quite patient in waiting for just the right time to enact their revenge. A battle is a sprint, but a geopolitical war is a marathon, and in the grand scheme of things several decades isn't really that long on the timeline of human existence and blood feuds throughout history."

"My dad was down there in the eighties," added Ray from the group.

"I know. And Rob, you may not know this but your grandpa was right there with Ray's dad."

"Excuse me?" I asked.

"I know this is a lot, but we'll have to cover that later. For now, let's just say that the underground portion of this base was built years ago. It's a strategic location that we chose based on terrain and the tunnels across the border that the cartels thought we didn't know about, as the place we could most easily funnel them to in order to choose our battlefront. Once the invasion happened it only took a few diversions and breadcrumbs to have them right where we wanted them."

"So Austin isn't the HQ, is it?"
Jim seemed as if he were about to answer but hesitated, waiting for me to turn the wheels in my head and pull the string just a tad further.

"This is the HQ. That's why the General is here. Jumping Jesus on a pogo stick, you put the HQ smack dab on the front lines?'

"Where's the best place to hide something Rob?" Jim asked wryly.

"Directly in plain sight."

CHAPTER 3

RETURN TO COLORADO

After yet another insightful lesson from Jim, he walked our team to meet The Templars.

"Moshe," he called out to the man at the front of the room as our group followed him across the hangar.

"Meet the men of 022. These are the guys we told you about from Colorado."

"You mean the ones who let Jacob die?" he asked with a snarl.

"This is neither the time nor the place for that. Settle down," Jim ordered.

Moshe diverted his attention from Jim, giving me a full once-over from head to toe, then turned to the team behind me and scanned every man in the same fashion.

"These guys are supposed to be Special Forces?" he asked skeptically.

"I thought they would be be bigger."

"You don't look like you'd win any strongman competitions yourself," The Major chimed in.

He had a point.

Moshe stood a few inches taller than me, standing just around six foot. While he didn't exactly have a barrel chest or look like he'd win any deadlift competitions, it was obvious from the sinewy muscles in his forearms, exposed from his rolled-up uniform sleeves and veins bulging without any exercise or tension that he was in far better than average shape.

He had shoulder-length black and curly hair, and from his facial features and olive-tanned complexion I could tell that he had Israeli DNA coursing through his body...which made perfect sense.

Looking around at the rest of his team, seated in the chairs and obviously perturbed that we had disrupted their briefing, it was apparent that the same basic genealogy or at least ancient nation of origin was shared by all.

I had so many questions for them.

Were they all bred from the original Templars? Was this the same bloodline that had stayed together, breeding new generations of knights and warriors to uphold their sacred oath and duty, or had they been admitting new members and growing?

If they started with only few dozen knights hundreds of years ago and had at least two sons each, the sheer number of these guys would be incredible by this point.

Who would the wives be? Could knights even have wives, weren't they sworn to an oath of chastity along with piety and bravery?

My spinning head was snapped back to reality as Moshe motioned to more foldable chairs stacked against a wall and seemed to be reading my mind verbatim.

"We can answer all your questions later, Rob. For now you and your team get your chairs and have a seat. We need to be on the road as soon as possible."

Looking back to The Major he motioned for me to grab chairs for the team, turned to J-Lo and directed him to help.

Grabbing enough chairs for our team J-Lo and I began to set them up behind the Templars. After we had taken our seats, Moshe moved to the map affixed to a whiteboard at the front of the room and started to speak.

"We'll start back from square one for the newcomers."

If they had been any military unit I'd ever been a part of, you would expect at least a few audible groans and wisecrack comments to have erupted from the peanut gallery at the news that the time they had spent briefing already was wasted, and they would have sit back through it all over.

Instead, there was nothing more than silence and rapt attention.

None of the Templars even blinked, fidgeted or did anything besides devote all their focus to Moshe as he laid out our personnel (*how did he know every one of our names and specialties),* which trucks we would be traveling in, our route back to Colorado, actions in the event of enemy contact or emergency, frequencies for communications and go-to-hell plans.

When he finished, he turned back to the group and asked the obligatory "any questions?"

Seeing none, Moshe began to fold his telescopic pointer away and at once The Templars stood and got to work on their trucks.

I wondered if they were nothing more than robots from the absolute precision and efficiency with which they moved, and that once moving they didn't stop to chat with one another, crack jokes or do anything aside from working towards their objective of getting the vehicles ready to move.

As we had left our vehicles in Austin we would be riding in The Templar's trucks and would have to bring extra vehicles for our families, the additional people that we had picked up at DIA & the prisoner camp and our equipment.

This was probably for the best, as Moshe had chosen to take their trucks that bore the Cyrillic writing, flags and designators of Russian military vehicles.

Josh called our team into a huddle and ordered us to begin going through the trucks they had designated for us to ensure we knew where everything was, and most importantly that the drivers knew how to operate them.

He next instructed the Bravos to pick out our weapons systems & ammo and the Charlies to choose any necessary explosives.

Moshe had ordered that we needed to roll out in less than thirty minutes, so once Josh gave his order we became a flurry of movement.

I was astonished that our men had taken on the demeanor of The Templars and, contrary to any time that I had ever prepared for a mission with our guys, not a word was spoken in jest or sarcasm.

The Templars were in their trucks ten minutes prior to our time set by Moshe, as our team was still scrambling to load the new weapons and gear.

The Charlies walked around and gave new frag, concussion and smoke grenades to each man in our party, and as Jim watched and smiled we were seated in our respective vehicles two minutes prior to the stated departure time.

As the large digital clock on the wall closest to the vehicles ticked down, Jim walked to the passenger side of the lead Templar vehicle where Moshe was located to have a quick discussion with him, ending with a head nod and salute as he made his way back to us.

As usual I was in front with The Major, but due to the reshuffling of the trucks we had Dave and Buckeye in our truck as well. I was extremely hesitant at first, as every Green Beret I had ever met was more superstitious before a mission than even the crustiest old school baseball player before a big game.

But I figured that since so much had changed from our normal SOP [Standard Operating Procedures] already, a simple change in seat assignments wasn't enough to get worked up about.

Stopping outside of our truck on The Major's side, Jim crossed his arms on his chest and took a deep breath.

"Take it easy on these guys," he remarked to The Major.

"They are going to be different than anyone or anything you have ever dealt or worked with before."

He paused after the last word to glance back towards Moshe's vehicle.

"Understand that they are a force to be reckoned with, and hell hath no fury like men with a single purpose and absolute dedication. They don't joke, they don't play and they don't stop moving forward. Ever."

"Laying it on a little thick sir, don't you think?" The Major asked.

"You'll see what I mean," was Jim's response.

"You boys had lives before you joined the military and while it may be hard to remember now, childhoods full of friends and playing. These men have been bred and raised for a single purpose, and have been trained to enact that purpose for generations."

Jim paused again as each of The Templars engines roared to life, and looking on the wall it was precisely 1800 hours, our designated time to leave as ordered by Moshe. As I cranked our engine to life, Jim shot me a nod.

"They'll take care of you, but remember that you are not their mission. I'll meet you back in Austin in a few days."

With those parting words, Jim came to full attention and rendered a salute to our vehicle. After I returned his gesture the pressure changed in the hangar, and looking in the direction of Moshe's truck I understood why.

The rear wall, that which the vehicles were lined up facing, began to lower into the ground rapidly, showing a great concrete tunnel leading up at an angle, nearly the size of the Holland tunnel in New York City.

As Jim stepped back, Moshe's voice come to life with a single word through our Peltor headsets.

"Moving."

And with that, they were off.

Like everything else in The Templar's being there was no gentle easing the vehicles off the line to a gradual start. The lead vehicle lurched forward and began to speed through the tunnel, followed in close pursuit by the rest of the convoy.

The screeching of our tires against the hangar floor was replaced by a silent whir as they met the concrete of the tunnel and commenced our ascension to ground level.

After several hundred meters the tunnel made a sharp turn to the right and soon we were traveling 180 degrees in the opposite direction, steadily climbing up. Again, a few hundred meters later we made another sharp, 180 degree turn and I understood what the tunnel was.

The steady climb and turns were reminiscent of days spent trying to find a parking spot in an airport or shopping mall garage, although I believe they would put anyone in jail for moving at that speed back in the real world.

After several turns and what seemed like hundreds of meters of upward elevation there was yet another pressure change as the ceiling above us began to retract.

I watched as Moshe's vehicle accelerated and shot out of the tunnel, disappearing from view. I understood that he must have come out above ground, wherever that was.

Soon the vehicles in front of us disappeared from view as well, and as we were traveling close to them to keep up with their rapid pace it wasn't long before we also emerged into another dark tunnel.

The vehicle headlights illuminated more dark grey concrete. Rather than one single block as the hangar had been these seemed to be the same T-barriers I had seen at ground level earlier, along with concrete blocks on top.

Those on top, I suspected, must have been positioned to ensure that drones, satellites or planes flying overhead wouldn't be able to view the tunnel from which we had emerged.

After about thirty seconds I began to see daylight, and soon the T-barriers were gone and we found ourselves driving along a dirt road.

As we drove past the plywood huts we had seen earlier, I caught a glimpse of the helipad that our Black Hawk was still resting on and we made a sharp turn toward the main road of the FOB.

Looking in our side view mirrors to ensure everyone on our team made it out I was relieved when I observed all of our vehicles in tow complete with armored trucks, APC's [Armored Personnel Carriers] and supply trucks. Before long we were nearing the front gate, and as I began to wonder if Moshe was going to blow through it opened in just enough time for our convoy to speed through.

"He didn't even slow down," I said in disbelief.

"Yeah I don't think that's his style," Dave added from the back.

"This should be an interesting trip."

The Templars may have entranced us in their no-nonsense approach while getting ready to leave, but it only took a few miles of road outside of the FOB's gate for Dave and I to strike up a conversation.

He explained that he had been raised Mormon, and for reasons he wasn't inclined to share with someone he barely knew (let alone the rest of the truck) he had left that faith in his teens.

We immediately hit it off amongst the long stretches of highway and dirt that is desolate West Texas, continually talking along each route and only pausing to take nature calls and switch seats every few hours.

Dave reminded me once again just how careless and callous it was to judge a book by its cover, for even though he was built like a linebacker and spoke slowly with a midwestern accent he was one of the most intelligent and insightful men I had ever spoken with.

Our conversation continued without stopping through Texas and into Oklahoma, where we decided to pull over and try to rest.

Truckers and dads on long distance car trips love to play the macho angle and go as long as possible without sleep, but we knew just how dangerous that would be in our situation.

We finally had enough people to have adequate security while the others slept, and having everyone alert greatly reduced the chances that our sleep-deprived and blurry eyes would miss an IED, ambush or enemy gunship that had avoided our radar.

Fifteen hours into our trip and conversation neither of us were ready to take a break, so Dave and I each volunteered to be a part of the first group to stay up and pull security as the others found a comfortable patch of dirt to lay down on.

We were still running our mouths about the similarities between Masonry and Mormonism an hour later when J-Lo tapped me on the shoulder.

"Hey guys," he quietly uttered in his growling southern accent.

"I hate to break you two lovebirds up, but Josh says if we don't get ambushed he's gonna kill you both himself if you don't shut the hell up and get some sleep."

Looking down at my watch and realizing what time it was, there was only one way I could think of that would appropriately call an end to such an invigorating and enlightening conversation.

I held up my fist, which Dave met with a bump. We nodded to each other, and before turning to find my own patch of dirt I repeated my assessment from earlier that day.

"I don't care what they say about you big guy, you're alright."

Finally getting it, he chuckled, turned around and walked off into the cold, black night to find his own piece of respite for a few hours.

The scent of coffee first got my senses stirring, and as I opened my eyes Tex was kneeling over me, gently wafting the aroma from a tin soldiers mug towards my face.

"You seemed to be having a pleasant dream there Rob. There aren't many of those left anymore, so I didn't want it to end too suddenly for you."

"Thanks Jason, that was mighty nice of you."

"Did you find what you were looking for?" he asked in his cool and friendly Texas accent.

"How did you know I was looking for something? Was I talking in my sleep?" I asked.

"Naw man," he said, grinning.

"You just strike me as the kind of guy who's always looking for something, and won't rest until he finds it. So, did ya find it?" he repeated.

"You know Jason...I don't know Brother. Sometimes I even know that I'm looking for something, but just don't know what it is I'm looking for quite yet. Does that make sense?"

"Yessir," he replied.

"I know those kids mean the world to you. I heard a little bit about your background, and I get it. My family history is pretty similar, but instead of losing a mom to cancer I lost mine to divorce. I don't have any kids o' my own quite yet, but I can tell you nothing would make me happier."

"It changes your life Brother, that's for sure. You'll be a great dad when the time comes, but let's focus on making the world a better place for you to raise yours in before you start knocking girls up, how about that?"

He laughed to himself, took a sip from his cup and started to walk away but had a second thought. He turned and knelt back down next to me, now up on my elbows nursing my coffee.

"And you know what, just so it's not confusing, can you call me Tex like the other guys?"

"Of course," I replied.

"I wasn't sure how you felt about that. I've gone by a lot of nicknames over the years, I know how important the right nickname can be to a guy."

"Yeah, well I'm actually from Texas, born and raised. Small town named Rosethorn, population not much more than a couple a' hundred on a busy day. It was the Navy that took me outta Texas, and if I'm honest it's kinda like I've always been waiting for someone to give me that nickname. It's like I know I'm finally in the right place."

"Well ok Tex, that sounds right by me. Thanks for the coffee Brother, anybody say how long we have until we roll out?"
He glanced down at his watch and grinned.

"I think that conversation just cost us most of our time to get ready. If nothing's changed I think we're heading out in about five minutes."

"Yeah that sounds about right. That gives me just enough time to hit the little boys room and move to the trucks. Thanks again for the coffee."

Tex nodded in affirmation, shot me a wink and walked back towards the vehicles before I was off the ground.

I had slept on plenty of cold rocks during my time in the Army and had woken up with my face frozen to more than one. And even though there wasn't any ice or snow around us, the aches and pains throughout my body were just another way of my body telling me that civilian life had made me soft.

"Hey Tex, did you have a chance to see where The Templars slept?" I shot my question to him as he sauntered away.

"Yessir," he replied.

"So did they plug into the cigarette lighters in their trucks to recharge or did they actually sleep like real human beings?"

Tex chuckled a bit and kept walking.

"You'll have to see that for yourself."

I let out a groan as I rolled to my knees to stand and Klint laughed at me from a few feet away.

"Yeah Rob, that'll happen. Guess medical school left out the sleeping on rocks portion that we got in the 18 Delta course, huh buddy?"

The cobwebs in my brain and soreness in my body prevented me from having any reasonable or humorous answer for him, so I gave him the best response I had ever learned in the Army: I shot him the middle finger.

"Well at least you still have your sense of humor buddy. They can't take that away from you," he laughed.

As I was relieving myself behind an outcropping of boulders not far from the camp I began staring at an arrangement of small rocks and dirt just in front of me that had somehow found their way over time into a miniature pyramid of sorts.

I contemplated the sheer statistical odds that a group of a dozen small stones would fall in that arrangement as the top one became dislodged and rolled to the ground.

As I brought my gaze up from the fallen former Capstone, the rest of the formation began dancing around ever so slightly.

The fogginess in my brain couldn't understand why in the world the earth was acting so funny in this place, but then I started to perceive the vibrations in my feet and the cold rock I was straddling.

I peeked my head up like a prairie dog looking for predators and noticed that I wasn't the only one who felt something strange: several other men in the camp had stopped dead in their tracks and were scanning the horizon.

"GUNSHIPS, TEN MILES OUT, COMING FROM THE WEST," someone shouted from inside one of the trucks.

"Throw the nets over the vehicles, now! Everyone get under a rock or in a truck and put a weapon in your hand! All radios off," The Major yelled to our group.

As I sprinted to the trucks to help with the camouflage netting I couldn't believe how lax we had become. It hadn't been long since the original trip back to Colorado, but given that we hadn't seen enemy gunships in a few weeks it seemed like a lifetime.

After pulling the netting over my truck I jumped in the passenger seat and pulled the charging handle back on my rifle to glance through the ejection port and ensure I had a round chambered.

Seeing that I was ready to fight if needed, I began to scan our temporary base camp to check that everything was hidden from sight.

The dashboard in the truck started to rattle with the vibrations being emitted from the gunships as they moved closer, when I caught something out of my peripheral vision that made my heart jump.

Amidst the rocky, barren terrain I squinted to make out a camouflaged woobie [Army blanket] flowing in the wind.

Looking out over the horizon I identified three Mi-28N Russian gunships, escorted by two smaller Ka-50 attack helicopters.

"Shit," I exclaimed under my breath.

"What's up bro?" Dave asked from the driver's seat in a hushed voice.

"Someone left a woobie out. It's flapping in the breeze over there," I said, pointing to the spot.

"Well it's camouflaged, maybe they won't see it."

"Yeah, but it's camouflaged for the woods. We're in the mountains."

"Damn it. That's not going to end well."

With my right thumb I pulled the selector switch on my rifle from safe to fire while moving my left hand up to the door handle. If things went bad they would do so fast, and seeing my movement Dave followed suit.

I looked through the netting to the formation of helos coming closer, then back at Dave.

We both winced as the gunships came closer, while the reverberations in the truck became so loud and forceful that it was almost painful, then back at each other as they flew over top and kept moving.

The team was staying off the net in case the enemy had the ability to listen in, but I was pretty sure we were all thinking the same exact thing.

Please keep going along on your merry way.

As the reverberations began to dissipate we each let out a sigh of relief and started breathing again. I peered through the netting and back window to find the formation flying away from us.

Somehow our team’s lucky horseshoe was still paying dividends.

From the rear seat of the Mi-28N Dmitri pointed a thick, gloved finger to the ground as he spoke to the pilots and other gunships over the radio.

"There."

"I don't see anything," the comrade piloting his helo responded.

"11 o'clock. Five hundred meters. Do you see the green thing flying around on the ground and the strange, rounded rocks around it? Those aren't boulders, those are trucks with the men we're looking for in them."

"Do you want to engage Major?" the pilot asked.

"Nyet," Dimitri responded.

"Stay on this course. They are going back for their families. I think it would have much more of an impact on their people if we wait until we have all of them together, don't you think? Their wives and children will make a much better example. Mark this location; we can be assured they won't take the same route back. And since there are only two routes they can take to travel quickly, we know where to wait for them."

Dmitri smiled to himself and began to daydream. Not about medals, nor accolades nor the praise that he would receive from catching the American rebels he had been sent to hunt.

That wasn't Dmitri's style.

Rather he started to daydream about things that would be considered nightmarish to other, normal and well-adjusted people.

He began to plan the logistics behind flaying them alive, in front of an audience of course, and finding a way to televise it to the rest of the American dogs.

He thought about how entertaining it would be to waterboard them with gasoline, setting their writhing bodies to flame after he was finished to show people what real torture looked like.

He smiled as he imagined the most brutal methods that could be used to keep them fully lucid as he deliberately cut limbs and sliced the skin from their bodies, forcing them to scream and cry and wail while their people watched their "heroes" being reduced to nothing more than a puddle of weeping blood, flesh and bone.

He learned of a technique to pop someone's eyeball out of its socket, yet keep the retinas intact and, if you were very careful, would allow the sight to remain so you could actually turn it around and make the victim view their own empty eye socket as you put the blowtorch to it.

They wouldn't see the results, of course, but they would feel the immense pain and scream for mercy that would never come.

And it made him grin in anticipation.

Down on the ground, the team began to exit the trucks and come out from their places of hiding when the gunships disappeared over the horizon and the vibration from their rotors ceased. As Dave and I exited our truck and started folding the netting to put back in the trunk, Josh spoke up.

"Alright boys it looks like the Ruskies just ate up our five minutes to get ready. Pull your heads out of your rears and start the trucks, we ain't home yet."

Just a few short minutes after the gunships disappeared from sight we were driving back to our families, eyes glued to the horizon and fingers on our triggers.

The worry began to fade from our minds rather quickly, and Dave and I picked back up on our previous day's conversations within the first hour of the drive.

Pulling into the front gate of the fallback compound outside of Colorado Springs put me on high alert. We radioed ahead when we were a few minutes out and Chad had given us the all-clear to pull in, but as we rolled through the gate I observed several men in the guard towers whom I didn't recognize.

Just as I was pointing it out to the others in our truck, two more men I had never seen before emerged and started moving towards the trucks with weapons drawn.

As I began to open my door to provide cover for what I thought was going to be a firefight, Bulldog burst from the building with his hands up, yelling at the two figures.

"What the hell are you doing, do you want to get yourselves killed? Put those damn rifles down."

Seeing the men hesitating, he stepped in between them and our lead vehicle to prevent anyone from making a stupid mistake.

"These are our guys. Back off," he barked to the men with their weapons drawn.

"Who the hell is that?" I asked him.

"Long story. Good guys. Let's just say we've all met before," he answered before yelling out to the whole group, who were getting out of their vehicles and beginning to stretch.

"Download your gear and hurry into the office. We've got a lot to catch up on."

I looked to the front of our convoy while stretching my back, arms and legs, as Moshe left his truck and made a beeline for the two strangers.

"Doesn't even need to stretch, huh?" I asked Dave.

"What are these guys made of?"

I watched as Moshe and the two strangers, who I now noticed both had gray ACU uniforms but shared the same Maltese Cross patch on their shoulders, huddled in a small circle and their demeanor indicated that the two were filling him in on something.

When one pointed to the guest house of the fallback compound, I found something that had escaped me when we pulled in.

Well-hidden given that our fallback compound didn't have much cover and concealment, there were four uniformed soldiers lying in the prone at each corner of the guest house, facing out with rifles drawn and eyes on their scopes, scanning the horizon outside of the chain link fences.

In addition there were two more standing on either side of the front door, unmoving and reminiscent of the British royal guard who tirelessly stand their posts at Buckingham palace.

Before the stranger's hand was down, Moshe was heading straight for the guest house.

As I squinted and racked my brain to try and figure out just what in the world was going on, Bulldog began shouting orders from his own pow-wow with Josh.

"Move into the team room men. We don't have much time. Everything is ready to roll and these guys are going to be on their way soon, with or without us. And we want to be in their convoy, trust me."

I glanced back to Dave and the rest of our group, hoping someone else was a little sharper than me and had an idea of what we had gotten ourselves into.

Seeing nothing more than shrugs and similar looks of puzzlement on the other guys faces, I decided the only place I would be getting any information was in the team room.

Bulldog and Josh walked towards the team room when we began moving, and once the team was seated Bulldog walked to the front of the room and began to fill us in.

"So you guys saw that we have some new friends, and I see you came back with a few of your own," he began as he was met with a sea of blank and questioning faces.

"These are a contingent of the GI Joe Space Command that we ran into at DIA the night of our operation. When you linked up with their leader in Texas and rolled out to come this way, they showed up and filled us in. They didn't call, they didn't send any signal that they were coming, they just appeared at the front gate. Let's just say that was an interesting event."

Chad let out a chuckle from his seat at the side of the room next to the radios, confirming Bulldog's comment.

After a sharp glance at Chad, Bulldog continued.

"We still don't know exactly who they are, but they're friendly and have been helping us man the security until you got back. Well that's not entirely true...they made sure that the attachments we brought home the night of the DIA hit were secure, and didn't care too much about the rest of us."

I raised my hand to try and add what little information we had gained on the trip, but Bulldog waived me off.

"These guys have been very clear that their only mission is to protect those attachments, and that their plan was to move out the moment their leader arrived with you. From talking to them and seeing the firepower they have, if we're going to be moving out to Texas I want us to be in their convoy. Which means there's no time to sit here and debate or run our mouths."

I looked around the room as each of the men in our team nodded in accordance.

"You each will be back in the same trucks you came in, and we'll be putting the families in the APC's. The guys here are already loading our stuff on the supply trucks, and as we never really unpacked after getting blown out of the first compound and had about twenty-four hours to prep, we should be ready to go in no time. Rob, go say hi to your family, everyone else eat some hot chow and then hurry right back to your vehicles. Go."

On his final command the room erupted into a flurry of activity, each man moving with a purpose. Part of me was pleased that The Templar's focus had rubbed off on our group, but another was beginning to miss the catcalls, humor and closeness that had been such a mainstay of our team to that point.

Following orders, I moved out of the team room and began to make my way to the living quarters to search for my family.

The fallback compound had been nothing more than a contingency plan from the beginning, so while it was livable it was nowhere near what our original compound had been.

Given the sparse accommodations I was relieved that we'd be moving our families to Texas and to a location that was not only much more secure but would also be more comfortable for them.

And having grown up in Texas myself a part of me had been waiting for the day that I could relocate my kids back there from the moment they were born.

Walking down the front steps of the team room I observed Moshe and his men move with the precision and quickness that was their style.

As I stepped off the last stair their truck engines started up outside in unison. There were groups of Templars ferrying the families out of the guest house and into the trucks, and I knew we didn't have much time.

Our own vehicles were being loaded with supplies as I walked towards our living quarters, but before I began my descent down the stairs I heard an engine shift from idle into drive.

I turned around and observed the lead truck, complete with Moshe and its crew, begin to pull around and move towards the gate.

They really aren't messing around.

I jumped down the final steps into the living quarters and found Ray's wife Sarah walking towards me with my children.

"Daddy," Robert squealed in excitement and pulled away from holding Sarah's hand to sprint to me.

Even in his young age, he was already showing that he would be built just like his dad, and quite possibly turn out to be even larger and stronger than I had been in my best days.

His shoulders had begun to broaden, and his legs were getting the thick build that looked as if he ever found protein and squat machines he could be a professional athlete if he so chose.

If professional sports ever became a pastime again.

Barreling towards me at full speed, he ran into me just as I squatted and picked him up to envelop him in a hug. I rubbed his hair and gave him the biggest squeeze I could muster, being exhausted from the road.

As Sarah reached us I moved Robert over to my right arm and took Avery in my left, pulling her in for a hug and giving her a kiss on her forehead.

Smiling at me in the way that a little girl reserves only for her father, my heart melted and I lost all sense of war, travel, vengeance and battle. I was always a dad before anything else, and I forgot the world and what was going on in it, happy to once again have all that I loved cradled in my arms.

A call from Griz at the top of the stairs broke our little family love fest after only a few seconds.

"Rob, Sarah, the convoy is pulling out. Get your butts up and in the trucks, it's go time."

Nodding a thank you to Sarah we turned and began walking together.

"I'm going to have to ride in the front truck with Dave, The Major and Buckeye on this one, can you stay with the rugrats during the drive?" I asked her.

"Of course, that was the plan!" was her reply.

Ray and Sarah didn't have children of their own, but she was one of those strong, intelligent yet loving women that you knew would make a wonderful mother one day. And by all means, our entire team had been pulling for that to happen as well.

Sure, we wanted them to be happy. But selfishly we all hoped that these great people would be able to pass their genes along and put another generation of amazing human beings back into our society.

As we reached the convoy I saw that The Templar trucks had already left the compound, and each of our team were seated in their vehicles with gun turrets up top, ready to roll.

I led Sarah to the APC they would be riding in, and as she walked in the rear door first and turned to take my children I hesitated for a moment and took one last long hug with both of them.

As I tried to pry Avery off first and hand her to Sarah's waiting arms, I was met with resistance and her stronger grip around my neck.

Deciding to give her another moment with daddy, I tried next to pry Robert off, but was once again met with resistance from my children who didn't want to be separated again.

JLo turned to me from the driver's seat and gave the "hurry it up" signal, so I took a knee and stood both of my kids in front of me.

"Robert, Avery, we're going to a new home that is much nicer and safer than this one, but it's far away."

I looked up into the APC and found the other children playing together and reading books their mothers had packed for the trip.

Turning my gaze back to my children, I continued.

"This is going to be a long ride, but you'll be with all of your friends and we'll be there before you know it."

"But why can't you come with us dad?" Robert asked.

"Daddy has to stay up front to make sure that we keep you kids safe. Mrs Sarah and Mrs Deanna will take very good care of you, and will be a lot more fun than daddy would be. So can you both be tough boys and girls for dad and be good listeners for the trip?"

"Yes dad," they replied in unison.

"Good," I added as I picked them up and handed them off to Sarah.

"I love you guys, and I'll come visit you every time we stop. Have fun, play with your friends but most importantly be good listeners and I'll have a surprise for you when the trip is over...if Mrs Sarah tells me that you were good on the drive. Deal?"

Seeing both heads nodding in affirmation, I reached up for a final kiss on each forehead.

I watched as Sarah took them to their seats and began to fasten their seatbelts.

The voice in the back of my head started whining about taking a seat right there in the back with them, spending precious time with those who I held so dearly and using the opportunity to tell them everything that was going on, catch up on what they had been doing the past several days and having fun with them like I used to before this all began.

But looking beyond them and to my Brothers seated in the front, guns at the ready and holding steadfast to go upon this new leg of our mission, I knew that sitting in the back of that APC wasn't where I was needed, nor where I would provide the most safety for my children.

Sometimes being a good dad is about doing the right thing rather than doing what you want, and with that I shot them a smile and moved back to the driver seat in the lead vehicle to begin our movement.

While we hadn't been ambushed on our trip to Colorado to get our families, to be safe we opted to take a different route on the trip back to Austin in case a spotter had seen us along the way.

Knowing that the front lines had been drawn north of the Texas/Mexico border we chose to start by traversing cross-country into Kansas and then making the southerly drive south through Oklahoma and into Texas.

We wouldn't have the safety of the mountains to provide cover in the event that we came upon an enemy ambush, but we hoped that our increased numbers and the speed of flat land would make up for it.

We caught up to The Templars moving east along I-70 in Kansas, and as had been our initial plan moved their convoy into the middle of ours to keep them safe with our families.

And we were driving along I-35 south nearing Edmond and Oklahoma City when they hit us.

The lull of our tires rolling along the highway combined with the lack of sleep from the constant movement over the past week had put each of our minds into a state of unnatural relaxation.

I hadn't even perceived a change as the plains of Colorado and Kansas had given way to the lush greenery of central Oklahoma.

We should have been alert. We should have fallen back on our training and realized that if the enemy were going to hit us, that would be the perfect spot.

Tired from a long movement and unaware, I hadn't even considered the choke points formed by the dense, encroaching trees and forest on either side of the highway leading to the optimal circumstances for an ambush that nature had provided for our enemy.

The IED rocked us so hard that before the sound of the explosion reached our ears the truck was rolling on its left side, still moving forward but now spinning and tumbling.

We were no longer on the highway but now in the well-manicured median between north and southbound lanes leaving us absolutely nowhere to hide.

Once we stopped moving I looked around in a daze to ensure that everyone in our truck was alive, if not shell shocked and doing their best to gather their wits.

Our vehicle had come to rest on its roof, and as I checked our side mirrors to check on the convoy that had been behind us, I realized that both mirrors had been crushed and torn off in either the explosion or subsequent rolling.

As I saw Dave, The Major and Buckeye begin working to unfasten their seatbelts, I knew that everyone was alive and put all of my focus into finding and securing my children.

I pulled the knife from my pocket to once again cut myself free from a seatbelt in a downed vehicle when I heard the "whoosh" of a shoulder fired rocket and subsequent explosion.

Understanding the logistical steps of an ambush I knew that after they had the lead vehicle (ours) disabled, they would likely next target the trail vehicle to trap everyone in between with no way to escape.

But it was what would come last that scared me the most: eliminating everything in between.

I freed myself from the seatbelt and kicked my door open, seeing that Dave, The Major and Buckeye had done the same.

The Major began yelling something as I exited the truck, but my ears were ringing so loudly and thoughts of my children racing so fast that nothing else in the world existed to me at the moment.

Taking a knee at the rear of our overturned vehicle I worked to assess the situation as quickly as possible.

Ours was the only truck that had been blown off the highway, and the rest of the convoy had continued driving and stopped several hundred meters ahead of us.

That was good, as the standard ambush would have put crew-served weapons and any shoulder-fired rockets at the far end, near where our trail vehicle was.

By pushing through the killzone (which I was now firmly in) our team had opened up an opportunity for survival.

Tracers and small arms fire began to erupt from the treeline on the western side of the highway, aiming both at our truck and the convoy ahead of us.

Looking for muzzle flashes and point of origin for the shooting I realized that it was a linear ambush, meaning all enemy was situated on the same side of the road.

These were definitely not un-trained cartel soldiers. These guys knew what they were doing.

As I braced myself to begin running for the convoy to check on my children Dave's large hand took a firm grip on my shoulder to prevent me from going.

Looking back I could see his lips moving and his head nodding side to side, but couldn't discern any of the words coming from his mouth.

Just as I returned my gaze to surmise our situation, I found that my hearing was not so diminished as to miss the opening salvo from the enemy heavy weapons squad.

As the flurry of red tracers continued erupting from the woodline several hundred meters behind us, I thanked all that is Holy that this was nothing more than what I had assumed, a linear ambush with their heavy weapons situated at the far end of the objective.

If their heavy weapons had been emplaced in the center of the ambush, or our team hadn't been smart enough to push through the killzone, we would have lost a considerable amount of people.

After only a few seconds of their heavy weapons opening fire it was met with a fury that I had never seen before.

While I couldn't hear anything coming out of my Peltors, I assumed that Bulldog or Josh had come over the net, telling our turret gunners to hold tight until they showed their hand.

Because once we knew where their heavy weapons were, we had enough firepower on top of our dozen trucks to decimate just about any small enemy element.

Our team met force with force and the cannons from the Bradley, .50 caliber machine guns on top of HUMVEE's & MRAP and MK19 fully-automatic grenade launchers began to make short work of the foliage which our enemy was hiding behind.

The flurry of red tracers coming from the forest slowed at first and then stopped altogether as the trees were felled around them from so much lead that I didn't think anything would ever be able to grow in that area again.

As the small arms fire and heavy weapons tracers from the woodline began to die down, there was another clinch of Dave's hand on my shoulder and then a push.

Knowing that was the typical signal to tell the first man in a squad preparing to enter a house and conduct Close Quarters Combat [CQB] to go, I set off racing towards the APC in our convoy, not hesitating or looking back.

Reaching the last vehicle I transitioned to the highway shoulder and continued running until I ensured that the APC containing my children was untouched and idling.

Looking back I found Dave, The Major and Buckeye sprinting towards me.

I glanced forward in the convoy to find Josh, his door open and motioning for us to come to him for instructions. But before I could take my first step, vibrations began to rattle the ground underneath my boots.

Looking at him it was obvious that I wasn't the only one who noticed, and hoped that the incoming gunships weren't so close that the families in the APC would hear it.

Looking back towards the overturned truck, my worst fears became reality as the same formation of Russian helicopters we had seen on the way to Colorado was now heading in our direction, flying low and over the highway following our route.

The vehicle that I was bracing my body against began to vibrate, and I tried to attain both a tiny bit of protection from what I knew would be incoming rounds and stabilization to take aim and begin to fire.

I stared in horror as each of the helicopters opened their arsenal and let loose a salvo of bullets and missiles toward our convoy as the men from my truck sprinted towards the safety of the armored vehicles.

Dave was first to reach our trail vehicle, but as The Major and Buckeye began to near us the gunships shifted their field of fire.

I felt rounds scream past my body and the Russian S-8 rockets impact on the highway and median.

I lifted my M4 to return fire, expending my first magazine of 5.56 rounds. I knew that it was next to useless but was steadfast that I would do anything necessary to protect my family and take everything I had back to the enemy.

The gunships were still out of range of my M203 grenade launcher, but if they came close I'd be sure to get one inside of their open bay doors, even if they took me down trying.

As Dave turned and followed suit, the attack helicopter pulled ahead of the formation and began to walk its rounds up the highway towards Buckeye.

I screamed for him to hurry, but the deafening cacophony of the firefight drowned out any hope of his hearing my cries.

I prayed to God, hoping he would find the strength to push faster, stay out of their aim and that the Russian gunners would be out of focus or miss their mark.

Another gunship let loose its next volley, and my heart sank as the 23 mm rounds cut my Brother down while he sprinted towards us, his forward progress stopped dead in its tracks in the middle of the road.

I felt as if a part of my own soul were being ripped apart as the bullets tore through his body.

The trousers of his uniform changed from ACU grey to crimson red as the projectiles nearly cut him in half and his legs fell out from under him.

The spray of fire continued along the ground, now moving through his entire body.

He was wearing body armor, but the velocity and caliber of the rounds were much more than it had been built to withstand.

Despite the chaos I heard them impact and splinter the ceramic plates on his back and chest, meant to protect him from at most 7.62mm.

His plates were pulverized by the massive size and velocity from the 23mm rounds, which turned them into nothing more than a cloud of dust and blood.

Sparks began to fly as the rounds from the massive gunship ricocheted off the pavement in front of him and continued their search for more victims.

Those very sparks ignited a flame in my soul.

The Major reached our trail vehicle and turned to fire at the oncoming helos.

The truck that I was bracing against violently pushed forward as my ears popped, bringing sound back to my world in time to hear several audible "whooshes" of a rocket launch.

While my eyes were trained on the enemy, four orange streaks screamed towards the unsuspecting gunships.

As the attack helicopters on the outside of the formation broke away, one of the slow and laborious gunships erupted into a ball of fire, dripping flaming fuel and the bodies of its crew to the waiting pavement below.

I looked up and observed that a turret had risen from the top of the vehicle that I was braced against, and one of The Templars had opened a door on the back and was handloading replacement missiles into it.

Looking back to our enemy in the sky, the formation had broken and were flying around to make another pass.

The attack helicopters were stretched out far over the tops of the trees, and the remaining gunship stopped over the area where the ambush had come from and rapidly lowered out of sight.

Moving my gaze back towards our convoy I found another, peculiar looking turret atop one of The Templar vehicles, shifting its direction in accordance with the attack helicopter's flight path.

Rather than a missile turret with several rounds, this was nothing more than a large, rectangular black box that was constantly changing its elevation and aim.

I moved my gaze back to the helicopters and there was a tingling in the back of my neck like I was about to be shocked by someone who had rubbed their socked-feet along shag carpet and was getting close enough to me to deliver their static electricity.

Instantaneously a vibrant green beam shot from the black box.

There was no firing, no seeking and no projectile moving through the air towards its target.

One moment I was looking at an attack helicopter making an arc to fly around and hit us again, and in an instant there was a solid green line emanating from the box on top of The Templar vehicle and connecting with the helo.

When the beam made its connection, the rotors on the helicopter stopped turning and its arc became a rapid descent.

Rather than completing the turn to come back at us, it fell out of the sky like a rock and the beam vanished.

Hearing a whirring I glanced back and found the rectangular box moving again, this time taking aim on the second attack helicopter which had been making the opposite arc of its comrade.

Again I felt the hair stand up on the back of my neck, and within an instant the green beam had locked on to its target, the rotors stopped turning and the helo fell out of the sky, this one erupting in a ball of fire when it landed on its side on the highway.

I looked towards the front of the convoy saw that the expression on Josh's face matched my astonishment.

Knowing that we needed to move before their reinforcements arrived, I knocked on the passenger side of the Templar truck I had been bracing myself against.

When the door opened, I pointed back towards to road behind us.

"I need you to reverse about fifty meters to cover us while we grab Buckeye."

The Templar took a moment to look in the direction which I was pointing, look briefly at the driver and shook his head.

"Negative. We're not moving back into the killzone to pick up someone who's already dead."

"We don't know he's dead. We need to get to him as soon as possible," I replied, having to force down an intense rage that was beginning to well up in the pit of my stomach.

"You're lying to yourself, Rob. He's gone. We haven't done any BDA [Battle Damage Assessment] to ensure the ambush is gone, and unless you can tell me where that other gunship went I'm assuming it's picking up their buddies and heavy weapons while we're wasting time talking."

While I stared incredulously at The Templar and wondered how he could be so cold and callous, Josh began to bark out orders over the net.

"We've got to get to Buckeye, and The Templars are saying they won't move the trucks back into the killzone. Rob, Dave, Major, you guys are already there. Do we have any other volunteers to go do a BDA? We need a complete fire team on this one."

I heard familiar voices come over the net to volunteer, and estimated that I had at least enough time before a fire team was assembled to move Buckeye and begin trying to save his life.

I winked at Dave, gave him a nod and started running at a full sprint, moving my rifle from my hands to the sling across my back as I neared him.

Along the run I put my complete attention on Buckeye, looking for any signs of life, attempting to assess what I would need to do when I had him back to the cover of the trucks.

Reaching his body I knelt and grabbed the shoulders of his armor to begin dragging him back to safety, as another hand came down and took hold of his left shoulder strap.

I looked to find that it was Dave, and without a word we began to pull our Brother back to the security of the trucks.

Just a few meters into our movement towards the trucks the small arms fire erupted again from the woodline, along with the "whoosh" of shoulder fired rockets aimed in our direction.

The incoming rounds began to move closer and closer to our feet, so Dave and I each turned to hold Buckeye behind us so that we could run forward much faster.

We were nearing the rear bumper of The Templar vehicle we had been taking security behind, and I watched in horror as its engine engaged, the truck pulled to the left and sped past the rest of the convoy along with the other Templar vehicles.

No time to stop and complain, Dave and I continued on our path to Josh's vehicle, which was unloading fire and fury into the treeline along with the others from our convoy.

As we neared the bumper of Josh's truck, Tattoo stood in the gun turret and released a Raven into the sky.

Good thinking.

Josh stepped out of his vehicle and pointed to the rear hatch.

"Don't put him in the APC with the families. Get back here and see what you can do. We're not going into those woods until we know exactly what's there. If we don't have anything in two minutes we're rolling out, so do your best but hurry up."

Dave unlatched the rear hatch of Josh's truck and helped me load Buckeye's body inside.

I jumped up and stood over him, pulling medical kits out of the back to begin my assessment as Dave turned and returned fire into the woodline with an intense ferocity.

Looking down at Buckeye I knew that he was gone, but I still had to try.

Even if I could revive him and bring his vital signs back, the amount of damage he had taken from the high-caliber rounds of the attack helicopter would be unsustainable in anything less than a level one trauma center, and only there if we had him on the operating table in a matter of minutes.

But I wasn't going to give up on him.

Pulling off my shooting gloves and searching for a pulse at his neck, I found none.

I knew that the neck pulse was the last to go as your body shut down and saved the very last of its blood pressure to keep the brain alive, and if he had no pulse there he wouldn't anywhere else.

Still not wanting to quit on my Brother, the Godfather to my children, I pulled open his eyelids and shone my penlight to test for any reaction in his pupils.

Nothing.

In a last-ditch effort I rolled up my sleeve and pushed my left hand through a gaping hole in his uniform and into the blood-filled open cavity in his chest, feeling for an artery or even the smallest sense of a pulse to tell me that he was still alive.

Nothing.

Grabbing a stethoscope from the med kit I pulled his body armor completely off, ripped open his blouse & shirt and listened intently, hoping there was still at least some pattern of life left in his heart.

Nothing.

Throwing the stethoscope at the wall I buried my face in my hands, dejected.

Being a surgeon was easy, working on people I had only met in the pre-surgery assessments and never having to know them personally, just in case the worst happened.

But being a medic, working on your best friends, being the last hope and the final one to hold your Brother's lifeless body in your hands, racking your brain for some piece of knowledge that maybe you missed, praying to God for some miracle to bring life back into his body.

It was earth-shattering.

Josh's voice came to life through my Peltors, parting the clouds of dejection and hopelessness.

"We only count six fighters on the objective, and the helo is still on the ground with rotors on. If we just hightail it out of here there's a good chance they'll take off and hunt us down while we drive, or be there to tell their QRF [Quick Reaction Force] when it arrives to reinforce them. Let's go get these bastards."

In that instant I lost all sense of thought and reason.

My vision turned red with anger, now wanting nothing more than vengeance for my friend, my Brother, the man I had spent so much time with and who had been so close that he was Godfather to my children.

Reaching down to shut his eyelids and prevent him from staring off into nothingness, I grievously whispered my goodbye.

"Via con dios, Brother. May your warrior soul find peace now."

Awash with hatred and anger, I put my shooting gloves back on, gripped my rifle with such force that I thought it may bend the steel under the strength of my hate, opened the rear hatch of the truck and started towards the woodline.

There were immediate protests from Josh yelling through my Peltors, but nothing registered.

I felt and heard the turrets on top of the trucks erupt along with small-arms fire to cover my movement, but there was nothing stopping me.

In less than ten seconds I was across the highway and into the woodline.

I was vengeance.

I was hate.

I was violent retribution.

I was everything awful in the world comprised into one unstoppable and unconsolable being of fire.

The cover fire must have truly masked my movement, or the enemy hadn't expected me, because at my full sprint I came upon their line while they were still laying in the prone and directing their aim on the convoy.

Slowing to a fast combat walk I fired double-taps in rapid succession into the first four men I came to as each of my boots landed on the ground.

First the man on the heavy machine gun, "tap-tap."

Next his assistant who was feeding ammo into the weapon, "tap-tap."

Next the man another few meters away with an RPG, "tap-tap."

Another in line with an AK-47, "tap-tap."

The fifth and final man on the line began to understand what was happening, and he rolled over to his side in an attempt to take aim, save himself and kill the enemy.

But he was too late.

By the time he was beginning his roll I was on him, serrated-blade knife in hand.

I stepped on his rifle to pin it to the ground as I brought the full-force of my weight into a knee on his right shoulder.

I was going to enjoy this.

Taking joy in the sheer terror I saw in his face, knowing the inevitable of what had to happen next, I raised the knife high above my head with both hands and buried it square in the center of his throat.

Facing straight down into his windpipe I turned the blade to the side, opening up a hole so big that I could have fed him a porterhouse steak through it.

I next moved my grip to the opposite side, then shifted my weight to bring the blade completely through his throat with my fist ending in the dirt under his left ear.

With the gurgling of blood and air escaping through what was now an opening that took the entire left side of his neck I picked my fist up, inserted the blade back to the middle and repeated again, this time widening the wound to his entire neck and cutting clear through his spine.

I sat for a moment, now with knees on both of his shoulders and blood covering each of us to marvel at my accomplishment, hoping there would be another to whom I could repeat this task.

As the life slipped away from his eyes and the gurgling stopped, I wiped the blood from the blade onto my pants as a branch snapped behind me.

I jumped and turned just in time to meet the crack of an AK-47 buttstock across the side of my face.

Everything went black.

When I regained consciousness I was staring at a sterile white ceiling full of interlocking squares, reminiscent of those I had seen in office buildings, schools and hospitals.

My head was pounding with a headache and my fingers & toes were tingling like they had just fallen asleep.

As I tried to sit up and scratch my head I realized that I wasn't just lying down...I was strapped to a table with my arms and legs each extended on its own board.

I started to panic, and as I squirmed and pulled at my restraints a voice with a thick Russian accent began to speak from somewhere in the room but out of my vision.

Craning my head up and attempting to find the source of the speaking was to no avail; I couldn't see the person from whom the voice was coming.

"Good morning Doctor Lewis, how did you sleep?" the voice asked.

"Who the hell are you? Where am I?"

"That doesn't really matter now, does it? If it makes you feel better we are still in your home country, for now, but we are far away from your friends and family. No one is coming for you," the voice said.

"Ok, nice touch, thank you for that," I responded with the thickest sarcasm that I could muster.

"Who are you and what do you want?"

"My name doesn't matter. And where you are really doesn't matter. Since I know your name, you can assume that I know who you are, what you've done, where you've been and where your friends and family are at this very moment. I know that you're an intelligent man, so we'll skip the pleasantries."

As the voice took pause, a form began walking around the table I was on, from behind my head to my feet so that I could see him out of my periphery.

Craning my head up again I noted the man was wearing a green and red Russian dress uniform with no name, rank or unit insignia.

The Russian had an expensive-looking video camera and tripod in his hand, which he began to expand and set up in front of me.

"I'm not going to lie to you or attempt to make your situation seem any better than it is. We are going to torture you. Actually, my comrade Dmitri is going to come in to torture you. While you were asleep I gave you a dose of a special chemical compound that we have been developing for some time. One could say that you're both a human trial and a pincushion at the moment."

"What do you want?" I asked again.

"It doesn't matter," the Russian replied arrogantly.

"You understand pharmacology, Doctor Lewis, so perhaps you will find this interesting. The compound we are working with is a combination of chemicals similar in psychotropic effects to LSD and another similar to PCP with of course the obligatory sodium thiopental used for these types of things."

"What's the point of that?" I asked again.

"It doesn't matter," he again responded.

"But, if you must know, our Chinese comrades stole this compound from your own CIA, which they developed for interrogations. So perhaps it will add a little respite to know that your own nation created this compound that will put you through so much pain very soon."

"What's the camera for?" I asked.

"It doesn't matter," again came his response.

A loud knock sounded at the thick metallic door, to which the interrogator smiled.

"Ah, just in time."

He turned and the lock twisted in its housing as the heavy door was opened.

My vision had begun to blur, but I saw the interrogator stand aside for the shape of an enormous man to walk through the doorway.

"Who are you?" I stammered.

"Hello Doctor Lewis," the giant man answered in an accent much deeper and heavier than the interrogator.

"May I introduce you to my comrade, Dmitri. Or as we have taken to calling him, Creeping Death," the interrogator spoke from behind a smile.

"What do you want?" I asked.

"At first, I just wanted to kill you," he replied and took a short pause.

"But since you decided to make it so easy for me and walked directly into my hands, now I have other plans."

"What does that mean?"

"People have always told me that I should watch my temper. Even my friend the psychiatrist here is on me about it all the time. But who would have known that yours was enough to send you into a fit of rage at your friend's death that would result in your being here?"

"My government won't negotiate for me. I'm not a soldier anymore. Hell, I don't think there's even a government anymore *to* negotiate for me."

"I don't want to negotiate, Doctor Lewis," Dmitri chuckled as he tugged at the laces and pulled off my right boot.

He turned and picked something up from a table behind them as he continued.

"I'm going to torture you, long and slowly..."

He turned back to me with a metallic object in his hands, and the bright fluorescent lights from the ceiling cast a schism of light across my face as he manipulated it in his hands.

"Most of it we will record and televise for your countrymen, to show them that they don't want to mess with me."

There was a sudden pinch of pressure on the big toe of my right foot and a flash of excruciating pain as Dmitri quickly pulled his hand up in front of his chest.

It took all of my energy and effort to hold back the reaction to scream and writhe in pain that should have come along with the agony he had just delivered.

"I'm sure we can even find a way for your children to watch their father die a terrible death," he continued as I pulled against my restraints with every bit of strength available.

"That won't do you any good, Doctor Lewis. Nobody can hear you, no one is coming for you and those restraints are not moving."

I began to kick wildly as there was another pinch of pressure on the next toe, but despite my best efforts not to scream, another wave of sharp pain pulled the guttural sounds of agony from deep inside my chest.

Dmitri once again pulled the pliers up with my next toenail, this time with the nail bed and a small amount of flesh attached.

"What is wrong with you people?" I screamed as the nerve endings in my toes sent a barrage of pain through all of my senses.

"What do you want?"

"Shall I turn on the camera?" The interrogator asked, not bothering to answer my question.

"Nyet. Not yet. This is just a little warm up to let the good doctor know what is coming," Dmitri replied, walking along the table towards my head.

Crouching next to my restrained body I could now see that his neck was nearly the size of my thighs, and his face bore a jagged scar from forehead to left cheek.

I turned my head to meet his stare, and the demons behind his eyes caused me to look away in a wave of panic.

"What I want, Doctor Lewis, is for this to be over. I don't want to be here any longer than I have to."

Dmitri glanced at the interrogator and then back at me to gauge whether his comrade would share his secrets outside of that room.

"I do not enjoy doing these things...ok, that is a lie," he grinned.

"I do enjoy doing these things. But more importantly, I am one of the few people who can do these things, and who does them well. Just like when you were in the military or working at the hospital in Los Angeles, I have a job. And my job is to strike fear in the hearts of everyone in this country and crush anyone who dares get in our way."

The radio on Dmitri's belt chirped to life with a man's voice speaking Russian in a fast and excited tone.

Looking down at the radio for a moment, Dmitri locked eyes with me again as he pulled the radio from its place on his hip.

"You are an example, Doctor Lewis. Nothing more, nothing less. Don't take this personally...but it will hurt."

Dmitri stood and walked to the door, keying his radio and responding in Russian.

The man on the other end continued to speak in a rapid and frantic tone as Dmitri walked past the interrogator and opened the door.

"I will be back shortly. Do not touch him or start recording until I am back...he is mine," Dmitri snarled the last comment as the heavy door once again opened and closed.

Silence filled the room and I was left to contemplate the horrors of what was to come along with the searing pain in my toes.

"How are you feeling, Doctor Lewis?" The interrogator asked as my mind raced to find a way out of my predicament.

His words began to reverberate in my head, as if in an echo chamber or dance music tune, and the periphery of my vision started to turn black.

I twisted my head from side to side to check if the lights were in fact going down.

The blackness slowly crept into the rest of the room, enveloping all that it touched and creating a darkness that became so cold it seeped into my bones and made me begin to shiver.

The Russian interrogator laughed as I began to struggle with all my might to free myself from the bonds which held me.

"It doesn't matter."

The cold black monster started to grow and envelop the room, growing more terrifying and bone-chillingly frigid with each nanosecond.

The interrogator's words echoed again.

"It doesn't matter."

The physical properties of the room began to defy the laws of physics, first with the steel instrument table from which Dmitri grabbed the pliers twisting into a vortex and spinning ever quicker as the blackness began to absorb it.

"It doesn't matter."

I was suddenly more afraid than I had ever been. A terror that crept into the deepest recesses of my soul began to overtake me, and as each corner of the room started to allow the darkness to creep in I began to do the only thing I knew how to do: fight.

As the interrogator's chorus started to echo again, I continued to wriggle in my restraints.

This brought a smile to the interrogator's face, and with the latest "it doesn't matter" his face started to transform, twisting into the horrible grimace of a demonic being from the very world of the darkness that was now coming to take me.

Although I could no longer feel my body, I heard the metal of my restrains banging against the table as I wriggled at first, and the clanging grew ever louder as I began to pull and kick furiously at that which held me down.

The room was now nothing more than the open vestibule of a ship careening through space, but a different kind of space than that we've seen with pictures of happy astronauts and stories of human achievement.

This was a biblical kind of space. The dark and cold void that reverberated the deepest, darkest and most horrific secrets of the evils of humanity. It was my own personal hell coming to take me.

But I wasn't going to give in that easily.

I smelled the metallic scent of iron, and as the interrogator repeated his mantra and started pulsing to a rhythmic beat of his own making, I pulled my head up to find that my wrists and hands were now covered in the dark red blood of my fighting for freedom from the restraints.

But I continued to struggle.

As the darkness began to creep into my feet the interrogator let out the howl of a demon hound and I decided I'd had enough.

Sitting up on the table my body was upright but arms and legs were still splayed like a hog ready for slaughtering.

I pulled with everything I had, struggling and straining with all of my might, rage, love and determination to make it back to my family.

The interrogator's eyes turned the same dark cold as the black of the energy in the room. He snarled and walked towards me.

With a final herniating pull my right arm became free.

The interrogator took a step back in horror but it was too late. The left arm pulled free, then the right leg and lastly the left.

As I lunged for him a beam of light opened in the blackness and I saw Matty run through it with his weapon raised and fire two well-placed rounds into the interrogator's head and chest.

When I looked back up from the crumpled body of the interrogator laying on the floor Josh, Jason and Tattoo were through the door and finished clearing their sectors of the room.

"Jesus Rob," was all that Jason could muster as he gingerly but rapidly bandaged my toes and the flesh of my wrists that had been chewed away under the restraints.

"We gotta move," Josh announced as Jason completed wrapping his field dressing.

As I switched my gaze to Josh, there was no need for words.

"Thank you," I communicated without opening my mouth.

"You're welcome," his eyes replied.

CHAPTER 4

SPLIT TEAM OPERATIONS

The next time I opened my eyes I was once again staring at a sterile white ceiling consisting of interlocking squares, reminiscent of those I had seen in business offices, schools and hospitals...and interrogation rooms.

Feeling my heart drop I looked towards my right arm in horror, expecting to see metal bands restraining me.

Instead, I found my daughter, nestled gently in my arms with her head on my chest. To the other side lay my son, also in a deep sleep but smiling as he lay cradled in my left.

Blinking a few times to ensure this wasn't a dream, I sat up in bed and tried to gather my thoughts.

My head was so tangled with cobwebs that I couldn't tell what was real and what wasn't, and had no recollection of anything after Josh burst into the interrogation room with the team.

I looked around the room for any clue of the recent past but found none. I was in a barracks of some sort, complete with sparse institutional furniture and drab grey sheets on our bed.

There was another bed on the opposite side of the room which had my kid's belongings on it, which made it seem like we may have been there awhile.

Hearing boots walking down the hallway outside of our door I jumped out of bed to try and figure out what was going on, reeling with a twinge of pain from the missing toenails of my right foot.

I braced my shoulder against the door in case we were somewhere that we didn't want to be. Cracking the door just enough to see a sliver of the hall, I watched a soldier in ACU's walk past our door.

"Hey," I softly called to him, but he kept walking.

"Hey," I tried again a little louder to no avail.

Not one for patience I swung the door open and stepped out into the hallway.

"Hey soldier," I called out after him.

That got his attention, and when the soldier turned around and saw me he immediately snapped to parade rest, showing me the front of his uniform which was adorned with name tape, US Army indicator and the rank of Private, First Class on his chest.

"Sir, I'm sorry sir. I didn't see you there. Can...can I help you with something?" he asked stammering, obviously caught off guard and mistaken that I was someone important.

"Don't call me sir, I work for a living," I replied.

"Where are we?"

"Excuse me sir?"

"Pretend I'm a guy who just woke up from a coma and has no idea where he is. Where are we?"

"Is this a test, sir?" the young Private asked cautiously.

"No Private. I think I may have actually just woken up from a coma. Where the hell are we?"

"Uh, The United States of America, sir."

"Good Lord son, I know that. Specifics."

"Um, uh, sir, I don't know how you want me to answer that."

I took a deep breath, cocked my head to the side in a "really?" motion and tried again.

"Do you see locks on the door I came out of, Private?"

"No sir."

"Don't call me sir, son. Do you see chains on my wrists?"

I glanced down and remembered tearing the flesh from my wrists as I struggled to free them from my restraints the previous...day? Week? Month?

The Private followed suit and also moved his gaze down to the thick, blood stained gauze wrapped around each of my wrists.

"Um, no s...."

When I held my hand out to him as the first syllable of a sir began to emanate from his mouth, the former NCO [Non-Commissioned Officer] in me roared back to life as I made a knife hand and pointed at him with force, fingers extended and joined in an action that any junior NCO in the US Army knew was *never* followed by anything good.

"So, Private, you can safely assume that as I'm not restrained and just came from an unsecured room that I'm supposed to be here, can you follow me on that?"

He shifted uncomfortably in his feet and stammered again.

"Roger that...uh...mister?"

"Just call me Rob."

"Holy crap. Are you Rob with the team guys from Colorado?'

"Now we're cooking with Crisco. Yes, I'm that Rob. Where are we and more importantly, where are my guys?"

"Your guys are gone. They took off a few days ago. The Colonel has been waiting to brief you, but wanted to let you rest. There are even signs at the end of this hallway to be quiet so we wouldn't wake you."

"Hold the phone there, Private. They took off a few days ago? How long have I been out?"

"I think it's been about a week."

I took a deep breath and tried to contemplate what that meant.

We were only in Colorado for a few weeks after the invasion. If I had lost an entire week to sleep I could only imagine what I had missed.

Snapping out of my thoughts I saw the Private, still standing at full parade rest and waiting for my next words.

"Thank you, Private. Let me get dressed, I'll find the Colonel shortly. Do you know where the families who came here with us would be?"

"They refused to stay anywhere far from you to ensure they'd be able to check in on you and take care of your kids. Your team..." he paused, chuckled to himself and continued.

"Once the docs cleared you and put you in this room, your team, uh, *removed* everyone else from this hallway and took these rooms. They literally pulled people out of bed and threw their stuff in the hall as they moved their own gear in."

"Yeah that sounds about right," I laughed in response.

As much as I would have hated to be one of the people woken up by Tony and Chad's python arms and menacing faces telling me to find somewhere else to live, it was nice to be on their side and the object of their actions trying to help out a Brother.

"Thank you, Private."

I turned and began to walk back into my room. Seeing the Private still standing at parade rest I turned back to him as I opened the door.

"I'll tell Jim, uh, The Colonel that you were a huge help. Carry on, Private."

With that the Private, being a good soldier, came to attention, enacted a drill-perfect facing maneuver 180 degrees and carried on along his merry way.

In a free-standing closet the likes I hadn't used since basic training I found several duffel bags full of my clothes and gear, picked out a set and started trying to figure out what I had missed.

Walking to the room next to mine and knocking lightly on the door I was relieved when I saw Sarah's face.

"Rob, you're up!" she smiled and came through the door to give me a hug.

"Yeah, but I still don't know what in the world is going on or what I missed."

"There was a lot of action around here after they got back with you. Something very hush-hush, and the guys left a few days ago. They split up with half the team going to the east coast and half to the west. That's all I know, but Ray told me to track down Jim as soon as you woke up."

"Thank you, that's a huge help," I replied.

"But I have to ask another favor...would you mind watching the rugrats while I look for Jim?"

"Of course," she answered.

“Those kids have been attached to my hip since we got here. They refused to sleep without you, so we've been putting them in bed with you every night once the docs cleared you to be out of the clinic."

"That's a relief. Thank you so much for all of your help, it's..."

In mid-sentence I began to hear the ring of a sat phone [Satellite Cell Phone].

Concentrating on the sound I could tell it wasn't coming from Sarah and Ray's room, but it was close.

"I think that's been coming from your room. We've been hearing it on and off again over the past few days."

My eyes widened. There were only a few people who had my sat phone number. My parents and sister were one group, and as I hadn't heard from them since the invasion I moved with a quickness.

Without saying another word to Sarah I raced to my room. The ringing was coming from the closet, and I tore through my duffel bags to find the sat phone buried in the bottom of one.

"Hello," I whispered after pulling the antennae out and walking into the hall.

"Hello?"

"Bubs!" exclaimed my dad, who had nicknamed me Bubba as a kid due to my chubby, Buddha-like appearance as a toddler.

"Dad. What...where…how...are you ok?" I asked, not sure where to begin.

"Yes, we're all ok. We're together on the boat. We never thought the day was going to come when we'd have to follow your crazy plans, but your sister was the first to see what was going on and forced us all onto the boat. We've been out at sea since the whole thing started and we're fine. How about you?"

"Jeez. I don't even know how to answer that," I responded and paused.

"I'm good and the kids are with me. Where are you?"

"We made our way towards the Caribbean, figuring it was best to be as far away as possible. Where are you?" he asked.

"I can't really tell you that right now. But I think I'm somewhere that I can find out what's going on and how we can get you back here. I'm in a very secure place and there is plenty of room here for you guys."

"Well, we kind of like it down here. We still have lots of supplies on the boat, there's fish in the ocean and no fighting going on down here."

"Dad, I'm not sure how much information you're getting but this is pretty ugly. I would prefer to have you here so we can ensure you're safe, and the kids would really love to have you around as well. It's been rough on them with me having to do what I do. I haven't been around much and if you were here, well, it would help me out a lot."

"Ok, but how in the world do we meet up with you if you can't even tell me where you are?"

"I don't know that just yet. Let me figure something out. Do you have a power source to keep your sat phone on and plugged in?"

"Of course, we have the generator on the boat."

"Ok, keep someone near the phone at all times and I'll get back to you. Keep your head down, dad. Being an American abroad may be a very dangerous thing right now."

"Understood. We'll stay on the boat and wait for your call."

"Ok dad, I love you. Glad to hear you're ok. Send everyone my love and I'll get back to you."

I hung up the phone and closed the antenna as Sarah looked on. Knowing I had a lot of information to gather in a short amount of time, I shot her a smile and a nod and moved out to find Jim.

Walking in the direction I had seen the Private moving earlier, I found signs marking the hallways and soon made my way to an elevator and up to ground level, recognizing that we were back in Austin at the Scottish Rite Temple, the de facto rear command of the resistance.

Having a slight memory of the layout I made my way to the TOC [Tactical Operations Center] and found Jim at the front of the room, locked in a conversation with several uniformed soldiers.

Seeing me walk through the room he broke off his conversation and made a bee-line directly for me.

"Rob, so glad you could join us!" he stated in a manner laden with sarcasm.

"How was the nap?"

"Was I really out for a week?'

"Yeah, you took some pretty tough licks, soldier."

"Besides whatever they used to knock you out, they also roughed you up a little. Actually a lot. The guys brought back the vials of drugs they had been feeding you to give our docs, and let's just say it's a miracle that you're still alive. I bet you had some crazy dreams, partner."

I nodded and followed along with every word as he spoke.

"You spent two days under observation here in the clinic, but once the docs flushed that crap out of your system and cleared you, we put you in your room for some rest."

"Thank sir, it was very much needed and appreciated. But now I'm rested and need to get to work. What's the SITREP [Situation Report]?" I asked.

"Take a walk with me, Rob. Let's go visit the SCIF [Sensitive Compartmented Information Facility]."

Once again I followed Jim to the SCIF, a trip that it felt like we had just taken. When we entered the room he asked the analysts inside to take a coffee break, grabbed himself a chair and motioned for me to sit as well.

"Your team was worried about you when they got you back, Rob. But as The General said, time is of the essence and they had to get moving."

"I appreciate that, sir, but moving where?"

"We've been communicating with other freedom fighters around the country. As I briefed you previously the east coast is in the process of being overrun and the west coast has completely fallen. There are groups of Marines, Special Forces and some conventional military units still holding the line. We held the east coast for about a week with our massive naval presence there, but once the enemy ground forces moved in from their landing points in New York they took everything north of North Carolina."

"Good Lord."

"Good Lord is right. Fortunately we have some former operators who owned a rifle manufacturing company up in New Hampshire and had a team of their own. They've been keeping quite an arsenal to themselves for years, and when the fighting got heavy they communicated with the teams we have in North Carolina and moved there to link up, cutting a swath of dead enemy in their wake. So while we may be outnumbered on the east coast, those boys are well armed and ready to start some trouble."

"Roger that. And the west coast?" I asked.

"The west coast is a bit trickier. The California politicians succeeded in disarming the public there. All the while one of the most fervent anti-gun senators was selling automatic weapons to the cartels and, as it turns out, sleeper cells who were waiting for this to kick off. There are a few small pockets of resistance in northern California, but the only teams we have been in communication with are some SEALs and Marines from San Diego. They've fallen back to the mountains about 50 miles east of San Diego to regroup, wait for us to refit them and begin their unconventional warfare operations."

I sat staring at the map behind Jim for a few minutes, contemplating the grand scale of our enemy's operations and just how in the world they pulled this off under everyone's noses.

"Doesn't San Diego have a huge military presence?" I asked.

"Yes of course," he replied, paused and continued.

"But our enemies have been planning this for a long time, and were brilliant in the way they neutralized our greatest assets. They knew we had a Navy they couldn't compete with, so just like on the east coast they moved massive ground forces up through Mexico to take out our ships while they were still in port. The guerrillas and sleeper cells they've had in place for years caused enough distraction so that when the land forces came in, they caught everyone off guard. Marines are some of the fiercest fighters on the planet, but by their very formation there just aren't too many of them. Once the enemy came in force, they were the proverbial meat in the grinder."

"Great. So what's the plan, and how can I help?"

"I'm glad you asked, Rob. Since you have more experience in southern California than anyone on the team, I'd like to send you out there. Understand that you will be surrounded on all sides, greatly outnumbered and outgunned. But if we want to take back the country, we need to take back the ports in Long Beach, Los Angeles and our bases in San Diego."

"Well sir, a Green Beret is supposed to be outnumbered, outgunned and surrounded, so that sounds like precisely what I was built for. I do have an issue I need your help with first, and it's not in southern California."

"Well Rob, I think you've earned a few favors. What can I do for you?"

"I hadn't heard from my parents since the invasion started, and I just got off a call from them on my sat phone before I came to find you. They're on a sailboat in the Caribbean and I'd really like to bring them here."

"Rob, we can't exactly risk sending a rescue mission to the Caribbean at the moment."

"I understand that sir, but what if they can make it back on land in the continental US? Could our teams on the east coast link up with them in Georgia, Florida or something like that? My dad was a Navy pilot, he may be of some use helping us train pilots or getting more planes off the ground."

Jim thought this over for a moment.

"Well ok Rob, now you're speaking my language. Do they have a sat phone of their own?"

"Yes sir."

"Call them before you leave and tell them we'll be in touch. I'll procure a unique identifier that you can pass along so they will know it's us. While you're gone I promise we'll do our best to get them linked up with a team and back here."

"Roger that, sir. But my dad is where I got my cynical nature from. If he doesn't buy the identifier, tell him that my childhood nickname was Bubba because I was such a chubby baby."

Jim chuckled and nodded.

"Roger that, Rob. Go back to your room, spend some time with the family and pack the gear you need. The Russians took your weapons, so I'll have one of my aids escort you to the arms room where you can take anything you like. Stop by the aid station and fill a med bag as well; the team in California has been at it pretty hard. There are already a few medics from your group out there with them, but they need anything they can get. This will have to be a HALO mission as the team is between two enemy fronts right now, so pack light but pack well. We can't fly any resupply drops into them at the moment so you'll only have what you can carry in. Roger?"

"Roger that, sir," I replied, stood and rendered a salute.

"I think we're past having to salute each other at this point, Rob. But thank you."

Jim stood and returned my salute, as I made my way out of the SCIF and back to see my kids.

Our room was empty when I arrived, and as I could hear the joyful cheers of children playing down the hallway I figured they had been woken and scooped up by Sarah.

I had the option of bringing the kids back in with me while I packed, but quickly dismissed it as I knew that would slow me down considerably. I opted instead to pack as fast as I could and spend the extra time playing with the kiddoes until I had to move out to my next mission.

Packing was a peculiar thing on an ODA, and much different than I had experienced among infantry guys. On an ODA everyone had their specific job, which had been mandated by the Gods of Special Forces after you passed Selection and Assessment.

This made packing an exercise where you truly understood that those choices of putting a certain man in a particular job were spot on.

I say that because nearly every Green Beret I had known packed their gear not like every other Green Beret, but rather like every other member of their specialty.

For instance, you could always tell which HUMVEE had the 18B's in it by backpacks full of ammo and small arms. Ammo was heavy, and for a Bravo there was never enough of it, so whenever the trucks were around that's where it went.

18C's, the engineers, had explosives for their toys. Since C4 needs to be fashioned into an explosive complete with blasting caps and wire before use, they would build the bombs pre-mission and hand them out amongst the team based on the operation.

18E's, the communications guys, had to deal with military radios which never quite kept up with the civilian sector mantra of "always make it lighter and faster."

The Army seemed to make everything as heavy as possible, and so it was the way of the Echo to hand out whatever they could, mainly the large batteries that we referred to as "useless anchors," to the others on the team.

But the 18D's, selected for some trait we must have shown during the psychological and mental testing in Selection, were much too empathetic and caring towards our guys to ever burden them with our gear.

To add to that same sentiment, we cared for our men so much that we wanted everything we could potentially need on us at all times, but didn't want to load others with our weight.

Given our packrat tendencies and desire to take pain away from our guys rather than add it, every medic made each movement with bags packed so tightly it seemed a misplaced sharp object would pop it like an over-inflated balloon.

This mission, however, was going to be a HALO insertion, meaning I could only bring one bag, in which I would have to take enough gear to last me an undefined amount of time. And if I packed too much on this one I ran the chance of breaking my legs upon impact with the ground, which would put everyone in a precarious situation.

Our training in the 18D course had used some of the most high tech and not yet on the market medical and trauma technology, but also had a strong focus on knowing how to improvise anything possible in case we ran short of supplies.

The "sticks & rags" section in our trauma education had taught us just that: how to treat any battlefield injury with nothing more than sticks and rags fashioned into tourniquets, bandages, slings, etc.

Given that the team was now in the middle of a small mountainous forest, I figured we could find plenty of sticks, and in a worse-case scenario the legs of my pants would make great rags.

Next I focused on what would be an extremely important part of long-term sustainment for injuries and our resistance fighters: antibiotics and medicine. But I would have to go to the medical locker to find those, so I made a mental accounting of what I would need.

Back in Afghanistan we had been way out "on the wire," so I knew none of us had major issues with not showering or changing uniforms for a few months at a time. With that in mind, I focused my clothing on the most integral gear for any light-fighter [light Infantry or grunt-type]: plenty of socks and underwear.

I didn't know what types of vehicles the teams I was going to link up with would have, but figured that in any situation we would be doing quite a lot of moving on foot.

Being outnumbered to this extent meant you could never afford the risk of being seen, lest your entire team be decimated in one sitting. So we'd most likely be walking in the last several miles of any ambush or raid, and I needed my feet in the best shape possible.

Athlete's foot or crotch-rot from dirty socks or undies would be a mission-stopper in that situation, so in the end I packed one extra uniform, a few shirts and as many socks, gold bond [talcum powder] and undies as I could fit, along with a healthy amount of beef jerky and meal-replacement bars I had found in the TOC.

There was still room for ammo and meds, which were my next tasks to find.

Thankfully that left me a relatively light bag. Unfortunately, if we took any heavy contact with the enemy and sustained significant injuries, we'd have to kiss those guys goodbye unless we could either call them an EVAC back to our friendly lines or find a Level I trauma center.

Neither of which sounded likely.

With my bag packed to satisfaction, I set out to find Jim's aide and equip myself with a new weapon.

The Russians had also taken my body armor, but given that speed would be our greatest asset on an Unconventional Warfare [UW] mission and any heavy contact would leave us dead anyway, I didn't think the weight would be worth it to replace.

The aide was easy to find, as when I walked into the TOC someone tracked him down and led him my way.

He brought me through a set of hallways I hadn't seen yet, taking us downstairs and walking into an unmarked room with a middle-aged soldier sitting on a stool behind a counter.

"Janski, this is Rob, one of the Colorado team guys."

Janski stood up, gave me a once-over and looked back to the aide.

"The Colonel says to give him anything he desires. So, make it happen. I've got to get back. Do you need me to sign anything?"

"Negative, sir," was Janski's response.

"I'll fill out a DA-2062 [US Army hand receipt for equipment issued] and take it to The Colonel for his signature."

As the aide turned and left the room, Janski shot me a smile and a wink.

"Ready to go shopping?'" he asked.

Seeing my face light up like a kid who was handed the keys to a toy store for a Christmas present, he lifted a movable section of the counter and motioned for me to follow him.

Walking me through a locked metal door and into the arms room, my mind began to race with the possibilities.

"Where do you want to start?" he asked.

"We won't have enough ammo so I'll need to be able to scrounge whatever I can in battlefield recovery. That means I'll need something Russian that shoots 7.62. Do you have AK's?"

"Sure do, follow me."

The room was filled from floor to ceiling with large, grey lockers, situated in columns as if it were a library full of weapons rather than books. I followed Janski down a corridor through the middle, passed six rows and turned into the seventh row as he moved to the left side.

I recognized the Russian makeup of the weaponry housed in these lockers, and halfway down the row he turned back towards me.

"Any preference on color?"

I thought about what we would be doing and made my decision.

"Everything we do will need to be out of sight, nothing shiny, nothing colored. Do you have anything in all matte-black that won't shine or reflect?"

"Yes indeed I do."

Janski walked a few feet further, turning to a locker on his right and opened the top gate. Pulling out an AK-103 with an already-mounted scope and grenade launcher, he let out an "ain't she a beauty" whistle as he handed the rifle to me.

"She take 7.62 rounds?"

"Yup."

"Does she jam if not regularly cleaned?" I followed.

"Nope, you know the Russians. They make their weapons simple, sturdy and dependable. Not exactly as accurate as our American ones, but that's why you have full auto!"

I cracked a smile at the last comment.

"Is that it?" Janski asked as I inspected the weapon, felt its weight, checked the boresights and ran through a few dry-fire exercises.

"Not on your life Sergeant," I replied.

"I don't trust this Russian crap as far as I can throw it. I need an MP5 and 1911 for my secondaries."

There had always been some contention amongst our guys on what the best sidearm was. In the Army we had been allowed to use either the M9 [Beretta 9mm pistol] or 1911 [.45 caliber pistol], the SEALs had their own go-to pistol, and after leaving the service it was a sure fire way to start an argument if you were to ask a group of vets what the best pistol was.

For me it was a simple choice, and boiled down to a few main thoughts I held firmly to.

The 1911 was so named because its design was made in 1911, and although it was a true pain to clean and put together it worked like a charm when you needed it. So much so that they hadn't had to make any major design changes since, well, 1911.

Secondly, my hands were too wide for the Glock or many Heckler & Koch pistols. Some people loved them, but I was the only person in my middle school rock band who could play the bass guitar because I had hands big enough at thirteen years old.

So the oversized handle of the 1911 fit quite nicely in my extra-wide hands, and when choosing a pistol, fit is an incredibly important factor to consider.

Lastly, and perhaps most importantly for this mission, the 1911 is built like a rock. It's big, it's tough and it's heavy. As I had vowed to never go down without a fight, I figured if worse came to worse and my last bullet were gone, I could bash somebody's head in with it if I were backed into a corner.

After Janski and I were finished toy shopping, we were walking to the front for him to begin transcribing the weapon serial numbers onto my hand receipt when I realized something was missing.

Seeing my head jerk in recognition and looking up to see what the matter was, I had one last request for Janski.

"You wouldn't happen to have any knives back there, would you? You never know when some Russian will need a little cultural appropriation via a Columbian necktie."

"I think we got you covered, sir," he smiled back at me.

I walked out of Janski's office with a brand new Russian rifle complete with shooting optics and a grenade launcher affixed to the bottom, one submachine gun, one pistol, a few knives, a lot of ammo, a handful of frag grenades and rounds for the grenade launcher, two tactical vests with plenty of pouches for missions and a pistol holster.

It didn't look like my bag would remain light for long. And I still had to go to the medical locker.

By the time I was finished packing, as per usual, my bag was packed to the gills and heavy as a rock once I added my new toys, ammo and medicine to the load.

Oh well, ain't getting resupplied and this isn't going to be a walk in the park.

Jim's aide had found me while I was picking out antibiotics and pain meds for the trip, and informed me that the plane taking me in would be leaving at 8pm that evening. He suggested I rest up as I wouldn't be getting much sleep for quite awhile, but I had a more important mission first.

It was still late afternoon when I finished packing, so I found my kids sitting in a circle around Deana listening to her reading a children's book. Rather than interrupt I took my seat next to them, which caused them both to crawl into my lap.

Every time I was with them between our operations I would constantly worry about how I would answer their questions, but they never seemed to come.

It was a constant battle in my parenting mind of whether I should try to explain our situation to them about what was going on, where we were going and why this was happening.

And although I had always made it a point to have full disclosure with them and not sugarcoat the hard truths of life to prepare them for growing up, I couldn't bring myself to try and explain war and the horrible things people did to each other in the name of whatever it was they were fighting for.

I knew at some point I would, and I would have to explain why their Godfather was no longer with us and what happened to him...but not yet. I wanted to preserve their innocence for as long as possible.

They never brought it up, and I wasn't sure if it was their somehow sensing through our subconscious connection and karma that it was something I wasn't ready to talk about, that they were so bright they already surmised from overheard conversations and seeing the actions around them, or perhaps they really were just too young to comprehend what was going on.

Deanna and Sarah had been doing such a great job of keeping the kids entertained and busy that the last option was a real possibility. And I hoped it was correct.

By the time Jim's aide found me and told me it was time to move to the bird we had listened to stories, eaten a snack, taken a nap, played a game of tag outside and sat down for dinner together.

I had given them showers and was reading a bedtime story when he knocked on the door and peeked his head in. I nodded to him in affirmation, finished reading and took the kids to Sarah's room for bed.

Speaking to them as much as to Sarah to let her know what was going on, I took a knee next to the bed after tucking them in.

"Robert, Avery, daddy has to go back to work tonight."

"No daddy, can't you just stay here with us?" Robert asked.

"No son, I can't. Daddy has to go to work and meet up with the rest of the guys. We have a lot of work to do, so I may be gone for awhile this time."

Both sat up in bed to protest, so I kissed them each on the forehead to try and put their minds at ease.

"You both know I love you more than anything, and there's no place on earth I'd rather be than with you. So if I am going, you have to know it's so important that daddy has to leave everything he loves to make sure we do our jobs."

"I know dad," Robert replied wistfully.

"We just miss you when you're gone."

"Believe me buddy, I know. And I miss you very much when I'm gone. But just because I'm not here with you doesn't mean i'm not thinking about you. I miss you every second I'm not with you guys, and that should help you understand how important this is."

"Even more important than when you were saving lives at the hospital?" Robert asked, puppy eyes gone and now replaced with an inquisitive look.

"Yes sir. Much more important than saving lives at the hospital. Now I have to go and make sure my friends are safe. I have to go and make sure Uncle Ray, Uncle Chris, Uncle Bulldog and all of the guys get back here safely."

"But dad, they're the toughest guys in the world. Why do they need you to keep them safe?"

I heard a slight chuckle from Sarah, and turning I saw that it was coming through a tear-stricken face, that of her own worries for her love, reminding me of just how much we had at stake.

"That's right buddy, they are. But everyone needs someone to look after them. And while I look after them to keep them safe, they'll be looking after me to keep me safe. And we'll all come back here together."

I looked to my daughter, who was listening intently through pouting lips and sad eyes. As I struggled to come up with what fatherly advice to give next, Jim's aide knocked on Sarah's door and walked in.

"Rob, wheels up in ten mikes. We need to start moving."

"Give me a moment here," I held my hand up to him without looking.

Recognizing the importance, Robert leaned in and kissed me on the forehead, repeating my nightly ritual to them.

"It's ok dad, we understand."

He looked to his sister and gave her a hug.

"I'll watch over Avery while you're gone, and we'll be good listeners for Mrs Sarah and Mrs Deanna."

I smiled and had to fight back the coming tears with every part of my being, knowing that seeing their dad cry wouldn't do anything to help the situation.

"Thank you buddy. I'm counting on you. And you Avery, be a good listener and daddy will be back soon to play with you two again, deal?

Both nodded their heads in affirmation.

But I didn't want to go either.

I knew it was needed. I knew it was my job, I knew the guys needed me, not only as another gun in the fight but also as their Brother, medic and the only trained doctor on the team. As my head screamed one thing and my heart sank for another, Jim's aide stepped back into the room.

"Rob, eight mikes."

"Got it, sir."

Looking back to my kids I was at a loss for words. I stood to kiss them both on the forehead, and as soon as I leaned in I was met with two pairs of arms around my neck.

I held them with everything I had, cherishing the moment and asking the Lord to bring me back to them quickly.

Their grips loosened after a few moments and both sat back.

"Go dad. They're waiting for you," Robert commanded.

"Roger that, buddy. I'll see you two soon. I love you guys."

"We love you too," they replied in unison.

As I began to walk down the hallway with Jim's aide in tow, he started to brief me as we walked.

"Sir, I'm going to need you to shut up for a few minutes. Just let me collect my thoughts."

I wasn't sure if he was a father with little kids of his own running around the facility somewhere, possibly a father who had lost his children in the invasion or was yet to sire his own progeny.

But whatever the case, he understood and we walked silently, shoulder to shoulder, down the dimly-lit hallway.

Once we were standing in the elevator I knew it was time to make the transition back from loving father to the cold & calculating warrior.

"Sorry sir, it's just..."

"No need, Rob. I understand. You good?"

"Yes sir."

"Ok, here we go. We're getting on a helo now that will take us to Austin-Bergstrom airport. Once we're there I'll walk with you to an MC-130 that is waiting to take you to the guys. You'll be making the flight to California, which should take a little over two hours. There is a jumpmaster on board who will help you get your chute and gear on, will give a heads-up when you're nearing the objective and when it's time to jump. Clear?"

"Clear, sir."

"Normally you'd have an IR chemlight or strobe to mark your position after landing, but you're going straight into enemy territory. And this ain't the Taliban, we know they have night vision."

"Roger that sir, so what are my actions upon landing for linkup?"

"Yeah. About that. We've communicated your DZ [Drop Zone] to the team, but they're going to have to leave their cover to come grab you. They're on the southwest corner of the mountain range, but we don't want to fly over their area and alert anyone to their presence. We'll be dropping you about five miles northwest of their position, and given that it's a HALO drop we had to find a DZ that was open and flat."

"So i'm not going to have any cover or concealment once I hit the ground, will I?"

"None at all."

"Ok, so how do I know if the trucks that come get me are good or bad guys?"

Jim's aide handed me an MBITR [Multi-band Intra Team Radio] as he spoke.

"We've programmed this radio to their team frequencies. Once they're close they'll try to raise you on the net to let you know they're coming in."

"So if I see trucks but no radio call, start running?"

"Well you know how commo goes, Rob. It always works fine in the rear but seems to lose its mind whenever you actually need it in action."

"Ok sir. So hold tight and hope for the best?"

He looked at me and winked.

"From what they tell me your team has a lucky horseshoe hidden somewhere, and most of them think it's lodged somewhere you don't want to show."

I shook my head and chuckled. It was true that 022 had a lucky horseshoe hidden somewhere on the team, I just hoped it would be with me on this one.

The flight gave me a lot of time to think, which wasn't always a good thing.

Once we were airborne I grabbed an insulated pad to lay down on the ground, pulled the woobie out of my bag and attempted to get an hour of sleep before it was time to meet my destiny and jump into the night sky.

It would only take a few minutes to put my gear on when I got the word we were getting close, but the crew chief came over as soon as I began to lie down.

"Sir, I don't think we can let you do that. You'll need to stay strapped in on this one."

"What? Why? Don't we have a couple of hours to burn?"

"Yes sir. But we're flying through a lot of enemy territory. We're going up pretty high and trying to fly a path around their lines but we can't guarantee that we won't encounter resistance. They still have aircraft in the air and anti-aircraft guns on the ground, so...."

I held up my hand to tell him he didn't have to continue.

"Got it, I'll strap in."

Sitting down in the webbed seating of the C-130 gave me another reminder of how soft I had become in civilian life.

I had grown accustomed to the creature comforts of the finer things of life, and shifting around uncomfortably I longed for the padded, fully-reclining seats and service of the first-class commercial airlines which I had traveled exclusively since my first year as a full-fledged surgeon.

When I had been a knuckle-dragging grunt one of the first skills I learned (as any soldier will) was to fall asleep, at will, regardless of the situation.

The Army had a strict culture of "hurry up and wait," meaning no matter what unit, rank or specialty you were, there was always someone above you rushing you to get somewhere to either stand in line, wait for others to arrive or just sit around a radio for days on end waiting for your orders.

As such, Army-types learned that there were a few skills even more essential to survival in the military than moving, shooting and communicating: keeping yourself occupied and always rested on the chance you would start a mission with little notice that would last several days without sleep.

In my new life however, with billable hours in the hundreds of dollars for my time to operate on or consult with patients, people made sure that when I arrived everyone else was ready to go. I didn't step into a room until a patient was on the table, prepped and the staff was already moving.

And because of the hospital regulations I was on a rigid time limit for seeing patients, not allowed to spend any time on pleasantries or dilly-dally.

It seemed that with those new experiences and dramatic life-shift from always being on someone else's clock to everyone being on mine, I had lost the unique grunt-acquired talent that was shared by all soldiers.

It was a vital life skill, having spent time in the Army training under someone else's thumb and timeline to be able to quickly fall asleep in any office, supply room, tent in the desert, airplane, back of a moving truck or pile of rocks on the side of a mountain when you had a few moments with nothing to do.

And on this trip, I knew I'd have plenty to do, and was not likely to be finding much time to sleep any time soon.

Hell, these were actually very conducive conditions for a quick twenty-minute nap, as all lights were off lest the enemy on the ground or in the air spot anything to give away our position and movement.

But when it got to the point I was beginning to get angry that I couldn't sleep I realized it was a futile attempt.

It was impossible to stop my mind from running back to my kids, how much I missed them and the time I had enjoyed spending with them.

Looking at the nanny cam and catching my son climbing out of his crib when he was still too young to even walk. Teaching him how to throw a baseball, putting him in his play truck and pushing him as fast as I could along the long tile floors of the downstairs in our home.

The day my daughter was born, the first time I held her tiny newborn hand in mine, reading her bedtime stories and hearing the magical sound of her first words: da-da. She had my heart from the moment she came into this world and I longed for when I would be back to hold them both in my arms again.

Thankfully my thoughts never went to those dark places that could have pulled me into a descent of worry and self-doubt, but I knew they were lurking just beneath the surface.

What would happen to my children if I never made it home from the operation? What if my chute didn't deploy? What if the guys weren't there when I landed and I found myself in another interrogation center?

What if one of these missions went wrong and we were compromised...or worse yet, what if the guys had already been compromised and I was walking straight into a death trap?

When the jumpmaster walked over and told me we had ten minutes to showtime I was thankful to be able to concentrate on the job at hand.

I had kept the monsters hidden away in the darkest parts of my subconsciousness, but I knew it wouldn't be long before they came out to play and muddy my thinking when it was so important to keep my head clear.

By the time the jumpmaster signaled to me that we had two minutes until the ramp lowered I was fully geared up, my rig double-checked by him and was standing by my seat waiting for the word.

I made my way over to stand near the ramp and when the red light next to it turned to green I said a silent prayer, walked to the edge and jumped into the dark oblivion of night above the desert.

We were at 35,000 feet Above Ground Level [AGL] when I leapt into the darkness, convincing myself that everything was ok and doing my best to not gulp the oxygen from my mask too rapidly. I reached terminal velocity as expected, keeping a careful eye on the altimeter affixed to my wrist.

The entire reason we selected HALO for insertion was the highly likely chance of being seen by the enemy, so I'd be opening my parachute low, somewhere between 600 and 700 meters AGL.

We chose the DZ based on natural topography; I would be landing in a wide open desert expanse, around ten square miles, which should be a walk in the park. If I had exited the aircraft either too early or too late, however, we could easily have problems.

Not only would I run the possibility of coming down in the very woods that our team was hiding in, but there were also mountains in every direction except north outside of the DZ.

The worst-case scenario had been lingering in the back of my mind since the location of the drop was briefed: a casino, located a few short minute's drive north of my DZ had become a favorite of enemy officers and support personnel looking to blow off some steam.

It hadn't been turned into a headquarters so I wasn't concerned about radar or the plane being seen. But all it would take would be one enemy soldier stepping outside for a smoke or looking in my direction at the right time.

If I opened my chute too high, jumped too far north of the DZ or the wind carried me far enough that way to be spotted, I could very well be dead before I hit the ground.

But it was the only DZ available that would put me close enough to our guys to be feasible, so it was what we had to work with.

As Napoleon famously said, "you don't go to war with the army you want, you go to war with the army you've got." And it was what we had.

Movie screenwriters and war novelists love to make HALO jumps seem like a super-sexy and sneaky infiltration method that was so easy it should be used for any mission. But the reality was much different.

Falling 35,000 feet from a moving plane, at terminal velocity and so high up that an oxygen tank is required to breath on the way down provided a long list of opportunities for a deadly mistake.

Even after I had left the service I continued to receive calls from the team that various friends of ours had been lost, and horrifyingly two of those notifications had been for Brothers who died on HALO training jumps.

And now I was doing it in the dark, alone, near a known enemy hangout, close enough to a mountain range and ocean that the winds would be far from normal.

The speed at which I was falling pushed every inch of my face not covered by the oxygen mask, goggles or helmet back so tightly that it felt as if it would be peeled from my face like a tangerine before I hit the ground.

As I passed through the last bank of clouds I could see the lights of the world below, just as if I had been in the first class seats I had become so accustomed to, looking out of the window as I handed my drink to the stewardess and prepared to land.

But there would be no landing gear to depend on nor music to listen to as we came back to the earth. This was all on me, and any misstep meant I would either be so broken I'd die in a heap of bones on the DZ or get caught and never make it home to see my family or Brothers again.

Concentrating on the landmarks screaming towards me at around 200 kilometers per hour I saw the bright lights, far enough to my north that unless an errant gust pushed me once I opened my parachute I would stay out of sight.

I began to see the area of darkness formed by treetops in which the team was hiding, and the great expanse of desert that was my DZ.

The map had shown that everything would be clear land for about five miles northwest of the southeastern edge of the mountain range, so I altered my course by shifting the position of my arms and legs.

While my eyes scanned the surroundings below, I could feel the rucksack was still in place between my legs, waiting for me to pull the strap and lower it to meet the ground long before I did.

This would slow my fall as I positioned my feet for impact without having to also move 75 pounds worth of weapons and gear.

Looking back at my altimeter I was getting close.

I was down to 3,000 meters AGL, meaning I would have to pull the chord releasing my parachute soon.

Doing the math in my head, I knew that if it failed to deploy I would be nothing more than a pile of broken bones on the ground in about 54 seconds.

I focused my complete attention on the altimeter affixed to my wrist as I screamed past 2,000 meters AGL.

1800.

1500.

1000. This is the point where, had I been jumping in with my team I would have touched my hands to my head to "wave them off" and let them know I was about to deploy my parachute.

800.

700.

I reached for the cord attached to my harness and pulled it free, feeling the movement in the rig on my back and thankful that the parachute began to release from its housing, as it enveloped the sky around it and yanked me jarringly from falling at terminal velocity to a leisurely descent towards the ground.

Because of the possibility that a HALO jumper loses consciousness from any number of incidents (loss of oxygen supply, hitting the plane upon exit, losing control and spinning all the way down, a piece of his gear coming loose and knocking him out) there is an emergency system that would have automatically deployed at 500 meters if I hadn't pulled the cord.

But, given the casino, ocean breezes and mountain range I thought that would be more of a death sentence than a saving grace.

I reached up and grabbed the controls to steer myself down.

Looking again at the altimeter I was down to 100 meters, which meant it was time to drop my gear and turn back into the wind.

One of the most important lessons of jump school, especially landing on a DZ in a windswept desert full of cross breezes from the ocean and mountains, was to be sure you landed while facing into the wind, not "running" with it at your back.

There were several reasons this was so important: firstly, it helps slow you down and allows you to ensure a steady footing when you touch down.

"Touch down" is a bit of a misnomer...while it looks easy in movies, every time I've ever jumped I hit the ground like a bag of bricks, coming perilously close to eating my kneecaps.

Secondly, a jumper who really knows what he's doing can pull down on his parachute controls at the very last moment, capturing a final pocket of air and lifting him up for a soft landing.

Pull too early, you lose the air and, as I stated, hit the ground like a bag of bricks. Too late and your attention is on the controls rather than footing, giving the same end result of a dirt sandwich.

But running with the wind rendered all of this useless. With the wind at your back adding inertia to your forward movement as you descend toward the ground, it becomes a bully along with your parachute, driving you forward and knocking you over the moment your feet hit terra firma.

Even worse, once you hit and try to stand up to get your life together, the wind stays in your chute and topples you over, dragging the inexperienced jumper along the ground until he can either dig his boots in enough to stop the torture or release his risers and parachute from its harness.

Luckily the horseshoe was with me on that day and I turned just in time to have the wind in my face, hit the pocket and dropped my gear in time to have a nice soft landing.

Maybe everything's going to work out on this one.

As this was a jump into enemy territory I went straight to task gathering my parachute and stuffing it into the rucksack. We didn't want to leave any trace that I had ever been there.

As I crouched on one knee, rucksack open and packing my chute into it with weapon at the ready next to me I began to hear the rumble of several engines driving toward me at a high rate of speed.

Looking around I saw no headlights, but the sound of vehicles was unmistakable.

No lights. Is that a good thing or bad thing?

With the desert wind screaming I couldn't make out the exact direction, and straining my eyes I couldn't find any dark masses to show me where the sound was coming from.

And then I saw it.

Tiny, and in the distance, I noticed a light blinking in morse code. I counted in my head and hoped I could remember Chad's morse code refresher.

Five dashes. Pause. Three dashes. Pause. Three dashes. Long pause. Five dashes. Pause. Three dashes. Pause. Three dashes.

I thought for a second, realizing that it was a short message being repeated.

Doing the translation in my head I was relieved.

0-2-2.

The message stopped after three cycles, and looking towards the dark edge of the trees lining the reservation I saw the outlines of several vehicles speeding in my direction from where the flashlight message had come.

I looked toward the casino behind me.

Seeing no matching outlines of vehicles moving towards me I stood, put the rucksack on my back and began jogging out to meet my Brothers for the next leg of our mission.

CHAPTER 5

BACK TO CALIFORNIA

From the bed of a Toyota Hilux I scanned the horizon for enemy vehicles as the team drove me deep into the mountainous and wooded terrain which they had chosen as their base camp.

We started our journey on hardball roads, which turned into smaller country roads following the mountain crests and finally dirt roads leading off the beaten path.

After we pulled off the last actual road I saw a man-made dam to our southeast, pinpointing our location from studying Jim's map after his pre-operation briefing. We parked the trucks in a heavily wooded draw between a grouping of hilltops and I marveled at the spot they picked.

Pulling my rucksack from the truck bed and helping Ray pull netting over the vehicle, I spoke to him to ensure I had my proper bearings.

"Barrett Lake is to our east, the dam on its southernmost border and the major road up here to our north will take us back to the area of the DZ, am I correct?"

He replied without looking up.

"That's right, but if you look directly to our west there's another, smaller road. We didn't want to count on one road alone in case we need to make a hasty exfil, so we've prepped some motorcycles over there in the treeline near a big bend in the road."

He switched his complete attention to me, ensuring that I understood his message.

"If we get blown out of here Brother, run as fast as you can that way, hop on the bikes and don't look back. We're keeping a low profile but this entire state is crawling with enemy. That's our go to hell plan, and there's a good chance we may have to use it."

Pointing past the woodline to our west, he showed me so that I would understand exactly what he was telling me.

"Just about four clicks [kilometers] that way. Once you leave the woodline the last click or so is completely exposed, so just be aware of that."

I could tell from Ray's eyes and voice that something was different.

He was typically the first one to crack a joke or lighten the mood, but when it was time to be serious and go to work Ray was all business.

The team had been there for several days before I arrived, and his demeanor told me they hadn't been holding hands and singing songs.

As we finished pulling the netting over our truck, a fit and good looking blonde haired man in his late twenties who I imagined was more comfortable on a surfboard in board-shorts rather than his current fatigues came over to give us a message.

"Ray, take Rob to the sand table and we'll read him in on our SITREP."

He stepped closer to me and extended his hand for a shake.

"Rob, I'm Tyler. Welcome to Camp Santa Cruz."

I gave a puzzled expression as I reached out to meet his handshake.

"Maybe my bearings are way off, but aren't we pretty far south of Santa Cruz?"

"Yeah," he acknowledged dryly.

"But that's the point. We've got enemy everywhere and are relatively sure they can pick up our radio traffic at will. We've named our camps by the names of other cities, mostly ones that we love surfing in to try and confuse them if they intercept our communications."

I nodded in understanding as Tyler turned and walked further into the canopy of trees, and felt Ray put his hand on my shoulder.

Turning to stand face-to-face with him, I imagined that I wouldn't be hearing any wisecrack comments from him as long as we were there.

"I'm glad you're ok Rob, and it's good that you're here with us. We could definitely use the help. But..."

He looked in the direction which Tyler was walking, then back to the trucks.

"But I kind of wish you weren't here. This is a whole new ballgame. We won't all make it home from this."

After a brief pause Ray picked up my rucksack and started to walk on the same path as Tyler and disappeared into the night.

Not knowing where I was going I hurried to catch up to him so I didn't get lost in the darkness of night and cover of trees. After a short climb up a modest incline I began to see a camp, the likes of which I hadn't seen since Robin Sage.

Robin Sage was a section of the Special Forces Qualification Course and is known to many as the largest Unconventional Warfare [UW] exercise in the world.

Positioned near the end of the Q-course, it is where Green Berets-to-be learn one of the most important parts of their job, and the skills which prepare them to do the job that separates them from the rest of the military and Special Operations.

Taking place in the hinterlands of North Carolina, teams are paired up at Camp Mackall and given a mission by their instructors.

Once they have their mission the students have a week to prepare, research the terrain they'll be in, the enemy and friendly SITREP and gather any intelligence they can about what they'll be moving into.

All of this is made up of course. But the exercise has been going on for so long, with generations of ODA's inserted to help the People's Republic of Pineland fight a brutal dictator and win control of their land that, although only an exercise, it has become its own little world and very real country for several months out of every year.

But now, many years later and several wars beyond my time in the Q-course, I felt like I was walking right back into Robin Sage. And on a primal, freedom fighter level, I was right at home.

This was exactly the type of place in which we had learned to wage UW, and so it was only fitting that this would be the fire base from which we would take back the west coast.

I walked past camouflaged tents and ponchos hung between trees, placed both to mask the camp from enemy overflights and to serve as a cover from the elements.

In the middle of the camp I came upon a sand table around which stood Josh, Chad, The Major and a handful of men whom I didn't recognize.

Looking up and seeing me, Josh offered a nod but no smile, which was quite unlike him.

"Welcome back Rob," Josh said.

"Come here so we can brief you on the current SITREP and our mission tomorrow."

I walked to stand around the sand table with the group and marveled at another relic which I hadn't seen since Robin Sage.

A sand table is used to brief a mission as a depiction of the target area. This one stood three feet high, looked like it had been a dinner table with sides nailed on and was full of roads drawn in the sand, representations of buildings and soldier figurines to denote our actions on the objective.

As he laid out the operation, he briefed that we would be taking a team through the backroads to a small town just north of the mountains. The team had a contact there who was holding an SUV and several pairs of enlisted Russian soldiers uniforms for us.

They had learned from a source who worked in the casino that a particular Russian intelligence officer had a tendency to sneak away from his unit one night every week to go boozing, play the craps tables and steal one of the casino women away with him: at the very casino I had been so worried about north of my DZ.

And the following night would be his night.

As I began to wonder how reliable this source was or why they would jeopardize themselves by offering us that type of information, Josh answered all of my questions.

"Last week was the third time in a row that the women this officer took from the hotel never showed back up again. And last week it was our source's sister that went missing and she wants some answers...and his head on a stake."

"Wait a minute," I interjected.

"Why is this casino operating in the middle of a warzone? I thought the west coast had fallen and has enemy crawling all over this place."

"It is, and there are," responded one of the men whom I didn't know.

"But the Ruskies like their booze and women. They consider this area to be totally under their control. Much like the enemy controlled areas far from the front lines in World War II, the Russians insisted the casino and other entertainment venues like bars and movie theaters open back up for the morale of their troops."

"So taking that a little further," I said, looking around the table and ensuring they got my point, "this intelligence officer isn't going to be the only enemy in the joint, is he?"

"Far from it," Josh answered, paused and continued..

"But we need to gather some better intel if we're going to make any progress here. We can't just drive around and do area reconnaissance or we'll get greased any time we go out of the woodline. A private isn't going to give us any intel worth a damn, and we have a prime target of opportunity here. And if we don't kill him the Kumeyaay Tribe who owns the place, and to whom the last chick who disappeared belongs, is going to do it on their own."

"So why don't we let them?" I asked.

"What would we gain from that? One enemy lost without the chance to interrogate them first?" Answered one of the men I didn't know from the other side of the sand table.

"Now hold on a second, hear me out," I continued.

"We could let them dump his body in a shallow grave, sure, but why don't we let them pull him out of there *for us*? They have access to the casino, which we don't. And I'm sorry, but unless we have some fluent Russian speakers laying around that I don't know about, the uniform idea sounds like a terrible one."

"We have two Russian language speakers with us," countered another of the men.

"I think you're missing my point here, guys. If they want to grease this guy anyway, and we want intelligence, why don't we get what everyone wants but with minimal risk? Tell them to let him do his normal thing, have his drinks and play craps but place a specific woman with him this time. When they're leaving she can signal someone inside and they roll him up on the way out. After which they hand him off to us, we bring him back here and put the screws to him."

"Who the hell do you think you are?" Snarled one of the men.

"No, he's right," said Josh.

"I think we can make this work. It's my source, let me send the load signal. Rob, twenty minutes and you're rolling with me to meet the source. Put your stuff in Ray's tent and I'll come grab you to head out."

I glanced around the sand table and was met with unhappy faces. I wasn't sure if they had become upset that I was changing their plans, that they didn't know me or just didn't like my face.

Whatever it was, Ray grabbed my shoulder and we walked off to his tent without another word.

Twenty minutes later Josh and I pulled out of the canopy of trees and onto the dirt road, along with Tattoo and a machine gun in the back seat.

"Don't take it personally Rob," Josh told me in a consoling tone.

"These guys have taken some significant losses, including all their senior leadership. After they lost their intel guy apparently any desire to run safe and quiet missions went out the window. Let's just say they prefer to put a heavy hand on every operation."

"Even if it means running unneeded risks?" I asked.

"It doesn't look like they have room to lose too many more guys."

"Especially if it means taking unneeded risks," answered Tattoo from the back seat.

"Their team has a death wish. They think they're all as good as dead, and their families already are. They just want to take as many bad guys down with them as possible before they go."

"That's no good," I said.

"It ain't perfect, but it's what we've got," replied Josh.

"They don't know you, and barely know us. But you're the new guy again, so just hold your horses until you have a few ops under your belt with them. They seem to ease up once they fight alongside someone and that will happen soon enough."

"What else can you tell me about the situation here?" I asked.

"It's ugly. Uglier than we thought. We knew about Hezbollah and every terrorist group who wanted a piece of America activating their sleeper cells on the east coast, but it seems the Russians also made landfall in the northeast and brought the heavy equipment. At the same time they and the Chinese also had sleeper cells all over the west coast. While they were causing havoc, Russia brought their Navy to the west coast and put more troops and firepower on land, from Washington down to Los Angeles."

"I thought the west coast had been taken by China?" I asked.

"Both. The Chinese have been buying up South America just like they've been doing in Africa. But in South America they set up dummy corporations and freighting companies which allowed them to bring massive amounts of troops in without anyone knowing. They slowly moved land forces up through Central America and then Mexico. They aligned with the cartels to smuggle some in, but once the chaos started they rolled everything in through the Mexican border."

"And the Russians?"

After the Chinese and cartel land forces took out our bases in San Diego, the Russian Navy sailed in with their part of it. Most of their brass is based in Los Angeles, and from what I hear they took over Hollywood and have been sending some pretty perverse pictures back to their friends."

"How much worse can it get?"

"Glad you asked," Josh responded.

"The Chinese and Russians have some sort of deal. The Chinese are going north from their Mexican entrance, and Russians are moving from coast to coast. Whoever finishes clearing the country first, wins."

"What do you mean wins?" I asked, horrified.

"Not sure about that yet. But whatever it is, it ain't good."

As Josh finished the last sentence he started to slow the car and turned off the road at an abandoned restaurant. He steered the truck to a parking lot in the rear, obscured from the view of any passers-by.

"Be on your toes. When we stop, you and Tattoo pull security outside. Stay well-hidden just in case; we don't want to fight unless we have to, because with only three of us we'll likely lose. I'm going to meet the source inside the restaurant and propose our new deal. If I hear shooting I'll come out, but if you can make it inside to warn me first I'd really appreciate it," Josh told us.

"How do we tell your source from a car of bad guys?" I asked.

"Tattoo knows the car. It's an old beat up Honda, gold colored, dent in the front left bumper with license plate XJH 34R."

As we exited the vehicle, Tattoo and I each moved into the woodline on opposite sides of the abandoned building while Josh made his way inside.

Shortly after we settled in our concealed positions, an old beat up and gold-colored Honda, complete with dented bumper and license plate matching Josh's description came into the drive.

Maybe it was because it was dark, maybe it was because I hadn't seen or been with a woman in quite some time, but when the Honda drove to the back and turned off its lights I could see from the shadowed outline which emerged that she was young, attractive and had an amazing figure.

As she walked towards the building I watched her long black, Native American hair coming to a stop just above her very tight and well-fitting jeans. I hoped this wasn't just a honeypot, an informant for the enemy using her beauty to bring down our guard and lure us into a trap.

If that were true, we would be as good as dead.

Even though Josh and Tattoo were some of the deadliest warriors I had ever met, and surely the best shots, if she were a honeypot the amount of force they would bring to take us would mean there would be no way for us to make it out alive unless in their custody.

And I was not going back into their custody while I still had life in my body.

Less than five minutes after I watched Honeypot's tight jeans walk into the restaurant I saw her once again emerge, and the vision of her from the front held my attention much stronger than even the rear had.

Native Americans, like many cultures, are one that have certain bloodlines that scream at you from first glance that they are cut from a different mold than the rest.

With her regal high cheekbones, perfectly fit body and stride that had an air of royalty to it, I imagined her not-too distant family members and what they would look like in their full regalia of leadership.

She stopped at the Honda, placing her key in the door but suddenly startled, as a deer that is too far to see or smell, but somehow has the third-eye intuition that a hunter is waiting or creeping towards it from somewhere.

Honeypot finished her scan of the surroundings and, not looking entirely satisfied, turned her keys and hurried into her car, starting the vehicle and racing out of the parking lot.

Soon after her car was gone Josh emerged from the doorway himself and began walking to our truck. Tattoo and I each materialized from our hiding spots, making our way out of the treeline and towards the vehicle to meet him.

As we took our seats, with keys in the ignition and engine prepared to roar it to life, Josh paused.

He turned, looked at me and raised his eyebrows in the "what do you think about that one" gesture that many a man has given to a friend when a beautiful woman walks past them.

"Let's just say I've made her nickname Honeypot, whatever you say about how vetted she is," I responded to his gesture.

"Wait until you get a load of her voice," Josh answered, pulling a micro tape recorder from his jacket pocket and putting it on the arm rest.

"Play that bad boy."

After pressing play we proceeded to listen to him have a conversation with one of the most sultry voices I had ever heard and a part of me was immediately jealous.

I couldn't remember the last time I had spoken with a woman who wasn't either one of their wives, a woman on a combat operation or one of the families we had pulled from the DIA hit or prisoner camp.

As hard as it was to actually pay attention to the conversation beyond that sweet and sultry yet commanding female voice, the content of their discussion was much more interesting.

She confirmed that it was her sister who had gone missing, and as I suspected she wasn't just your ordinary croupier at the gambling tables. She and her sister, along with their older brother, were the heirs to the Kumeyaay nation leadership and wanted both justice and answers.

Honeypot agreed that the plan could work. She would assemble a group who would organize the snatch and grab to take place the following night.

They would drug the Russian officer's drinks and take him to the high rollers section where he wouldn't be seen by many of the other soldiers.

Honeypot would approach him as his "date" for the evening, and once he started showing the effects of the drugs she would invite him upstairs to her room.

The Russian wouldn't make it beyond the elevator, as they would be met at her floor by several armed men who would knock the officer out and ferry him, hogtied, down the service elevator and to a waiting car.

The Russian usually arrived at the casino around 11pm, so she expected to have him in their possession and delivered to the restaurant between one and two am the same night.

Josh raised his eyebrows and again looked at me in the "what do you think" gesture.

"It's just crazy enough to work," I replied.

"But what do we do with him once we've got him. I didn't see any cages or back rooms to interrogate this guy in once we bring him back to the camp."

"Oh we can't take him to the camp," Josh answered.

"You're right, too many chances for him to make noise or escape."

He looked at me and Tattoo to make sure we were paying attention, and Tattoo finished the answer.

"We checked out the dam the first night we got here. There are a lot of thick, reinforced concrete walls with little rooms deep in the dark pits of that place that we can take him to. Nobody will ever hear him."

"Doesn't that dam supply energy to this valley? How are the Russians not controlling that place already?" I asked incredulously.

"People from Honeypot's tribe run the entire dam. The Russians made a smart move by leaving the people in place who run important operations, from power plants to casinos and strip clubs. Yes, morale for their troops is something they take much more seriously than our current American generals ever did."

He shot a smile to me after the last statement.

"She'll inform the people who need to know that they should take the graveyard shift off tomorrow night."

"And you're sure she's not living up to her name and a real Honeypot?" I asked.

"Her tribe may not have a whole lot of affection for the US government, but they understand that the Ruskies are much worse. And they don't want to go through another battle for land with another government. They'd rather help us repel the enemy and maybe get some favor after this thing is over than have to deal with those guys," Josh responded.

After we got back to the camp and started emplacing the nets over the trucks, Josh stopped me before walking up the incline to the others.

"Stick with Ray tonight. Get some rest and I'll take you around to meet the other guys tomorrow. They're pretty rough right now and have been on edge since this whole thing started. Just stay in the tent and we'll all sing kumbaya or something together in the morning, roger?"

"Roger that," I responded.

"Maybe we can do a trust building exercise like catching each other while falling or something like that."

"I think killing a few Ruskies will do a whole lot more for you than that," answered Tattoo.

I had set my gear down, built a small bed with my sleeping bag and was just laying down to sleep across from Ray in our tent when Tattoo poked his head in.

"Rob, Ray. We just got the call. The Russian intel guy showed up tonight, switching up his pattern or something. Honeypot is taking him in a few hours. Be in the trucks in twenty to move out. We're bringing a fire team this time so we don't get hit with our pants down in case she earns her nickname."

Ray and I looked at each other and shook our heads from across the tent.

"This is why you just can't get comfortable Rob. The Gods of War can feel it, and have to throw something your way to keep you from getting soft."

We packed our bags, grabbed our weapons, extra ammo and my med bag. We stood ready at the trucks when Josh arrived with Tattoo, Dave, Chad and four of the others whom I didn't yet know, plus Tyler.

Josh led the mission brief, but since we weren't sure how the night would transpire it was limited.

Our plan was to go back to the abandoned restaurant.

While Josh went inside to wait on the package, six of us would hide and provide cover as the other four moved in groups of two, further along the woods lining the road to act as recon and early warning.

As we parked the trucks and began getting out, Josh gave out the assignments.

Ray and I would form the recon element heading north, so we should see the vehicles coming in from the casino before anyone else.

Our job was both to give the rest of the team notice that we had cars inbound, but also to provide a "sniff test." If anything seemed out of the ordinary our job was to give the guys a minute or so of preparation to either fight or run.

Chad and Tyler would be the southern recon element, with the rest of the team setting in place for Josh's security. We knew we had to kick the recon teams out as soon as possible to clear enough distance to give our team a fair warning if something was amiss, so we checked everyone's radios and prepared to move out.

Before Ray and I left to find our position, I put a hand on Josh's shoulder.

"Be careful Brother. She's too hot to not be trouble."

Josh looked at me and winked, his version of letting me know he heard me loud and clear.

I hesitated for a second but Ray grabbed my shoulder and we started running.

As we moved through the treeline skirting the road I had a few questions that I couldn't wait to ask.

"Ray, how do we know that we can trust these guys?' I asked with labored breathing.

"You mean the hot Native American chick?" he replied.

"No, the guys I don't know. How do we know they're on the level?"

We were both out of breath from running in our gear, so Ray took a moment to gather some wind and stay on the run.

"You missed a lot Rob. These guys are the real deal. They've lost a few guys since we got here, and I've seen them do some amazing stuff. It's good they're on our side."

"Ok," I asked, catching some air myself.

"What about Honeypot?"

"Who's Honeypot?" Ray asked.

"Josh's source, the hot chick he's meeting here," I said as I jumped over brush and weaved between trees at a fast run.

“Well, he hasn't slept with her. I think if she were a true honeypot she would have tried as soon as they met, don't you think?"

"Good point," I said while gasping for air.

"Do you think we're far enough yet?"

Ray stopped in place upon hearing the last question and took a look around, speaking between labored breaths.

"Yeah, this distance should give them at least a minute heads up. Let's find a good place to take cover and set in. If something bad is coming this way we don't want them to see the two of us or we're toast."

To check the feasibility of our location, Ray and I each edged all the way to the woodline to get a picture of our fields of view.

We had about five feet of open terrain between the edge of the treeline and the road, and found a natural defilade [small ditch] a few meters away which would mask our position even further.

As I lay down in the defilade to ensure I had a clear view, Ray stepped out to the road to check that they couldn't see us. He jumped up to check the perspective that someone would have from a military truck or SUV.

As he gave me the thumbs up, several engines roared as headlights started to come around a curve in the road a few hundred meters ahead of us.

I motioned for Ray to hurry up, and he ran towards me and jumped in. He was positioned a few meters to my south in the same defilade, and was settled just before the vehicles rounded the curve and sped along the straight section of road in front of us.

The moment the vehicles passed us, Ray got on his radio with the rest of the team.

"Hey dad, heads up; we have five tangos headed your way. Three school buses and two speedboats."

"Roger that," came Dave's reply through our Peltors.

We opted to stay in place so that we didn't miss anything or get caught with our pants down while running back to the team.

We both were a little surprised when Ray and I heard more engines roaring down the road and once again saw headlights coming around the bend.

Getting on my radio this time, I keyed the mic to signal the team that they weren't alone.

"Keep your head on a swivel guys. We have more kids coming to the party."

Ray and I watched and listened intently as two more SUV's and one truck sped past us in the direction of their location.

"Two school buses, one freighter," Ray spoke into his microphone when the vehicles had cleared our position.

He and I looked at each other from our spot in the dirt.

"We gotta get back there," I said.

"We're the only eyes out here. They'll let us know if they need us."

"By the time they tell us they need us it may be too late for us to make it back there in time!" I yelled back at him in a forceful whisper.

"Patience Rob," Ray retorted in a voice that told me he was serious and wouldn't take no for an answer.

"We can't abandon our position and I'm not staying out here alone. Sit tight buddy."

We sat patiently, splitting our watch between staring at each other and keeping an eye on the road.

I started to relax given that we hadn't heard any gunfire yet, and at the speed the vehicles were moving they would have been at the restaurant by that point.

I began checking the time incessantly, feeling it had been an eternity since the vehicles had passed. But the digital readout of my watch told me that it had only been two minutes.

As my worry grew with each ticking second, Dave's voice sounded again through our Peltors.

"Come back home boys, we have the birthday cake."

That was our cue to fall back to the restaurant, and without a moment's hesitation Ray and I took off running through the woods.

We ran out of the woodline and into the parking lot just in time to see a group of heavily tanned men and women, each with dark black hair, wearing various assortments of jeans, boots and flannel shirts helping Josh lift a hogtied and violently struggling person with a black bag tied over their head into the rear bed of the Hilux.

Seeing Honeypot standing off to the side, not lifting but barking orders to the others and dressed to the nines in a black dress so tight it seemed painted on her, I knew what was going on.

She shifted her gaze and I froze in place.

"I don't think they were supposed to see us," I whispered to Ray, trying my hardest to stand still and pretending that maybe they hadn't seen us yet.

At first I saw fire in her eyes, the kind that made me believe that if she were a witch she would have cast a spell forever freezing Ray and I in place, and purely out of spite would have next summoned lightning bolts or firing hot lava to ensure the job was done.

Instead she paused for a moment, just as surprised as us, and doubled over laughing.

Adrenaline can do some strange things to the human mind and body, and while spastic fits of laughing at very inappropriate events can be one side effect, when our eyes met I was sure that wasn't it.

She just thought it was hilarious.

And in hindsight the thought of two figures, in full gear for a recon mission with lightweight vests lined with magazines of ammo, night vision goggles and rifles in hand stopping frozen, not moving a muscle but in the middle of a parking lot surrounded by people...well it was kind of funny.

"Come on over here guys," she laughed in her exotic accent.

I had spent time all over the southwest of our country, met handfuls of Native Americans but had never heard anything like her accent. It was intriguing.

I glanced over to Josh and then at the prisoner who, having finished being loaded into the pickup bed was able to turn all of his attention to us.

I expected to see fire in Josh's eyes as well, angry that we had exposed ourselves and let the group know that not only didn't we trust them, but that we were also putting teams out to ensure they weren't up to no good.

Instead he shrugged and nodded his head in her direction, motioning for us to go to her as requested. Unfreezing ourselves and walking over to the group, Honeypot stuck out her hand for a shake as we neared her.

"Hello gentlemen, my name is...."

As she prepared to formally introduce herself, Josh loudly stopped her with a "shhhhhhhhh."

Each of us turned to look in his direction, to which he pointed at our new prisoner.

"Let's play it safe guys. This guy is a pretty high ranking intelligence officer. Keep the talking to a minimum until we know we're not being monitored."

At his words the hooded prisoner began cackling maniacally from his position in the truck bed.

"Do you really think that will help, you silly Americans?" He asked between evil laughs.

"You really don't think that I knew something strange was going on when you offered yourself to me tonight and gave me drinks with drugs in them after I raped and murdered your sister last week?"

As the hooded prisoner commenced laughing again, one of the tanned men with dark hair, this one with an especially fine, pressed button down shirt festooned with rhinestones and turquoise took a step towards him and punched at the hood with all his might.

"What did you say? What did you do to my sister?" he snarled, reaching his right arm back to take another swing.

"No matter. Hit me as much as you like," the prisoner cackled between words.

"You will all be able to see her again soon enough. I will even put your bodies where I put hers."

Josh raised his hand and motioned for the angered brother to hold steady for a second.

"What are you talking about, sir? You're currently tied, hoodwinked and in the back of my pickup truck surrounded by armed men."

"For the moment. But the moment I knew something was strange I pressed the little pin on my right lapel, the one that looks like my unit insignia to the untrained eye. It started transmitting my GPS coordinates within one meter, recording everything around me and sending both back to my unit. It's been over an hour since I did that, so I must say that I am thoroughly disappointed in them."

At this he shouted something loudly in Russian, which if his last statement were true was likely some sort of "I'm going to put your butt in a vice," to the analyst listening on the other side of his transmission.

He continued.

"But, it's ok. They will be here soon."

I began to feel the dull vibrations under my feet which had become so terrifying to our group and saw the recognition and brief terror flash in Josh's eyes.

Yelling for everyone to prepare to move, Josh directed Ray and I to give him a hand.

He started pulling the hooded prisoner towards the gate of the pickup, and by the time we reached him Josh had pulled the man flat down onto the pavement and was cutting the laces from his boots with a knife.

"Strip him. Bare. Everything. No time to check his pockets for intel, get this guy naked."

As we began to see the security detail emerge from the woods, Josh was shouting more orders as we finished stripping the officer naked and threw him up into the truck bed.

"Alamo Alamo Alamo," he shouted into his microphone, letting both us and the men left back at basecamp know that we had been compromised.

"What do we do?" asked Honeypot.

"If he is telling the truth they know you were a part of this. Your best bet is with us. Do you have weapons?"

"Yes," answered her Brother.

"Good. Get them out and start your vehicles. And stay with our trucks, this is going to get a little hairy."

Josh motioned for Ray and I to jump in the truck bed as he got in the driver's seat and roared the engine to life.

As the seats filled up in our trucks the prisoner began to laugh again, madly and ever louder.

A quick kick from my boot to his face stopped that...or perhaps it was the back of his head hitting the rear windshield so hard it broke a hole and formed a spiderweb.

Regardless, he shut up so we could concentrate.

"Butt naked in the cold, in the rear of a truck bed full of enemy about to go careening through the night trying to outrun your own unit. I don't know if it can get much worse than that," I remarked to Ray.

"Ever had gonorrhea?" he asked.

"That's worse. So I hear."

And with that, my funny Ray was back. Now if only we could survive the night and keep him there.

Josh laid on the gas so hard in reverse that the rear wheels of our Hilux screamed in the night and kicked up fumes of black smoke.

When the rubber finally caught road we careened back like a race car with Josh enacting a rear facing maneuver, slamming the truck into drive and speeding through the night.

Racing down the narrow mountain roads was dangerous enough, especially for Ray and I in the truck bed.

But with our convoy in close pursuit I soon found another terror: we emerged from the tree-lined road near the restaurant and into another part of the mountainous road, this one wide open with no cover whatsoever.

Josh gave the command over the radio to kill all headlights as we left the protection of our tree cover, and each car in the convoy behind us followed suit.

It wasn't long before we saw the origin of the ground shaking below us just a few minutes previously, and the full force of it was terrifying.

We had seen Russian Hind gunships and attack helicopters, but never like this. The most I had ever seen were three gunships and two attack helicopters, those which had attacked us in Oklahoma.

But my heart sank as I watched a dozen gunships flying toward us from the direction of San Diego, all in formation with twice as many attack helicopters in tow.

That meant that not only did they have massive firepower (and ground troops) in the gunships but also agility and speed in the attack helos.

I knocked on the rear plate of the windshield and motioned for Tyler to slide it open. When he did I pointed to the sky and told him "we've got company."

He passed my message up to Josh, who never took his eyes off the road.

Both hands were on the wheel as we sped 60 miles an hour down a path that wasn't safe to drive at 30, screeching along curves with Ray and I hanging on for dear life in the back.

As we careened through the night, we stretched our legs across the prisoner's body and shifted our centers of gravity to keep him from flying out of the bed.

My eyes widened as the gunships stopped and went into a holding pattern in the direction from which we had come, likely stopping over the restaurant thinking their officer was still in the parking lot.

Without a word of warning Josh exited the mountain road still at 60 miles an hour, going briefly airborne as our tires left the pavement and switched to a dirt road at a steep decline.

He slowed the engine as we made the transition, but due to the steep decline our speed still increased.

Having taken our team through several tactical driving courses including some off road, four wheel drive and ATV courses we all knew what he had to do: if he stepped on the brakes he would lose control and the truck would careen off the side of the dirt trail to a steep death.

Well, maybe not the guys with seat belts but surely Ray and I in the back.

If he downshifted at this speed he'd blow the clutch and the truck would be undrivable, something we couldn't afford in our current situation.

So we just had to hang on, grin and bear it while trusting Josh had retained all those skills we learned in the off road courses.

I couldn't see Josh from where I was, but from spending years together and getting to know him both as a warrior and leader, and also having been positioned in a truck with him for several deployments, I knew the expression that would be on his face.

For all the carelessness and joking that Josh exhumed in public, inside he was as straight as an arrow and a fireball of determination.

I had memories of the face he made when he was laser-focused and blocked the rest of the world out, lost all sense of time, noise, oxygen and the space around him.

When Josh was determined and focusing on something, he made it happen. Period. And I knew that we would make it safely through this death race down the mountain side.

As I felt the steep decline start to level out beneath the wheels of our Hilux, Josh began to decelerate and I could breathe again.

I knew in my heart that he'd find us a way to get us out of there, but the automatic responses from my body hadn't been so sure.

I was able to release some of the death grip which my hands held on the side of the truck and loosen the pressure of my legs that I'd kept on top of our naked prisoner.

Feeling the pressure start to lessen and our truck decelerate the prisoner began to wriggle under our legs and make noises.

A square kick to the face from Ray this time and that promptly ended, to which I shot a wink across the truck bed to Ray, which he met with an air smooch.

With the headlights still off I could only make out the edges of where we were with the small amount of moonlight available. I saw a vast rock overhang ahead of us, along with patches of huge boulders scattered around the ground below it.

Josh had found us a natural parking garage big enough for all the vehicles.

As he slowed the truck to a crawl, I realized that it would be more than just our convoy. I remembered Josh calling out "Alamo Alamo Alamo" over the radio, which explained how the other vehicles, the rest of our team and the team we had come to help already had their trucks parked.

Pulling the truck into a space between two boulder outcroppings and below the cover, Josh brought us to a stop as two more vehicles pulled in alongside us.

Each of the vehicles nervously kept their engines on and idling until Josh turned ours off. Looking to the top of the boulder we parked under I saw Tattoo, having just climbed it, with NODs on, binoculars in front of his face and giving the thumbs up.

The helos and gunships weren't following us.

As soon as the engines stopped, small groups of the team brought netting to all of the vehicles and covered them. Dave came to our truck and helped Ray and I pull the prisoner off and on to the ground.

"Should we give him some clothes or something?" Dave asked.

"Nah. Screw him. Let em' freeze," was Ray's response.

"Don't let him freeze to death, or this was all for nothing," came Josh's interjection from behind Ray.

"The whole point of this was to pump this guy for some intel. Let's keep him alive but uncomfortable."

Tattoo stayed perched on top of the boulder as Josh and The Major pulled our group in for a wide huddle underneath the outcropping of rocks.

"Good job getting the package and making it back here men," started The Major.

Hearing a loud "ahem" from Honeypot, he continued.

"Sorry, ladies and gentlemen. Good job. It doesn't look like the gunships followed you. There was something at the restaurant they seemed pretty focused on, but that won't last long. Why is that dude naked?"

"He had a tracking and recording device on him. For some reason he was dumb enough to tell us what and where it was, so I think we need a very thorough inspection to ensure he doesn't have another one hidden anywhere. Doc, can you do the honors?" Josh asked, looking at me.

"Roger that," I answered and began moving towards the prisoner to make him extremely uncomfortable.

"Uh, Josh," I asked as I was walking.

"I think I'm going to need to pull his teeth out to be safe. Do you want to start asking him questions before I do that?"

"That's not necessary," answered Chris.

"Old school Russian spies had cyanide tablets hidden in wisdom teeth, but even that is a thing of the past. It failed more often than it worked. And nobody has the tech to fit a transmitter in a tooth that could sustain a signal this far or battery life this long. You can let him keep his teeth."

With a look from Josh, he added a final piece.

"For now."

He turned to Honeypot with a question of his own.

"What did you give this guy? Why would he give that up and let us pull it off of him?"

"GHB," she responded.

"It's a party drug that people started bringing in from the city a few years ago, and some local dealers learned how to make it in their bathtub. We've confiscated quite a bit of it in the casino.

Knowing what it does to people and the fact that it's a liquid, we put a little in his first drink. He didn't seem to taste it, so we added more in each drink until he was on the ground giggling."

"That creates a problem," I said to Josh, remembering my pre-Army party days as a young college man without a care in the world.

"How's that Doc?" asked The Major.

"GHB is some pretty powerful stuff," I said.

"Some people started calling it the new date rape drug when Rohypnol was outlawed. Just a few capfuls of this stuff can make a person a giggling pile of nonsense until they pass out, completely incoherent and unable to remember the previous night."

"So you're telling us we can take advantage of him sexually but can't pump him for any good intel tonight?" replied The Major.

"That depends," I replied, looking to Honeypot.

"How much did you give him?"

She turned to one of the fit, tanned and black haired men who had come along for the ride with her.

Meeting her gaze then turning to me, he held up his thumb and forefinger, showing a size estimate that looked to be about one-quarter of a standard 12-ounce water bottle.

"And this was bathtub GHB, not from a lab?" I asked.

The man nodded in the affirmative.

Taking a second to think, I added my two cents.

"The problem with that stuff is that the homemade chemists are all over the place. Just like North Carolina moonshine you have pros that can make it at 80 proof so it still tastes good but packs a punch, but novices who don't know what they're doing and crank out high octane, nearly 100 percent alcohol."

I looked back at the naked prisoner, lying on the ground with his hood still attached, giggling uncontrollably while rolling around like a dog rolling on a freshly-cut lawn.

"He already gave up his tracking device, so there's a chance he's still coherent and in a pretty good space to give up intel without knowing what he's doing. He's a decent sized guy, but you gave him a heavy dose if this stuff is strong. It takes anywhere from 20 to 30 minutes to take effect and the plateau high can last from 45 minutes to an hour and a half. He's going through a massive dopamine response at the moment, hence the uncontrollable giggling."

"English Doc, what does that mean for us?" The Major interrupted.

"It means he'll be high as a kite for the next hour or so. His walls are as down as they'll ever be...if you can keep him awake and he's not about to die from overdose."

"How can he overdose if he's not still taking the stuff?' asked one of the dark-haired men.

"Good point," I added.

"I never saw him vomit, and there's nothing seeping from the bag on his head. We should be good, but when he comes down from the high our window will close. He'll go into the typical drug comedown and will be uncomfortable, unhappy and realize what's going on. Get on him now."

The Major shot a glance to Josh and Chris, nodding in the prisoners' direction to lay it on him.

"But no need to go rough. If he's as high as I think he is there's no need to use fear or pain as a tactic. In fact that may make him aware of what's going on and he'll put up his defensive walls. It's a club drug, so pump him for information the way you'd press someone over drinks at a nightclub."

"Do we have any more of the stuff?" Josh asked the group with Honeypot.

The man who had given us the dose estimate nodded in affirmation, walked to the trunk of their sedan and threw a bottle to me. Catching it in my hands I saw that about three-quarters of the bottle still remained of the clear liquid.

"Any more?" I asked.

"If you gave him one-fourth of this dose we'll need the same if we decide to hit him again tomorrow, but this will be pretty handy if we take any more prisoners."

The man shook his head negative.

"We still have loads of stuff back at the casino, but this is all we brought with us. Didn't think you guys would be looking to party."

Smiling and nodding, I turned back to Josh and The Major.

"The window is closing. Get to work."

Pulling a blanket from a bag in the rear seat of one of the trucks, Josh and Chris took it to the prisoner, covering his body from the cold and picking him up to walk, cutting the restraints from his ankles and each putting an arm around his shoulders.

In another world it would seem just as if two friends were stumbling while helping their drunk and stoned buddy to a taxi or ride home.

But in this world, it meant they were about to convince this intelligence officer to help us kill as many of his comrades as possible.

The three men disappeared around one of the outcroppings of boulders and The Major called to Tattoo on top.

"How we looking Tattoo?" he asked.

"They're going into a search pattern," he responded.

"Looks like they found his uniform and tracker and are combing the area with flood lights. They're still quite a ways from us, but are starting a linear search. They have a lot of manpower over there, so I don't know how long we have until they're over us. Or until they have vehicles on the roads and find the path we drove here."

The Major combed this information over in his head and started forming a plan.

"Somebody go ask those guys how long they think this will take," he ordered to the group.

"Negative," replied Chad.

"If they're trying to flip this guy, any interruption or reminder to the prisoner of what's going on will set them back. Let's leave them be."

Not the type of man who enjoyed being corrected, especially in front of the group, The Major visibly bit his lip and held back the barrage of insults and anger queued to spew from his mouth.

Hesitating, he thought better of it and took a different approach.

"Well whatever we're doing we need to move the hell out of here fast. There are only a few roads in and out of this area and it's about to be swarmed with soldiers looking for their buddy. As I see it we can either stay in place and try to find a really good hiding spot, go further into the mountains and hope to escape their search perimeter or head towards San Diego where they will never expect us. Any suggestions?"

Hearing The Major, a man who wasn't known for pleasantries (but was well known for his conviction) asking for suggestions meant that he didn't have any good ones of his own.

"I have an idea," spoke Honeypot from her place in the circle.

"We own a golf course not far from the casino, but on the highway heading towards El Cajon in the direction of San Diego.

It's not that much closer, but the Russians forced us to keep it open so their officers can play golf whenever they like. We have to keep it ready to go at any time, day or night, in case they want to play a round and relieve some stress."

She looked around at the group, unsure of how her suggestion would be taken.

"Because we receive calls late at night to prepare for officers working the night shift, we have staff there around the clock, living on the property, and have food and supply trucks going at all hours to keep everything ready for them. If we can make it there, it wouldn't be strange for vehicles to arrive at this hour."

She once again watched the faces of our group for any hint of acceptance or outright denial of her idea.

The Major, spinning the option in his head, was the first to break the silence after her suggestion.

"If we were to do that, how would we get there? We only have one primary road going around the mountains and the north exit is crawling with helicopters."

"You are correct," she responded in her alluring accent.

"But if we can move a little further south before the helicopters expand their search, the road splits off into many directions and smaller roads. We have a few options to either circle deeper south, where they won't be looking yet, or cut north through the lowlands and go as fast as we can."

Taking a knee, pulling a map and small penlight from his jacket pocket The Major motioned for Honeypot to take a knee next to him.

"Show me," he ordered when she was kneeling alongside him.

For the next several minutes, she used a finger to point out several roads and trace the options we had for routes.

Standing, he called out to Tattoo again.

"How are we looking up there?"

A thumbs up was his only response.

"How far west and south have they expanded the perimeter?" he asked.

"Not far," was the answer from Tattoo.

"I don't know what's going on down on the ground, but they're still only covering a few square kilometers around the restaurant. They're going to be doing this for a long time, and at some point soon they'll need to go back for fuel."

The Major took a moment to think the last part over.

The Russian Hind helicopters were absolute feats of engineering, and had no direct match anywhere in NATO.

While our American arsenal had airframes that could act as troop transport, like the Black Hawks we used now or Huey's used in Vietnam, we didn't have anything that could act as both: our helos were only either a fighting vehicle or transport.

But the Hind was built from the very beginning to do both. The Russians didn't like to waste economy of motion, and for all of the jokes about communism and the outdated, shoddy equipment their military had, they always had more than one purpose for everything.

Yet however grand these death machines were that could ferry a handful of shock infantry troops along with an enormous payload of ammunition and missiles, like many feats of Soviet-era engineering all of that multi-purposed usage came with a price.

They were heavy. Extremely heavy.

Putting an airframe into battle didn't only depend on the amount of weaponry you brought to the fight or number of troops you could drop into the war. It also depended on dwell time, the amount of time that airframe could stay in the fight without needing to return for fuel.

He knew the maximum range of a Hind, one that wasn't fully loaded down with troops and ammo, was less than 300 miles.

Given that we were over 25 miles from San Diego, if that's where these gunships had been scrambled from, at a minimum they would need to leave when they had just enough fuel to make the trip home plus a margin of safety.

Not that Russia cared about the crew. But they surely cared about millions of dollars worth of gunships and their pilots more than a single intelligence officer.

The Major stood and addressed the team, now standing in a circle and shooting puzzled looks his way.

"Tattoo is right. Those gunships can't stick around much longer and the attack helos will need to exfil with them to cover their flight back to refuel. I can't even imagine how many trucks full of enemy are headed this way from San Diego, but we have to be ready to move. If those birds see us while they're flying home, we're toast. They can drop enough payload to blast us to kingdom come without even pausing along their flight path."

He moved his gaze around the group to gauge their feelings with his plan.

"We need to get all our gear and people in the trucks. The moment Tattoo sees them turn and head west, we roll."

The group stood in a circle, not sure of exactly what they were waiting for.

"**GET!**," he barked, sounding like someone who had seen one too many cowboy movies and fancied himself The Lone Ranger or Outlaw Josey Wales.

As the circle broke and each member moved toward their respective vehicles, Dave approached to ask The Major a question.

"What about the interrogation, sir?"

"We'll let them have at it until it's time to go. But when Tattoo gives the word, throw them in the closest truck and get your butt in there too. This has to be near perfect timing; missing the helo overflight but getting to the golf course before reinforcements arrive from San Diego."

Lifting his left arm to glance at his watch, he spoke over his wrist to Dave while still holding his forearm suspended in the air in front of his chest.

"Which by my estimates, even if they took an awful long time to muster and get their QRF moving, should be very soon."

He continued to stare at Dave, who wasn't quite sure what to do next.

"Move, big guy," was his final order.

He decided the right place to be was just out of sight, leaning against the boulder but far enough away from the interrogation that he didn't disturb our guys and wouldn't be seen by the prisoner.

Dave had always been the model example of a good American kid: straight-A student, starting athlete on every sports team he ever played for, Eagle Scout and he even led the student council through high school while other kids were getting themselves into adolescence-induced trouble.

When teenagers like me were doing everything they could to find mischief, sneaking out of their parent's houses to meet up with girls or run wild-eyed through the woods hopped up on any booze they could steal from the parent's liquor cabinet, Dave always stayed on the right side of things.

Although most kids who are the product of a divorce chose to act out and attain attention through making trouble or getting their parents called in for meetings with the principle, he opted to make life as easy as possible for his mother.

He had seen the pain in her eyes growing long before his parents even told him they had filed for divorce, and he couldn't bear adding any more trouble to her life.

Seeing how hard it was for her to make ends meet when his dad left, Dave took up a job after school. He would run straight from football, baseball or whichever sport he was involved in at the time to bag groceries at the local grocer.

When that didn't fill all the gaps, he took up another job stocking the shelves at night. When the opportunity and idea had first been presented, his mom disagreed abhorrently. But seeing how much it hurt her to not be able to afford things for her boys that other families in their neighborhood enjoyed, Dave lied to his mother for the only time in his life.

The model student and Eagle Scout began to sneak out of his house in the dead of night; not to party and cause trouble like I did, but to ride his bike back to the grocer to pull the graveyard shift stocking shelves when the delivery trucks arrived.

He told his mother that the team was starting morning football practices again, and that he'd have to leave early in the morning before everyone else woke in order to study a little before putting on the pads and going to practice.

In reality, he kept a blanket in a locker in the store's employee break room and would sleep on the hard bench for just a few hours before getting up, using the dirty bathroom sink to comb his hair and splash cold water on his face.

His mom could never quite figure out why, after the Friday night football games, he never wanted to go hang out with his friends or go on dates with pretty girls.

Not that he couldn't: he was painfully handsome, with his growth spurt at the end of middle school making him not only one of the largest kids in their entire football division, but also built like one of the models adorning the cover of trashy romance novels from the time he turned fourteen.

No, Dave didn't party after the game with his friends who snuck in ice coolers full of beer bought from older brothers and degenerates who had never left their little town.

Although the prettiest teenage girls and every cheerleader from their school (and every surrounding one that heard the story of "Dreamcakes" as they nicknamed him and wrote on the walls of girls restrooms for miles in every direction of his town) pined for a date with him, he wasn't interested in those things.

Dave wanted to sleep.

He would sleep from Friday night until church on Sunday, again collapsing into their living room couch after lunch with the congregation. His mother had been so worried she had taken him to a number of specialists who could never quite pinpoint the problem.

He had always insisted to his boss that he be paid under the table, so his mother would never have to cash an extra check for him and figure out what he was doing.

She had thought that she was losing her mind for several years when every week it seemed there were always more bills in her wallet than she remembered putting in it or taking out from the bank.

Of course a man with that sort of teenage life, much different than those of us carousing all night, wild-eyed and full of piss & vinegar, wouldn't understand the drug-fueled ramblings of the Russian intelligence officer.

Having attended the Air Force Academy, learning to be a fine young officer and being a starting member of the football team, Dave's college experience was much different than mine.

Sure, by the time I got to medical school I had a purpose, a promise to the men of 022 that I was only leaving them to fulfil two obligations: become a doctor and start a family.

My undergraduate studies, however, had been much more gregarious than Dave's.

I too was an athlete in college, but playing on the lacrosse team at a Texas university was a hair shade different from playing football at the Academy.

On the east coast lacrosse was a varsity sport, and one that well-heeled kids played with a love and dedication (to large audiences as well) from the time they could walk, just like Texas kids growing up with football in their veins.

But in Texas the lacrosse players came from one of two pools.

Either they were football players trying to keep in shape during the offseason (and enticed by the idea of having a big metal stick to hit people with), or they were athletes who loved competition but were too rebellious to put their sweat and dedication into the football team, where all the straight-A and "all American" types congregated.

I had been a member of both, but moving along to college I found that our lacrosse parties were even more raucous than those of the fraternity I was in. I had always been smart enough to pass my tests without even attending many of the classes, and spent much more of my focus on social activities than my studies.

Dave had assumed I was able to rattle off the characteristics of a GHB high because of my biochemical knowledge and background as a doctor, especially an orthopedic surgeon who had to know what to look for in case a kid hopped up on drugs got into an accident and found himself on my operating table.

Sure, that was true, but I spoke my insights on the effects of GHB through experience, not something learned in a book or gleaned from a news special about the dangers of the new party drug.

I knew it all too well, and had even operated a nice little side business moving the stuff with a friend I knew in college. When we started making enough money I had even figured out how to make it in my own bathtub to cut out the middleman and increase our margins.

As Dave was standing out of eyesight but in earshot of the Russian intelligence agent, who was taking turns giggling hysterically, mumbling incoherently and only pausing to answer some of Josh's questions, I was recalling the formula for the stuff in my head while seated in the passenger seat of the Hilux.

Genius. Why hadn't I thought of that earlier?

In less than ten minutes, with the right household ingredients I could synthesize all of the truth serum that we would need for future battlefield interrogations like this one.

The onset was fast, the duration was plenty long enough, and as its nickname "liquid ecstasy" indicated it would produce massive euphoric highs that could make any soldier release his inhibitions just enough to divulge the information we needed.

The short whistle of a bird call from Tattoo told us that our time was up. As he began to crawl down the boulder and find his seat in the vehicle, Dave stepped out and gave the "time to go" motion to Josh and Chris.

Knowing that any hesitation or argument wouldn't be a prudent idea in the situation, both men grabbed the prisoner under his arms and lifted him, still giggling, to move back to the trucks.

The sight of a naked man covered by an Army blanket flowing in the breeze may have been enough to get us stopped, seen or killed by a soldier who decided to take a closer look, so they shoved him in the trunk of the sedan Honeypot had arrived in and found their own seats, with Josh again taking the driver's seat of the Hilux.

"Did he give you anything good?" I asked as he roared the engine to life.

"Yeah, I think so," he responded.

"But that guy is so whacked out of his mind it will take Chris and I putting our notes together to see just what it means. Where are we going?"

"We're going golfing," I chuckled.

"I hope you brought your clubs."

CHAPTER 6

DESTINY

Through the scant light of the moon I could see that the golf course wasn't any run-of-the-mill municipal course with dying brown grass and greens workers who didn't know crabgrass from Perennial Ryegrass.

No, these courses were first rate.

Honeypot, in the front vehicle to lead our way, stopped to speak with the security guard housed in a beautiful guard shack keeping watch over the tall wrought iron gates complete with brass inlays, extremely high-end decorative columns and festooned with ivy crawling up its sides.

"That guard shack alone looks like it cost a million bucks," remarked Tattoo from the back seat.

"It very well may have," I replied.

"This place ain't exactly just outside of San Diego. If they want to bring rich muckety-mucks out here to play the links and lose money at their casino, everything has to be top notch."

With a wave from the guard Honeypot shifted her transmission into gear and led us down a long, winding drive.

We soon passed the turnoff that would have taken us to the clubhouse which resembled an Ivy League university or one of the mansions that adorn the lands just a short commute from New York city, where the real money of the United States live to escape the scrutiny of prying eyes and the "regular people" they so despise.

Continuing we found ourselves turning onto a side road, hidden from view by high poplars and a descending elevation.

We had our headlights on so as not to arouse even more suspicion by driving like we were, well, suspicious, and she stopped her sedan in front of a building with large rolling bays that looked like an enormous garage.

As the men jumped out of the vehicles one ran to a door on the side, opened it and emerged after a few minutes from one of the tall doors which was now being lifted automatically.

Five more giant bays began to open, revealing garage spaces with enough room for three of our vehicles in each, and the man motioned for us to enter.

Stepping out of the Hilux I observed that it was some type of maintenance or repair facility.

There were golf carts in various states of repair in the several spaces to our left, and work trucks suspended in the air by hydraulic lifts to our right.

Dave let out a long whistle as he took in the full scope of the garage.

"Nice place," he said, not quite to Honeypot but in her general direction.

"Thank you," she responded.

I couldn't hide the puzzled bewilderment on my face.

"You own this place?" I asked, this time directly to her.

"No. My tribe owns this place," she answered nonchalantly.

"Ok, but your family leads the tribe?" I followed.

"My father and brother, yes," she replied with a "where is this going" tone.

"Maybe this is rude of me to ask, but why do you drive that beat up jalopy if your family is in the leadership of a tribe that runs a place like this?"

She laughed, showing that I wasn't the first person to ask the silly question.

"This is a small town, one of those places where everybody knows everybody and loves to be in everyone's business."

I nodded in understanding, as I had grown up in a small town very similar in that respect.

"Plus, the Russian brass who come here to play and out to our casino took a very keen interest in my family when they first approached us to open the places back up for their troops," she continued.

"I don't know what impression you have of me, but I'm not really the silver spoon and designer clothes wearing princess that you might think."

I couldn't keep the grin from my face as she spoke, and as I moved my gaze from her eyes down to the skin-tight, thousand-dollar designer dress she was wearing a small laugh escaped her mouth.

Even as she spoke I kept just a few extra moments of my attention on her dress... specifically the figure under her dress, before I met her eyes once again.

Will I ever see another woman dressed in that type of outfit again in my life?

"Okay, you got me there," she said smiling.

"But everyone in town and even the Russians would recognize my truck. Hell, they probably have a tracking device on it somewhere. So every time I go to meet Mr. Bryce here," she said motioning to Josh, "I drive a worker's car so that nobody will ask questions as to why I'm driving into the mountains."

Tattoo pointed at Josh and let out a laugh.

"Bryce? Really?"

Tyler spoke up from the other side of Josh.

"What's wrong with Bryce?

Josh looked over to Tyler with a grin.

"Let's just say the name Bryce fits in a lot better with you guys down here in SoCal than it does up in Colorado."

Turning his gaze back to Honeypot, he gave an explanation.

"I guess, given our circumstances, that isn't going to hold up for long. I'm Josh," he said, and then proceeded to introduce each man in our group who promptly held up a hand when his name was called, with some even adding the special touch of a sarcastic bow fit for the royalty that she was.

After introducing her team as well, Honeypot finished by introducing herself as Meda.

Meda.

I repeated her name in my head, realizing that it suited her, aligning perfectly with the exotic mystique and sultry energy which she exuded.

The Major was the first to voice the question in all of our heads.

"What does it mean?" he asked matter of factly, almost as if he didn't really care but felt obliged to inquire like every other white guy she met before him.

"It doesn't mean anything important, and it's not as cool as you imagine."

The men in her company shifted their feet awkwardly in an indication that we weren't getting the whole truth.

Looking to her brother, I posed The Major's question to him.

Glancing furtively at his sister, our group and then back at me, he answered using a single word as if with an err of caution.

"Prophetess."

"It's just a name, it doesn't mean anything," Meda argued.

"That's not true," her brother disagreed.

"It means everything. It means you should listen closely to anything she says."

Sparks of fire flashed in Meda's eyes, a volley of momentary betrayal-fueled anger shot at her brother which, realizing that we were all in this together, was followed with a sheepish nod and her gaze shifting to the floor.

"She sees things," he continued.

"Things that nobody else can see. Even amongst the wisest ones in our tribe, she finds the path when everyone else's vision is clouded."

He opened his arms wide and looked around, from left to right.

"All of this is from her. When she was born our tribe had nothing. We were confined to the reservation to slowly die away poor and hopeless. But she had my father's ear from the day she could talk, and became his closest advisor. And our sister..."

He paused, suddenly remembering that the Russian intelligence officer had confirmed their worst fears regarding the sister's fate.

Closing his eyes for a moment in what I imagined was a brief but solemn memorial for her memory, they reopened with visions of pain hidden behind happy memories of a brother's love and the internal anguish he tried to bury with the knowledge that she was gone.

"Our sister was Nacoma, or Strong Warrior, and she was the enforcer."

Meda smiled half-heartedly and fought back tears as the memories flooded her mind, while the men lowered their eyes to the ground and paid silent reverence to her memory.

The brother continued.

"Between Meda's ability to see the correct path, Nacoma's absolute fearlessness and my father's leadership they were unstoppable. Nothing could stand in their way, and they began to build this empire."

"And what about you?" The Major asked.

"What's your superhero power?"

"I'm a man," he said with an obvious tone of shame.

"Before my mother died, father told me on more than a few occasions that a truly wise man finds the strongest and smartest woman he can, and listens to her."

Seeing The Major's puzzled face, the brother elaborated.

"No matter how strong my sister's abilities were, it is still a man's world and, especially in the world of the tribes, the ideas may have come from them but the orders had to come from my father and I."

Hearing the chagrin in his explanation that may have never been said out loud before but seemed as if it were contemplated often, with the brother's head hanging lower than necessary for mourning, even The Major knew it was time to change the subject.

Clapping his hands together and looking from side to side at the entire group assembled in the expansive garage, he asked the most important question that we hadn't quite broached.

"Okay then, what do we do now?"

A shout came from the trunk of Meda's sedan, and we realized that we had completely forgotten about our prisoner.

"Oh yeah. That guy," The Major said dryly.

"Did we pump any good intel from him yet?"

"A little," answered Chris.

"But Josh and I need to put our heads together to make sense of it."

"Well then," The Major added.

"Somebody shut him up and keep him out of sight before I cut his freaking throat out."

Josh and Chris walked to the trunk and when they were positioned on either side, Meda clicked her keys and it opened to reveal the Russian officer lying quietly on his side in the fetal position, no longer giggling uncontrollably.

"Looks like we missed our opportunity," said Chris.

"Not so fast," I said.

"I can make as much of that stuff as we need from a few ingredients I'm certain we can find here."

A dozen confused faces turned to me, unaware of how it was that medical school taught me how to make party drugs.

"Did you take some extra party drug chemistry classes in med school doc?" asked The Major.

"Not quite, but it's not important how I know."

I grabbed a pad of paper from a nearby workbench and began to scribble a short list of ingredients I would need.

Handing it to Meda, I conveyed just how simple it would be.

"Find me those ingredients and a kitchen for ten minutes and I can make enough to dose a hundred people into the giggling mess we saw earlier."

Taking the list and looking back at Josh, Meda shook her head affirmative.

"Let's take this guy to the back room," she said.

"Follow me, and after that I'll start working on this list. I think I know where I can find everything."

As she disappeared through a door at the rear of the garage, Chris and Josh followed carrying the prisoner suspended by his arms and legs.

I turned to The Major.

"And I've got a mission that I need to go on alone," I told him rather than asking.

"What the hell are you talking about Rob?" he asked.

I looked at the array of vehicles lining the garage and pointed to the sedan that Meda had driven.

"I'm going to take this car and go away for about twelve hours."

"You taking a vacation Doc?" Tattoo asked.

Shaking my head and laughing, I answered his joking question with all seriousness.

"My usefulness here comes from my medical knowledge, as it's no secret that i'm probably the worst shot in our group."

"And don't forget the biggest tactical moron we've got," added Ray.

"Thanks Ray," I replied.

"No problem buddy," he smiled with a kiss in the air.

Pretending to catch his kiss and put it in my pocket like a lovesick teenager, I continued laying out my idea.

"To Ray's point, I'm not going to do any good helping you guys plan operations. But I can offer quite a bit of help if I were to have a truckload of medical supplies to help sustain those operations."

The Major frowned, not understanding my train of thought.

"I was able to bring some bandages and enough antibiotics to cover maybe a few people for minor illnesses. And from what I've seen that's about all we've got around here."

I looked to Jason and Klint, the other medics who had jumped into this mission ahead of me with the team. Their nods in the affirmative confirmed my point.

"Between school, residency and work I've spent almost a decade at a major hospital that's only a few hours drive from here. Since I left straight from the operating room when the invasion started, I should still have access to the entire place."

Staring at me blankly, not giving any indication that he understood what I was outlining I laid it out for him bluntly.

"After I make a batch of GHB for you guys to continue the interrogation I'm going to drive back to Los Angeles, use my access code to sneak into the hospital and gather all the medicine and supplies that I can to better outfit these guys."

Shaking his head The Major didn't seem to agree with me.

"We have enough medical gear to sustain us Rob, that's a chance we can't afford to take right now."

Filing back into the garage Meda, Josh and Chris took their spot behind the open circle of the group as Jason added his views.

"He's right sir. We have enough medical supplies to handle maybe a few injuries, but not much more. We have basic antibiotics, but hardly any IV fluids and no blood or plasma. If our group increases at all, or we take more than an injury or two we'll be down to zero."

The Major turned to look at Jason, shot him an angry squint of the eyes and then turned his full attention back to me.

"Who's going to go with you?" he asked.

"I don't think anyone wants to volunteer for that suicide mission."

"Nobody," I answered.

"I'll be faster on my..."

"Negative," was his cold and no-nonsense response.

"I don't want to do anything to inflate that giant ego of yours Doc but we need you, terrible tactician or not."

"I'll go," shot Dave from across the garage.

"No," Meda added loudly from the back.

"Rob, you go. There's something you need to do and it's very important that you get there before it's too late. But Dave..."

She hesitated, a scared expression coming over her face.

"This isn't for you."

"All due respect," Dave added.

"Rob can't really look after himself and definitely isn't strong enough to lift boxes of medical supplies on his own. I mean, look at that civilian potbelly and puny little arms."

He laughed, sauntering past the circle to poke me in the belly like a Pillsbury doughboy.

The Major, not happy that his power was being subjugated on several fronts, insisted that he give the final word.

"Rob, get on your way. Dave, watch his back. Any questions?"

Meda stood in the back of the garage and visibly shook her head to make it clear that she didn't think it was a good idea.

"Sir," she began but was immediately met with a knife hand from The Major.

"I'd like you to wait to give your opinion until we ask for it missy," he barked angrily.

"You may be a big shot and have an ominous sounding name for your tribe, but this is my team, not yours. And I decide who goes and who stays. Got it?"

Meda, having never known the feeling of someone so unashamedly refusing her guidance continued to shake her head.

She only stopped to glance up at me, shifted her gaze to Dave and then walked back out of the room.

When the door closed behind her, Josh extended The Major's orders.

"You guys need to stay off the grid and out of sight. Change into civilian clothes..."

He stopped and looked to Meda's brother.

"Do you have some clothes that will fit these two?"

After their confirmation, Josh continued laying out the logistics of our movement.

"Keep a submachine gun in your laps and ready to go at all times, with a pistol under your clothes. Load up your rifles and keep them hidden in the trunk, along with a double basic load of ammo [14 loaded magazines] and some frag grenades. If you guys get into trouble, do not engage. Just lay down enough suppressive fire to get their heads down, find a place to hide and hightail it back here as fast as you can. We won't be able to offer any help from here if something happens."

Dave and I were dressed in poorly-fitting civilian clothes, hiding our weapons and ammo in the trunk of Meda's car when she entered back into the garage carrying a cardboard box loaded with all the supplies I had given her on my list.

Motioning for me to come to her, I nodded to Dave telling him to finish the preparations without me and made my way to her.

Taking a mental note of the contents while walking toward her I smiled and took the box out of her hands.

"Now all we need is a kitchen," I said to her.

"Follow me," she responded as she turned and walked back towards the door she had come from, leading me through an employee break room furnished with benches, dining tables and televisions, through a long hallway with administrative offices on either side and finally stepped into another break area, this one complete with coffee machine, refrigerator, microwave and stove.

Upon entering the room she turned to me and spread her arms.

"Will this suffice?" she asked.

"This looks great," I answered.

"But there was one thing that I forgot on my list. I need a permanent marker to label the bottles. We don't want someone filling their canteens with this on accident and rolling out on a mission high as a kite."

Smiling at the thought she nodded, letting me know that she would go find one for me. But as she began to walk passed me, she stopped and gently put a hand on my arm.

"When you see her," she said, almost in a whisper while looking at her hand.

"You will know she is the one. Protect her with everything you have," she spoke just loudly enough for me to hear above the soft hum of the refrigerator.

"But your friend Dave," she added and hesitated.

"You must allow him to find his own destiny. Whatever you do, do not get in his way."

She lifted her eyes to meet mine briefly, and seeing the puzzled look on my face she shook her head ever so slightly.

As I formed the words to pose a question she put a single finger on my lips and shook her head in a wider arc from side to side, telling me that I would find no more answers with her.

I stood in the middle of the break room puzzled as she walked away from me, out into the hallway and made a left turn without looking back or acknowledging me any further.

Unsure of what happened or what any of it meant, I knew the clock was ticking and we had to start moving. The team wouldn't sit still for very long, and I was sure they would begin planning operations while Dave and I were on the road.

As always, time was of the essence.

I never noticed Meda come back into the room, but as I finished the last batch and put the bottles of clear fluid into the refrigerator I found a permanent marker on the counter next to me.

Had that always been there? Was I just so tired or tuned out that I didn't notice Meda come in and put it right next to me?

Looking around the room for a moment with a puzzled expression on my face I found the notepad my list was written on, which Meda had left in the cardboard box with my supplies.

Taking a brief moment to write out the dosages, effects and duration of GHB with the strength that I had just created I walked back to the garage.

The team was already huddled around a map that someone had put up on one wall, and when Dave saw me he motioned to the car. Nodding, I handed the GHB instructions to Klint, said a quick goodbye to everyone and took my place in the driver's seat of Meda's car.

I cranked the engine and was pulling the transmission into reverse when Meda came running to my window with a piece of paper.

"Here, take this," she said as I rolled down the window and she thrust the paper into my hands.

"What is it?" I asked.

"It's authorization for travel," she explained.

"The Russian's and Chinese have roadblocks all over the place and this will allow you to pass through."

"I don't think it will help much if they find our weapons in the trunk," Dave added from the passenger seat.

"With this you shouldn't have to worry about that," she responded.

"Like I said earlier we get calls at all hours of the night from Russian officers who want to use the course or have a special party at the casino. The seal and signature on here tells anyone who pulls you over that they'll be in deep trouble if they make you late. It works like a charm."

Smiling and nodding to her as I carefully placed the note in the glovebox, I saw a momentary glimpse of something that I couldn't quite place wash over her face as I pulled out of the garage.

What was that? Fear? Regret?

I couldn't help but wonder what types of thoughts or premonitions would make a prophetess scared, but we didn't have time to think about such things.

Dave and I were on a mission.

I had driven between San Diego and Los Angeles countless times, and often late into the night as we were now doing.

The drive only took about two and a half hours on the highway, but given the situation we chose to stick exclusively to the route which skirted the pacific ocean and beach.

We knew that while enemy on the major highways would be looking for anything out of the ordinary, soldiers on the Pacific Coast Highway [PCH] would most likely be enjoying the view and gentle ocean breeze instead.

This doubled our travel time, but after traveling the entire route without being stopped for a roadblock we knew it was the correct decision.

As we came closer to our objective and the road forced us to follow its path further inland, I realized somewhere around Long Beach how important proper planning is, and why no matter how well you think you know a route you should always take at least a cursory glance at your map.

Had I not rushed us through that integral piece of any mission and taken a moment to lay out a map to show Dave what route we were taking, I would have realized the massive error I made in planning: while the PCH kept us off major highways and away from enemy eyes for over three hours of the trip, the end would make up for it.

To continue our path, we would have to pass directly by Los Angeles International Airport (LAX), one of the largest airports in the world and likely an enemy stronghold.

As the signs on the side of the road began alerting us that we were passing Redondo Beach, then Manhattan Beach and finally entering El Segundo, I knew it couldn't be long before we were forced to come face to face with enemy soldiers.

Wanting to keep my MP5 submachine gun close but out of sight, I put the car on cruise control while I moved the seat back as far as it would go, placing my weapon in the space underneath my seat alongside its electric wiring.

Dave watched and followed suit, and when they were both out of view I motioned for him to get Meda's authorization to travel out.

While he was pulling the official paper out of the glove box the traffic began to slow. Our choice to take the scenic route meant the sun was just starting to make its appearance on the horizon, and those people who still had jobs were making their way to them.

Warzone or not, traffic in Los Angeles is always one of the worst experiences imaginable.

After about fifteen minutes of moving forward at a snail's pace I saw the problem.

We were less than a mile away from the airport and there were large piles of sandbags on either side of the road forming checkpoints, funnelling traffic into a single lane in both directions, complete with a giant metal arm rising and lowering after each vehicle showed the appropriate documents.

The guard checking those documents was a gaunt-faced Chinese soldier, AK-47 slung around his shoulder and hatred in his eyes.

From his demeanor and movements I recognized the type of soldier he was.

He thought that when he joined the Chinese Army and prepared for its greatest military campaign in a millennium, that he would be faced with arduous battles and given the opportunity to perform with such bravery that people would sing his name for ages.

He was the best shooter in his class. His athletic performance was outstanding and mental acuity tests showed that not only was he faster, but he was also smarter than most. If you asked him he was even smarter than his instructors, who clearly were just jealous because of what a great soldier he had turned out to be.

He screamed the loudest in the war drills, was always the first to volunteer for extra duties and show his dedication.

The explosions in training simulations never bothered him or caused him to lose even the slightest bit of concentration, lest he flinch and miss one of the American swine coming for him.

When he held his knife in his mouth and crawled through sand and barbed wire, machine guns firing over his head and the sounds of agonizing screams playing through loudspeakers, he never hesitated.

Not once.

He told his mother he would make her proud, told his father he would bring honor to the family name. He was destined to prove his might and tireless devotion to his nation.

But instead he was guarding a road in a sleepy little beach town, waving Americans along as they made their way to whatever servitude his superiors had chosen for them.

I had seen the dead and disappointed look on his face in multitudes of soldiers faces over the years.

The National Guard troops guarding the gates of our headquarters in Bosnia, watching us go out on missions in plain clothes with nothing more than a pistol in our pocket and hunting some of the most vicious war criminals and mobsters the world have ever known, bringing new ones back to base with a black bag over their head and rips along their Bosnian Business Suits (Adidas track pants and matching jacket) from where we roughed them up while asking questions that even the interrogators back at our headquarters didn't have high enough clearances to hear the answers to.

The young Marines in Africa who, although they had been trained to be ruthless and efficient warriors, had been resigned to guarding an embassy or, as this young man, guarding the front gate of a base or standing watch over a roadblock.

The infantrymen in Iraq and Afghanistan who, having showed promise on the ranges of the bases we inhabited, would be taken aside and released from their units for a few hours a day so that we could train them to go with us on missions.

They were hard, they were mean, and they soaked up everything we taught them about Close Quarters Battle [CQB] and how to enact violence of action on an enemy objective.

But after weeks of training, tireless hours of sweat and gaining our complete trust to watch our backs on a mission, their commanders would pull them at the last minute from running actual operations with us for fear that it was an unnecessary risk.

I knew that look.

I knew that despair.

Most importantly, I knew the dangers that it posed and the fire it caused to rage under the skin of a young man prepared to kill and, if needed, die as a hero with honor in the name of his family and nation.

"Don't look this kid in the eyes when we get up there," I told Dave.

"What?" He asked incredulously.

"Just don't look him in the eyes. And don't stare at him. Look at that kid. Don't let him see you, but take a good look at him. He's just waiting for a reason to shoot someone and earn a few medals. I don't want it to be us."

As we drew closer to the warrior-to-be I began to rehearse what we would need to do.

"We both work at the hospital," I said under my breath.

"The morning shift will be coming in about now, so it's logical. And if he asks any questions about the facility, just let me answer. I know everyone in and everything about that place."

"Roger that," he replied quietly.

I unknowingly flinched for a brief moment when the car in front of us was waved along and the young soldier looked directly at me.

I didn't know why, but everything inside of me froze momentarily.

Maybe it was his demeanor.

Perhaps it was the hype I had been telling myself about how dangerous he was in an attempt to cool my own mind.

Possibly I caught something subconsciously that flashed when I looked into his eyes for the first time.

I had been stared down by men much harder and more dangerous than this kid in my day, from Bosnian death squads to Taliban warlords and men who would skin you alive, go eat dinner and then kiss their children goodnight without ever having a second thought about you.

Whatever the reason, I committed the two cardinal sins of low-visibility operations and making it through a checkpoint in enemy controlled territory: don't look an agitated guard directly in the eyes and never give him a reason to think you're hiding something.

Unlike the previous cars who he had waved through without a word, the soldier began furiously screaming at me in Chinese.

After a brief moment of yelling he started to advance toward our vehicle, pulling his weapon from the sling on his shoulder.

As he advanced, Dave turned to me.

"I think we were supposed to drive to him."

"I see that now, dude," I responded.

"But if we start driving while he's got a gun in his hands he's definitely going to shoot us."

The soldier lowered the rifle and pointed it at the windshield of our car, lifting his barrel up in a motion that, I thought, meant to put our hands up.

I raised my hands, shoulder width apart and palms facing the front, to which Dave followed suit.

I was unsure if Dave was cursing out loud or I was screaming it in my mind, but every expletive that I had ever known, in multiple languages, began streaming through my head at a rapid pace.

Finishing his advance to our vehicle and pointing the barrel of his rifle in my window, perilously close to my face, the soldier continued screaming in Chinese.

Having been married to an Asian woman and having two kids that were both mixed and mandarin speakers I knew a little of the language. But the speed, ferocity and his audacious accent hurt my ears and confused any attempt I made at translation.

"What's he saying Doc?" Dave asked, eyes forward but able to see out of his peripheral that the soldier's rifle was placed firmly against my temple, with him using it to push my head, attempting to provoke any response that would allow him to paint Dave's face with my brain matter.

"Dengdai. Buyao pai. Women you wenjian, " [Wait. Don't shoot. We have papers] I spoke, still looking straight into the windshield and praying the little mandarin that I could remember wasn't telling this guy, on accident, that his mother licks toads or that his sister was the object of my affection.

The screaming paused for a second, as the soldier seemed as stunned as Dave that this ignorant American scum actually understood his language.

"Ni shi shui," [who are you?] the soldier responded, his tone no longer angry and now tinged with a hint that he realized what would happen if he shot, not only the wrong person, but someone with papers.

While the American military was more than happy to skewer her own service member who committed the most trivial crimes against the indigenous populace in a warzone, willing to send them back home on the first thing smoking for dirtbag Judge Advocate General [JAG] officers, politicians and journalists to make a name for themselves prosecuting a soldier who had made an error, our enemies didn't quite have the same perspective.

No, if he shot some average civilian on the side of the street, it would likely only take a quick call to his boss and a few more soldiers would expeditiously arrive to strip me naked, harvest anything of value from my pockets and dump me in the ocean.

Probably even minus my teeth and fingernails to prevent identification when the UN War Crimes people started poking their nose around (as they always do when it's far too late to actually help anyone in a warzone).

But if he shot someone important...if he shot someone important with papers...that was a whole new ballgame.

He wouldn't go home a hero, having brought honor to his family.

He wouldn't be the subject of ticker tape parades and songs sung by Chinese youth for generations.

He would be the one finding his grave in the ocean.

"Yisheng," I replied, telling him I was a doctor.

"Wo you wenjian," I repeated, saying again that I had papers.

The cold barrel was pressed against my left temple so hard that my skin stuck to it as it was pulled back, slightly at first and then out of the window entirely.

"Gei wo kan," [show me] the soldier ordered as he nervously dropped his rifle to a low ready, sure he saw a look in my eyes that told him something, he wasn't sure exactly what, but something was amiss.

Keeping my left hand raised and in clear view I cautiously moved my right hand over and, still staring straight at the windshield, accidentally stuck my hand in Dave's face.

I laughed a little inside but could tell, mostly from the expression which was resting against the palm of my right hand, that he was not amused.

Also moving as slowly and deliberately as possible, he reached down and lifted our fake papers with his left hand, using his right to pry my dirty, smelly, greasy hand from his face.

Papers in hand, I remembered one small Chinese tradition that could very well bridge our communication gap even further and let him know that, even though I may be American swine, I understood his culture and was showing him a sign of respect.

And if I knew to show him this subtle sign of respect, well maybe I just was the type of person that he wouldn't be able to kill and dump in the ocean.

Firmly taking the papers from Dave in my hands, thumbs on top and hands below clutching gently to each corner I slowly swiveled in my seat, held them out with both hands extended and bowed my head ever so slightly.

The soldier, having been manning the same checkpoint since the post-invasion occupation, was stunned.

None of the American dogs had shown him that respect.

Sure, they were all terrified of him and gasped when he snarled at them on days in which he was especially unhappy to be there, but none had shown this traditional Chinese form of respect.

Maybe this one is different.

Awestruck and slightly ashamed for being so harsh towards us, the soldier put his rifle back over his shoulder, used both hands and offered the same sign of respect in taking the papers as had been offered to him, adding a slight bow.

His face eased, tension in his belly subsided and he almost began to smile, thinking about how high-strung he had been, questioning why he had reacted in such a way to these obviously wise and intelligent men.

Until he looked down and saw what the papers contained.

Caught off guard and feeling that he had been tricked into a false state of ease by the two men in the car, the blood rushed to the soldier's face as he gritted his teeth and imagined how satisfying it would be to put a bullet in each them.

Still holding the paper in one hand the soldier started to raise his rifle again.

Fake.

The word continued to echo in his head, allowing him to understand where the brief look of fear in my eyes had come from.

"Russian?" the soldier yelled into the window of our car.

"Russian?" he repeated.

"Ni zai nali zhongwen baozhi?" [where are your Chinese papers] he screamed.

"No Russia. China. Where China?" he bellowed.

As the barrel once again found its way through the open window and to the flesh of my temple, we heard a voice with a thick Cossack accent in the distance.

"What is this, Russian? What Russian?" the voice asked.

"No Russian, American," the Chinese soldier replied.

"American with fake Russian papers."

Astonished that the soldier spoke, not perfect but good broken english, it made sense.

The members of most European and Asian nations were made to learn multiple languages as children, and if you were going to use several countries to invade another, it was necessary that all soldiers be able to communicate in a common language.

Although they were united in their communistic roots and hate for America, I knew enough about both Chinese and Russian generals to understand that neither would bow to the other and allow their language to be that common identifier.

They were cultures who followed the "death by a thousand paper cuts" mentality, and allowing the other's language to be the official would deliver too many paper cuts to let it go.

It just so happened that the common language for the world was english, and given that it was also the national language for the nation they were invading...well that made sense even to communists.

"Why fake?" the thick Russian accent continued.

"How fake?"

I saw the unmistakable grey jacket of a Russian uniform appear in the periphery of my vision, and watched as a pair of gloved black hands took the paper from the Chinese soldier.

He began to laugh in that hearty, remarkable and manly laugh that all Russians share, the kind that seemed to emanate from the very depths of the earth and echo from the heavens as if caught in its own cavernous chamber around your being.

"Oh boy," the Russian continued.

"No fake...important person."

He paused to bend down and take a closer look at me, glanced over at Dave and then stood back to square off with the Chinese soldier.

"Let them go," he spoke calmly yet with absolute authority.

Seeing the Chinese soldier unprepared to move, his patience was running thin.

"Ho-kay," he continued.

"I tell you what."

The Chinese soldier shifted nervously in his boots while the Russian, entirely at ease, rapidly became annoyed by the Chinese soldier's insolence.

"I will let you do what you want. But if you don't leave now, my comrade and I will assume you don't want us to relieve you."

The Chinese soldier again shifted uncomfortably.

"And I will go to my superiors and tell them there is a car with papers signed by our colonel, specifically saying to let them pass, and that if they are slowed down the blame will be on the soldier reading the papers."

A knot began to form in the Chinese soldier's gut, realizing that not only had he made a mistake, but that he had made a mistake with the kind of people you couldn't make mistakes with.

Knowing the culture and that a Chinese soldier would want to save face above all, the Russian added a comfort.

"It's ok. We all make mistake. I won't tell anyone, mine comrade won't tell anyone..."

He leaned once again into my window, looking at Dave and I.

"And I'm sure they won't tell anyone."

While the constant barrage of expletives had stopped their incessant loop running through my head, I still had the cold barrel of a rifle pressed firmly against my temple.

Noticing this and my resulting hesitation to so much as breathe, the Russian stood again and faced his Chinese comrade.

"So, let these men go on their way."

With the last words, seeing the Chinese soldier still unmoving the Russian gingerly placed one hand on his shoulder and the other on top of the rifle, moving it away from my head and helping guide it back and out of the car.

"Good work comrade. Food is ready in cafeteria. Go enjoy."

When the Chinese soldier turned and walked away the tension dissipated from the inside of our vehicle. The Russian soldier handed the papers back through the window, smiled and rendered a short half-salute.

I felt the sharp ingrained desire to return his salute, but knew that would be as good as a death sentence.

So instead I nodded, put the car in drive and moved through the barrier when it raised.

Dave didn't launch any insults my way on the final ten minutes of our trip, and he didn't need to. He was classier than that, but I sure wasn't. While there were no words spoken in the vehicle, a constant barrage of loathing from my brain were creating their own war in my head.

I couldn't believe I had been so stupid. I knew better.

That type of sloppiness and laziness was going to get someone killed. And if it had been me, I would have deserved it. But if it had been Dave I don't think that I could have lived with myself.

When we finally neared the hospital I was dumbfounded by what I saw. While Austin had seemed like it wasn't even part of a nation under attack, Santa Monica looked like a downright warzone.

Santa Monica boulevard was lousy with Russian and Chinese troops, and every street corner had fighting positions.

Built from sandbags, they were each manned by soldiers at the ready and some even held anti-aircraft guns pointed up at the sky with bored operators standing next to them, smoking cigarettes and waiting for something to shoot.

Turning onto sixteenth street I was amazed that the garage in which my parking spot was located was still open. I devised a cover story as I entered my code into a small grey keypad, having no expectations that it would still work.

But much to my amazement the gate rose, we pulled in and, though my reserved spot had been taken by a Russian military vehicle, we were able to find an empty spot without much effort.

I looked over to Dave while pulling the keys from the ignition and stuffing them in my pocket.

"I saw guards at the front door but no metal detectors. They were searching bags, which means we can't take the submachine guns in there."

"Yeah," he added.

"And I saw them patting someone down, so we can't take the pistols in either."

After taking a moment to pause, I turned and looked him square in the eye.

"There's no need for you to take the undue risk of going in there with me, unarmed. You stay here, guard the vehicle and be ready in case...."

Dave cut me off.

"Negative ghostrider."

He met my gaze to tell me he was as serious as a heart attack.

"I told The Major I'd be here watching your butt, and I fully intend to stand by my word. Now, how are we doing this?"

Much like Ray had communicated the night before when I arrived to meet the team, I was glad he was there with me but wished that Dave wasn't in this dangerous situation of my making.

But, realizing that Dave was a man of his word and wasn't going to break it just so I could feel better, I laid out my plan.

"My office, if it's still there, is on the third floor of the old hospital. There have been a lot of renovations over the years and when I started my residency they built a brand new wing of surgical theaters. We need to get to those new theaters to grab the supplies. I always kept a small pistol taped underneath a false bottom in a drawer of my desk in the event of a psychopath trying to shoot the place up, or, well...this."

Dave and I each paused for a moment.

With a quick glance in each other's eyes we were thankful that whatever it was inside of us that knew this was coming one day had never subsided, but constantly scratched at our brains to stay vigilant and never forget that we had to be prepared.

"Okay," Dave repeated.

"So we have to go to the surgical theaters and your office. Anything else?"

"Yes," I answered.

"The pharmacy. If my credentials still stand here I can checkout whatever we need. If there are no enemy soldiers in there I plan to convince the pharmacist to let us get in the back and go shopping. This place is also a staging center for environmental disasters or mass casualty incidents [MASCALs], so we have more trauma kits, packed and ready down in the basement, than we could ever need."

Dave shot me a look that I knew too well.

"Rob," he stated in a no-nonsense tone.

"Be realistic. We have to carry whatever we take out of there. I don't think the guards will be ok with us walking out of the front doors with the whole hospital, and a dozen or so trips are sure to arouse some suspicion."

"Damnit big guy...you're right." I buried my head in my hands and thought.

"Ok. Let's grab the pistol first so that if something goes wrong we can at least have a fighting chance. We can swing by the employee locker room and steal a few backpacks. The orderlies and scrub techs always bring their personal stuff to work in backpacks."

Dave gave me an unhappy look, telling me that he didn't like something I had just said.

"Ok, sorry. We'll borrow the backpacks. If it makes you feel better we can leave cash in the lockers to pay them for it."

Seeing him smile let me know that we were back on the right track.

"The pharmacy is our next priority. We can always make trauma gear or find bandages, but drugs are something we aren't able to make. I had really hoped to walk out of here with some high speed gear, but let's save that for if we feel froggy enough to make a second run. We have to grab some trauma kits from downstairs, but with all of that I think we'll be set."

As the surly Russian soldier patted me down at the front entrance of the hospital I was thankful for Dave's keen eye. I hadn't seen it on our drive in, and the absence of metal detectors had me planning to bring a pistol tucked into my waistband, which was now being patted down by the military guards.

Once inside, Dave and I began to move with a quickness, passing people in the hallway as I focused on the list of items we needed and the routes we should take to get them.

I kept my head down, moving quickly in the hopes of blending in, not catching any extra attention like I had at the roadblock and being in & out before anyone realized we were there.

A voice rang out behind me when we stepped off the elevator onto the third floor and turned to move towards my office.

"Doctor Lewis."

Just put your head down and keep walking. Damnit Dave, don't react big guy.

"Doctor Lewis," the voice repeated.

I could tell from the volume she was following me.

Mind racing, I tried desperately to scan my memory banks for that voice as I walked, faster now, doing my best to look like a busy surgeon who didn't have time to talk to anyone.

At least I had a lot of practice at that .

I walked as fast as possible, hoping and praying that Dave was staying just a step behind me and not reacting to the voice that I couldn't for the life of me place who it belonged to.

It felt like it had been decades since I had been at the hospital, and couldn't remember any of the people who I had worked most closely with.

We rounded the corner which took us on the final straightaway to my office, meaning we'd be there in under a minute at our pace.

"Doctor Robert Lewis," the voice stomped in defiance, bringing back memories of my childhood, raised by a strict and strong southern mother who, once the full name came out, told you that it was time to take your medicine.

I stopped dead in my tracks so suddenly that Dave, all six foot five and 250 pounds of him, kept walking right through me.

I felt him picking me up and ushering me to continue our walking race down the hall, but I held up my hand to let him know it was all right.

"Cecile!" I exclaimed.

"So good to see you, it feels like it's been ages."

Not looking amused in the slightest bit, the icy stare she gave me was so cold that it felt as if the shards of ice would rip straight into my chest and pull my heart out while it was still beating, freezing every drop of blood in my veins and causing it to shatter, along with my ego, when they hit the ground together.

"Something wrong?" I asked with the nicest smile I could muster.

Surgical nurses and the surgeons to whom they are assigned, much like military soldiers and officers in smaller and specialized units, share a few things in common.

But none is more steadfast than the two rule books they share: the written and the unwritten.

In the written rule books, in both cases, one is mandated by the very essence of their job and station to pay nothing but the utmost respect to the other, especially in public, with fear of significant reprisals and punishment if they don't.

But the unwritten rule books are drastically different.

For instance, in Special Forces an ODA typically has one officer, one warrant officer and ten non-commissioned officers [NCO's].

By the written rulebook, the officer should always be saluted, should always be called sir, should always be treated with respect and his word should be the absolute final, as if it came from God himself.

But in reality, and the unwritten rule book, life gets in the way.

A team sergeant, who is not an officer but may have been in the Army for twenty years or more with dozens of combat deployments, can help the officer. While one of the best and brightest the Army officer corps has to offer, he is normally a Captain with only five to ten years in the Army, several of which have been spent in training.

On the closest of teams, and those who have shared the most intimate secrets and earned the respect of their peers in trials by fire and combat, they may throw the written rule book out of the window and the officer, as is his right, may ask the team to call him by his first name as the NCO's do to each other.

And on the teams which house an immense amount of both combat experience and NCO knowledge, the officer may defer to the team as Subject Matter Experts [SME's] in their respective fields and ask that their word be the final.

And sometimes, on the very closest teams, those which don't fear reprisal because they know that each would walk through a mile of fire to take a bullet for the other without question, the officer holds himself as a member of the team.

He demands the same level of respect as they hold for each other, and, on occasion, may be told that one of his ideas is the dumbest they've ever heard.

The written rule book would not look very highly upon this, but in the unwritten rule book it is par for the course on only the closest of teams.

I had taken those wise lessons in leadership, the understanding that true leaders don't lead from behind an inferiority complex or from high in an ivory tower, and had worked hard so that every civilian team I led emulated those lessons I learned from the greatest leaders I had known.

If I would have honored them by taking a bullet in combat for them, it was my way of honoring them beyond combat by providing the finest honor a great leader can ever hope for: in his men applying his lessons throughout the rest of their lives.

So I should have seen it coming and shouldn't have been surprised in the least bit when Cecile, a five-foot nothing Filipina with a fiery temper and mean right hook slapped me so hard that Dave laughed and then gasped, holding his hands up to his mouth so he didn't laugh out loud again.

I saw an orderly, ten meters ahead of us in the hallway, turn around and begin to laugh, point and exclaim "OH DAMN!"

Seeing who was on both the giving and receiving ends of the award-worthy slap, however, promptly changed his mind and led him along his way.

"Wow," was the only response I could muster.

"Wow is right," chimed in Dave.

The fiery ice stare was hurdled in Dave's direction and, wiping the grin from his face which it was apparent his mother had done, like a good mom, he held his hands up and shut his yapper.

After a few choice words in Tagalog that I recognized from late nights in the operating room but had never needed a translation for, Cecile steadied herself, pulled her scrubs taught and began her line of questioning.

"First, who the hell do you think you are walking down the hall, pretending you don't know me and acting like you didn't hear me. Second, where the hell have you been? We all thought you were dead! What's wrong with you, not telling us you were ok and letting us think you had been killed or ended up in one of the prison camps?"

Her second point seemed to stir something loose in her mind, something even stronger than the slap which still had my head reeling and certainly left a mark that wouldn't be gone anytime soon.

Tears welling up in her eyes, she jumped and put her hands around my neck to embrace me in a hug so strong that it reminded me of my children.

After a moment of the embrace I put my hands up and tried to step back but, with Cecile unmoving and my having a daughter, I knew she wasn't ready to end it quite yet.

Just when I thought the weight of her hanging from my neck would pop my head clean off she released, pulled her scrubs taught again and looked me dead in the eyes.

"I need to speak with you."

"Well my friend Dave and I were just going to stop by my office. Why don't you join us so we can speak in private."

"Is that how you introduce people, Doctor Lewis?" she asked politely.

Remembering that Cecile was a mother of four whose practice lecturing children routinely carried over to everyone else in her life, I opted to indulge her rather than suffer another blow to the face.

"I'm sorry, where are my manners. David Lyon, meet Cecile Pimentel.

Turning to face Dave and offer her hand, I watched as in an instant the fire-eyed and steel-spined woman who I thought could make the devil run with his tail between his legs if he caught her on a bad day, transform into the dough-eyed teenage girl with big blinking eyes and love in her heart as, I imagined, all women did when they laid their eyes on Dreamcakes.

It took her several long moments to recover, and watching her cover the handshake with both hands I could only wonder where this would have led under different circumstances.

I loudly cleared my throat, the ticking clock still running in my head.

"Right," she said when it seemed the blood had made it back to her head from the other parts of her body, to which it had be rerouted in a sudden action of the most primal human physiology, that which had been designed to ensure that our species would continue.

Turning again to face me, but with a few glances back at Dave, she composed herself and raised an alarm in the pit of my soul.

"We can't talk here. Get what you need from your office and meet me down in the sterilization room in five minutes."

Preparing to deliver my argument, as it took a minimum of five minutes to ride down the elevators and to the sterilization room located in the deepest depths of the hospital, she stopped me before I could begin.

"I won't take no for an answer," she told me, stole another glance and a wink to Dave and began walking down the hall to the elevators.

I looked at Dave, still shell-shocked and seeming like he was trying to decipher what had just transpired, and motioned for him to follow me.

Pleasantly surprised that my office had not been commandeered as my parking spot had been, I was even more delighted to find my SIG Sauer P238 pistol still taped in the same place I had left it, along with three loaded magazines.

We hadn't had time to borrow any backpacks from the locker room just yet, but pistol or not I didn't want to face Cecil's wrath for being late (something she hated even more than absent-minded surgeons) and walked out of my office as I tucked it into my waistband.

Stepping off the elevator with Dave in the hospital basement made me immediately remember why I used any excuse available to keep from going down there.

It was so hot and muggy from the massive steam cleaners and autoclave ovens that could fit several carts at a time, six foot tall and two feet across to cook them at just under 300 degrees, that I started sweating before we were five steps out of the elevator.

The heat and humidity reminded me of my childhood in Houston, a place we would jokingly refer to as "the devil's armpit" from its mercilessly humid summers.

And the noise...that was what really got me.

There was a constant clanging of metal as the unseen workers pulled used surgical equipment from trays to clean off the heaps of flesh and prepare the tools for sterilization.

The constant hum of the ovens and washing from commercial-grade jets began to gnaw at the back of my brain, remembering just how similar the sounds down there were to the hum of large military bases in combat zones.

Cecile saw us and waved to catch our attention.

Well, Dreamcake's attention; I didn't think she cared if I were there or not.

She led us to an area next to one of the autoclaves where the noise was so loud that it could have been a kitchen at peak traffic during the lunch rush.

Glancing around the sides of both Dave and I to ensure we were alone, she motioned for us to come down to her level.

"I know where you've been and what you've been doing," she whispered just loud enough for us to hear.

As I began to stand and think of some denial or protest, she grabbed the collar of my shirt and pulled me back down.

"Nuh-uh," she said.

"Don't start with me. Don't forget that you told us what to look for to know this was coming. And even though you didn't talk about it much, everyone on our surgical team knew what you did before medical school."

Taking a second to contemplate her statement, I saw her eyes begin to tear up.

"I just wish we had been smart enough to actually listen to you," she added.

"You didn't bring us down here to tell me I was right, Cecile...what is this?" I asked.

"I need you to do something for me, and I swear to everything holy, *ayudame Dios* I will hunt you in the afterlife if you say no, *comprende*?"

From a mixture of both healthy fear and absolute respect, Dave and I each nodded that we understood and were willing to listen to her request.

"My sister and her two children are hiding just a few blocks away from here in the basement of an apartment building that a friend owns."

I tried to stand again but she yanked me back down by my collar, refused to let go and pointed her finger in my face, springing to life the memories of the most stern conversations with my own mom when I was young and in trouble.

"Say whatever you want to whoever you want, but don't lie to me. I was in the operating room with you the day this started. I saw you back away from the table when the music stopped and leave, not even pausing to say goodbye. We all saw the news and had to operate on the Russian soldiers flown here from Colorado, where we know you own property."

She took a second, not to compose herself but to bring the ice daggers back out to tell that she wouldn't be taking no for an answer.

"You may not like this, and I surely don't like this, but if she doesn't get out of here I don't want to think about what will happen. She's a seer, and her kids have the gift as well. Somehow the Chinese know about everyone that has those abilities and have been using lists to round them all up."

"Seer?" I asked.

"It means she's sensitive," answered Dave.

"Like she cries a lot?" I asked.

"No stupid," Cecile shouted under her breath and smacked me on top of the head.

"It means they see things before they happen. Sometimes little things, sometimes things that don't happen, but sometimes..."

She paused for a moment, unsure of how much to divulge.

"Besides you, she's the only person who knew this was about to happen and started moving. She came here to get me out before it got too bad, but she got trapped when the troops shut down the highways leading out of Santa Monica and locked everything down."

I looked at the sudden change in her face, the replacement of fire and ice now turned to melancholy.

"But what about you Cecile?" I asked.

"I'm fine for now. They need us, so nobody from the hospital is in danger. Southern California is the only territory they seem to have won outright, and because of the stronghold and top-class hospitals in L.A. they fly all of their most critically wounded soldiers here."

She hesitated and smiled a devilish smile to Dave and I.

"And you guys have been sending us a lot of patients, which tells me that you know what you're doing."

Dave and I met each other's gaze to make a decision that didn't need words. Shrugging and winking at me, he gave me his choice.

"Ok," I began.

"But if we're going to do this...how in the world are we going to do it? How do we get them out? And where do you want us to take them?"

"Anywhere but here," she responded, already beginning to smile knowing that we would help her.

"I'll take you to the apartment building, introduce you to our friend and then it's all on you. I don't want to know where she's going just in case I'm questioned, but I know they'll be safe with you."

I took a moment to plan it out, and decided I may as well say it out loud given that the noise would block any recording devices the enemy had planted in the walls. And I needed Dave's mind working on the logistics as well.

"We have special papers that should be able to get us through checkpoints, but I'm a little worried that five people in a car will raise a lot more suspicion than the two of us."

"Her kids are young so they can lie on the floor while you drive."

"Ok, but I don't think you understand. Where we came from, where we're going back to from here, it isn't safe."

"Anywhere but here," she reiterated.

"They know she and her kids are in this area and they're searching high and low. Just take her away from here, to anywhere she's not on their radar."

"We still need to find some supplies, that was our whole point for being here," I reminded both Dave and Cecile.

"What exactly do you need?" she asked.

I rattled off a list of the medicine, supplies and trauma kits that we had planned to take back with us.

"That's going to be easier for me to get than it will be for you. I don't know if they're looking for you or suspect you of anything, but they've been asking a lot of questions about you. I chalked it up to your military background but now...why don't you guys stay down here while I gather the supplies. The pharmacist likes me better than you anyway, she always thought you were too full of yourself."

Beginning to feel offended, I realized there wasn't any point to getting upset about a the opinion of a person who I would never see again.

After I jotted down the specific items that we needed on a pad of paper, Cecile took them and headed towards the elevator.

We agreed that the longest we could wait was an hour, at which point we would have to assume the worst and that she had been compromised, meaning we would have to get out of there in a hurry.

I had put my white lab coat on before we left my office, thinking that it would allow me to blend in better than the poorly-fitting clothes did.

But, remembering that Cecile said the enemy soldiers had been inquiring about me and knowing that any pictures of me in the hospital would have me in the exact uniform I was now wearing, I decided it was best to change it up.

Thankfully the sterilization room had its own bathrooms and locker room downstairs, so we wished Cecile luck while I took Dave to find us each a pair of scrubs.

Dave wasn't an easy guy to shop for, and I could only imagine how difficult it had been on his mother, watching him quickly outgrow every new pair of clothes and shoes she bought for likely the entirety of his teenage years.

It took a lot of work and a little mixing & matching but we emerged from the locker room wearing scrubs, with a purchased backpack each to carry the clothes we had come in wearing.

We walked back to the area in which we had been speaking with Cecile, prepared to wait an hour with eyes glued to our watches and waiting on the worst.

But just a few moments after we found a comfortable place to sit and wait the elevator bell rung, alerting us that it was about to open on our floor.

Knowing that it hadn't been nearly long enough for Cecile to be back, I told Dave to help me load a cart of used instrument trays into the autoclave to appear busy.

I fought every urge screaming at me to watch the elevator to see who walked off, perhaps giving me the extra second of notification that could mean life or death.

But on the other hand, a shootout in the most heavily-guarded facility I had seen outside of the enemy bases we hit in Colorado wouldn't end well regardless.

Sure I may get the jump on one or two bad guys, but hundreds more would be on us in no time to guarantee that we didn't make it very far.

As I resisted the proto-warrior inside of me pulling like a dog on a chain the rational part of my brain, the one that had learned so much wisdom in the halls of this very institution, told it to take a back seat.

That was, of course, until the Chinese soldiers were upon us.

There were two of them, and if they hadn't gone down there searching for us specifically, they sure did take an interest in us immediately.

I whispered to Dave to continue loading trays on the cart just like I was doing, taking time to ensure every single instrument was nicely aligned, lest we finish with them and have to wander around looking for something else to do.

I had one eye on Dave & the instruments and with the other I saw the soldiers make a beeline directly to us from their elevator exit.

My mind was rationalizing it with every step they took, telling me not to overreact, it was perfectly normal. After all, we were the only people visible down there in direct line of sight to the elevator.

Of course they would mess with us if they had it in their mind to mess with someone.

Doing everything that I could to pretend I didn't notice, I focused on my peripheral vision and watched them walk, never pausing to stop at the mountains of used equipment or search for others in the basement.

When the sound of their boots come to a stop just a foot away from the cart we were stacking, I looked up briefly and gave them a nod, acting like we were just too busy to take a minute to chit chat.

The pair continued to watch, and my brain screamed with all its might and rage that the jig was up, that they could tell we didn't belong there and had already sent the signal for reinforcements to come.

The darkest parts of my brain began to wonder what it would be like to wake up strapped to an interrogation table again, only this time the victim of a Chinese captor rather than the Russians.

They wouldn't even waste the short time he had on the small talk and tormenting me. They would just start cutting.

Using every bit of restraint and concentration that I could muster, I worked painstakingly to ensure that it appeared like we were just a couple of regular sterilization techs giving painstaking attention to detail for trays of instruments.

I imagined how it would start.

Would one of them try to be sly and circle around out of my field of view, hitting me on the back of the head with the butt of his rifle?

Or would they just come at us from our side, where they were already situated, rifles in hand and ready to either turn us in or shoot us on sight?

As I tortured myself with the gory details, angles of their potential attack and best ways to respond, the first spoke up.

"Hey, you like America movie?' he asked, not indicating either of us in particular.

"Excuse me?" Dave asked.

"You know. America movie. John Wayne. Marilyn Monroe. A Gone with Wind. Casablanca."

I smiled.

"Sure. We love American movies."

"Wha abou moosic," the other added in broken english, which I could tell from the start of it was about to get much worse.

"Rolling Stone. Snoop Diggity Dog. The Beebs. I love hip hop. I love punk rock yah yah yah."

I couldn't hold back the smile any longer.

They didn't want to kill us. They wanted to practice their english.

The first one continued his original line of questions from before his friend had so rudely interrupted him.

"What kind movie you guy like?"

I shot a glance to Dave, who seemed to agree that talking about American pop culture was much better than a firefight.

He decided to join in the conversation and have a little fun.

"Did you say that you like The Beebs? Who is that?"

"Jushen Beeper. You know, he sing, he dance, he good looking he get all the girl."

Dave, a serious fan of classic rock and hater of all things pop couldn't resist his urge to set the soldiers straight.

"No. He not get all the girl. He need music lesson."

Our pair of english conversationalists fell silent.

I knew a little about Chinese culture, but wasn't sure if Dave had just crossed a line that would get us killed or at the very least buy us a room with no windows and a man with a pair of pliers who would yank all of our fingernails out.

Instead, the pair erupted with laughter.

"Ok smart man, who you like. Who good America music?"

As Dave paused from pretending to organize dirty surgical instruments and looked around, searching for the best America music to share with our new friends, we heard the elevator ding letting us know we had more visitors to the party.

I was at first relieved to see Cecile step off rather than a dozen shock troops coming to hogtie us and put black bags over her heads, but seeing her reaction I realized that might have been a better choice.

We couldn't blame her.

She didn't know what was going on and she was scared.

All that she knew was when the elevator doors opened, instead of seeing us twiddling our thumbs and waiting for her to return we were talking to armed Chinese troops.

In less than a second they saw her terrified face, glanced back to our calm and collected ones and knew something wasn't right.

And it was hiding right in front of their faces.

"Hey, where you ID badge?" one asked, pointing at my chest where there should have been an ID with my smiling face affixed to my breast pocket.

"You too," he pointed at Dave.

While the wheels were still turning inside the first soldier's head to make the connections and fully understand the situation, the second had already begun to react.

As the soldier moved to pull the rifle from its sling on his shoulder, in one deft move Dave was on top of him, grossly outweighing him by more than two-to-one, throwing him on his back and laying on the rifle he had been reaching for.

Dave pinned the soldier's arms with his massive legs and began to pummel him viciously while I made my move.

Thank God my guy's an idiot.

The full situation still hadn't formed its understanding in the soldier's brain as I threw one forearm into his windpipe and kicked his legs out from under him.

Following him to the floor I had him unconscious before the back of his head hit the ground a second time, standing up with his rifle while Dave stood over his victim victoriously.

Cecile was still frozen in fear with the bags she had brought for us scattered at her feet by the time we reached her and the elevator.

"Let's go Cecile, time to move," I told her.

Still paralyzed with fear, Dave put his hand gently on her chin and lifted her head up to look at him.

"Are you ok," he asked her.

Good Lord, he really is a Dreamcake.

That seemed to have been just the antidote Cecile needed, as I watched the fear leave her face and be replaced with a gentle smile.

"I am now," she replied with teenage lovestruck eyes peering up at him again.

"Jiminy Christmas, let's go lovebirds," I ordered from the elevator door.

The worry train hit Cecile the moment the doors closed and we started our upward climb back to the world.

"Oh my God, we need to hide the bodies," she said, looking up at Dave (I don't think I even existed to her anymore).

"Do we need to hide the bodies?"

"Won't do any good," I answered.

"Those guys are patrolling a portion of the hospital, and when they don't check in a few minutes from now when they should have been finished clearing the basement, someone will send a team to check on them and the sirens will start wailing."

As if on cue, the loud wailing of an alarm system began to sound.

"Or now," I added.

"What do we do?" she asked.

"We've got what we came for, now we need to get out of here. All of us."

Cecile began to protest, but Dave cut her off.

"There are cameras all over this hospital. Even if they don't have a clear view of you walking and talking with us, those two will be able to identify you. You're coming with us."

Not one to argue with Dreamcakes, Cecile fell silent.

"What's the fastest way to your sister?" I asked.

Seeming not to have realized she was still part of our plan, Cecile thought for a moment.

"There's an employee entrance on the other side of the hospital that won't be shut down with the lock down. It's the closest to the building where she is and if we hurry we can get to it before they put a guard there."

Pulling the pistol out of my waistband and putting it in my pocket for easier access, I saw Dave check the pistol he had lifted from the soldier.

He stuffed it in his pocket just as the elevator stopped at the ground floor, and we stepped out into a sea of confusion and people running in every direction.

Still wearing our scrubs we blended into the chaos effortlessly.

Cecile took us down a main corridor and then through a side door into another, smaller corridor that I knew from my time at the hospital was part of the outer perimeter of hallways.

We were moving along the outer wall of the building, meaning the door had to be close.

As we turned a final corner and saw the door Cecile had told us about, we watched in disbelief as a pair of armed troops ran from another direction and posted in front of the door.

"Keep moving. Same plan," I said under my breath as we continued quickly walking down the hall.

The soldier must have thought that we would turn at the last minute and move in the direction from which he had come, because we were almost on him before he impatiently shouted his warning.

"No exit. Door close," he stammered.

I held up my left hand and pretended to dig deep into my right pocket with the other.

"No, no, I have ID, we need this door."

But my right hand wasn't digging for an ID.

It hadn't left the grip and trigger of my pistol since we got on the elevator.

Shooting from the waist I had the perfect angle to put two rounds under his chin, causing the bullets to explode through the top of his skull, bounce around in his helmet and enter back in for extra damage.

I used the left hand which was already raised to push his dead but still standing body back into the other guard, and as he braced himself for the impact I placed another two rounds directly into his face, one between his eyes and the other in the middle of his forehead before he was thrown back from the velocity and crumpled into the ground like his friend.

Not wasting a moment of hesitation, I continued my forward movement and went through the door, pushing the bumper handle along its center with my left hand as I ejected the magazine from my pistol with only two rounds left and popped a fresh one in while using my waist to finish opening the door.

I briefly glanced back as Cecile bent down to pick up one of the dead soldier's rifle.

"Don't do that," I told her, which was met with a confused expression.

"Right now they don't know who they're looking for. A rifle will make us a target to every soldier on the street. And there's a lot of them."

I saw recognition flash in Cecile's eyes as she dropped the weapon and followed Dave out of the door.

"We don't have much time. Take us on the fastest route to get where we're going."

True to her word, we only had to travel a few blocks to arrive at our destination.

The chaos inside the hospital hadn't spread to the surrounding area by the time we entered the lobby of a middle-tier apartment building and Cecile led us to an elevator.

I watched the streets outside of the floor-to-ceiling glass lobby windows while Dave and Cecile waited for the elevator, and moved to join them when the doors opened.

"Still nothing crazy outside," I said as we traveled upwards. "Not sure if that's good or bad."

The elevator stopped on the top floor and Cecile knocked on the penthouse apartment's door.

The man who answered was a fair-skinned Filipino man, and I couldn't shake the feeling that I saw more than just a little resemblance between the two.

As if to confirm my hunch, no words needed to be spoken and the man grabbed a set of keys from his wall and joined us in the hall, leading us back to the elevator.

As Dave, the man and I stepped in, Cecile stayed back and watched us re-enter the elevator and make a spot for her.

Dave motioned for her to join us, but Cecile shook her head.

"She'll never go if I'm downstairs and tell her I'm not going."

"You are going. You have to come with us Cecile," shouted Dave.

"No," she responded.

"There's no room and besides, my place is here."

She stared at me and showed a soft side that I had never seen in all the years we had known each other.

"Take care of them. All of them. And they will take care of you."

As the elevator doors closed, I knew that was the last I would ever see of Cecile.

We were less than a floor into our elevator's descent when I heard the loud sirens begin wailing from the streets outside of the apartment building.

"Do you have a car?" I asked the man.

Without words he produced a pair of BMW keys from his pocket and handed them to me over his shoulder.

"Natalie knows where to find it," he said in heavily accented english, still not turning to face us.

"Natalie?" I asked.

"We are going to get Natalie, her son Noah and her daughter Ava Luna so you can take them far away from here. I will lead you to them, they will lead you to the car, you will lead them somewhere safe."

"By chance do you have any weapons?" Dave asked.

"Of course," the old man replied.

"But this will do you much more good than weapons."

As he spoke the old man took a carefully folded piece of paper from his right pocket.

Unfolding it in my hands I could see that it was a set of new travel authorizations, these ones written in english, russian and chinese, compete with seal of approval and signature from a Chinese general.

My head was spinning with questions by the time the elevator stopped at the ground floor.

"Don't bother your head with useless questions, Robert," the old man spoke as he stepped out from the elevator and turned to face me.

"All will be answered in due time. Focus on getting away from here with your precious cargo, that is all that matters in the now."

Holding his left arm out and motioning for us to move in that direction, he used his keys to open a thick metal door at the end of the elevator lobby, leading to a vestibule which was lined with lockers on one side and another door opposite the one we walked through.

Quickly opening the lockers we saw the contents were full of rifles, pistols and ammunition.

"Take what you want," he said to Dave and I.

"But we must hurry."

Knowing we wouldn't be able to make it back to the car which had our weapons, I reached for a black AK-47 and pistol, along with several loaded magazines for each. By the time Dave pulled an AR-15 and Uzi the man had opened the other door and was walking through it.

On the other side, seemingly waiting for us, were a dark-haired woman and two children standing in a dimly-lit room with an assortment of furniture.

I couldn't see much of anything, and heard the old man speaking in hushed tones to the three. After sharing a quick but strong embrace with the group, the old man turned back to Dave and I.

Looking to Dave, the old man pulled Dave down to his height and touched their foreheads together, with each man closing his eyes. When both pairs of eyes opened, Dave stood and nodded to the old man, who slapped him on the shoulder.

"Good man," he said.

The old man turned to me next and and repeated his previous statement.

"Lead them somewhere safe."

With that the old man stepped toward and walked around me, exposing the dim light in the small room and I was frozen in place, rendered speechless.

Once he moved and I saw the full light of the room I was struck with a sense of bewilderment. Standing in the middle of the room, with a child on either side of her was the most beautiful woman I had ever seen.

I had called women strong before, but she was the true embodiment of a swirling symphony of gorgeous features, from her long, black hair which appeared to have been spun from the finest silk ever known to the faint hue of olive-colored skin and large almond-shaped eyes that seemed to see right through me and speak directly to my soul.

But there was something else, something both alluring and alarming that exuded a kind of strength I had only read about in novels about the ancient goddesses and priestesses of war, who would soothe the gentle souls of Vikings, Celts and Romans before they set off to wage war in her names.

A sort of untamed and unspoken power that had existed through the ages with a different name for the songs sung by each generation: Tiamat, Lilith, Maleficent, Hel, Cleopatra, Helen of Troy and on down to the very sirens whose temptations ran so deep they could drive men willingly to their deaths.

The hair stood on the back of my neck as shockwaves ran under my skin and through my spine, and I could not shake the premonition that this was not the first time I had met her.

Not only met her, but had been there...not at that very location but in the same place.

My world clouded as every emotion and faceless memories ran through my being: love, anger, lust, fear, hate, joy and sorrow.

I felt it was going to overtake me and leave me in a pile of broken bones when I heard both men walking out of the door behind us.

I turned just in time to see the giant silhouette of Dave walking away, following the old man.

Reality came screaming back like a crash of lightning as Dave disappeared through the doorway.

Stepping out I called to him.

"Dave, what are you doing? Get in here and help me with their stuff, we have to go!"

He paused for a moment and turned to speak.

"This is where our paths split, Brother."

"Dave what in the hell are you talking about?"

As he smiled the kind of smile that best friends give when they know they won't see each other for a long time, machine gun fire erupted outside and I felt the impact of a shoulder-fired rocket against the outer wall of the building.

Unfazed, Dave continued.

"He will lead you to them, they will lead you to the car, you will lead them somewhere safe," Dave repeated the old man's words.

Continuing to smile and adding his own part of the puzzle, Dave concluded.

"I will lead them away."

He turned and walked out of the doorway, and I tried to follow so I could slap some sense into him. But an unseen force anchored my feet to the floor and wouldn't allow me to take another step.

Suddenly I heard Meda's voice, the words she spoke in the kitchen the night before as clear as if it were being spoken in the room I was now standing in.

You must allow him to find his own destiny and whatever you do, do not get in his way.

I turned, half expecting to find Meda offering her guidance but was instead met with the gentle stares of Natalie and her children, looking at me as if they knew what I would do before I did and were simply waiting for me to take the first step.

"Are you ready?" she asked.

Still unsure of what planet much less dimension I was on, not believing this was real but sure it wasn't a dream, I felt my head nodding in accordance.

"Good," she said.

"Follow me."

When she stepped aside a third door which I hadn't previously noticed came into view, situated against the far wall of the room.

Holding her children's hands in hers they walked to the third door together, opened it and waited for me to join them.

As a glorious firefight ensued in the streets above us the three led my way through a dark tunnel, illuminated by nothing more than their Light.

And when we emerged on the other side, all that was left for us to do was go home.

CHAPTER 7

UNITED BY FIRE / BOMBS OVER LONG BEACH

"Sir, there's a group of men at the front gate insisting they see you," said the young Private through the radio.

"Excuse me?" Jim asked, picking his radio up from the desk to respond.

"Four civilian trucks just rolled up, and I'm not quite sure what's going on but they look tired, mean and insist they speak with you."

"Well who in the hell are they?" Jim asked, hastily becoming annoyed that the soldier should have known better than to bother him when they had teams out running missions on either side of the country.

"I'm not sure sir. They're all wearing civilian clothes but I know they're military. Or at least paramilitary. And I've only been speaking to the men in the first truck but I can hear several different languages and accents coming from the group."

Jim turned and asked his aide to put the video from the parking lot cameras up on the main screen. Once it was displayed he walked to the front of the room to have a better look, staring intently at one of the faces in the lead vehicle.

Although Jim couldn't be certain and wasn't able to place a name, there was a strong pull from deep inside his mind that told him he recognized the man now sitting angrily in the passenger seat and burning a hole with his eyes through the guards barring his entry.

With nothing more than a quick glance from Jim his aide, still seated at his desk, picked up the phone and called down to one of the highly-secured rooms buried deep in the ground below them.

A few minutes later two men stood inside the door leading to the TOC [Tactical Operations Center], each with shoulder-length curly black hair, tan baseball caps and the stubble from their face rapidly becoming beards after only a few days not shaving.

Jim walked to join them.

He spoke to the men as they followed him closely down the hallway, bringing their Scorpion submachine guns to the low ready as one stepped in front of him to exit the building first.

"Let me know if one of you recognize these guys," Jim told them as he walked through the door.

Seeing the man's face sitting in the light of day rather than through a closed-circuit camera shot a sudden recognition through Jim's mind, finally remembering where he knew the face from.

"Sir," the man said to Jim from under a pair of dark sunglasses as he strode around the front of their truck to say hello.

"What brings you to this side of the pond, Harry?" Jim asked the man as he began to smile.

"I heard you Yanks got yourselves into a little predicament," Harry started in a thick cockney accent.

"My mates and I figured we'd come help you find your way out of this bind. Ya' know, given that you helped us out of our tight spot last time we found trouble on our doorstep."

Bulldog was exhausted. It had been many years since he was stationed at Fort Bragg during the Q-course, and the moment he left he was glad to kiss it goodbye.

Nicknamed "The Flagpole" by Special Forces soldiers, the US Army Special Operations Command [USASOC] was littered with officers who had been far removed from the teams and front lines for decades, having long traded in their tradecraft and fighting skills for bureaucracy, politics and PowerPoint skills.

The men under them were out taking the fight to the enemy and doing great things to defend their country, but back at the flagpole Bulldog was required to give full operations orders and brief their plans to several groups before being told whether they had the permission to run their missions, or if he needed to go back to the office to rewrite his presentation.

Not to restructure their actual operation, mind you. But to tighten up the presentation.

In the rear, with the gear. Where these guys seem to prefer it.

The disdain of that thought had been playing on a constant loop in Bulldog's head since they first arrived.

He longed for the freedom of Colorado or the hands-off approach from Jim where they could simply acquire targets and do what he knew they should be doing: finding, fixing and destroying the enemy.

But he was given strict orders from Jim and The General. If this war were to truly progress and they wanted to take the upper hand and put the enemy on their heels, they needed a cohesive battle plan.

A national battle plan.

The team which had gone to the west coast was tasked with a relatively simple set of orders from Jim: refit the teams out there, figure out what they were doing, let them know that reinforcements would arrive soon, get an accurate picture of the enemy and exfil back to Austin to brief Jim on what they had learned.

Bulldog's orders would have sounded much simpler to the layman, but an experienced officer like him knew the multiple layers of commander's intent hidden beneath the black and white.

"Liaison with the leadership, report the enemy SITREP back to me and lay the groundwork for future operations between all forces," Jim had ordered on the runway as the rest of the team moved to the planes for their flight.

He instantly knew what it meant, and had been jealous of The Major from that point forward.

The west coast teams would be running missions and doing what they needed to disrupt the enemy men, weapons and equipment as they had not only been trained for but were excited to do.

Bulldog, however, was chained to a desk.

Upon arrival at Fort Bragg they had linked up with another group of former Green Berets who moved to New Hampshire after their time in uniform ended to start a weapons manufacturing company.

Being from the "Live Free or Die" state the men had no trouble assembling a team of freedom fighters, men who fancied themselves the rebirth of the Minutemen who had helped to save this great nation from enemy on her shores hundreds of years before.

And being weapons manufacturers, in a state which still believed in individual freedoms, meant they were well armed.

The name of their company, Daemon Defense, had either been a catchy idea or an omen from God, because it was an extremely well-fitting name given the havoc they had begun to reign on the invaders.

They caused so much havoc in the enemy ranks on their journey from New Hampshire to Fort Bragg that orders were sent from Russian generals and Hezbollah commanders alike to execute anyone found with their OPR-16 rifle.

The Daemons had been using them to tear holes through their troops from distances so far that the Daemons were packed up and on the move before their targets even dropped.

Daemon had even designed an ultra-compact 300 blackout pistol that was so concealable it allowed their team to walk unnoticed through the streets with one tucked under a jacket.

Yet these weapons were so accurate and powerful that one round sent its targets flying. The casualties were knocked so violently back from a range of fifty meters that the enemy thought they were being engaged by snipers, and took cover rather than looking for the shooter.

Who was in fact right in front of them.

When Martyn, the wizard behind these death-dealing weapons introduced himself, JLo immediately recognized him from his legends and asked Bulldog if he could tag along with the Daemons while Bulldog was tending to his officer duties.

Once JLo was cleared to go, Tony wanted to join. And once Tony was cleared to go, Griz wanted a piece.

Before anyone else had to ask, Bulldog asked the entire detachment if they'd like to join Martyn and the Daemons on their mission crushing the souls of enemy on the east coast.

They were in to a man, leaving him alone at The Flagpole briefing other officers and doing the one thing he thought this war would have allowed him the opportunity to forget.

Every time the men would come back to Fort Bragg to refit and head out for another mission taking down roadblocks or snatching unwitting soldiers off the street for interrogation, someone would come by to check on Bulldog and tell the stories of what they'd done, make fun of someone for dropping the ball or saying something stupid, and of course to ask him if he wanted to lead them on the next op.

But he had his orders, and had to decline every time.

Each request landed a blow directly to his heart.

There were many soldiers who would have relished his position, the opportunity not only to lay down in a soft bed every night but also to eat hot meals three (or five every once in awhile) times a day, and most importantly not have to worry about whether he would make it home to his wife and daughters.

But that wasn't Bulldog.

He wasn't the officer bent on political aims or counting the days until he pinned stars on his shoulder. He hadn't hurried through his team time to start working up promotion points in administrative positions like many had done before him.

He relished every moment of his time with the men, believing full heartedly in the "leaders eat last" mentality and savoring every operation he had led men into throughout his career. Loving the sweat, cherishing the camaraderie and imparting any wisdom that would help them be stronger soldiers, better men and wiser human beings.

Taking a man like Bulldog away from the front and missions with his team was like taking sun & water away from a flower, or the warm embrace of a child away from a new puppy.

Not that he was all sunshine and rainbows.

In the two years that he spent active with 022 he earned their respect in more ways than any could keep count of. To begin with, he had previously led one team and been working an administrative job when 022 needed a leader.

He was already promoted beyond the knuckle draggers on the front lines, chosen for his wit and cool head under pressure to take on a new position implementing strategy rather than tactics.

There he could begin amassing promotion points to his next career objective, while his peers who started with him clawed feverishly and unsuccessfully at the same promotion ladder which he had so easily climbed, due to the very essence of leadership which he exhibited naturally and to his core.

And the instant that word was given that there was an ODA who needed a leader, he asked to be demoted to go back with the men.

He thought it had been a well-guarded secret, but the men knew what he had rescinded to take the reins of 022 and lead them back into battle.

And the amount of respect which that action immediately gained in their minds for him was something which may never be expressed in words, not even the most ancient of them from blood-stained warrior proto-cultures whose language consisted entirely of synonyms for human emotions like respect, war, carnage, love and honor.

Their reverence for him was not told through words, because it never could be; the ears of man cannot withstand the absolute gravity of something so significant.

But it was shown through their infinite love for him, and the respect he had gained from men who did not give it to most, and guarded the right to even earn theirs as it were the Holy Grail, Fountain of Youth, Secret of Life or the very name of God himself.

But part of their respect for him came from an almost programming code that Bulldog had which required him to do what was right, not what he wanted to do (but for what could possibly have been considered as one of the "last good guys left," there often wasn't much discrepancy between the two).

It was almost as it were his Prime Directive to choose the hard right over the easy wrong.

And while the men didn't know how much inner turmoil it caused him every time they asked, they knew that they must.

Even though they knew he would say no, even if it took the only precious minutes they had between dropping prisoners off at the base and heading back out for more operations, even if they hadn't slept or eaten in days, asking Bulldog was their first priority of work anytime they had even a few precious moments at Ft. Bragg.

Because regardless of rank, location or mission, he was their leader.

And they would walk the ends of the earth to hear his commands, and charge headfirst into certain death at the hands of Satan's legions if he so ordered.

There were no limits to their loyalty.

Yet even though he hated it and longed for his place leading the men into battle, he was accomplishing his mission from Jim.

Unlike the west coast, the east had been full of mountain men, Special Operations units and militia who, while not planning for this specific event, had been prepared for anything.

And they were not taking this war sitting down.

Forts Benning and Bragg were the homes of the Infantry and Special Forces, respectively, and had successfully repelled the enemy at every turn.

Much like Texas they each had airplanes, anti-aircraft weapons, intelligence operations and a plethora of ground troops, meaning that they could wage war on any front from which the invaders came.

As such, they had put out word through their clandestine agents, radio stations, HAM radios and every other method available that any freedom fighters, partisans and would-be guerrillas were welcome to come in and become a part of the plan to take back the country.

Or at the very least to let the military leadership know where they were operating to deconflict areas of operation and not waste additional units in regions where the enemy was already getting their butts handed to them by Americans with guns.

And there were legions of them.

Mountain men from the forests and mountains of North Carolina, men who had been unknowingly training and preparing for this very day.

While the rest of the nation had grown fat and lazy, eating fast food and ready-to-eat meals on the way home from their desk jobs, these men had maintained the ancient ways. It was their life, and now their prey was not only dinner, but also enemy.

The Apex Predators were back on the hunt. And having a hell of a fun time doing it.

Bulldog had not only become ever more familiar with the local warlords as they came in, but was likewise beginning to gain a very clear understanding of what the brass at Fort Bragg had in mind and how they would shift their forces when new information was received.

He was starting to notice a pattern; he didn't quite have it yet, but he recognized it was there.

I was greeted with a mixed reception upon arrival at the golf course.

The men were happy that I brought back the medicine and trauma kits, Meda was not pleased that I'd lost both her car and her authorization to travel and The Major scowled at me like I had killed Dave myself when I delivered the news.

After losing his brother and team in the invasion he didn't have any tears left for Dave, but the fire and disdain I saw in his eyes while delivering my report were enough to know that some sort of emotion was flowing under it all.

He wasn't dead inside. Sure, maybe everything under his skin was made of an inextinguishable flame, but at least it wasn't dead.

After a few moments of The Major staring at me with hate-filled fury, Josh decided to speak up and deliver the events that I had missed.

"Jim called and ordered us back to Austin," he said.

"What? I thought we were going to be here at least a month?" I asked, surprised.

"He didn't go into much detail, but said something about new friends that we need to bring out here. He wants us to give these guys all our gear and guns, exfil back to Austin tonight and return in a few days with these new friends and an airdrop of weapons and supplies."

"What good is an airdrop of weapons and supplies going to do if there's only five dudes on the team out here?" I asked.

"Dudes aren't the only ones who can fight you sexist bastard," smirked Meda.

I saw an enormous grin emerge on Josh's lips and shot him a confused glance.

"Meda here offered their tribe to get trained up and go on the offensive with us. The whole thing."

Looking to Meda for confirmation, I could see her shaking her head in accordance.

"How many?" I asked.

"At least a hundred fighters, probably two hundred more that we can use for support or logistics," she said with a smile.

"Good Lord," I exclaimed.

"We've got an Army now."

I glanced around the room as the men nodded their heads in agreement. This was excellent news, and meant that we could really begin to make a dent in the enemy stronghold.

The Office of Strategic Services, or OSS, had been the predecessors of both Special Forces and the CIA, and to many who knew their history had been the primary reason the allies won so many victories in World War II.

They operated in tiny three to four-person teams (we can't say "man" because there were women on the teams...even the famous chef Julia Child) of enlisted and officers who were typically Ivy League or highly educated. Many had been American citizens born in a foreign, then occupied nation so that their first language had been French, Dutch, German, Italian or an east European one.

These small teams, called Jedburgh teams, would jump into their missions via a night time airborne drop with as many weapons as they could carry.

They carried with them only a radio, weapons and money, and their missions were either to link up with local partisans to train and fight or cache the cash and weapons around Europe for future operations.

And European nations are still digging up old caches of money and weapons to this day.

These small teams of commandos would then spend what time they had been allotted training the partisans in the arts of unconventional warfare: guerrilla fighting tactics when using a smaller force to fight a proper military, how to make and use homemade explosives, how to communicate with them once they left, how to collect human intelligence and many other invaluable fighting skills.

Those Jedburgh teams had trained tens of thousands of partisans across Europe by the time the war ended, and they had been only detachments of three or four. We had fourteen men plus whatever friends Jim was telling us would be coming back with us.

As I began recounting the days when 022 had trained entire battalions of local troops to fight with us in Iraq, Afghanistan and Africa, Josh continued.

"Our exfil bird is due here at 2200 hours tonight, meaning we need to get a move on."

"Where and how are they picking us up?" I asked.

"The enemy has a strong presence on the coast and along the Texas/Mexico border," Josh responded.

"But there's a large swath of land which they still haven't occupied. Jim sent us an encrypted message with grid coordinates about an hour and a half drive inland, near the Salton Sea. It's a whole lot of nothing but hills and desert out there, and according to his intelligence the enemy hasn't found it very important to put troops in that location."

"So they're going to land a plane in the middle of hills and desert to pick us up? What is it, a single prop or something?" I asked.

"You know Rob, I know you have to be smart to be a doctor, but sometimes you really are an idiot."

Josh grinned at me and shook his head while he continued.

"They're sending a Chinook with a few attack helicopters for cover. There will be two pallets for these guys inside. The crew will drop ramp and hover, kick the pallets off and we run up the ramp. They don't want to be there for more than two minutes, so we have to be quick."

I raised my eyebrows in doubt.

"We can do it," The Major replied dryly.

"Isn't that going to create a sandstorm around the bird?" I asked.

The Major repeated himself, sounding a little more perturbed to be doing so.

"We can do it."

Looking down at my watch and starting to do the reverse planning in my head, I realized that meant we didn't have much time to get on the road.

"We want to arrive at least two hours before the birds so we can do a little recon and make sure there isn't a surprise waiting. The last thing we want is to be running up the ramp and have an enemy sniper or machine gun tear us all apart," added Josh.

"That means we're leaving in..." but The Major cut me off before I could finish.

"Thirty minutes. We downloaded and divvied up our gear in the break room for these guys. We'll hold on to our weapons and ammo until the bird touches down and be back with more in a few days."

The Major looked over my shoulder to Natalie and her kids and shook his head slightly.

"Rob, you gotta stop picking up strays every time we go out. Get with Meda and find a place for them before we leave."

"No," replied Meda from behind him.

"She can't stay here. She stays with Rob."

The Major, obviously fresh out of patience for the woman who kept defying his commands and orders, turned and took a deep breath, seemingly preparing himself to dig his heels in and project his authority.

But upon making a complete turn and coming face-to-face with Meda, his demeanor changed when their eyes met.

The two stared at each other for a moment and The Major's face softened, muscles loosened and jaw became unclenched. He lifted his gaze from her to look at me, then back at Natalie and returned his attention to Meda.

"I'm not sure how many men are coming on the bird already for our security. But if we have seats, I guess they can stick with you."

"If they don't have seats, you'll have an extra because I'm staying with them," I stated.

With his eyes still locked on Meda's, she reached over and put a hand on his shoulder.

"That won't be an issue," she added.

Still seeming more relaxed than I had ever seen him, The Major capitulated.

"Ok Rob. Whatever. Just make sure your gear is ready and find a seat for them in the convoy. We roll out in thirty."

I looked around at the faces in the room, with everyone but the few of us off in their own separate directions working on tasks.

The medics were walking the team who was staying through the drugs I had brought back, the Charlies were building more explosives and Bravos were oiling up guns and loading magazines with the little time we had left.

Ray and I had been out with Josh meeting Meda when the men had to leave the old camp in a hurry, so someone had moved all of our rucksacks which were now lined against the rear wall of the garage.

I picked mine up and began to walk back to the break room, making a mental inventory of what I could give Tyler and his team before I left, and what I needed to bring back to Austin with me.

Thirty minutes later we were all loaded in the trucks along with Meda, her brother and helpers.

If they wanted us to train their people in the new ways of war we decided it was a good time to get started, especially since this sounded like a simple movement.

I didn't want to go back in the truck with The Major, given that two of the former occupants of our normal travel team were no longer with us.

Two men in less than a week. Two men who meant a lot to me.

I couldn't afford to dwell on it, but at some point, whether I wanted to or not I would have to deal with that reality.

Josh assigned me to a suburban that Meda's team brought, giving plenty of space for Natalie and her kids to sit in the rear row with myself and Ray taking the middle, Meda riding shotgun and her driver behind the wheel.

Meda had been eyeing Natalie since we arrived, but I couldn't put my finger on what was going through either of their minds.

They didn't want it to be obvious, but each would steal looks at the other whenever they didn't think they were being watched...but we saw every stolen glance.

"So Rob, you gonna introduce me to your new girlfriend or what buddy?" Ray asked when we took our seats in the Suburban.

"Shut up Ray," I muttered through clenched teeth.

"Rob and, hey what's your name?" he asked her.

"I'm Natalie," was her response.

"Rob and Na-ta-lie sit-ting in a tree...."

Before he could progress much further I landed a well-aimed right cross directly into his sternum which seemed to effectively put a pause on his antics for a little while.

I was anxious like a teenager on my first date with butterflies buzzing around my stomach, sweaty palms and a million terrible lines going through my head. But I couldn't understand why; I had plenty of other things to think about, with no time left for infatuation.

Come here often? No, she won't get the joke.

Is that a mirror in your pocket? No, too crass.

Did it hurt when you fell? Come on, stupid, say something or it's going to get really uncomfortable.

Amidst the ongoing dialogue in my head I stole a glance to the back seat.

Natalie's young daughter was resting with her head on her mom's lap, and as I watched her gently stroke the girl's hair she looked up and met my gaze.

Not knowing what to do and feeling like a kid who had just been caught with a hand in the cookie jar, I dropped my gaze to my hands for a moment.

When I looked back up she was looking down at her daughter's head just as before, and I wondered if I had imagined her catching me staring.

Looking next to her I saw her son sleeping with his head on the window and decided to stop being nosey.

Turning back to face the front and keep an eye out for any possible enemy, I began to contemplate the near future.

What do we even brief the command about what we've seen here...it's been absolute chaos since I arrived.

Who are the strangers Jim wants us to meet and bring back?

How many more of our Brothers will be gone before this war is over?

The last thought resonated with me.

Part of me had thought that leaving the Army to go to medical school and start a family would mean that I would be finished getting calls telling me a close friend had died.

But in reality, although I had gone to the civilian side our Brothers-in-arms stayed in harm's way as the role that Special Operations played in Iraq and Afghanistan began increasingly leading to the vast majority of combat deaths.

Tallying up the numbers in my head, I had lost nearly as many Brothers after leaving the service as I had while I was in.

And now there I was, brought back together with those Brothers who were left, those who I had missed so much but with whom I was right back at the tip of the spear.

The mountains sped past my view from the Suburban's window as I said a silent prayer for Buckeye and Dave.

Not only had they been close to me, but I had been with both of them when they died.

Buckeye had watched my back and saved my butt numerous times while we were in the service, and without Dave we never would have made it out of Santa Monica and home from the hospital.

As my heart grew heavier with each passing mile outside of the window, I felt a hand on my shoulder. Turning I saw that it was Noah, Natalie's teenage son, now leaning forward with a hand outstretched.

"How can I help you son?" I asked as I turned in my seat.

"I don't need any help, I just thought you could use some support. And I never said thank you for getting us out of there. Thank you."

I looked back at him for a moment, his tall and lanky teenage frame leaning towards me, his square and taught face covered almost entirely by glasses with buzzcut hair and eyes that seemed much older than his years.

"You're welcome son, and thank you for the support. I need you to keep an eye on your sister and mother when we stop the vehicles. We're not expecting anyone to be there until our friends arrive, but in this environment you can never be too careful."

"Can I have a gun?" he asked.

"Not quite yet Noah. We need to be sure you know what you're doing before we put a weapon in your hands. But keeping your eyes open will be more helpful than anything tonight. Our guys who do have guns are very good with them, so if you point them in the right direction they'll take care of any problems we may have."

"Like killing bad guys?" he asked.

I took a second to look at his mother, her gaze now locked on both of us and our conversation.

"Hopefully no," I answered.

"But if needed...then yes."

"But aren't they bad guys?" he asked.

"Don't you *want* to kill all of the bad guys?"

"It's not as easy as that Noah," I countered, wondering how I would answer the same question when my children grew old enough to ask.

"We have a saying in Special Forces that i'm quite fond of...one man's terrorist is another man's freedom fighter."

I paused for a second, contemplating how best to pass on this very important lesson to a teenager caught in the middle of a warzone.

"Nobody likes killing. Well, some do...and those people have serious problems. We have a respect for any warrior, given that they are fighting for something they believe in, just like us. And just like us, they are soldiers with orders. None of the bad guys we'll meet actually gave the orders or devised the plans to invade our nation. They're just doing a job, and many of them have families themselves who are waiting for them to come home."

Ray shot me a glance, being one of the only other people who knew the importance of understanding that stark difference between the real enemy and those merely following orders.

"But I thought you guys loved killing. I mean, to be a Green Beret...don't you go into that just to kill bad guys? I mean, like, how many bad guys have you killed?"

I stopped for a second to compose myself, having been asked that same question countless times in my post-military days by nearly everyone who discovered what my job had been in the Army.

"Firstly Noah, that's a question that you should never ask a military veteran. It's a very personal thing and is quite rude."

I took another moment before continuing, seeing a puzzled and ashamed look come across his face when he realized his inquiry was insulting.

"But it gets asked a lot, so don't feel bad. One of the most important parts of selection, where they decide who amongst us is good enough and allowed to train to be a Green Beret, is a psychological profile. You'll notice that most of us have a very similar personality type. We're family men with big hearts, driven by a purpose that you don't find in other people. That purpose can be anything...our families, our love for our nation, our dedication to making the world a better place."

Looking straight into his eyes to ensure he was paying attention, I continued.

"But none of us are driven purely by a desire to kill...that's what makes a psychopath, and none of those types are selected to wear the Green Beret. We believe down to our core that we are doing what is needed to protect our families and our country...which I'm sure many of the people we are fighting are driven by as well. We don't do this merely because we enjoy it, but because we know that the world needs sheepdogs to protect the innocent, and there aren't that many like us who are willing to do anything that is necessary to do so."

Noah nodded his head, and I nodded back to him and turned around in my seat to continue watching outside of the window for anything out of the ordinary. It took a few minutes before I realized his hand was still on my shoulder, but I decided not to say anything about it.

It was nice to feel his support.

I was still gazing out of the window as our vehicle began to slow and we pulled over to park next to some open terrain that looked like farmland.

Getting out of the trucks and stretching my legs to look around, I suddenly came to a realization.

"Holy crap, I know where we are."

"Congratulations Rob, do you want a prize? We should all know where we are buddy," joked Ray.

"No, I mean I've been here before. Coachella is not far from here."

"Huh?"

"Coachella. The music festival."

Looking over at Ray I could tell from his blank stare that he was awaiting more information.

"Seriously? You've never heard of Coachella?"

His face remained completely unchanged.

"You really need to get out more, man."

Josh made his way up to the front of our vehicle and motioned for us to form a circle around him.

Pointing to the large body of water to our west, he began giving out his instructions.

"Over to our west you can see the Salton Sea. To our north is Joshua Tree national park, where we'll move should we make contact here while waiting for the bird. And for those of us who weren't paying attention, the golf course is about ninety miles to our southwest, as the crow flies. Our LZ is just over this ridge to our immediate east, and the birds will be picking us up in a valley on the other side. Any questions?"

Looking around at the group, mostly checking their bags and gear to start moving, Ray raised his hand.

"Yes Ray?" Josh asked, exasperated and expecting sarcasm.

"Can we go to a concert?"

"What?" he asked incredulously.

"Rob says they do music festivals here. Can we go check it out?"

"I tell you what, Ray," Josh replied as he looked around the group.

"We'll go catch our bird to get more troops and weapons, you can do whatever you damn well please. Everyone else follow me, we're moving out."

It took over an hour for us to reach our position to wait for the birds, as the moon rock and dust-like ground made the movement slow and laborious.

As we neared the crest of our observation point, Josh gave out instructions for who would be situated where, as we would string out along the ridgeline keeping a low profile so that we could have eyes in every direction but try to remain undetected should any enemy pass below us.

Josh and Tattoo took up their positions next to Meda and her brother. As we moved further down the line to set in and wait I heard them begin to discuss the importance of picking out a good observation point for any mission, along with the obvious advantages of high ground.

"Mommy I'm cold," Ava Luna remarked to her mother as we were walking to our position, and I began to feel the frigid desert wind begin sapping the cold from my skin as well.

I decided we had gone far enough, and as I instructed her children where to lay I took a knee to fish the woobie from my bag and set it over them.

"Now I need you to take good care of this, Ava Luna," I told her as I used it to cover their three shivering bodies.

"This is not just any ordinary blanket. This is a woobie. Actually it's my woobie and we've been through an awful lot together over the years."

"Woobie?" Ava Luna asked, brushing her long black hair aside to reveal big brown eyes.

"Yes," I answered.

"It's much more than just a regular blanket. A woobie is made of special material to reflect your heat back to you while you're under it, and it's camouflaged so that soldiers can use it on missions or out in the field like tonight. It's kept me warm on some very cold nights in some very dark places before."

"But we're not in a field," she countered.

I chuckled, remembering that I was speaking with a nine-year-old girl who had never been around the military before.

"The field just means anywhere away from home or your base. You're right, this is the desert, but we're in the field because we're not at home but out on a mission."

She smiled and nodded at the explanation.

"Ok, I get it!"

As Ava Luna and her mother worked to find comfort under the woobie, Noah began to wriggle out of it to stand next to me.

"I'm not cold and I want to help," he said to me, pushing the glasses back up on his face.

Looking at his tall and wiry frame I couldn't imagine that to be true. I was 200 pounds and my teeth were about to start chattering, so I could only guess how cold his slender body must have been.

But I admired his determination and willingness to help.

"I tell you what," I responded.

"We need eyes on both sides of this ridge; north and east to watch for the helicopter coming to pick us up, and south to look for bad guys. Which do you want? Enemy or friends?"

"Definitely friends," he answered.

"Ok then, you three lay on the ground this way and keep your eyes peeled in this direction. We should see several shadows appear low on the horizon in about two hours. There will be a big one in the center that will flash on its red beacon lights to let us know it's friendly. When you see that, let me know...quietly."

Noah got a big smile on his face and rendered a salute.

I couldn't tell if he was happy to help or because he'd be able to sit under the woobie while doing so.

Either was a win for everyone, so as they settled in to watch for our exfil birds, I lay down on the opposite side of the crest to keep an eye on our vehicles and for any enemy who found their way to our location.

Natalie and her daughter snuggled up together under the warmth of the woobie, and before long I heard the light sounds of their sleeping.

I glanced over at Noah every few minutes, expecting him to fall asleep as well. Instead he watched the horizon with silent determination.

And we waited.

With about twenty minutes left before the helos were scheduled to arrive, Josh walked our line to ensure everyone was awake, keeping an eye out and was ready to go. He took a knee and reminded us the crew would kick off the supply palettes for those staying behind, and as soon as they were cleared we would run up the ramp.

Meda and her team would then drive the trucks around the mountain range to pick up their supplies, and we would see them in a few days. Josh had given them our encryption key and times to call on specific frequencies so that we could coordinate with them later.

He stopped next to me along his walk before heading back to his spot on the ridge.

"See anything moving out there?" he asked me.

"Not all all boss. All quiet on the western front."

He shook his head.

"I hope that's good news."

When the clock read ten minutes out, I packed up the woobie as we moved in a line down the other side of the hill into the valley, so we would be ready to run up the ramp the moment the pallets were out of the way.

We stood at the bottom with a few minutes to spare, so I took my woobie back out for Natalie and her children to keep warm while we waited.

And waited.

As the hit time passed, Josh incessantly scanned the horizon for shadows, lights and the sound of muffled rotors but found none.

Ten minutes after our hit time he sent Tattoo back up to the crest to see if he could find anything in the distance. When the answer was negative Josh ordered our team back up to the top.

An hour past our hit time, Josh sent us back to the vehicles.

We had to maintain radio silence on the drive to ensure our signal wouldn't give us away, so the ride back to the golf course was silent.

Meda and Tyler had planned on returning with new weapons and gear while we had hoped to see our families that night, so nobody was in a good mood.

As the bay doors opened, one of the men from Tyler's team raced out to meet us and confer with Tyler, riding shotgun in one of the other vehicles. After a short exchange of words, he leapt out of his seat and ran through the door leading into the hallway at the rear of the garage.

Ray and I exchanged glances.

"That can't be good," I said.

"No kidding," he responded.

As the garage bay doors closed we each made our way hastily to the first breakroom, which the Echoes had converted into a communications room before we left.

We had to maintain radio silence on the road and while waiting for the helos, but they had stayed on to communicate with Jim and let him know if we encountered any enemy or had bad news en route.

But the bad news came from Jim's end.

As we filed into the room, Tyler's communications man filled us in.

"The birds went down man. All of them. They got hit somewhere in New Mexico. I'm not sure if it was ground fire or aircraft yet, but we just got word about thirty minutes ago. You guys were on the way back when we got the news and I didn't want to risk a message to you being intercepted."

"What does that mean?" Meda's brother asked.

"It means we're on our own," Jason responded.

"No," added The Major.

"It means we start preparing the tribe tomorrow and we hit them where it hurts."

It took a full week of gruelling around-the-clock training to get the tribe ready and select a target of opportunity, but we had a few factors on our side making it a much better situation than we had originally anticipated.

Because the reservations are considered sovereign land and not under the uber-leftist policies of the rest of southern California, the tribe hadn't been forced to give up all of their weapons along with the state's populace.

They also had their own tribal police, and thanks to some very conservative and government-fearing members of the force they had amassed an arsenal on their own.

They had stockpiles of automatic weapons and rifles, a handful of explosives but enough ammunition and gunpowder for our Charlies to rig up plenty of bombs to do whatever we needed.

And a large cache of dynamite bought under the guise of demolition for construction meant that we were on pretty good footing in the "make things go boom" department.

The tribe had been both more eager to fight and easier to train than we had anticipated. After a few days of getting familiar with the weaponry and tactics, we began to see their fierce warrior souls emerge from the shells that had been hiding them for generations.

As our team would meet to AAR [After Action Review] each day of training, we were reminded of the stories about the basis and traditions of Special Forces coming from Native American warriors.

The unit patch adorned by Special Forces soldiers was centered around an arrowhead representing the Native American warriors from whom our base of fighting tactics were born.

They were the original tacticians of guerrilla warfare, even being the first to launch their attacks in the early morning before dawn, leading militaries around the world to initiate a "stand-to," requiring security to be at 100% just before daybreak while in the field or on missions.

And now we were handing the torch which had been lit by their ancestors back to them. Each of us felt as we were witnessing their forefathers emerging from the dust, shaking the rust from their skills and tools of war and preparing once again to defend their land, honor and culture.

While it took some time for them to become acquainted with the weapons of our day, each warrior had the most vital tool necessary to train for and wage war: determination.

The skills we could teach to anyone, but the heart was something that had to come already forged from fire and hard as steel.

And they had more than we could have ever wished for.

After much deliberation, we selected our first target.

California is the port of entry for the vast majority of goods coming into and out of the US, and due to its proximity to China was the point from which most of our nation's resources that were heading back to their homeland were leaving through.

While we had once possessed the greatest Navy in the world, the Chinese and Russian attack had obliterated everything that was docked in port on the west coast, and it was time for us to return the favor.

There were two major ports in our area, those of Long Beach and Los Angeles. The port of Long Beach was not only closer to us, but was also the second busiest in the nation behind Los Angeles.

Having seen the massive enemy presence in Los Angeles recently, I pushed strongly for our mission to be in Long Beach where we had a chance of getting in and out without being seen.

It would be suicide to attempt to take those forces head on, and would go against everything that we were trying to do.

Guerilla warfare depends primarily on stealth and speed over size, and even with a hundred fierce Native American warriors by our side we wouldn't last long in a full man-on-man battle with the enemy in the area.

But even though Long Beach would be less heavily guarded than Los Angeles, they are fewer than twenty-five miles apart. That meant that we would have to sneak in, do what we needed and be far away before anyone even noticed we were there.

Being seen on the way in would mean that we all would die. Being seen while emplacing explosives would mean that we all would die. And being seen on our exfil would mean that we all would die.

Long Beach moved more shipping containers than any other port in the country, and we decided that would be a great opportunity to cause some real damage.

As the enemy was working to move America's resources to their own nations, we knew that shipping containers would be a large part of that operation and we could put a stop to it.

At least temporarily.

More importantly, the rumors that would circulate amongst their soldiers that someone got into the deepest stretches of their stronghold and were able to wreak havoc would do major damage to their morale, and potentially even bring more troops back from around the country to guard their operations on the coast.

If we could cause that action and coordinate with the rest of our teams across the nation, we would be able to move them where we wanted for a large-scale coordinated attack.

We had a few options available to do that, and deciding which option to pursue took more time and deliberation than any other aspect of the mission.

Our first thought was to place explosives on an actual ship, turning it into a smoking heap in the middle of one of the ship channels and blocking passage for others.

But the idea was discarded, as it wouldn't take long for them to move the wreckage and wouldn't really sustain any long-term damage to anything besides the one ship.

The next thought moved to oil. Texas gets the notoriety of producing US-based oil, but a lot of it comes from California as well.

If they were moving the California oil out of Long Beach and we could locate the terminals from which it was flowing, setting them ablaze would not only cause an enormous fireball but also catch the attention of their entire force.

But that could require a lot more intelligence than we had time or resources for, and would be a massive failure and waste of time if not done correctly.

We would only have one opportunity, as the resulting strengthening of enemy security posture would ensure that we wouldn't be able to get back in to try again.

We moved our thought process to their logistical operations, and what would create the most terror and put the greatest strain on their ability to move equipment.

The cranes used to lift the shipping containers were enormous, alien-looking contraptions which rose high in the air above the water and, if done right, could possibly both limit their capacity to maneuver containers and impede ships in the channel if we took out the correct legs and caused them to fall into the water.

After a full day of deliberation trying to decide on our best option, we agreed that we were just spinning our wheels until we had eyes on the ground to let us know if any of the ideas were even feasible.

We didn't have internet access or imagery from Jim, so we would have to do it the old-fashioned way: kick out some recon teams.

We decided to send out four detachments of two men each, a significant part of our team but also necessary to get in fast and have a full understanding of their entire operation.

There were suburbs located around the inland perimeter of the port, and with good binoculars each team would easily be able to acquire an accurate picture of their assigned quarter section of the port and report it back to us.

For the first time since this all began, I wasn't itching to be one of the men going out. I knew that my place was to be there with Natalie and her kids to both keep them safe and comforted with a familiar face.

The drive would be almost as long as my trip to Los Angeles with Dave had been, and in the same manner as I had done they chose to leave under the cover of darkness, find a place to set in for the night and spend the daylight hours observing the port, looking for targets of opportunity.

Each team would reconnoiter a quarter of the objective and look for a few primary things to help us determine our best target: ease of undetected travel in & out, targets that would cause the greatest amount of damage both to their morale & logistical operations and the enemy security posture that was in place.

Standing at the bay door to see the recon teams off, I soon discovered that Natalie shared my fondness for cheesy pickup lines but had significantly more bravery than I in delivering them.

"Come here often?" she asked, joining me as the last team drove off on a pair of motorcycles.

"Huh?" I asked her.

"Oh come on, cut me some slack. I haven't had the chance to say thank you yet, and you keep yourself so busy that it's nearly impossible to get your attention."

I smiled and turned to face her, giving her my complete focus.

"Well, mission accomplished. Can I buy you a cup of coffee?"

I led her back to the breakroom, which had a perennial pot of coffee either full or brewing since our arrival. Taking a seat across from her it was my turn to start the conversation.

Starting with the obligatory questions about her kids, I became once again entranced by her entire being. It was like we had known each other forever and were just catching back up, and the first time that I glanced at my watch I realized we had been talking for hours.

Her having children in the next room sleeping and me having a mission to go on soon, we both laughed and decided to part ways to get some rest.

As I watched her walking away from the table and to the room in which her kids were asleep, a magnetism began pulling me toward her that I hadn't felt in a long time.

But I couldn't allow myself to be distracted. Not while we had recon teams out in heavily guarded enemy territory and a mission of my own to go on soon after they returned. Any emotions that I felt would have to wait.

I was asleep on the break room couch when the recon team's engines roared into the garage, and bringing the group together to hear their intel we found that we had two viable options which would accomplish our objectives.

Each team reported they had found the massive cranes used to load shipping containers on and off ships, but there were so many lining the waterways that taking one or two down wouldn't even put a dent in the enemy's operations.

And while they were massively tall, the channel was so wide that it wouldn't impede much progress of the ships moving in and out.

There were, however, two opportunities which we decided upon unanimously as our targets.

First was a major road and train track which led into the port, going over the channel and splitting it in half.

The tracks were more important than the road, as this was the only way to move trains in and out of the port. Once those trains crossed the channel bridge, they came to an oil terminal.

If we could blow the bridges for both the road and tracks, the enemy would lose their ability to bring trainloads of vital resources onto ships for export to their countries and off the ships to import their own weapons and supplies for their troops.

The added bonus, of course, was that if we blew the bridges into the water it would render that part of the port unusable, as ships would no longer be able to move beyond the wreckage. And with an oil terminal situated on one side of the bridge it was too good of an opportunity to pass up.

The second target identified by the recon teams was on the southwest corner of the port, and was the largest oil terminal it contained.

Being on the corner meant that it had access routes nearby if we had to get out quickly, and densely populated suburbs in which we could disappear just a few minutes away.

That gave one major advantage we had never held before in our wars on the soil of other nations: if we needed to hide, we could blend right into the populace, our people.

Having identified the targets, the Charlies got to work building explosive charges that could be used to destroy the columns of the bridge and others that would be strong enough to blow through the walls of the oil terminals and ignite the precious cargo inside.

While they went about creating our new toys, the rest of us put our heads together to plan the logistics of our operation: who would go, how we would get in and most importantly, how we would get back.

We had two options for getting in and out: move to the water and sail up the coast or drive straight onto our objectives.

One of Meda's team knew the port well, and once he informed us that the port employed underwater sonar to detect incoming watercraft, that plan was out.

After I mentioned that Dave and I had driven the PCH unhindered for our trip to Los Angeles, it was decided that would be our way in.

We would need a lot of people on this one, and although the tribe couldn't be trusted quite yet to emplace the explosives, they would make a great QRF should we get into trouble.

The bridges would require multiple teams emplacing their charges at the same time, and with two targets (the train and road) and four columns on each to take down, that would be the bulk of our manpower.

The oil terminal was much simpler and wouldn't take many people. We could send a team of two to each terminal, set a handful charges and blow them off the face of the earth.

All that we really needed was for one of the charges to work, as the ensuing explosion would ensure the rest of the terminal went up in a fireball.

Suburbs or not, if we amassed the QRF with a hundred fighters in any one location it would be a dead giveaway, alerting the enemy that something was going on.

Even though the recon teams were tired, we'd need them back on this operation to walk us in on the target, lest using radios to communicate give away our plans and positions.

We decided to split the entire group back up into four sections, each led by one of the recon teams operating as their command and control.

Unlike normal missions we couldn't risk a single element coordinating all of the forces, as that much radio traffic to one location would be way too risky.

We decided to leave twenty men back to guard the golf course. We split the remaining 80 tribal fighters amongst the four units, with four men in five trucks as QRF for each element.

Getting in under the guise of a normal day was paramount, and although we hated that many moving pieces, vehicles with four people each ran less risk of arising suspicion from any enemy they passed along the way.

The QRF would remain scattered throughout the suburb closest to the element they were supporting, and would carry a radio each for the sole purpose of a call for help.

Once the teams went to emplace their explosives we couldn't risk any communication, guidance or help aside from a call to the QRF to save their lives.

If the QRF could even get there in time if the call was needed.

We had three medics amongst us, so although one unit would be without a medic on their objective, three of the units would be working less than a hundred meters away from one another. It was a calculated risk we could afford to take.

We opted to stagger the units by thirty minutes, with each vehicle leaving five minutes apart.

The recon teams would lead their respective units back to the same place they had set in the day previously, using their same route in once it got dark, emplacing the explosives and coming back the same way, picking up their QRF element on the way home.

Each team carried a radio transmitter to blow the charges, so we didn't expect any explosions until all of the teams were on their way back to the golf course.

But the road to hell is paved with good intentions, and no mission, no matter how meticulously planned, goes off exactly as expected.

I was on the team designated to take out the largest oil terminal. It was fitting, being that I was the only Texan on the team and they thought that we had been raised on black gold, much like kids on a corn farm in Iowa grow up with an innate understanding of the crop.

Mine was the last team to leave, as our objective was the shortest distance from the golf course. This meant we were able to see each of the teams off and would be prepared to react if anyone got into trouble on the way in.

By the time my team arrived, several hours after the first team set off, the sun was beginning to set behind the ocean.

As we neared the objective, the SUV's which carried our QRF would peel off, one by one from the convoy, and we passed them parked on the side of a residential street on the way to our control point.

The locations in which we left our vehicles would be our rally point, meaning that if anything bad happened, we would call the QRF while moving to those vehicles and hopefully would make it back unscathed to meet them and fight in force.

All went according to plan until I was climbing the stairs on the side of one of the enormous cylindrical tanks which housed the oil waiting to be shipped.

I had a pack full of charges, needing nothing more than to be emplaced along the side of the terminal and out of view to await the small radio signal that would trigger it to explode.

With a half-dozen charges in my pack, I climbed twenty feet up on the ladder circling clockwise around the first tank and got to work.

I started using one hand on the railing to hang down and emplace the explosives on the containers, to conceal them and ensure someone walking on the ground below would not spot the mounds of demolitions I was putting in place.

Four of my charges were in place, and as I hung down to emplace the fifth a crack of automatic weapons fire shattered the silence around us.

Jamming the charge against the tank with the putty that was already affixed to it, I pulled myself back up to the stairs and crouched down, straining my ears to locate the source of the gunfire.

I was in the center of a semicircle of nine tanks, so the echo and reverberation caused me to jerk around wildly looking for the origin.

Being so close to completing my objective I decided it was better to hurry and place the last charge. I grabbed the railing to hang back down as Ray shouted in his best hushed tone at me from below.

"Rob, get down here man, we need to get moving."

Using the explosives-filled hand to wave him off, I didn’t like how close the five charges were to each other and decided to climb higher.

Ray began to protest as I climbed higher, but I was on a mission and would be damned if I didn't at least take our target down.

Once I had emplaced the last charge and ran down the stairs, I couldn't find Ray and my head was swirling with the cacophony of a full-fledged firefight. There hadn't been any explosions yet, but it sounded as if the entire port were engaged in a battle.

It had only been a few minutes since the initial volley of fire, but remembering that Los Angeles was only several minutes away by air I knew the gunships were either on their way to come find us or that at the very least pilots would already be racing towards them on a helipad.

I found Ray on the far side of the grouping of containers, listening intently to surmise the situation.

"Do we wait here for the others?" I asked him in a hurry.

"No, we're the only ones here. The shooting is coming from right where they are, so we need to get to the trucks and get the hell out of here."

From our new vantage point we heard automatic weapons and small-arms fire erupting from the direction of our other teams, and I hesitated as he grabbed my shoulder to run.

"There's only two of us, Rob. We can't do anything to help them right now. We need to follow the plan and get back to the trucks."

I thought for a second.

"There are only two of us, but we have twenty fighters waiting for us with a trunkful of heavy weapons."

He paused for a moment to think, then nodded his head.

"Ok, let's go get help."

It took us ten minutes of sprinting to get back to our vehicle and gather the QRF from our team.

Ray and I had driven in a sedan, but with their numbers each QRF element had come in an SUV, which was perfect for what we were planning.

There was only one primary road going directly to their location, but it had two routes of ingress and egress to get to it.

As the alternate route would add an extra several miles that we couldn't afford the time for, we decided to go straight in following the way the other teams had taken.

Ray directed the men in the last three vehicles to arm themselves with automatic weapons and line the truck floors at their feet with as much ammo as they could.

The men with belt-fed weapons lined it around their necks and at their feet, while those with canister and magazine-fed weapons continued to load extra magazines as we drove.

I echoed the same command to our first vehicle, took over the driver's seat in the lead and directed the men who had been in front to move to the trunks and be prepared to shoot from the rear and make room for our guys, should we find them.

Several minutes later we were racing to the bridge with the train tracks situated on our right hand side. A few hundred meters ahead of us we saw a couple of our guys, running along the tracks and stopping to shoot behind them in a leapfrog maneuver.

Ray rolled down his window and yelled to them as we pulled alongside, opening his door and laying down suppressive fire as they moved to our vehicle.

It was Josh and Klint, and as they jumped into the opened trunk of our SUV they pointed ahead of our truck.

"We made contact while placing the last explosives. The others were following us but they must have been pinned down," Josh yelled as I laid on the gas and vaulted the SUV forward to save the rest of our Brothers.

As we drove over the elevated bridge I began to see the full situation.

I wasn't sure exactly how many soldiers it was coming from, but there was a heavy base of fire directed under the bridge from the other side of the road, a large parking lot now littered with muzzle flashes and enemy troops.

I yelled to the back of our SUV to establish covering fire into the parking lot, and stopped the vehicle just before coming to the other side of the bridge.

The SUV's behind us followed suit, circling the wagons and erupting a grand volley of gunfire into the parking lot.

Ray jumped out of the truck before I could say anything, and as I opened my door to follow him I heard Klint yelling at me.

"Rob, you stay here. We need these vehicles ready to go as soon as we get the guys. Shoot from here but stay ready!"

Before I could respond, he and Josh had popped the rear hatch and followed Ray under the bridge to find our other teams.

Looking back at the other trucks to see if I needed to adjust their fire, I erupted with a swelling of pride.

They were "dueling guns," as we had taught them, taking turns laying down suppressive fire by alternating M240 belt-fed machine guns.

Even using the "dueling guns" method we taught them so as not to burn out their barrels or need to reload at the same time, they were still slinging nearly 200 rounds per minute each of hot 7.62mm lead fury and painting the parking lot red from the enemy soldiers' demise.

Because we had five trucks, each following this same tactic, we had an endless stream of heavy weapons fire emanating from our vehicles, keeping the enemy head down and taking away any advantage they thought they had.

As I kept my head on a swivel to look both for our men and any new enemy coming in, I saw a convoy of five more of our SUV's speeding towards us, now also laying down their own volleys of fire.

While the reinforcements sped to our location, Ray emerged from under the bridge carrying Tattoo, followed by Chad and The Major.

The last two dropped Tattoo in the trunk of the SUV behind us and immediately ran back under the bridge.

Ray grabbed a few more of the QRF from the trucks behind us, and I understood what was going on. The parking lot wasn't the only source of enemy; there must have been a firefight going on underneath us as well.

Turning to the men sitting in the seats behind me, I directed them to go under and help the guys get everyone else.

To their honor, it didn't take me asking a second time.

They knew what I was asking the moment I turned to them, and before I could say anything they each took an arm full of ammo and moved out.

The shooting sounds echoing from under the bridge soon matched that coming from our trucks, and before long the men re-emerged, this time with Tyler and Chris.

Keeping my eyes on the sky as the men popped open the hatches behind us and found places for everyone to sit, I saw what I had been dreading since hearing the first rounds fired: gunships on the horizon, speeding down the coast from our north.

As the last of the rear hatches were closed behind us, I slammed the truck into drive and jammed down the accelerator as hard as I could.

Given that our position was already given away, I pressed my push-to-talk and let the rest of the team know what I saw.

Josh spoke over the net as soon as I was finished, directing everyone in the trunks to find a shoulder-fired weapon and get it ready.

As I sped along our alternate route we were soon crossing over another bridge, this time onto the smaller Ocean Avenue rather than the expansive causeway we had driven in on.

Keeping an eye on the rear-view to see how long we had, I watched the formation of gunships closing in.

As we reached the opposite side of the bridge and leveled off onto a flat road, The Major spoke into his radio to give the command we had been waiting for.

"I have control, I have control, I have control."

Each of the Charlies, the men holding the radio transmitters for our charges, knew exactly what he meant and picked up their detonators, excitedly waiting for his countdown.

"Three...two...one, execute."

There was the briefest of silences after his final command as each man held their breath in anticipation of what we knew what would come next.

As I kept one eye on the rear view with the other dodging parked cars in front of us alongside the road, I took my foot off the gas for a moment as our creation engulfed the port behind us.

One second I was watching the skyline and a formation of Russian gunships bearing down on us just a few miles away, and the next the entire world behind us and sky above it were filled with a beautiful artwork of fire and chaos.

The explosives hadn't done that much, really. They were man-carried batches of dynamite, C4 and homemade munitions.

But the tanks of oil, both the ones we had emplaced charges on and the others next to them became death and destruction to anything in their wake.

I kept one eye on the rearview mirror as the fireball began to subside, now replaced with thick, black acrid smoke.

And to my horror, I watched several gunships fly directly through the black cloud and slice through it with their rotors as they came down on us.

"Rob, look out!" I heard Ray yell and looked back just in time for the impact.

We had driven in to the objective on a fairly wide road, but the egress route had been the smaller, residential type of a beachside community, still littered with the beat up vehicles of surfers and residents who had parked before the invasion began, many of which hadn't been moved or started since.

As the front right bumper of our Suburban plowed through a Prius parked on the side of the street, it sent the back of our truck sliding in our direction of movement, as the sheer power of the physics of momentum meant that while the front of the vehicle stopped rapidly, the rear wanted to keep going.

I maintained a terrified consciousness as the Suburban began to roll down the street, toppling over several times before coming to a stop on our side.

I brought my knife up to pop the airbags out of our way as the unmistakable hiss of several shoulder-fired rockets sounded behind us.

Cutting free from my airbag and seatbelt I climbed out of my door, now sticking straight up into the air, and jumped down to move to the back and help the others.

I moved to the hatch, which had already been opened by its passengers.

Josh and I stood together and marveled at the smoking wreckage of three gunships falling out of the sky. They crashed into the middle of the suburb, taking several multi-million dollar beach houses and off beach condo buildings with them.

Thankfully the vehicles in the rear of our convoy had been paying better attention to the road than I, and we began to move our men to the QRF trucks behind us.

As the last were loading into their new ride, Ray slapped a few leftover charges on our Suburban, now laying on its side in a smoking heap.

"Wouldn't want to find out the hard way that we left something in there, would we?" he asked me with a wink as he jumped into the trunk next to me.

Josh came over the radio and gave his next orders.

"Blow it when the last truck has passed. We can't afford any more injuries on this one."

The rest of the convoy pulled ahead of us to pass, and as we took our position in the tail of the convoy, Ray sported a naughty grin when he pressed his initiator to leave one final fireball in our wake.

CHAPTER 8

INITIATION

Upon arrival back at the golf course, I first noticed something strange as the bay doors opened and we began to see inside.

The men were arranged in a semi-circle around a figure in the center of the garage. A figure who didn't look entirely...real.

We exited the vehicles to unload the injured as Jason shouted orders to take them to a room in the back so we could fix them up.

When I ran out of the passenger-side door of my truck to begin unloading our wounded brothers, a familiar voice called my name.

"Moshe?" I asked, slowly turning to recognize the strange figure was in fact Moshe.

As I walked towards the group who had stayed behind, I couldn't wholly grasp what I was seeing. I squinted my eyes to try and understand why my mind kept telling me that something was off.

One of the men spoke out as I moved forward.

"Yeah, about that."

The man walked towards Moshe, pulled his right hand up above his shoulder and swung it in the form of a knife-edge directly through him.

"He's here, but he's not exactly here," the man explained.

I looked on, puzzled, as Moshe began to speak.

"Rob, we need you and Natalie to get back to Austin as soon as possible."

"What is going on here? And how do you know about Natalie?" I asked.

"There's no time to explain that," he responded in his thick Israeli accent.

"Get back here as fast as you can."

"Ok, but what is this? What are you?"

"No time. But we'll disclose everything when you're here. We know that you picked up Natalie, and we have a special project that we will read you two onto," Moshe answered.

Josh walked up behind me and must have been just as confused as I was.

"Moshe?" he asked.

Looking to Josh, Moshe repeated his orders.

"Get Rob and Natalie here with her kids as soon as possible. You and the team can stay out there if you need, but we need those two back immediately."

"I don't understand..."

"You don't have to," Moshe cut him off, becoming noticeably agitated.

"Just get them back here now."

As Josh began to formulate another question, Moshe disappeared before he could voice it.

Josh and I looked across the garage at the men who had stayed behind, each with a confused expression on his face.

"What the hell was that?" Josh demanded.

"I don't know," responded one of the men.

"He appeared just before you guys arrived and asked when you'd be back. He wouldn't tell us anything, just that he needed Rob and Natalie back in Austin with her kids.

"Did he speak with Natalie?" I asked.

"He didn't need to," answered Meda from the back of the room.

"She knew he was going to appear long before he did."

"What is going on here?" Josh repeated his question.

"You white people are so funny," she smirked.

"You make yourselves so busy with your daily life and striving to win accomplishments to get ahead that you completely lose sight of all the things going on around you that you can't explain. The world you choose to ignore is the world people like Natalie, Moshe and I exist in. And it's a lot more interesting."

Shaking his head and still maintaining a puzzled look on his face, Josh turned to me.

"Do you know what's going on here Rob?"

"He does, even if he doesn't realize it," responded Meda.

"But you're asking the wrong questions. You need to be asking how you're going to get them back to Austin. If Moshe showed these abilities to you, it's something very important...just understand that. If I were you, I'd focus on getting them back there before you do anything else."

"Ok Miss Prophecy Person or whatever your name means...how do we do that?" Josh asked.

Meda looked around the garage and pointed to one of the vehicles, a slightly beat up sedan that had been left behind during our mission to San Diego.

"Put them in that car and let them travel East," she responded.

"With all we've been through, with a helicopter having just been shot down en route to pick us up, with the Russians looking for us here and the Chinese looking for us on the coast, do you really think that's a safe option?" he asked her.

"I don't think, Josh," she answered.

"I know."

Josh shook his head, physically showing he was having a hard time grasping what was going on and extending his trust to Meda.

He also wasn't entirely sure that sending one of his medics along a drive through enemy-controlled territory, without any extra security, based off the orders from an apparition that had just appeared and asked it, was such a good idea.

He turned to me.

"I don't know Rob. I don't understand what's going on here, and we've got wounded to take care of. This is your call...what do you think?'

I glanced at Meda, who maintained a constant and determined stare towards both of us. As I looked back to Josh, trying to formulate a decision and answer in my own head, it came from someone else.

"We're going," Natalie spoke from the doorway, now standing next to Meda with her children and their bags.

"It's what we need to do, and we don't have a choice."

As I turned to look at her, she met my eyes with a stare so intense it made the hair on the back of my neck begin to stand.

I had become attuned through my life and experiences to whether someone was telling the truth, showing a false bravado or putting up a fake sense of assuredness while actually hiding massive insecurities.

And there was no doubt that she believed this was what we needed to do.

I held her stare for a few seconds and a tingling shot across my skin that felt as if I were being drawn to a magnetic field.

I heard whispers in the back of my consciousness, words I couldn't quite make out or understand.

"Rob, what do you say?" Josh asked, interrupting whatever transmission had been formed.

As my skin stopped tingling and hairs fell back to rest, I turned to square with him.

"I'll go. We'll take that sedan and be on the move in ten. Just let me gather my things and grab a little food and water. Can you have someone inspect the car and ensure it can make the drive?"

"It will make it," answered Meda.

"Look, I'm going out on a limb here for something that you two seem to be the only ones who have a good feeling about. Something is telling me this is the right thing to do too, but you'll have to understand that I have quite a few reservations about any of this. Just give me a little leeway and realize that as certain as you are, I still need at least some reassurance that I'm not going to end up back in an interrogation room because our car craps out on the side of the road during what is going to be a very long drive."

"Do we have a deal?" I asked.

Meda nodded and signaled to one of her men to have a look at the car, as Natalie and her kids began to carry their bags to the trunk.

I walked to the doorway through which she had emerged to collect my gear and our arms touched slightly as we passed each other. The slightest bolt of static shocked my arm, again sending unknown sensations through my skin and standing my neck hair at attention.

I arrived in a back room to get the bag I had packed the night before. As I took several extra bottles of water and began to secure food for the trip, Josh voiced his concerns.

"Are you sure about this Rob? I don't know if this is the correct move to be making right now. Can you help me understand why you're agreeing to go, or what you see in this to put my mind at ease?"

I finished filling my water bottle, paused to gather my own thoughts and turned to respond.

"I can't help you understand why I'm doing this, because I can't understand it myself. All I can tell you is that my entire life I've searched for rational answers to everything, and have understood for a long time that some things, quite a few things actually, just don't have rational explanations."

I paused for a moment to contemplate how to clarify.

"My search for answers has led me to some pretty strange places which I could never fully grasp. I've had experiences of my own that I know are real, that I felt down to my core but could never explain how or why they happened. But one thing I've come to learn is that there is a path for everyone, and when you're on the right one God or the Universe or whatever you want to call it gives you plenty of signs."

I looked up again for a second to ensure he was following my words.

"For some reason, this just feels right. I don't know why, but it does. We don't have any kind of projector that would have allowed Moshe to appear like he did, so I may know what it was. And if i'm right, there's nothing I can say in this moment that will help you understand it. But if he can do that, then I want to know what else he has up his sleeve, what he's got in store for us, and what in the world it was that brought Natalie and I together in the middle of all this and is pulling us back to Austin."

Josh stroked his beard in thought and looked at the floor, an action I had come to understand over the years as his form of meditation or deep thought when faced with a difficult decision.

"Ok," he responded, bringing the hand back to his side and looking up at me.

"I don't get it either, but you're a big boy and can take care of yourself. We'll stay here and keep taking the fight to the enemy, just let me know if you find whatever it is you're looking for."

"Roger that," I replied, put the water bottle into my backpack and walked over to exchange a fistbump with Josh.

Instead he pulled me in for a hug then pushed me back with a hand on each shoulder to look me square in the eyes like a father imparting wisdom to his son.

"You be careful out there. We'll keep the net open in case you run into trouble. If you need us, we'll come get you."

I met his eyes and nodded. With no words needing to be spoken in response, Josh turned and hurriedly moved back through the doorway to help tend to the injured and get an appraisal of their situation.

The drive took us a complete day, and when we pulled into the familiar Scottish Rite temple near the capitol building in Austin I was both relieved and surprised that we had made it.

Natalie had spent half the trip either playing with her kids in the backseat or resting.

I tried to keep a focused and watchful eye on the horizon waiting for gunships or an enemy roadblock that never materialized.

But after the second swerve due to my falling asleep at the wheel, Natalie forced me into the passenger seat to rest for the second half of the drive.

The soldier at the front gate recognized me and waved our vehicle through immediately, and once again as we parked our car Jim's tall, uniformed figure appeared and sauntered towards us.

As I exited the passenger seat and began to stretch my legs, Jim walked straight to the driver's side door and opened it for Natalie, then repeated the same for her children in the back.

"Nice to see you again, Natalie," he smiled as he spoke.

"And same to you, Noah and Ava Luna," he greeted them as they stepped out of the car.

"Do we know you?" she asked.

"We've been acquainted before," he responded.

"What does that mean?" I asked from my side of the vehicle.

"That's something I can't explain out here," Jim replied.

"Now Rob, I know you want to see your kids more than anything in the world right now, but there's something we need to do first. Can you hold off for a few hours? I promise I'll let you see them as soon as we're through."

Hesitating for a moment, I realized that if it weren't for Moshe's message I'd still be in San Diego either planning or preparing for another mission and nodded reluctantly.

"Oh and I have some good news for you," Jim added.

"We got in touch with your parents. We have a team linking up with them and are waiting for word on how long it will take them to be here."

I smiled and began to formulate a thank you, but he waved me off before I could begin to speak.

"No thank you's necessary," he told me.

"You're about to be offered something that will take every bit of your energy and focus, so let's get down to business. Follow me."

Jim smiled at the kids, turned and walked towards the door.

I picked up Natalie's bag as they gathered theirs, and we followed him through the doorway, down several halls and to the same elevator we had taken the first time we met Moshe and his team.

When we stepped off the elevator Jim walked to the right this time and began moving down a hallway exactly like the one I had previously traveled. But this time each door was adorned with a shape or symbol above it rather than a letter.

The first door we passed was marked with a triangle, sitting on its base with a line through the top one-third of the body, forming a capstone.

On the opposite side of the hallway, the first door was marked with a triangle again, but this one was turned upside down and now resting on the capstone.

I recognized a pattern in the symbols from the deep recesses of my memory, but it wasn't until we reached the third door, again on our left, that I remembered where I knew them from.

The next door on our left was another triangle, once again with the point on top and base on the bottom, but this one with no line of demarcation creating a capstone.

And, as I anticipated, the following door on the opposite side was the mirror image of this one, now again a triangle resting on its point with the long line of the base on top, and no capstone.

Images and symbols began to race through my mind, scanning my recollection for what symbol would come next.

As we came to the fifth door in the hallway, once again on our left side, Jim stopped in front of the very symbol I imagined, a door adorned with a cross. Each of its arms were a different color and the ends rounded in three small half-circles rather than a perfect rectangle.

I was staring at the various archaic symbols adorning every inch of the cross as the rest of our group came to a stop.

Jim turned to me and winked.

"Is this starting to look familiar Rob?" he asked.

Still reeling from the possibilities of what lay beyond this door, or any of the doors we had passed, my thoughts were spinning.

He gave a warm southern smile and lowered his face into a

control box to gain entrance to the room as we had with the original hangar to meet Moshe and the Templars.

We followed him into a dimly lit and cavernous room. The air was heavy and scented with smoke and incense, some burning and others which had long been extinguished.

In the center of the room I saw a figure, cloaked in robes, standing at an altar which was beset on each side by a tall column, one black and one white, both embellished with Egyptian hieroglyphs and other symbols from top to bottom.

I paused to observe the room as the group moved towards the cloaked figure.

The tops of the walls were embellished with more symbols which I didn't recognize, and where they met the floor they were filled with long benches. Either bas reliefs, grand pictographs or curtains of various colors rested above the benches, in black, red, white or green depending on the side of the room.

They reached the cloaked figure and were waiting patiently a few steps away for him to finish his ceremony.

As I continued to scan the walls to make sense of what I was seeing, I spotted movement out of the corner of my eye as the figure turned and spoke to Jim.

I couldn't make out his face due to my distance, the residual smoke and dimly lit room. But the voice was unmistakable.

"Jacob?" I asked incredulously.

As I began to walk forward, astonished and unable to comprehend the situation, the door behind me whooshed open to reveal Moshe as he walked in to join us.

Looking towards Moshe and then back to our group, my brain felt it was being critically overloaded with new information and questions, sending me reeling backward as I struggled to maintain my balance.

My head began to spin and I was forced to my knees by a sudden weakness and loss of equilibrium. The smoke of the incense overwhelmed my senses as I fought to grasp the events.

As I rested my forehead in my hands and took several deep breaths to try and regain my composure, I heard footsteps walking towards me and felt a hand on my shoulder.

As the energy raced back into my body, I opened my eyes to see the group, now standing in a semi-circle and looking at me with no words between them.

I stood up, focusing on the cloaked figure now waiting before me.

"Jacob?" I asked.

He smiled and nodded, his hood removed to show his shoulder-length and curly brown hair nestled just above his shoulders.

"I saw you die," I exclaimed.

"How in the..."

"You didn't see him die, because he can't really die," answered Moshe in a hushed voice.

Stunned, I turned to Moshe but didn't have any words to express the flood of questions his comment brought.

"Rob, let's go for a walk. We'll let the others get reacquainted, and I have a lot to catch you up on before we can read you on to what's going on here," directed Jim.

"You all know each other?" I asked the group as Jim began to lead me towards the door.

"You're asking the wrong questions," replied Natalie.

"Go with Jim, we'll see you when you get back."

She again put her hand on my shoulder and I felt immediately compelled to do just as she asked. Turning my gaze to the door, I could see the outline of Jim's tall frame waiting for me to follow.

After walking back down the hall and passed the elevator Jim led me into a room which was antiseptic white with an industrial atmosphere filled with chairs, desks, whiteboards and most importantly, a coffee maker situated on a counter.

After leading me to a seat and returning with a cup of steaming & dark black normalcy for each of us, he gently eased himself into the chair across from me, pushed my cup across the table and began another download of information that I would have never expected to come from a person like him.

"Rob, I know this may be a lot for you to take in right now. But everything I am about to tell you is something that you are familiar with, in one form or another. I think the biggest thing holding you back are the circumstances in which this is all coming together. Hopefully at the end you'll understand that the situation is what you make of it, and reality is quite different from what most people believe it to be. But of course, you already know that."

"Jacob?" I asked.

"He was dead. I saw the house explode. Even if that didn't kill him, the subsequent foo gas explosions destroyed everything on the compound. We made it specifically to destroy everything and leave zero traces of us, not even bones."

Jim listened, nodded and smiled.

"Correct," he said.

"So how is he here?" I asked.

"Well that's going to take quite a bit of backstory," he replied.

"And thankfully that's precisely what I had planned."

He took a sip of his coffee, the wheels turning in his head trying to formulate the best way to convey this lesson to me.

"It has been well known for a very long time that our government possesses the ability to monitor searches for information by people," Jim began.

"Before the days of Google, we kept records of books checked out from libraries on certain topics. Those could be books on topics we believed could help someone plot a terrorist attack, learn to build bombs, make illicit drugs, launder money and the sort. The internet provided an explosion of information directly into people's homes and cell phones, so of course when search engines came online, we were right there to follow searches. Now, with the millions of queries that happen every minute, or at least before the invasion started, it became a little more complex. We didn't have the manpower to handle each one, so we developed algorithms to alert us when certain searches or combinations came up that would indicate someone was searching for something which would be of interest to us."

"Do you follow me?" he asked.

I nodded, taking another sip of my coffee and wondering why Jim was telling me these things I obviously already knew.

"But while the FBI and NSA were scanning for people on the search for weapons of mass destruction, the same people who started building our deep underground bases built their own algorithm looking for another set of searches. People who were looking for something altogether different, but just as important in the scope of what it was that we were seeking."

"Now you lost me," I countered.

"Ok, let's pivot a bit," added Jim.

"Your whole life you've been searching for something. There is a very large majority of the population who, when authorities tell them the sky is blue, will take that in its entirety and just trust and believe the sky is blue because someone told them so. Within our population, there is a smaller portion of people who will ask why, and will press on for more information to ask why exactly the sky is blue. Upon further research they will discover that it is because of the way our eyes are built, the light refraction and environment that doesn't actually cause the sky to be blue, but rather causes our brains to perceive the sky as blue."

"Ok," I added.

"But even within that population, there is an even smaller segment who won't take that as the final word. They will again ask why it is, or more importantly what its ramifications are, what its metaphysical meanings are, and what it means for everything else in time, space and our reality. You, Rob, are one of the last group."

"How in the world do you know that about me, and why is that important here?" I asked.

"Up until pretty recently you weren't all that important to us."

He paused for a moment to check if I was taking this as an insult, but seeing I was unfazed he continued.

"You went through life as a troubled youth after the loss of your mom, stayed involved in sports, followed your parent's guidance and went off to college like a good young man. You were doing what you thought you were meant to do. Then 9/11 happened, and you felt a patriotic urge to join the military and defend your country, quite possibly to make up for the trouble you caused your family and on some level to bring honor back to your name and prove yourself. But even though you won your way into the coveted Special Forces, and your team did some extremely brave things and earned yourselves a substantial amount of accolades in war, you still weren't on our radar. Green Beret or not, you still didn't possess what we were looking for."

"What *were* you looking for?"

"One day, after you hung up your uniform and were trying to settle into civilian life, after beginning your road to becoming a doctor, you sat down at your computer and began looking for answers. I'm not sure what it was that preceded this search, but it's not important. This is where you appeared on our lists. Do you know what I'm referring to?"

"Not at all," I replied.

"Was it part of my studies?"

"Well, yes and no. Not part of your scholastic studies, but it became a significant aspect of your life and extracurricular studies. You showed up on our lists when you began researching some highly occult subjects one day. You stayed on that path for several months, finally finding your way to a Masonic Lodge just two blocks from the hospital you were working at and school you were attending. You were still pretty low on our radar, but our algorithms tracked you as you progressed to become a Freemason, studying every symbol you encountered to extreme detail. Our algorithms followed as you became a Master Mason, and still feeling as if there was more, found your way to the Scottish Rite and attained your 32nd degree, still searching for answers along the entire journey."

"So that's why I'm here? Because i'm a 32nd degree Mason?" I asked skeptically.

"There are a lot of us out there, why me?

"Because your search didn't end there," replied Jim.

It was all beginning to fall into place. This is why Jim knew I had recognized the symbols adorning the doors on our walk to the Temple, and why he knew that hadn't been the first time I had stepped inside one just like it.

"We followed your quest for knowledge and answers as you, feeling unsatisfied by Masonic texts and studies, continued to climb down the rabbit hole and arrived at The Order, a group started by other Masons generations before you who had the same unsatisfied urges."

"How do you know that?" I asked.

"I never told anyone outside of The Order that I was involved for fear of being banished from Masonry."

"Well, as I said...you moved from being low on our radar to being very high when you started that path. You see, Jack Parsons was, of course one of the more famous Masons and occultists involved with The Order. Back in the 1970's the CIA began researching ways to accomplish some of the tasks they needed done through rather unique methods. Most of this was based on our intelligence that the Russians were pouring a lot of resources into psychic research, and we couldn't let them beat us at anything during the cold war. A few highly-placed and open minded thought leaders turned their attention to the occult as a way to determine if, firstly, the phenomenon they described were real, and secondly if we could use them to find practical applications for our needs."

"What? How does that even fit together?" I asked doubtfully.

"Parsons was already working with the government on rockets and some of his research, and at some point he got into a philosophical discussion with someone he didn't know was a part of our Special Projects. He mentioned some things from his experiences with The Order and occult activities, which led us to

The Monroe Institute, a group of scientists who were working on the very same things we were looking for."

"Which was?" I asked.

"The ability to bend energy, time, space, create astral projections, do remote viewing, self-healing...all things which the occult groups have been saying were possible since the first Buddhist and Zen monks. After the run in with Parsons the idea was passed along that, if it really were achievable, it would have tremendous military applications. But unfortunately we weren't the only ones going down that path, and our enemies in the east had a millennia head start researching those practices."

"Ok, I've heard about that research in the CIA, but I still don't understand...why me, why Natalie and what exactly are you telling me?"

Jim thought for a moment.

"Perhaps it's time to pivot again. You've had physics, advanced chemistry and biochemistry courses in your medical studies, and given your occult background in Masonry and The Order I don't think I'm going to be teaching you anything new here. But I am telling you that we have been throwing an awful lot of money and government scientists at these practices for over forty years, and it's real."

He paused to ensure I was caught up and ready to listen, then continued.

"Dr. Bob Monroe had been studying a technology he called HemiSync, which used methods to communicate directly with the right brain to achieve things that people can't typically do, bypassing the filter of the left brain and allowing the right brain to fully control all of a human's abilities. Furthermore, we began studying highly advanced quantum physics to understand the true essence of energy, time, space and the like to discover how we could affect these laws of nature in order to accomplish our military and intelligence objectives."

"Using people's brains to bend time and space?" I asked.

"Yes, sort of. It's more accurate to say we found ways to allow people to become more in tune with the energy and consciousness of the universe, finding mechanisms to transmit their mental state beyond their bodies, giving them an ability to know things they wouldn't normally, do things that can't be done in the physical body, see things in places we had no access to and project themselves into other locations instantaneously, without the need for a plane flight to travel across the world."

"Remote viewing and astral projection?" I asked.

"Precisely," Jim replied.

Tapping on the table in front of us, he asked, "what is this table made of, Rob?"

"I'm not sure, maybe some acrylic on the top and metal underneath?" I answered.

"You're thinking about the table as we observe it. At its most basic level, what is this table made of?

"Millions of atoms?" I asked.

"Correct. But more importantly, even though we perceive it as a solid object, much like the sky that we perceive as blue, in reality it is comprised of millions of tiny atoms, held closely together but each maintaining its own frequency and vibration, not really sitting still but in a constant state of movement. Now, what is it between the particles *within* the atoms that makes up the majority of these objects we observe as solid?"

"Space," I responded.

"Empty space."

"That's what we used to think," Jim countered.

"But that space is actually comprised of energy. We have found there are two basic forms of energy in our existence, and this requires you to go beyond the thoughts of electricity or kinetic energy. The two types of energy in our world are constrained and unconstrained. While the energy which makes up the space between the particles in the atoms which form this table are constrained to the confines of those atoms, the rest of the universe is comprised of unconstrained, limitless and infinite energy that is in, around and between everything we see."

"Isn't that what Nikolai Tesla was studying?" I asked.

"Sort of," Jim replied.

"But our research was going in a different direction than Tesla. Not how to use that energy to power things with electricity, but how to change and bend the natural laws of matter and the universe."

"Those are some pretty heavy insights to come from a guy in an Army uniform, Jim," I joked.

"Boy you don't know the half of it," he replied with a laugh and smiled before continuing.

"Because energy is everywhere and in everything, if we could learn how to tune in to that energy, which we discovered an ability to do using the vibrations of the energy around us, we found we can do pretty much whatever we want. Almost like dialing a phone number to call the right corresponding phone, all we had to do was find the correct frequencies and tune in to them."

"Okay, I've been reading up on this kind of stuff for a few years, so I follow. But I still don't understand how Jacob is alive or why you need me and Natalie. And how did you find this technology?"

"That's all an extension of what I already told you. Like I said, we were searching everywhere and throwing money in all directions to accomplish these goals. We tried drugs like LSD and DMT, we tried the MK Ultra program, we tried a lot. But Dr. Monroe had been showing promising results in his own private experiments long before we got in contact with him. Jacob was one of the first people to go through The Gateway project with the Monroe Institute back in the 1970's. He's been doing this for decades, and has found ways to tune himself into just about everything. If the mind can imagine it, he can do it."

"But how is he alive again? Or still alive?" I asked.

"When Moshe said Jacob cannot die, it was a very high level and summarized version of the truth. Westerners believe time is a linear thing...there is a beginning, middle and end. That the moment in which you and I are currently is somewhere along a line going from one end to another, and is just a chain in a long string of events which will progress and be gone forever once it passes."

Jim took another sip of his coffee, the wheels still turning in his head and trying to find the best way to explain.

"One of the things we've discovered is that time is not linear. Rather than thinking of a line with a beginning, middle and end, time is more like a giant wheel with spokes emanating from the center out towards the different realities which are all happening at the same instant. Have you ever heard of string theory or the multiverse concept?" he asked.

"Sure, when I was doing my pre-med at UCLA there were diagrams and studies lining the walls of the hallways I would walk to my physics classes," I answered.

"No there weren't," Jim smiled.

"Excuse me? I think that's what got me so interested in the idea, from walking those hallways and seeing this science that was so far out there I could hardly contemplate it, yet was being studied at prestigious universities and research labs around the world," I responded.

"This is neither the time nor the place to get into that, Rob. Just understand those diagrams were a part of a reality you were meant to see, but others walking those hallways were seeing something else. We have enough big-brained information to download in a short time, we don't need to visit that now. Just listen."

"What we've found in our studies is that if you can use certain techniques which have been used by occult groups and mystics for centuries, you can tune yourself into the very vibrations which make up the universe and travel along the spokes of this time wheel as you see fit. It's by no means easy, but we developed technology to help people enact these feats after some minor training, rather than taking decades of transcendental meditation practice like it takes the Zen monks."

"So you're telling me Jacob was able to travel this spoke and get out of the house before he died?"

"No," replied Jim.

"What I'm telling you is the Jacob you saw today was a different Jacob than the one who died in the compound. Well, not really different, but the same Jacob from a different time. Not a different century or anything like that, but from a different point on the wheel of time."

"Ok this is getting a little far out for me, Jim," I said and began to push my chair back from the table.

"I've read about all this stuff and can kind of follow where you're going, and you've shown me enough that I'm going to trust you on this, but I still don't understand where Natalie and I tie into all this."

He looked around the room for a moment, seeming to be scanning for something.

"Do you remember when I told you that our enemies had been working on this for a long time before we even began?" he asked.

"I do."

"The reason they had such a head start on this is because many in the eastern cultures had been studying some form of meditation or meditative practices, whether it be Zen, transcendental, yoga or tai chi for their entire lives. What we've found is that, though we've built technology which can help speed up the process and allow people to jump into these vibrational frequencies at will, it seems the more practice the person has with it already, the stronger they are once we engage the process."

"So because Natalie is sensitive, you feel she would be well suited to use it?"

Jim's face lit up with a smile and he sat back for a moment, looked me in the eye and continued.

"Now you're starting to get it. She's at a place, having never used our technology, that would most likely put her on par with if not ahead of Jacob, who's been doing it for forty years."

"How in the world could you know that?" I asked.

"Jacob, Moshe and I have visited her. Like I said, this technology and the vibrations allow them to be anywhere, at any time, they see fit. She is powerful enough that she can hide her exact physical location, but her energy is so strong it creates a ripple in the universe's energy and stream of consciousness. So while we've never met in person, we've met in, let's say, our energy fields."

"You're starting to lose me again, Jim." I interjected.

"Ok, so she's really powerful, I got it. Why do you need me? Was I just a chauffeur to get her here?"

"This is where the algorithms kick back in," he responded.

"Do you remember your initiation ceremony for the second level of The Order?" he asked.

"Of course," I replied.

"I was working as a contractor in Afghanistan to save money for med school."

"You didn't think it would work because you weren't there in person, did you?" he smiled knowingly.

When I nodded in the affirmative, he continued.

"But the process of doing the remote initiation primed you into the specific energy we need right now."

"What are you talking about?" I asked.

"What happened when you performed that ceremony? I don't need the specifics about the preparation, but what did you see when you closed your eyes?"

"Well, my mentor told me to meditate and imagine being in space. He told me to open myself up to messages, gave me a grouping of symbols to picture should anything go wrong and envision a triangle in the center of my field of consciousness as I floated throughout the universe."

"Ok, and what happened next?"

"I did as they asked, but after what seemed like a few minutes I saw a bright light appear in the distance. It grew brighter and brighter, and then began to take the form of a symbol I didn't recognize. The symbol flew through the triangle and came into me. As soon as it did, another ball of light appeared and took the shape of another symbol I didn't know, and the process went on for a long time."

"Did you see any of those symbols today, Rob?"

"Yes. I saw them above the doors and in the temple...just who in the hell are you, Jim? How do you know this?"

"I was the person on the other end who was initiating you."

Bulldog was standing on the tarmac in North Carolina when the C-130 began its descent to land.

He toiled with mixed emotions as the plane's wheels touched down and he walked to meet the door as it came to a stop in an unmarked hangar apart from the rest.

The other men of the team were still off with the Daemons, fighting alongside some of the finest warriors of their age with the most powerful and accurate weapons to ever have been built. But while they waged war and decimated the enemy on our soil with each passing hour, Bulldog was still locked at the flagpole.

The cesspool and toxicity of leaders who had abandoned their training and SOF truths had grown ever more apparent to him. He had begun to believe the Generals and Colonels had completely forgotten they were now essentially warlords rather than military officers.

Yet instead of fighting and leading from the front with their men, they chose to work to preserve their legacy and future promotions.

They had taken to creating regulations for the men, trying not so much to bring order to chaos as add bullet points to their resumes.

While these so-called leaders were focused on how to further their careers after the invasion ended, those involved in the actual fighting of the war had become so disgusted with them they did everything they could to stay away from the flagpole.

The environment had devolved into something so unwelcoming and stifling to the real warriors that they didn't come back to the base unless absolutely necessary.

And why would they? Coming back offered nothing more than a reminder that the support personnel were no longer focused on supporting the warfighter, as was their duty, but instead were intent on stealing whatever new tools, weapons and equipment came in for themselves to look cool to others.

While the warfighters had to make due with battlefield recoveries and the good people of the land they were protecting for food and supplies, the men staying on the bases were decked out in the newest and best gear for their daily trips to the chow hall.

It had come to a head with the men of 022 on their last convoy to Fort Bragg to refit between missions and meet with the intelligence units for future target acquisition.

As always, JLo and a few of the others had gone to see Bulldog before anything else.

Caught up in the camaraderie and his joy of seeing the men and hearing of their exploits, he had forgotten to warn them about the new climate around the flagpole.

They had been living off MRE's, local farmers and meat from their hunts for about a month, so after an initial catching up Bulldog took them to eat some hot food from one of the base chow halls.

In line to receive their first real meal in quite some time, JLo had been accosted by a Sergeant Major who had, as the rest of the leadership, forgotten they were in a warzone.

The dirty uniforms and unkempt beards of unconventional warfare were not to the liking of this particular Sergeant Major and before Bulldog could step in to stop the escalating situation, JLo lost his ability to keep his disgust of the support team and leadership hidden any longer.

As the Sergeant Major flew back from JLo's blow he was unconscious in mid-air, and Bulldog knew they only thing they could do was run.

There would be no explaining of the stress of daily combat missions to this leadership team, those who had long forgotten that war did not exist within the headquarters and was not fought by delivering PowerPoint presentations or creating new and stifling regulations.

Their goodbyes were fast and brief, and Bulldog knew he would not be able to see them again until he left the flagpole...if even then.

His rank and position had been enough to get them out of the front gate and on their way, but as much as it killed him inside, that was all he could do for them.

But now the situation had changed.

As the crew door opened from the C-130, Bulldog watched as a few familiar faces from past wars emerged alongside new ones, each pair of men bearing the flag of a different country and insignia of a Special Operations unit from our allies.

The first two were British SAS commandos, led by Harry, with whom Bulldog and 022 had run missions and coordinated intelligence in Afghanistan on his first deployment with the team.

To his surprise, the next men were from the Polish Grom, both of whom had trained and fought with 022 as they helped stand up the unit.

Third to emerge were French Commandos Marine, one of whom Bulldog recognized from his second deployment to Afghanistan, who had worked with 022 and the French Foreign Legion in the murderous mountains of the infamous Tagab Valley.

The next grouping were a pair of tall, Viking looking men who, upon closer inspection of patches and flags were members of the elite German KSK. Having lived in Germany for several years Bulldog felt he should have known the two, but his mind drew a blank and he couldn't place any further connection than their nation of origin.

The last group were a pair of jovial Aussies, soldiers from the famed SASR unit who Bulldog had helped to gather intelligence for on missions but had never worked with.

Jim had sent him a heads up the men were inbound as soon as their plane took off from Austin.

The General, he and Jim each had doubts about whether meeting the self-serving politician officers at the flagpole was truly the best move, thinking it may sour any chances they had of help coming from abroad.

But this was a substantial part of the war as it was being fought.

As much as it pained them, it would be necessary for the allies to be read on to the current operations and meet those so called leaders in order to plan the logistics of bringing their units onto our soil for a final push to wipe out the enemy.

As Bulldog looked down at the pavement in front of him, hoping they had made the right choice he heard a familiar voice ring out.

"Oy, Bulldog, is that you? How you going mate?"

"Harry!" he exclaimed, pulled away from his regrets and happy to see an old friend and fellow warrior.

Bulldog extended his hand and walked forward to meet the group, but as they came within closing distance Harry dropped his bags, slapped Bulldog's hand away and went in for a bear hug.

"Brothers don't shake hands mate, they hug!"

Bulldog had forgotten that amidst all the missions and planning they had shared during their time in Afghanistan, there had been a lot of down time spent watching old American movies and drinking tea.

Especially early 1990's comedies, which for some reason the Brits and Aussies had really loved.

So much so, that one could predict which one of about five films would be playing on a loop in their team house all day long on any given day, and the tag lines from those movies had become their running jokes amongst the teams.

As they separated from their embrace, Harry took a step back and continued in his love-for-life and joking manner.

"So I hear you Yanks are in a pickle. Good thing your tougher older Brothers are here to help you out."

"Glad you could finally join us, Harry," Bulldog replied with a grin.

"We prefer to make a grand entrance. You know, you're never late as long as somebody will wait for you."

He took a moment to contemplate what in the world it even met, but Harry moved on without pause.

"Jim tells me I need to get my lips ready for some major butt kissing and told me to bring my waders. He says I'm about to spend quite a bit of time wading through large amounts of horse manure. What say you, mate?"

Bulldog smiled and winked at Harry.

"I'll fill you in while we walk. Let me lead you guys to your quarters and we'll talk about that somewhere by ourselves."

Along their walk, he filled Harry in on the current enemy situation, what was going on as far as the east coast was concerned, and when pressed about the other men from 022 Bulldog told him the story of the Daemons, the ever-growing constrained leadership environment and the uppercut via JLo which had banished 022 from the base.

"I freaking love that guy," Harry laughed after Bulldog filled him in about JLo.

"When can we go see him?"

"What do you mean?"

"Well, our mission here isn't to sit in offices and listen to stuffy old windbags all day. We need to get out and about to have a look at the real war here. If we're going to do that I don't want to roll out with a bunch of support personnel who've never fired a shot in anger before. How do we link up with the boys to get the lay of the land and see just how much trouble you Yanks are in?"

Hidden behind an outcropping of small rocks and partially buried in the ground, The Major carefully stared through his binoculars for a few minutes and spoke to Josh, who was looking through a pair of his own.

"Are you sure that's him?"

"Positive. Meda's people at the casino have been talking for several days about heightened security measures with the Russians. They've been overhearing hushed conversations in back rooms between the higher ups that Creeping Death was on his way. We thought it was some new weapons system they would be employing, but it was confirmed yesterday that it's actually this guy."

The Major stared intently across the casino courtyard and watched the figure emerge from his sleek, black armored car. It was readily apparent that everyone around the immense Russian man was terrified of him by their actions and inability to look him directly in the eye.

The reason became clear as he backhanded the first officer who emerged from the front doors, approaching with downturned eyes and a slight hunch of shame.

"I wish I could hear what they're saying," added The Major.

He watched as the figure towered over his now cowering comrade, spoke a few more words and finished the deed with a swift kick to his face while still trembling on his hands and knees.

The blow sent a spray of blood the men could see from even a mile away, and the colossal man stood up straight, grabbed his own uniform by the lapels to straighten it and walked into the casino.

"We will," Josh responded.

"The casino workers in their party are part of Meda's ears on the inside. They'll report back tonight with a very thorough accounting of what's going on in there."

When Josh and The Major arrived back at the golf course the team was assembled and waiting for their brief. Meda and Josh had been feverishly collecting intel since the operation on the port in San Diego, and it seemed their world had suddenly become a target-rich environment.

The physical damage had been minuscule in the grand scheme of things. The ships were stopped in the harbor for a few days and oil supply had been briefly interrupted, but before the team had returned to their base the enemy had already started repairing the carnage their explosives had delivered.

The deterioration to the enemy's morale had been much more significant.

It had been highly touted by the Russians in Colorado that the DIA hit several months previously had been nothing more than a fluke, an attack perpetrated by a rag-tag group of rebels who had been lucky in the commotion and chaos of the early invasion.

Their raid on the port, however, had not been quite so easy to hide or explain away.

This was not a simple airport in the middle of the country. No matter how big of an operation and how extensive the damage they had done in Colorado, that was still half a nation away from their main forces on either coast, and the leadership had been able to keep its true news quiet.

But the port had been the point of embarkation for both nations' soldiers making the trip into the combat zone which was now America. And there had been far too many prying eyes and loose lips for even the heavy-handed communist military leadership to keep hidden.

Fallout from the explosions had landed far north up the coast of California and south into Mexico. The fireball had been seen by troops on both the front lines of the war and those new arrivals coming off ships.

The minor cessation in the flow of oil had also disrupted their logistics.

Although it only lasted for a few days, the gossip which had started when soldiers couldn't fuel up their vehicles had been impossible for the leadership to stop.

The operation had been the first real dent in the enemy armor on the west coast.

Reports of guerrillas and partisans on the east coast had been slowly finding their way back to the headquarters in Los

Angeles, and the attack on the port had turned the gossip and horror stories into a reality.

They now understood that America was fighting back, and each of them were a target.

The Russian and Chinese leadership knew if they were to maintain their momentum and finish this war, they would have to eliminate those responsible for the attack with an immense amount of violence.

If they could take one or two alive and broadcast their deaths to the troops, or place their dead bodies on display it would put an end to the terror which had begun to sweep through their forces.

But the men of 022 had other plans.

"His name is Major Dmitri Gorbunov," Josh began from the front of the room.

"He joined the Russian military as an infantry soldier, but quickly found his way into the elite Spetsnaz. The man is an absolute bear, and if he were an American he's in the kind of pure, unadulterated and tenacious physical shape you typically only find in professional football players or MMA fighters."

Josh looked around the room as he flashed a picture from Dmitri's earlier days on the screen for everyone to see.

"He earned the nickname Creeping Death, or *Polzuchaya Smert* in Russian, for some of his deeds in the Afghan war. Not our Afghan war, mind you...this dude was there in the 1980's long before we started our campaigns there."

"What kind of stuff did he do?" Tyler asked from the back of the room.

"Your run-of-the-mill terrible and evil human being stuff. He likes to flay prisoners alive without even asking them questions. He finds it to be fun. He particularly enjoys bringing the families of his captives into the cell with them and orders his men to rape the women and decapitate the boys in front of them before he starts cutting off their skin. From some reports he prefers to leave the bodies in the cell so they have to stare at their dead families as they die. Oh yeah, and he cuts off their eyelids first so they can't look away."

"Jesus," replied Tyler.

"Sorry I asked."

"No, actually it's a good thing. You need to know the type of person we're dealing with here. I need each of you to understand that if we get caught going after this guy, as long as he lives we will not. And it will likely be the most terrible form of death you can imagine. Hell, this devil is so creative in his dark soul I don't think we have the capacity to think up the kind of stuff he does. Not even you, Ray."

Josh paused for a moment, anticipating a wisecrack comment from Ray. But there was nothing funny about this subject, so none came.

Sensing he needed a moment to continue the brief, The Major stepped in.

"It seems our hit on the port opened up Pandora's box and led the Russians and Chinese to pull out all the stops to find us. They've brought in their top intelligence officers and increased their number of Special Operations forces substantially after our operation, and have asked them to take the gloves off and do whatever needs to be done to put a stop to our missions."

Having composed himself, Josh stepped back in to continue the briefing.

"After the Russians left Afghanistan, Dmitri was brought into the KGB and then SVR when the former folded, and tasked as an operative doing some of the nastiest jobs that we know of to ever come out of the iron curtain. This guy is not only strong and hard as coffin nails, but he's also whip smart. Besides torturing people and burning kittens alive he's a bit of a chess aficionado and his position allowed him to play, and beat, several of the Russian grandmasters."

"What does that have to do with war?" Klint asked from his post standing against the wall on the side of the room.

"It means he's a smart son of a bitch," answered The Major.

"And he's been on to us for a long time," added Josh.

"What do you mean?" inquired Ray.

"Dmitri has been supervising the unconventional warfare and psychological operations for the Russians. As soon as we hit the airport in Denver he set his teams on finding us. He was leading the operation to attack our first compound, he was in the gunship that attacked us and got away on the highway to Austin and he's been looking for us ever since."

"Great," added Jason.

"So the devil is in our backyard and looking for us? Awesome."

"Not the devil," replied The Major.

"Creeping Death."

"So why him?" Chad asked.

"I mean if this guy is such a tough SOB, why not leave him alone and go after another big target to disrupt the enemy's operations. Isn't that our mission?"

"That's an option," answered Josh.

"But if we don't take him down, he's going to take us down. I don't know how he's seemed to find us at every turn, even after we left Colorado, but somehow he has. And as long as he's alive, he is our biggest threat."

"So how do we do it?' Klint pondered out loud.

"How do we draw him out from his security team and take him down without getting greased ourselves?"

"Every man enjoys a vice," was Josh's reply.

"Dmitri is no different, and he's enjoying as much of it as he can stand tonight at the casino."

"Meda's casino?" asked Jason.

"That very same one indeed," responded Chris from his seat.

"We had intelligence he moved from his base in Los Angeles down to San Diego after our operation. And as soon as he arrived, he began looking for a place away from their flagpole where he could let off some steam to clear his head before he started the push to take us down. Josh and The Major surveilled him arriving at the casino this morning, and we're just waiting for word from Meda's people to know when the time is right."

"When the time is right for what?" asked Tyler.

"Aside from murdering innocent people, Dmitri has a fondness for drinks, drugs and exotic women. Meda has ensured he'll have plenty of each, and placed a few specific ladies at his service tonight. We're going to have to be ready, when we get the signal we'll need to move fast. We're taking down the casino to get him."

"But that place is crawling with Russian soldiers, how are we going to do that?" Chad wondered out loud.

"Meda knows the casino's layout better than anyone else, and in case you're forgetting we have a hundred trained fighters on our side to help, along with the weapons and explosives that we've procured. We have people placed inside that will let us know what's going on. She has the access codes to tap into their audio and visual security systems both in and outside of the hotel, and of course we have us," answered Josh.

"Well okay then," smiled Ray. "Let's get to work."

CHAPTER 9

LOVE SONG / LAST DANCE OF THE WARRIORS

After Jim's new download of information I needed both a little fresh air and a dose of reality to bring me back to earth.

With my head still spinning to understand all that I had learned over the last hour, Jim begrudgingly agreed to allow me to go and see my kids, get some rest and then come back to him with an answer.

I still wasn't sure how I fit into all of it, or why he thought that I was a good candidate for The Gateway project. But I owed him the respect to at least take some time to think about it.

As always, seeing and wrapping my kids in my embrace was just what I needed to ground and pull me back to reality. It hadn't been long since I stepped on the plane to fly back to California, but it felt as if I hadn't held them in my arms for ages.

And the fear I had that I would never hold them again when the helicopter meant to carry me back to them had been shot down was finally subsided.

They had been playing with the other children when I walked through the doorway unannounced, and before I could even find them in the group I saw two short and fast-moving heads full of hair racing towards me screaming "daddy!"

We were still in the playroom sharing our reacquainting hello when the thought occurred to me: Natalie's daughter wasn't much older than my kids, and there were a few teenagers in our group that her son could potentially hang out and make friends with.

As I contemplated whether I should introduce them, there was a knock at the door.

As I turned, Jim's aide was standing with Natalie's children on either side of him.

"Rob, Jim thinks it may be a good idea for you to introduce Noah and Ava Luna to the other kids. So they can make new friends, you know? He and Natalie are pretty busy right now, but..."

Smiling, I stood and motioned for the kids to come in.

"Great timing, I was just thinking the same thing."

Without hesitation the kids walked into the room and knelt next to me. As Jim's aide turned to leave, I made the introductions.

"Ava Luna, this is Robert. He's a little younger than you, but I think you two will get to be best friends in no time."

As I stood to take Noah and introduce him to the other teenagers, Robert and Avery gripped my legs tightly for a moment, but slowly loosened and they approached Ava Luna.

"Let me show you our toys!" Robert exclaimed.

Smiling, I watched as the three made their way towards the toy bins and started pulling out their favorite ones to play together.

"Where are the teenagers?" I asked Jason's wife Deanna, who was sitting at the front of the room reading to a smaller group of the little ones.

"They're in the TV room playing video games."

She stole a brief glance at Noah and then back to me.

"Who is this, Rob?" she asked.

"Where did he come from?"

"These are Natalie's kids."

"Who's Natalie?"

"That's a long story, but I'm sure we'll get around to it sooner rather than later."

I looked to Noah and then over at the little ones, busying themselves with their new friend and blind to the rest of the world while playing with their toys.

"This is Noah, and the girl with my kids is Ava Luna. They joined our group in California and we arrived back here together this morning."

Deanna took a moment to look me up and down, knowing that I had a huge spot in my heart for children. But also that it had been quite some time since I had mentioned any woman's name who wasn't part of the group.

"Natalie, huh?" she asked.

"Is she cute?"

"We'll have to cover that at another time, but you can see for yourself. She's downstairs with Jim, Moshe and Jacob right now but I'm sure she'll be up for introductions later."

"Jacob?" she asked.

"Our Jacob?"

Realizing that none of the others had been in on my download from Jim and not sure if I had just let a cat out of the bag that was meant to be kept in, I sidestepped the train of conversation.

"No, no it's a different one. That would be crazy. I'm going to take Noah to meet the big kids, and I'll make sure Natalie comes up to say hello. Can you keep an eye on the little ones for me? It's been a few days since I've slept and I don't think I can stay on my feet much longer."

Deanna hesitated for a moment, sensing holes in my story but let me go reluctantly.

"Of course, Rob. But before you go, is everyone ok? Why didn't you all come back together?"

I hadn't thought about how strange it must seem that once again I was returning without the team. But having neither the time, energy nor approved information to pass along I did what I could to put her mind at ease.

"Jason and the rest of the guys are fine. It's been pretty busy over there, but we got some reinforcements and they have a nice place to sleep as their headquarters. Everything is ok, I'm sure they'll be back before you know it."

"Did you see all the foreign troops that were here?" she asked.

"Foreign troops?"

"A small group showed up in their trucks two days ago and flew out yesterday morning. I think they're going to meet with the guys on the east coast."

"Huh. No, I didn't see or know about that. There was word that we were supposed to bring some new friends back with us to the west coast, but that's all I know. I'll see what I can find out and report back to you as soon as I get some rest."

"Of course," she smiled.

"Sorry to pump you for information. It's just...there's so much going on around here and they don't really tell us anything."

"I understand, Deanna," I replied.

"Things are moving so fast now that it's hard for any of us to know what's going on. But I'll link up with Jim today and discover what I can for you guys."

"Thank you," she smiled.

"Now get some sleep!"

The teenagers were three doors down, in a recreational room that had a television and some couches which the small group had turned into their lair of sorts.

The sound of gunfire startled me as I opened and walked through the doorway, but seeing the tv screen put me back at ease.

"Is that Battlefield?" Noah asked as he entered the room.

Not recognizing the voice, each of the teenagers turned around to face us and focused their attention on him.

Seeing me with him must have been all of the introduction they needed, because they only hesitated for a short instant.

"Of course," one of them said from the couch, not removing his eyes from the game emblazoned on the screen.

"You any good?"

"Hell yeah I am," he answered.

"It's been awhile since I last played, but I've beaten it a few times. Where are you?"

Noah promptly left my side and walked to join the group, seemingly forgetting that I was even there. Seeing him being absorbed into the crowd so fast let me know that my job there was done and it was time to grab some much needed rest.

I awoke from a nightmare just a few hours later, sweating and startled. The room lights were off and Natalie was sitting at the edge of my bed.

"How long have you been here?" I asked her.

"Not long," she replied.

"Was I talking in my sleep?"

"No, but I could tell that whatever you were dreaming about, it wasn't pleasant."

Swinging my feet over and placing them on the ground I sat up to try and shake the cobwebs and terrible visions from my head. As soon as I could fully open my eyes, she handed me a hot cup of coffee.

"What was it about?"

"Huh?'

"Your dream. What was it about?"

"Can't you sneak inside my head and see that?"

"No, it doesn't work like that."

I thought for a few moments, still foggy from the sleep and sore from the days of missions and long drive from California.

"So how does it work, then? I'm still not entirely sure what *it* is. But I'm curious."

"I don't really know myself. All I know is that I've been able to see things since I was a little kid. Some are things that other people can't see, some are things that have happened long ago, some are things that will happen. As I grew older the visions became stronger, and I gained my discipline over them a little at a time. I met someone in my twenties who helped me refine my abilities, taught me about meditation and how to work with energy fields. Since then I've worked a little bit each day to learn to control it. Sometimes that's good, sometimes it's bad."

"Bad how?' I asked.

"Just don't make me angry. You wouldn't like me when I'm angry."

She saw my startled look and laughed as she slapped my shoulder.

"Oh my God I'm sorry. Noah is a huge comic book fan and, well, you set yourself up for that one!"

I laughed a little myself and the humor helped to clear my head.

"Ok wiseguy, funny stuff. Why don't I take you to meet everyone? Have you seen the kids yet?"

"No but I'd love to. And would you mind introducing me to some of the other people around the base also? I feel like a total stranger and have been getting some weird looks."

"Of course, if you don't mind giving me a moment to get dressed I'll take you to see the kids and meet our group."

Natalie sat at the edge of my bed still staring at me.

"Uh, that means can you please go outside while I put my pants on?"

"Why so bashful now? You know I've been able to see you naked anytime I wanted since we first met?"

I could feel the inside of my cheeks begin to blush as she burst out laughing and hit my shoulder again.

"Oh man, that's funny. No, in case you're wondering that's not how it works either. But you make it too easy sometimes. I'll be waiting in the hallway."

Natalie winked at me as she rose and walked to the door, pausing before opening it as if she had something to say but decided against it. When the door closed behind her, I laughed out loud to myself.

"Beautiful and funny. You're screwed, buddy."

We found the rest of the group outside, with the mothers mingling while the kids played on the playground. As I introduced Natalie to everyone and they began talking, Deanna answered her own question from earlier.

"She is cute Rob. You're in trouble."

Without affording me the opportunity to reply, she turned to Natalie.

"Rob's single you know. And he's a great father, decent cook and I hear he's amazing in bed."

"Oh is he now?" Natalie smirked in a sarcastic tone and hit me on the shoulder again.

"Thanks for that, Deanna," I blushed and smiled.

"Any time. Now why don't you two go find something to do without us. We've got the kids covered, you guys go get lost. Say Rob, aren't you from around here? Why don't you show Natalie the city? This town is so safe that the soldiers go home at night, and you do have a car..."

Still blushing from Deanna's previous comment, I realized that her idea wasn't half bad. I had spent my undergrad college years in Austin and hadn't been out in civilization for fun since the invasion started.

"There's just one thing that I need to do first."

I turned to Natalie.

"Would you mind excusing me for a few minutes? I have to check with Jim on something."

"Of course," Natalie responded jokingly.

"I'll just stay here and ask about your deepest and most embarrassing secrets."

I smiled and bowed to Deanna and the rest of the group.

"In that case, I'll leave you to it. Ladies..."

I found Jim in the TOC, the place it seemed that I could always find him. Brushing passed his aide, I was a little embarrassed to ask him for the favor I needed.

"Rob, what can I help you with?"

I glanced sheepishly down at the ground, trying to formulate the question. It was one which I hadn't had to ask since I graduated from medical school and starting bringing in a considerable amount of money, after being a poor college student for so long after the Army.

"Uh, Jim. I'm not sure how to ask you this, so I'll just ask...can I borrow some cash?"

"What?" he asked surprised.

"Well I wanted to go out and see the town, and I don't have any cash."

"Interesting," Jim said, looking amused.

"And what, may I ask, are you planning on doing?"

"I want to go out and visit some of my old haunts from college, you know, seeing if they're still around. Maybe grab a bite to eat, have a drink if I can still do that sort of thing."

"Alone?" he asked.

"Not really," I countered.

"I was planning on taking Natalie along with me."

"Ah, I understand," Jim smirked knowingly and rocked on his heels.

"She is pretty cute, isn't she?"

"It's not like that," I began, but he cut me off.

"I'm just messing with you, Rob. Of course, you can have anything you like."

Jim snapped his fingers and motioned his aide to come over to us.

"Give him all of your cash," Jim commanded.

"Excuse me sir?"

"Cash, give him all of your cash. Hell, give him all of my cash too."

"Sir?"

"It's not that difficult son. Take out your wallet, give him the cash inside, give him my cash that you keep for me and he'll be on his way."

The aide pulled a wallet from his uniform pocket and produced two crisp twenty dollar bills.

"Are you serious?" Jim asked.

"Don't we pay you?"

"Well sir, we had to pay for the deliveries this morning, and we still have the intel sources who get paid in cash, and..."

"That dog just won't hunt," Jim scowled back at his aide.

"I tell you what. I want you to take up a collection from every man in this TOC. Tell them we'll pay them back, but we need forty dollars from every man in here, now."

The aide hesitated and met Jim's immediate ire.

"First dates ain't cheap ya' dimwit. GET!!!"

As his aide began moving to the various men sitting at their desks, I turned to Jim to protest.

"Sir, I didn't mean to cause all of this trouble. I'll figure something out..."

"Nonsense," he cut me off.

"If anyone in this building has won the right for a little R&R, it's you. The boys in here spend all day at a computer and then go home to their families at night because of the warfighters keeping the enemy at bay. It's the least we can do."

Jim seemed to have another thought to add, but his aide reappeared with a fistfull of cash.

"Here you go sir," he stammered.

"Not for me, dummy. It's for Rob," he said gesturing to me.

Jim's aide moved his arm to the side to hand me the money. I looked back to Jim for a moment to make sure it was ok, and he nodded in affirmation.

"Have fun, Rob. We're safe here in Austin, but there are a lot of people looking for her. Keep your eyes open, but have fun. Get to know each other a little better."

As I stuffed the cash in my pocket and turned to leave I felt Jim's hand on my shoulder stopping me.

"But when you return, I'll need an answer from you about our previous discussion."

"Roger that sir," I called as I walked out of the TOC and towards the playground.

After a full day of briefings, puffery and dog & pony shows, both Bulldog and the visitors were at the end of their patience.

"I don't know how much more of this I can take mate," Harry whispered in Bulldog's ear as one Captain left the room after his briefing and another entered to begin setting up his own.

"The other blokes here hardly speak english, I don't think they even know what's going on."

"Welcome to my own personal hell," Bulldog scowled.

They both scanned the men seated at the conference room table, seeing the Aussies, Germans and Poles nodding off and fighting back tears of boredom.

"This isn't exactly what we had in mind when we were ordered to come help you Yanks win the war."

"Yeah, me neither," replied Bulldog in his most sarcastic tone.

"But we have to check this box before we can do anything else."

"Any chance on getting out to visit the boys?"

"I got a call out to Matty while you were settling into your rooms. They won't come back on base...hell I don't think they *can* come back on base. But when you're ready, we can link up with them at their camp."

"I'm ready," Harry smiled.

"We're ready."

"I think we have a few more hours of briefings before we're done for the day," said Bulldog.

"Not me mate. I just met my limit."

Harry stood up in his seat to address the room.

"Excuse me, Captain?" he asked.

"I'm sorry but we have an urgent matter that we have to attend to. Our HQ just sent a communique that needs our immediate attention."

The Captain, not sure what to do, paused and stared at Harry blankly. Not hearing any response, Harry continued.

"So...we're...going to go. Sorry for the trouble, I'm sure this is a lovely presentation but we'll have to get your brief later. Cheerio, mate, we're off."

Harry snapped his fingers at the other members of his team to wake them out of their stupors.

They may not have understood english perfectly, but they sure did understand when he pointed to the door and announced "we're leaving."

It took an unthinkable amount of paperwork and even more haggling for Bulldog to procure enough armored vehicles for their excursion, and although he hated doing it, in the end it was only by pulling rank that they were able to secure the equipment needed.

Thankfully the foreign SOF soldiers had come equipped with their own weapons, for Bulldog believed in his heart of hearts that he would never have convinced the young arms room sergeant to part with any from the base, even though they were doing nothing more than collecting dust in a locker.

Their convoy set off in the general direction of the team's basecamp. The Daemons and 022 had been operating so far off the grid that even the command, with all of the intelligence capabilities of USASOC, had been unable to track them down.

His call to Matty a half hour into their drive told Bulldog they were headed in the wrong direction.

"We're in Virginia," Matty informed him.

"A few of the Army of Northern Virginia guys showed up at our camp this morning and told us that they were going to take back DC. They already had the militias, ground branch and a uniformed army in place. They said that if we wanted to take part, we'd have to get on the road immediately. Sorry I didn't call, but we really couldn't risk the leadership at Bragg finding out or they'd screw the whole thing up."

"Jiminy Christmas," Bulldog replied.

"So where do we meet you?"

Matty conveyed a list of grid coordinates to Bulldog, and after looking at his map he redirected their convoy to Allie Freed park, a wooded area several miles from the Pentagon yet still across the river from the White House.

Bulldog instructed his driver to pull over to the side of the road for him to relay the new plan to the rest of the team, needing keep the information off the radio to prevent its being intercepted

"They're taking back Washington DC without any help from the military? Have your boys gone mad?" Harry asked incredulously.

"They wouldn't tell you this in the briefings, but our boys have been doing so much damage to the enemy here on the east coast that they only have strongholds left in DC and New York City. The guys from Daemon Defense equipped our boys with rifles that were so powerful and accurate that all they had to do was leave enough standoff to be out of range of their weapons, put a few good shooters on the trigger and take them out from a distance. It's been exceptionally effective."

"I don't know how many snipers you have but you can't pick off enough troops from several armies to do that much damage...can you?"

"Well no, but it's caused havoc in their morale to the point that enemy soldiers are afraid to go out on patrols anymore. Add that to the mountain men, militias, patriots and partisans that came out of the woods and started fighting back immediately, and the resistance here was much more than the invaders ever anticipated."

"You Yanks really are a lovable but stubborn bunch mate," Harry joked.

"Hell, we learned it from fighting your predecessors in those very same areas over two hundred years ago. The times may have changed, but the American spirit never died, no matter how much the politicians who allowed this invasion tried."

They were driving along I-95 in no time, in a race to link up with their men and add whatever help they could lest they miss the battle or lose their brothers.

JLo and Matty, knowing some old friends were on their way in, were the first familiar faces the convoy met when they arrived at the woodline to be led in to the rest of the team.

When the trucks slowed to a halt, Harry emerged from the trail vehicle and walked to JLo with his hand extended.

"Good to see you mate! I hear you've been a naughty boy lately."

Coming in close and slapping Harry's extended hand away, JLo crouched down and exploded into Harry, pulling him into a suplex move that could only be delivered by a former wrestler, but ended in JLo holding him in the air in an enormous bear hug.

"Brothers don't shake hands you limey bastard. Brothers hug!"

The entire group, now standing outside of their vehicles, erupted in laughter.

"Matty, are we safe out here?" Bulldog asked.

"Sure, we've beaten them back across the river," he answered.

"The Army of Northern Virginia guys knew more about the security in the Pentagon than its new occupants, so we cleared the entire building this morning with a few hundred troops. We're directing our new efforts..."

Before JLo finished his sentence, the men heard the short hiss of a shoulder fired rocket and the empty trail vehicle exploded.

"My bad, follow me," JLo ordered to the group as he began sprinting for the woodline.

A volley of returning fire enveloped them, with forces hidden amongst the trees shooting at unseen enemy, and the enemy returning fire from somewhere close.

Once inside the woodline, Bulldog located the shooting as coming from a school building nestled a half kilometer away.

With only hand signals needed, Harry and Bulldog coordinated for the team to surround the building and enter through a door at the front, on the opposite side from which they were taking fire.

As Bulldog, JLo, Matty and the Germans moved through the woodline to follow the far side of the school's walls and encircle it, Harry, the Poles and Aussies moved to the closer wall.

The French commandos set into place behind an outcropping of rocks several hundred meters away, laying down a field of covering fire and forcing the enemy situated on the roof down for cover.

Bulldog was met with hostile fire as he rounded the corner to begin his movement along the school wall, but JLo was right behind him and neutralized the Arab holding an AK before he took his second step.

While the men continued along the wall they heard loud shouting in Arabic as the men on the roof tried to coordinate their counterattack.

"Thank God these dirtbags aren't very bright," Matty said as he pulled a frag grenade from his vest and tossed it up on the roof.

Bulldog and JLo each paused long enough to follow suit, and the resulting explosions threw an Arab with a shoulder-fired missile system onto the playground next to them screaming.

If the explosion hadn't killed him, the crunch of his neck as he landed head first into the hard concrete of the parking lot did.

The team heard the cracks of a few rounds on the other side of the building as Harry and his fire team encountered resistance of their own.

Three bursts of rapid succession double-taps signaled it was Harry and the boys taking down a few bad guys, but the steady stream of automatic fire from a Dshk machine gun told them that there was still trouble on that side.

Rounding the final corner and crossing to the front of the building, Bulldog took a knee before reaching the doors and turned to face the rest of the team.

Hand signals let them know to split into two columns, with one stopping to cover the front door from any enemy coming out while the second column would push forward and take out whatever position housed the Dshk and its triggermen.

The first column stopped and deliberately pied-off their aim to ensure nothing would be shooting out of the front door as the second team crossed its pathway.

When Bulldog led his column to the other side of the building they were met with the scorching heat of an explosion and more screaming in Arabic.

They rounded the corner to find a pit of smoking sandbags with the bodies of several Arabs strewn about in various pieces.

"That was fun!" Harry called out as his team followed him along the wall to meet Bulldog.

"Well it ain't over yet. Let's take down the rest of this school and then go help our friends," Bulldog countered.

The team split into smaller elements to clear each room in the building, and after ten minutes and several dead Arabs they were lined up on the ladder that would lead them to the roof.

Looking at the open ladder door leading through the ceiling, Harry laughed.

"These Arabs put so much trust in their holy war that they always forget to watch their six. Do you think as they're dying they finally realize Allah isn't on their side?"

"Not likely," Matty answered.

"I think they hold their righteousness up until they find themselves at the gates of hell with no seventy-two virgins in sight."

Being the superb athlete that he was, Matty was chosen to be the first man up the ladder. Harry climbed up behind him with a shirt full of grenades, the other men in waiting to climb as soon as the pair emerged onto the roof.

When Matty gave the signal, Harry began pulling the pins from his frag grenades and handing them up to him, who popped their final safeties and lobbed them in every direction atop the roof.

He ducked down and covered his head after the last throw, and a half-dozen explosions sounded in rapid succession.

The team watched as Matty counted each explosion. After the last one Matty scaled up the ladder and through the hatch to the roof as fast as he could, followed closely by Harry and the rest of the men.

The roof was now red with blood and littered with body parts of dead fighters strewn about. The mush was so thick that their boots were becoming slick and sticky while walking through the mayhem with thick, dark blood drying to the bottoms of their pants.

"You know," began Harry.

"I understood why the Russians and Chinese would be here when we started getting briefings. That was destined to happen, I reckon. But the Arabs...I never quite got that."

"They had a bone to pick with the US, come from an unforgiving culture and were expendable to the Russians and Chinese. What's so hard to understand?" asked Bulldog.

"Good point," replied Harry.

"But until this moment I really thought it was some sort of hoax."

"No hoax," said Matty.

"The Russians and Chinese wanted our resources. The Arabs wanted revenge. And based on what we saw during our time in the Middle East, I would say that's a much more promising motivation for their culture than resources could ever be."

"And you still let them all in here," added Harry.

"The influx of refugees from Syria put an awful lot of enemy on each of our shores. Even though they created massive problems in the UK, Germany, Sweden and Greece we always knew there was something in store for you lot over here in the states. But you just kept letting them in..."

"We're starting to find that may have been part of a larger plan," Bulldog growled sharply.

"Of course it was. They knew what they were doing," Harry replied.

"No, from our own politicians," said Bulldog.

"This entire invasion was an inside job. Aside from allowing in thousands of refugees from enemy states with no real background checks, the same politicians who called us bigots for saying they needed better vetting procedures began disarming the American populace and weakening our military to allow this. This was all part of their treasonous plan."

"So American politicians are just as crooked as ours in the UK? Tell me something I don't know, mate," laughed Harry.

"I guess that's one thing we can all agree on."

"Time to go," Josh shouted from the communications room out to the rest of the group.

The Major set in motion, grabbing his body armor and heading to the garage to get everyone moving.

"We got the call from Meda's people on the inside. Start the trucks and take your seats, let's go get this son of a bitch," he barked as he moved along the corridors.

Meda had connected the monitors at the golf course into all of the casino's security cameras, and had been receiving a constant stream of updates from her people.

Although the enemy was on a heightened alert status, they weren't stopping their men from enjoying themselves in the midst of war.

And Dmitri had been thoroughly enjoying himself.

He had been drinking his favorite vodka since the moment he arrived in his room, and had his way with several women of the night who were in the employ of the casino.

To the team's surprise he hadn't killed or hurt any of them yet, but the night was still young.

He had, however, exposed a few rather peculiar fetishes with one of the women, unknowing that his every move was being watched by a team waiting for the right moment to wipe his existence from the earth.

"Do you think Sarah would let me try that?" Ray asked Josh as they huddled around the screens, watching Dmitri begin to set up some unusual props to be used in a sadistic role playing game.

"I asked Jane about it once," he responded.

"She told me that if I even mentioned it again that I'd wake up missing my...and her...favorite part of me. So no Ray, I think that's a hard negative."

The casino wasn't located very far from the golf course. That detail had worried the leaders at first, but was now proving to be an invaluable trait, as they'd need speed and stealth to pull this mission off.

The plan was simple, or as simple as an all-out raid on an enemy-controlled casino could go.

The beginning of the mission was set in a way that the men of 022 had done hundreds of times previously. Their well-armed and trained fighters, Meda's men, would begin by surrounding the target (the casino in this case) and launching an all-out attack from the outside.

Although the soldiers inside had some sidearms, the team didn't anticipate it being much of an issue.

There was a reasonable amount of enemy security outside. But with the men of 022 knowing precisely where they were situated, what they were armed with and how many more would come to supplement their defenses, they wouldn't last long.

Dmitri and his security team, however, were a different story.

Although it was well known that he could hold his own should the need arise, his position within the Russian military and role in this war meant that he wasn't one whom they would let go easily.

But even after 022 took care of his security team they would still have Dmitri to deal with.

The sudden attack from outside, and drunk soldiers inside the casino filled with alcohol and drug-induced bravery would provide an advantageous environment in which the men of 022 thrived: chaos.

With Meda sitting in front of the monitors at the golf course and speaking to Josh and The Major through an encrypted signal, she would help them stay abreast of Dmitri's location, what his security team was doing and any unexpected ripples in the plan they had developed.

While the men of 022 had prided themselves on collecting an excellent amount of intelligence and conducting highly-organized and inscrutable planning prior to any mission they undertook, this was an ace-in-the-hole which they had never held before.

The casino was surrounded by hills, mountains and trees, providing the perfect cover for Meda's fighters to approach unseen and set into place for their attack.

Since each of the fighters also had an intimate knowledge of the area, the inside of the casino and where every enemy position was situated, they had an inordinate advantage over the unknowing enemy.

As planned, the attack began with shoulder-fired missiles aimed at the two sandbag bunkers lining either side of the front entrance, in which machine gun positions, anti-aircraft weapons and a handful of soldiers had been located.

The next volley of missiles were aimed at the front doors, planned as such to both make escape extremely difficult for the soldiers inside and create the most ensuing chaos possible.

When the enemy soldiers began to pour out of the rear and side entrances, they were allowed to scramble a reasonable distance from the doorways only to be picked off by Meda's fighters laying in wait.

The men wanted the soldiers to have at least a little hope that they could either fend off the attack or escape with their lives, but chiefly to clear as much of an entrance for the team as possible on their way in to find Dmitri, who was under constant surveillance by Meda back at the golf course.

Dmitri himself had been resting after a rather physical romp in the sack with one of his women, but the first missile finding its target was enough to bring him up and quickly putting on his uniform.

The two members of his security team who had been guarding the door were inside his room before the second volley of missiles hit, and they scrambled to figure out what was going on.

One of the guards keyed his radio to transmit word back to San Diego to scramble the gunships and attack helicopters to no avail.

As he re-keyed the handset and struggled to understand why it wasn't working, Meda laughed.

Jamming radio signals didn't require the most high-tech equipment in the world, and thanks to Meda's access to and knowledge of the casino it had been easier than imagined to have her people on the inside place a few frequency jammers hidden amongst various wires and computer equipment in the building the night before.

Of course this meant that Josh and The Major would lose their communication with Meda when they entered the building, but with their fighters surrounding the place and minute-by-minute updates on Dmitri's movements until they went in it was worth it to keep the gunships at bay until Dmitri was dead.

When the ground outside of the casino exits became so littered with piles of dead Russian soldiers that no more dared exit the building, the men knew it was time for their grand entrance.

Dmitri had made his way into the security control center for the casino, but finding each of the monitors disabled, he understood there would be no easy escape.

It was time for battle, and the warrior inside of him smiled.

The team had split into two elements, with Josh leading one through the East entrance and The Major leading from the winding stairs of the West.

They encountered resistance instantly upon entering the corridors of the casino, but the occupants were not battle-hardened infantry types...they were mostly support, logistics and intelligence officers who had spent much more time behind a desk than in the thick of life-or-death battle.

Dmitri had last been seen in the security control room when the teams made their entrance, so each moved in that direction.

Although it would have made the search much easier had they been able to keep communication open with Meda, they knew that if the gunships came on station they would lose most, if not all of the fighters laying in wait outside, something which the team couldn't afford.

As Josh, Tyler, Klint and Tattoo moved down a long and beautifully decorated corridor and up a three-story marble staircase which led to the security control room, Josh was the first to hear it.

"Clink, clink clink."

"GRENADE!" Josh screamed in warning, but it was too late.

They were already halfway up the staircase, having ascended too far to run down, with no cover available and, judging by the sound of its trajectory, a frag grenade coming for them with only a few seconds left before it exploded.

He knew they had one more bounce until it would ricochet off the wall and into their group.

In an instant Josh saw his life flash before his eyes.

The smiling eyes of his loving wife, her shining red hair flowing through his fingers on their wedding day. The birth of their son, the pride he felt as he watched the young man grow up.

But in those briefest of moments, the adoration of his men and what they had meant to him grew a flame inside of him that told him what he had to do.

He was getting older, his knees sore and his body tired from the toils of over a decade of constant war.

His uniform soaked in sweat, his armor growing heavier by the moment, his beard long with years of experience and wisdom, all directed him that while his time was coming to an end, theirs did not have to.

In a final gesture of love, service to his nation but most importantly of the respect for the team behind him, Josh located the bouncing grenade and leapt as it bounced off the rear wall and towards the men for whom he held so much love and respect that even he could not put words to describe its depths.

The bullets from Dmitri's security team tore through Josh's body as he flew through the air, but nothing had ever been able to stop him once he put his mind to it, and a few lousy bullets were not going to change that.

As the AK-47 rounds riddled his body Josh grabbed the grenade in both hands, pulled them into his belly and flattened on the ground, nearly to the end of his time in this world before his frame even landed on the cold, hard and unrelenting marble floor.

He brought himself completely flat against the floor for his final moment, doing everything possible to maximize the impact against his armor and flesh so as not to allow any pieces of shrapnel to leave him and wound the other men.

When the time fuse of the grenade ticked its last moment, Josh looked back to the stairwell toward his men and smiled.

Whatever happened next, he was proud of them and all they had done together.

He hoped that he would see them again someday, in some other place far away from the fields of death and war, in a place where they could simply enjoy each other's company without the fear of losing one another.

But that would not be in this lifetime.

Tattoo had been the first man behind Josh climbing up the stairwell, and after being thrown slightly back from the explosion and watching his Brother's body ripped to pieces, his entire being turned red with hatred and fury.

He rounded the corner to be met with another volley of fire coming from the three men standing atop the staircase from which there was no shelter.

Tyler and Klint raced to stop him, but as Klint reached his hand to pull Tattoo back from the onslaught of 7.62 rounds raining down from the staircase above him, Tattoo stepped out in a fit of rage and let loose a hail of his own bullets.

The men looked on helplessly as their Brother, induced into no thought other than vengeance, stood and took each of the incoming rounds with full-force, standing with his feet shoulder-width apart to brace himself against the final fusillade of bullets that would be his demise...but not until his magazine ran empty.

His boots were surrounded with spent 5.56 casings from the rounds he fired and as the last one went off, while Dmitri's security team hunched and fell to the ground to begin tumbling down the staircase with their own lives having been extinguished, Tattoo felt his greatest sense of satisfaction.

Knowing that his last breath would be one of the next few, the two left standing watched as Tattoo walked to Josh, his leader, his father figure, his best friend and Brother, and took a seat next to him.

He grabbed Josh's outstretched and lifeless right arm, now laying on the marble floor, and held it against his chest.

"Dmitri ran off down the hallway. Don't let that Russian bastard escape," Tattoo spoke aimlessly into the air between he, Klint and Jason.

"Don't let this be for nothing," he spoke through bloodstained teeth as he took his final breath, moving from this life along to his own version of peace.

Leaving this world with fond memories of his wife, his life, his Brothers and the heroism he had been witness to and part of, Tattoo closed his eyes and his soul was set adrift, finally releasing from this mortal coil of pain and suffering.

Dmitri heard the American voices as The Major and his team encountered Klint and Jason on the staircase. He knew that his own end was coming, but he wasn't going to make it easy for them.

"What happened?" The Major asked as he began to climb the staircase.

"Josh and Tattoo are gone man," replied Jason as they came together.

"Dmitri ran down that hallway, we've got to catch up with..."

Before Jason could finish his sentence, a burst of automatic fire ripped into the wall at their back.

The men sprinted up to the landing to take cover as a squad of the Russian security forces begin to take up positions in the room below them and lay down covering fire for their comrades.

Hunched together on the landing, The Major laid out his commands.

"Klint, you come with me. The rest of you take these guys out so I don't have to worry about them on my tail," he barked and pulled a frag grenade from his body armor to hand to Ray.

"This should help," said The Major as he handed it off.

They were far enough down the corridor chasing Dmitri to hear the explosion of the grenade, but missed the concussion.

He knew the men were highly skilled warriors and up to the task of taking out a small element of enemy forces, so he didn't leave any part of his consciousness open to worrying about them or whether they would be ok.

His entire being was now focused on finding Dmitri and pulling every last drop of blood from of him.

The corridor was lined with doors on either side.

Years of training had burned the need to clear each and every room so deep into the American's psyche that Dmitri knew he had both time and the advantage of knowing how to turn a team of two men chasing him into one, which was much more manageable and offered him a chance to get out of there alive.

Counting the number of doorways ahead of them and unwilling to allow the Russian to escape, The Major gave the order for he and Klint to break up into two elements and each clear one side of the hallway; Klint on the left and he on the right.

They moved rapidly, each man only taking the time to open a door, expediently scan the room with their eyes and step in to execute a 360-degree turn to ensure Dmitri wasn't hiding inside.

These were administrative offices, so there weren't many available hiding places.

The Major was inside a room lined with desks when he heard a loud clanging followed by the soft thud of Klint's body crumpling to the ground in the hallway as the sounds echoed along the corridor.

Quickly but carefully making his way back out into the hallway, The Major saw Klint's body on the floor in front of the last door he had been checking, a dented fire extinguisher dropped hastily next to him with blood pooling at his head.

He could see that Klint's chest was rising and falling with his breathing. The bleeding not being enough to end his life, The Major lifted his rifle and expeditiously pied off the room using whatever angles he could from the doorway to check that Dmitri was no longer inside.

He spied an open window at the far side of the room and moved inside. Slamming the door hard into the wall with his back as he turned his rifle, he found no Russian hiding there and ran to the window.

Hearing boots slam into the ground before he could reach it, several rounds struck the windowsill and the explosions shot splinters into his uniform as The Major poked his head outside to see where Dmitri had gone.

Leaning his head back outside a moment later as the sound of gunfire still rung in his ears, he watched a large shadowy figure stand up in the darkness and run across the lawn.

He gave chase, knowing that even though they had a hundred fighters lining the perimeter of the casino, this was no ordinary target and it wouldn't take much for him to neutralize a few people who only had several weeks of tactical training.

As he made impact with the ground next to Dmitri's indentation in the soft, grassy earth and rolled into a parachute landing fall to reduce his impact, he heard several high-caliber rounds ring out.

When he looked up to where Dmitri had been running, Dmitri changed his path and began sprinting back in his direction, but towards the side of the casino.

Jumping to his feet and taking chase, Dmitri was several hundred meters ahead of him by the time he reached the full speed of his run.

Already sprinting along the wall, The Major chose to close the distance between them rather than take the chance of slowing down to take and missing a shot.

As Dmitri cleared the side wall of the casino and came to the open terrain of its rear, the crack of more incoming rounds filled the night around them.

He watched as the massive Russian slowed to a jog, changed his direction again to face The Major and stopped running.

Dmitri squared his footing and raised his rifle as more rounds erupted around his feet, kicking up dust and smoke.

As the dust cleared, he continued to close the distance between them, slowing to a combat walk to steady himself.

The Major looked through the close quarters optic on his rifle and brought the green beam of his laser sight up to mid-chest on the shadow twenty meters in front of him, his night vision goggles showing another green beam, emanating from the figure across from him and moving closer, aimed directly at his chest.

Dmitri and the Major crept steadily towards the other, neither willing to fire nor drop their aim.

This is the moment I was created for, each man thought.

Once the dark warriors were within ten meters of each other they naturally began moving in a clockwise circle, never leaving the sights of their rifles as they moved to encircle the dense and heavy night between them.

The Major was the first to drop his aim.

He calmly lowered the rifle to his side, knowing what had to happen.

He unsnapped the sling holding the weapon to his body and threw it in the dirt, three feet to his right.

The Major carefully pulled the battle axe from its position on his leg, gripped the handle with both hands and widened his stance.

Dmitri followed suit, and after throwing his rifle in the dirt removed the long and razor-sharp machete from his side, the one that had been used to flay prisoners alive, scalp indigenous warriors and decapitate countless women and children.

"**Prigotov'tes' k bitve,**" Dmitri screamed with a sound so terrifying it shook the ground between the two warriors.

"**PREPARE FOR BATTLE,**" The Major bellowed back in kind as he brought his battle axe up to the ready and faced his enemy.

The warriors charged at each other as if two knights from a battle whose blood had long ago dried and re-entered the cycle of life after laying in the mud in front of a castle or battlefield for a millenia.

The first swing of The Major's battle axe struck Dmitri's body armor and bounced off with a shower of sparks.

Staying true to the warrior code and knowing that only one could walk away from this battle, if any, both took several calculated steps back, unhooked their body armor and threw it to the ground atop their rifles.

"Much better," Dmitri snarled in his thick Russian accent as the men began towards each other again.

Dmitri struck first this time, a thrust meant more to throw The Major off balance than to strike flesh.

The Major, holding his battle axe in a defensive posture with one hand near the head and the other at the handle's base was quick to dodge and parry, deftly shifting his weight from leg to leg and throwing a menacing right kick into Dmitri's ribs.

The Russian smiled as he stumbled and snarled to The Major.

"Da. I've been waiting for you my friend."

His next chuckle was followed with a left jab so fast The Major didn't even see Dmitri's arm move, and the force of the blow knocked him back out of the path from Dmitri's immediate machete swing.

The Major spit the newly formed iron-rich blood from his mouth onto the ground and smiled at Dmitri through blood-stained teeth.

"You know I've heard about you," he grinned devilishly at Dmitri.

"Do you think you're going to enjoy Hell more than most?"

The Major leapt forward, brought the battle axe high over his right shoulder and attempted to bring it down into the left side of Dmitri's neck, but the Russian was too fast.

Dmitri quickly stepped backward and to the right, at which point he caught a mean left hook from The Major's steel-studded combat gloves.

Having been caught off guard the blow knocked Dmitri from his balance, as was intended, to which The Major followed with the butt of his battle axe into Dmitri's chin, knocking him back even further.

Sensing he was gaining the advantage The Major moved in for the kill, but this wasn't Dmitri's first rodeo.

He lured The Major in with his defenses down, but as The Major closed in Dmitri rushed forward and caught his chin with a direct blow from his thick and calloused elbow, then another quick left hook as he was flying backwards.

The Major tasted dirt and blood as his face landed in the ground, and although he was sure he was about to die, he wouldn't admit it.

He would do everything in his power to take Dmitri down with him.

He would fight to his very last breath as it was all that he knew, all that he had left.

He was vengeance, he was hatred, he was anger, he was violent retribution for his family, friends, countrymen and Brothers that Dmitri and his comrades had killed.

And he wasn't going to let this end while on his back.

The Major rolled to the left as Dmitri's machete landed squarely in the spot he had occupied with full force, hitting so hard that the blade bit six inches into the earth and Dmitri's body lurched forward with it.

Seizing his opportunity The Major, still on the ground, twisted, braced his hands and mule-kicked Dmitri square in the jaw, sending him lurching while his weapon was still buried in the earth.

Jumping to his feet, the predator lurched after his prey.

Getting up on all fours Dmitri turned to see the Major, two steps away with the battle axe held high over his head, both hands on the butt and prepared to bring it down with all of his might to end Dmitri's venomous ambitions.

With one short step left to finish Dmitri's terrible existence, The Major stopped.

If a bystander were to observe them it would have appeared as two statues of men in battle for the briefest of moments, as each man contemplated what the end truly meant for him and what peace it would bring them and the world.

With his eyes locked on Dmitri's, The Major lowered his battle axe and threw it to the side, just as he had done with his rifle.

He didn't care about any rules of engagement or man's laws of armed combat.

What did man's laws matter anymore, anyway? These two were engaged in the most ancient of religions, the most carnal of emotions, the most human of actions.

That of war.

And by the laws of war and warriors they would play.

The Major took a few steps back as Dmitri rose to his feet, dusted himself off and widened his stance.

Each man locked eyes on the other and drowned the rest of the world out. Watching every muscle fiber in the other, waiting to see who would act first and knowing they would only have split seconds to react.

This time it was Dmitri's turn to start the dance, and he ran as fast as he could toward his opponent.

The Major knew he couldn't take the full force of Dmitri's locomotive-like frame head on, so he sidestepped just in time for Dmitri's punch to whisp the skin of his cheek.

A kick to the back of Dmitri's knee brought him down again, but he had been running with so much momentum that The Major had to close the distance in order to jump on top of him and attempt to secure a rear naked choke.

He was able to bring his full force down on Dmitri's back and secure his top arm around the neck, but as he was bringing his bottom arm up to complete what would be the death blow, Dmitri brought his thick and iron-hard elbow back into The Major's face with such strength that his nose exploded in blood.

Dazed but not out, The Major held on and tightened the grip he had already won, crossed his left arm over the top of Dmitri's left shoulder, wrapped it around his arm and formed a crowbar.

It didn't take much pressure from that angle to completely dislocate Dmitri's shoulder, and when he felt the pop of the humeral head he pulled with everything he had.

Dmitri screamed as the ligaments in his shoulder ripped apart and The Major, not one for complainers, brought his left arm back up to secure the rear naked choke.

The extra pressure cut off all air to Dmitri's windpipe and his screams turned to gurgles in a feeble attempt to find oxygen.

As The Major arched his back to put as much pressure on the choke as possible and remove any possibility of escape for Dmitri, massive blows began to pummel the side of his head.

The first was a wild one, as Dmitri swung without aim in a last attempt to save his life.

The second hit The Major square in the ear, and as he felt the loud bursting of his eardrum his vision was filled with the stars of blunt force trauma.

Knowing his time was short The Major doubled-down on adding pressure to his choke, but when the third blow from Dmitri's massive cannonball fists struck him in the temple he lost consciousness.

He didn't know how he got there, but when The Major came to he was on his feet, once again squared off with Dmitri.

He felt fluid draining from his right ear, and looking across at his prey saw that the only thing keeping Dmitri's left arm attached to his body was blood-soaked skin, looking like freshly-cleaved meat hanging in a butcher's shop.

It took a few seconds for the stars to stop circling around The Major's head, and this time it was his turn to start the dance.

Making his full sprint towards Dmitri, he could see the Russian bear bring his right arm up in preparation for the attack, but wasn't where The Major was aiming.

When he reached a half-meter from Dmitri The Major hit the ground and slid toward him, pulling back his right leg and sending a kick with all of his momentum into the Russian's kneecap.

The enormous man fell like a brick house on top of The Major, which wasn't exactly his plan.

The right cannonball-sized fist was pummeling his face with Dmitri in a seated position on his chest before he could react, with the Russian seemingly feeling no pain from his knee or shoulder.

The Major pulled a move he had learned in Jiu Jitsu and at the same time brought his forearms up to protect his face and used every shred of available strength to lift his core and throw Dmitri forward.

As soon as the Russian was hunched over him The Major once again wrapped both arms around Dmitri's thick neck, used his off-balance to twist Dmitri to the ground and slide around behind him to crank down with every bit of strength he could muster.

As the breath stop moving through Dmitri's throat, suddenly The Major's body was lifted off the ground as Dmitri did a one-armed pushup, brought his feet under him and jumped upwards.

The air was forced from his lungs when his back hit the earth and the giant Russian landed on top of him.

His grip loosened just enough for Dmitri to break free, but the colossal man was on his last leg of energy.

The Major fought to catch his breath as Dmitri crawled away, still coughing as his windpipe had been badly damaged from The Major's choke.

The Major, sensing it was now or never, got to his knees and crawled after him.

As Dmitri fell to his side, The Major crawled on top and wrapped both hands around Dmitri's thick bear-like neck.

Dmitri, not one to go down without a fight, followed suit with his only working hand, which was still large enough to wrap entirely around The Major's throat.

The two men were sadistically smiling at each other as the life slipped from both of their bodies.

In their final moments, although neither could speak, their eyes spoke volumes.

Each man knew that this was his place, this was his destiny, this was his life's purpose.

And although it was the last moment of each of their lives, both were honored to spend those last moments locked in battle with a true warrior.

CHAPTER 10

MISSION SUPPORT

It was a surreal trip through the looking glass to travel around Austin, a city that seemed as if it were anywhere but the middle of a warzone.

I had been in and around plenty of war-ridden capital cities in my time, and none had ever looked so “business as usual” as Austin.

Baghdad in Iraq, even with its green zone, had been littered with burned out tank hulls, bullet holes lining the tall T-barriers as you drove around and the ever-present reminder of armed troops and armored vehicles at every turn.

Kabul, with its never-ending traffic jams and hustle & bustle, never allowed you to forget precisely where you were and that you were under constant threat of an IED, kidnapping attempt or ambush.

Afghanistan had, of course, played a key strategic role in military campaigns throughout the ages, so I imagined it had known more about war than being a capital city since the time of Alexander the Great and his campaign there.

Austin, Texas, however, didn't seem to have changed at all after my time living there in college.

Sure, some of the storefronts were different and the capitol building and some downtown areas were now heavily fortified. But once we turned on to Guadalupe Street, or "the drag" as it was called, all memories of war seemed distant.

The last time I had allowed myself to be lulled into a false sense of security we had been ambushed in Oklahoma, lost Buckeye and I briefly had my first experience as a POW.

To say that it was tough for me to relax would be an understatement, but every time I glanced at Natalie's carefree smile another chink in the thick armor-like shell I had formed was chipped away.

I knew that besides she and my kids there was only one other thing on the planet that could both help me relax and serve as an icebreaker for she and I to get better acquainted.

Food had always played a large role in my life...I've always believed that if you want to understand a culture, the best way to do so is through their food and music. The United States of America has long been a melting pot of cultures and civilization, a fact that was lost on many Americans.

Never had I been in another country in which so many cultures came together and were represented through their food.

In my travels in Asia I had found 7-elevens on every corner and the occasional McDonald's or KFC, but trying to find a good old American dinner was a test of endurance.

Germany had been close, with various forms of Asian cuisine everywhere and even a Mexican restaurant, opened by a British expat near my home in Stuttgart where we loved to go for their burritos, beer and sorry, watered-down excuse for tequila.

Austin, however, was still a veritable smorgasbord of both amazing food and eclectic music playing somewhere twenty-four hours a day. We started the evening at a unique place called Texadelphia that put a Texas twist on philly cheesesteaks.

The question of how they still served a full menu was completely lost on me, and quickly we were enough drinks and flirtatious smiles into the evening for the security-minded man inside of me to have left us to our own devices.

He may have been hidden for a long time but the hopeless romantic part of me, long buried from former wars and military service, was making his grand reappearance. And I was happy that he was back.

As it turned out I had a sense of humor that she loved, and the "accidental" brushes of her body against mine, her hand on my arm and the way her almond-shaped brown eyes twinkled and long black hair fell into her face when she laughed, fully and with her whole body, made me smile.

She brought a warmth back to my soul that I thought had long ago gone cold, like a once-raging bonfire extinguished by snowfall.

After a quick stroll down the infamous sixth street, strewn with homeless schizophrenics, drag queens and young college kids beginning their night of partying, we found our way back to Meda's car and began the drive back to the Scottish Rite temple and our temporary home.

But I didn't want to go back yet. The last social and unhurried meal I'd eaten was spent with the guys on our original compound several months before, after liquidating John's steakhouse of its best food & booze and him cooking it into a spectacular dinner shared amongst new friends and old Brethren.

I couldn't bring myself to go back there. Not quite yet, and I hoped that Natalie felt a mutual appreciation for the evening.

We made our way towards downtown, but instead of turning to drive to the temple I took the car onto Comal street.

Pulling into The White Horse parking lot just a stone's throw away from our final destination Natalie shot me a look that, even though I had been a single father and busy surgeon far away from the dating game long before even the war started...I recognized.

She wasn't ready for the night to end quite yet either.

What had begun as an idea for a stroll around town turned into an evening of fun until the lights came on and they kicked us out, the reverberation from the band still ringing in our ears.

I had forgotten that she was special, that she was some sort of mystic or whatever she was, and the thoughts and questions about her abilities had been completely wiped from my brain along with any other care in the world. There had been only one thing that I could see, hear or feel since we stopped at Texadelphia hours earlier and started talking.

Magnetism.

I had always been the sort who could talk to anyone, walk into a conversation with a complete stranger and not stop until whatever party or establishment we were at closed down.

The ability to create connections with strangers in an instant had served me well in the intelligence world, but for some reason I would become Forrest Gump whenever I was with a woman to whom I was attracted.

But not with her.

Everything felt right with her. The words that would have been normally gummed up somewhere in the transmission between my brain and mouth now flowed smoothly like aged wine.

Although I continuously found myself enamored by her presence and gently gazing at her silky and obsidian-like shiny hair when I thought she wasn't looking, I wasn't the love-struck and goofy mess that I would have typically been with another woman.

It was like we had already passed well beyond that point. I couldn't rectify it in my head, even though I knew that shared trauma had a tendency to form strong connections in people who experienced them together.

This was something else.

It was as if we had spent an entire life together. To passers-by we could have just as easily been an eighty-year-old couple sharing a fifty-year anniversary date rather than two thirty-something year old strangers getting acquainted.

I didn't want it to ever end.

But as with all things, it had to. The lights came on to tell us that our evening was over. Yet in the darkness of the night which enveloped us as we left The White Horse and walked to Meda's car, something was born anew in each of us.

The temple was only a short drive, and our arrival into its doors was reminiscent of my days as a young man coming home from a night out carousing around with friends.

We stumbled sloppily from the car and into the front entrance, and after making our way to the hall which housed our rooms I found Jim's aide waiting outside of mine.

"Rob, how was...."

As we came within speaking distance, the aide recoiled slightly.

"Well it sure smells like you guys had a good time. Is there any booze left at the bar you came from?"

"We gave it our best effort, sir, but alas we couldn't finish off the supplies of liquor before the enemy takes them. We failed our mission," Natalie replied with a half-assed and comical salute.

"Ok then. Well this may not be exactly the perfect time, but Rob you promised Jim an answer tonight when you returned. And I'm not allowed to sleep until he gets it."

"And I couldn't bring myself to sleep until you two lovebirds came back," Jim added as he walked around the corner.

Coming within smelling distance of us, Jim laughed to himself and rocked back on his heels as he spoke.

"I have a few pieces of news for you, but I think it's best to save some of it for tomorrow," Jim continued.

"Good or bad?" I asked.

"A little of both."

"How about the good news tonight?"

"Exactly what I was thinking. First, our teams on the east coast took back Washington DC this morning, including the Pentagon and everything else the enemy was controlling in the area."

I let out a short celebratory victory cry and raised my fist in excitement.

"And they had some help. I didn't tell you yet because, well, it just wasn't the right time. But some foreign SOF operators showed up here several days ago and flew out to link up with Bulldog and the team. They were with them on the operation, and their nations are sending troops to assist in the final push as we speak. The east coast is almost ours again, and your boys played a significant role in that along with some of their new friends."

"That's great news! Is everyone ok?" I asked.

"Bulldog, Matty, JLo..."

Jim cut me off before I could rattle off the list of our men on the east coast.

"All of our men on the east coast are fine. We'll be recalling them back here first thing in the morning. If all goes according to plan, you should all be able to have dinner together tomorrow night. Hell maybe tonight was a recon mission for you to take them out on the town when they arrive, they sure deserve it."

"Ok, how about the bad news? I don't think anything could dampen my day after hearing that!"

"Not so fast, Rob," he answered.

"I've got another piece of good news for you. Now that everything south of New York is pretty much clear of enemy forces, your family should be here in no time."

This time I lowered my head and held up two fists in silent celebration. It couldn't get much better than that.

"Ok Jim, lay it on me. What's the bad news?"

Natalie put a hand on my shoulder and smiled at me.

"Jim's right," she added.

"That's a lot of new information for one day. Why don't we hold the rest for the morning?"

Seeing the two exchange a furtive glance, a rock began to form in the pit of my stomach.

"My God Jim, what's the bad news?" I asked anxiously.

"This isn't the right time, Rob. She's right, tomorrow is better. And in the meantime, I've given you some news but you haven't held up your end of the bargain. Gateway. Are you in to start training?"

"Who would be training me? Who exactly would I be working with?"

"The tech does most of the training. But Jacob, myself, Moshe, the Templars and a few others will be helping. This is a very high-level project, Rob. I don't think I need to say this to you again, but no one outside of this group and those people I mentioned can know about it, whether or not you embark on this journey with us."

"Why is this so hush-hush? I mean people have heard rumors about CIA mind control experiments and sci-fi stuff for decades. What's the big deal?"

"We need to dive a little deeper on who we'll be fighting and how. But this isn't a place where we can discuss such things. We can get into that later, but I need an answer now."

I looked to Natalie, back at Jim and his aide, then again to Natalie.

"Are you in?" I asked her.

"I don't have much of a choice. They need me here, and this is why you found me in Santa Monica. This was written a long time ago, and every piece of my life before it was put into place for this very thing."

She paused to look back at Jim, nod and then meet my gaze again.

"So yes, I'm in. And so are my children."

"Huh?" I asked, wondering if I had missed something.

"Your kids? How are they involved in this?"

"Another time, Rob," Jim interjected.

"She's in, what say you?"

Looking back at him, I gave the decision I had made during our initial discussion.

"Of course I'm in. Just promise you won't leave me in the dark about whatever the hell it is that I'll be doing when we come to that point."

"Oh you won't have to worry about that, Rob. Once your training is complete, you will have access to all of the knowledge of the universe, and nobody will be able to keep you in the dark about anything for the rest of your existence."

"Three hundred and sixteen, sir," reported the young man, his clothes soiled from sweat and the blood of his friends and enemies spilled in a battle that seemed to have raged for ages.

"316, that's all?" Bulldog asked.

"Yes sir, we've checked and re-checked with each of the militias, the intel guys, the secret squirrel teams and the uniformed military."

"I want a list of every man's name who we lost today," ordered Bulldog.

"Those men are heroes and they need to be remembered as such. Every man we lost today died fighting to take back his country, our nation's capital, to bring freedom back to his people and keep our families safe. They deserve to be honored as the heroes they are, and I want it seen to that their names are etched alongside those from the revolutionary war."

Bulldog paused to ensure the young man was taking in the full significance of Bulldog's orders before continuing.

"If our nation ever forgets what they fought and died for we'll be right back here doing this all over. And I don't ever want to do this again."

"Roger that sir," he replied and moved out with a quickness to relay his orders to the requisite leaders of the various factions who had taken part in winning back the nation's capital.

"You've gone and made me a bit misty there, mate. Good speech and all, but I think I need a kleenex," Harry joked from Bulldog's side.

"Put a sock in it, Harry," he barked.

"We may be done here, but we still need to take New York. And after that, I have a feeling that it won't be long before you're back home, with us, doing the same thing on your shores."

For the first time in as long as he remembered, Harry didn't have anything funny to say.

Although a seasoned warrior who had spent many a night in countless warzones, he hadn't given merit to those deepest worries which had crept into his brain since they discovered the invasion had begun.

As Harry stood next to Bulldog, stunned and contemplating the absolute gravity of his comments, a middle aged but extremely fit man approached.

He was wearing dark sunglasses, a sizable Masonic ring on his right hand, khaki cargo pants, a black polo shirt and tactical khaki vest adorned with ammunition, pens and various equipment.

While Bulldog wondered how this man seemed to be the only person on the entire battlefield not soaked in sweat and blood, the man began to speak to he and Harry.

"Gentlemen, congratulations on the victory today. Harry good to see you again. Bulldog, we've never met but I've heard all about you."

As Bulldog extended his hand for a shake, Harry finally found his voice.

"Do I know you?" he asked.

"We've crossed paths before, but perhaps it wasn't significant enough to merit a memory."

"I didn't get your name, sir," Bulldog added.

"My name doesn't matter. Just think of me as a consultant."

"So what do we call you? Mr. Consultant?" Harry asked.

"You can refer to me as The Consultant."

Harry smiled and jabbed Bulldog in the ribs, but before he could let out any smart comments the man continued.

"Harry, yours and other NATO forces are currently en route and should be reaching land here before the day is done. Will you boys be joining us for the excursion up to New York city? It's quite lovely this time of year."

"How do you know that?" he asked incredulously.

"That was supposed to be highly classified and kept completely off the net so the enemy didn't know reinforcements were coming."

"It's my job to know that, Harry. Like I said, I'm a consultant."

"Look Mr. Consultant, if you know that Harry's men are on the way, then you should surely know that we'll be rolling out for New York at daybreak," Bulldog finished.

"We'll be rolling out, Bulldog. You'll be going back to Austin," The Consultant answered.

"Now why in the sam hell would I be doing that and not going along to finish this thing?"

"You haven't been told yet? Sorry, perhaps I'm a little early. You need to go check with Matty and see if any messages have come in for you. Maybe it was delayed in all the commotion of, well, you know..."

The Consultant held up his arms and gestured to the wreckage and battle scenes surrounding them.

"This."

"And in that case, Harry it was good seeing you again. Bulldog, it was nice to finally meet you. You should go find Matty as soon as possible."

Just as mysteriously as he had arrived, The Consultant turned and walked back into the thick of the men and soldiers celebrating their victory.

Bulldog turned to Harry and asked the question that was burning in his soul.

"Who the hell is that guy?"

Harry shrugged his shoulders and replied.

"I don't know mate. But you know those consultant types. They like it like that. Whoever he is, it seems you should find Matty."

Bulldog found Matty, JLo and Tony together and hunched over the front seats of an up-armored HUMVEE.

As he opened the passenger door Bulldog saw Matty holding the handset of a radio in one hand, his face dejectedly buried in the other.

"Matty, what's the matter? JLo, are you guys ok?"

"They're gone man," Matty sobbed.

"Who's gone? What are you talking about?"

"Josh, Tattoo, The Major. They're all gone. Klint has some sort of head injury, and the guys who are alive are pretty banged up."

"What? How? What happened?" Bulldog asked.

"I don't have a lot of information, I'm sorry. That's all they could tell me. But we're supposed to head back to Bragg immediately and fly to Austin first thing in the morning," Matty replied.

Harry put a hand on Bulldog's shoulder as he stood, stunned and silent, trying to contemplate the new information.

As Bulldog remained dazed, awash in his emotions, first sadness then doubt and finally intense anger, he felt the satellite phone begin to vibrate in his pocket.

As he lifted it to his ear Jim's voice began to speak on the other end.

"Bulldog, have you linked up with Matty yet?" he asked in a hurried tone.

"Yes. I'm here with he, Tony and JLo. What happened?"

"I can't go into that at the moment. But we've cleared a plane for you guys to fly from Bragg back here first thing in the morning. Your men need you, right now."

Bulldog knew in the deepest parts of his soul that, if what Matty had told him were true, he needed to find a way to move the earth and heavens to help his men.

The leaders who had been on the west coast were now gone, and the men needed a leader.

They needed Bulldog.

"What about the rest of the team? Are they ok? Matty said Klint has some sort of head wound and the others are pretty banged up."

"They're ok, but not for long. We intercepted communications that the enemy pinpointed their location and are heading there to take them out."

"How long do we have?" Bulldog asked.

"Not long. They stirred up the hornet's nest and have become the enemy's primary target on the west coast. They're sending a battalion to take them out and we don't have a whole lot of help in that area."

"If that's true then tomorrow morning isn't fast enough!" Bulldog yelled into the handset.

"I need to be out there now."

"I don't know what to tell you. We're short on resources everywhere right now. That's as quickly as I can move you there."

"Perhaps I can be of some assistance," The Consultant interjected from across the hood of the HUMVEE.

Josh, Tattoo and The Major's bodies each lay draped in blankets in a rear room of the golf course.

The medics were busy tending to Klint, now needing constant oxygen from their tanks and still bleeding profusely from his head while the other men, who had some good tactical medical experience but nowhere near the level which was now needed, tended to the less significant wounds sustained in the casino operation.

"I need some more fluids over here," Jason called to Chris as he watched one of the IV bags begin to run dry.

"That was it," he shouted back from the other side of the room.

"That was the last bag that Rob brought back from his hospital trip."

Jason bit his lip in anger and took a brief mental pause while calming himself and attempting to find a zen-like meditation in pumping short bursts of oxygen into Klint's motionless body.

He wasn't going to last much longer like this.

None of them were.

But he knew that voicing his frustrations wouldn't help the situation.

Quite the opposite. He knew that if the guys discovered how critically low on medical supplies they had become while trying to revive the lifeless bodies it would add another worry they didn't need at the moment.

As Chris patched up the wound from a bullet that had grazed his own leg during the mission, Meda stormed into the makeshift emergency room.

"We need to go," she said as calmly as possible.

"Excuse me?" Jason asked, dumbfounded.

"We have to get away from here, now," she repeated.

"She's right," Chad shouted from the doorway.

"I just got an encrypted message from Jim on the red side. Both the Russians and Chinese are amassing troops to come get us. They know we're here."

"How in the hell did they find us?" Jason asked.

"It doesn't matter," Meda replied.

"We don't have time to sit around and talk about it. We need to move now."

Knowing she was right but not knowing what to do about it, he barked out his orders.

"Chris, grab Ray and load every bit of weaponry and explosives we have left and put it in the vehicles. Chad, get any commo gear that we can take loaded into the trucks and prep some demolitions to blow anything we can't. Have Ray help with the demo so we don't leave anything behind to give away our frequencies with headquarters in Austin."

"What about the other guys?" Chad asked.

“Do you want me to transmit word to Bulldog or anyone at Bragg?"

"What good would that do us?" Chris challenged.

"They're on the other side of the country. We're alone on this one."

"It has a very long and technical name, but you would know it better as a Hyperloop," The Consultant answered to Bulldog.

"Wait, that's real?" Matty asked.

"I thought they were still a long away from being operational on those things."

"Well, the commercial ones that the public knows about, sure. But much like the highways that appeared all over the country after World War II, the military implemented this technology and put it in place for our use over the last decade. To be perfectly accurate, we developed it and chose the entrepreneur to bring it to the world when the time was right."

"What do you need these for?" questioned Matty.

"Well, when we built the deep underground military bases, we knew that we would need a way to connect them. Any event which would cause us to go underground would make the world above, well, what it is currently. So depending on what coordinates I set for you, you will end up at any number of underground bases around the nation."

"But how does it work?" Bulldog asked while tapping on the side of the white, egg-shaped pod sitting atop a landing pad as he peered down the long and dark tunnel.

"Quite simple, really," replied The Consultant.

"Do you know what the biggest impediment to long-distance, high-speed travel is?"

"Long lines and absent-minded TSA workers?" Matty joked.

"Funny. But I mean the physics. It's friction; anything going really fast creates quite a bit of it. So we took that out of the equation."

"How?" asked Bulldog.

"And how does that take us across the country in less than an hour?"

"Once you're in the pod, I'll go to the control room and seal off the door. This tunnel becomes a vacuum. The tracks around you are filled with magnets that will cause the pod to levitate and stay on track, and we'll propel you up to a pretty significant speed. It will slow you down enough to not crash into the wall at the other side, and voila. You're there."

"So what do we do now? How do we make this happen?" Matty asked.

"Give me your weapons and anything else that's not attached directly to your body, step in and I'll take care of the rest. You will stop at El Toro air base in Orange County and I'll have people there to take you to your friends."

"Weapons?" JLo interrupted.

"You didn't say anything about giving up our weapons."

"Look, I understand the hesitance for a warrior to give up his weapons. And as you'll be emerging in the midst of a battleground to go save your men, the gravity of what I'm asking you to do isn't lost on me. But please believe me that with the speeds at which you'll be traveling, anything unsecured inside the pod will become a missile should anything happen along the ride."

The men conferred with each other using nothing more than their eyes, unsure of whether this request was a bridge too far.

Tony was the first to hand over his rifle.

"This seems like the only chance we have to help the guys. If we're stopping at a base on the other end, I'm sure we can find a way to procure some guns. But we can't do anything for them sitting here like a bunch of pearl-clutching ninnies."

"He's right," Bulldog agreed.

"Hand over anything not attached to you. We need to get a move on."

The Consultant, Tex, Tony and Matty began carrying the large piles of weapons and ammo the men were now placing on the ground in front of them to the control room they had walked in through.

As the last trip to ferry the gear and guns was made, The Consultant looked at the group and smiled.

"Ok boys, make sure you strap in tight and enjoy the ride. Good luck and Godspeed, I'll be keeping tabs on your progress. And by the way, your team succeeded in killing Dmitri on the raid that killed your men, so take some solace in knowing they wiped one of our highest priority targets from the planet."

"Who the hell is Dmitri?" asked Griz.

"If you don't know, he is...or was...one bad hombre. We've been after him for over a decade, and he's been hunting you ever since the hit at DIA."

"With a name like that I'm sure he had it coming," Adam smirked.

"Right you are, Adam," The Consultant added.

"Right you are."

The Consultant led the men to the two egg-shaped pods, each with enough room to carry three rows of three people.

With plenty of room for the group of nine, they split up between the two pods with five in the front and four in the rear, leaving several empty seats between them.

He closed the pods' hatches and waved a goodbye from the window of the control room.

As the men were strapping on their safety restraints, each pod rose to levitate in the air.

With one hand The Consultant began tapping commands into the computer on the desk before him, and with the other he waved goodbye.

As JLo raised his hand to return the gesture, a loud humming enveloped them as the pods began to vibrate.

Before his hand returned to his lap, the men in the first pod heard a resounding "slap" when JLo's hand smacked his face as they were launched into their new journey.

CHAPTER 11

VICTORY OR DEATH

"What are the three properties which define God, as you know him?" Jacob asked as he placed a pair of headphones around my neck.

"Excuse me?" I asked, looking to Natalie for an indication as to what he was getting at.

"You told me that Jim filled you in on the basics. I know that you grew up going to Sunday school and studied all religions extensively during your Masonic practices and with The Order. So answer my question, Rob. What are the three properties which define God?"

"He's omnipotent, omnipresent and omniscient?" I responded in an unsure tone.

"Correct," Jacob replied.

"Now it's very important that you understand and grasp what I'm about to tell you, because its understanding will determine how successful you are and whether you will get where you need to go."

He took a seat in his chair across from me and next to Natalie, as we were seated in a circle of chairs in one of the dimly-lit and symbol-adorned rooms underground.

"Please define each of those three properties for me."

"Omnipotent means all powerful. Omnipresent means everywhere. Omniscient means all knowing."

"Correct again, Rob."

"We're going to take a slight departure from what you know as God, the benevolent being who created life on this earth, the stars and the heavens. You've grown up with pictorial representations of He and His Son because, well, it's just easier for people to comprehend. The idea is correct, but to try and put God into human form is not."

"Huh?"

"Jim explained unconstrained energy to you, yes?"

"He did."

"Knowing that energy can take many forms, whether it be lightning in an electrical storm, a thermonuclear weapon or kinetic energy which cannot be stopped until it meets an equal opposing force...would you say that energy could be defined as omnipotent?"

"I guess you could say that."

"And given the same lesson that energy is within everything around us, from the cells inside your body to the molecules of air between us and even between those, would you say that it is omnipresent?"

"Well if it's everywhere, then yes," I replied, feeling a chill creep into the deepest parts of my spine as I started to grasp where the line of instruction was heading.

"The last piece will take a little more of a leap of faith to understand. Have you ever heard of the scientists studying the memory of water, the theory that water can record events and maintain memory?"

"Yes, I had an old friend who described that and showed me a book he was reading. I thought it was a load of crap."

"Well, yes and no. Have you ever heard of the stone tape theory?"

"The one that says some ghosts are nothing more than certain parts of nature recording terrible events and replaying them throughout time?"

"Sort of," Jacob answered.

"Both of those were half right, and good hypotheses. When our scientists started looking into supernatural events and psychic powers, they made a few discoveries based upon those original studies. They found that it's actually the energy contained in those parts of nature that record memory and information."

"What does that even mean?" I asked, knowing the answer before the question escaped from my mouth.

"It means that all of the information in the universe, all that ever was, all that will ever be, is recorded in the energy all around us. It means, Rob, that energy is also omniscient."

"So God is nothing more than unconstrained energy?"

"No. And it isn't necessary that we go into a deep theological debate at this moment. Just understand that energy contains those properties. And this technology is going to allow you to get in tune, via vibrational harmony, almost like a homeostasis of your brain, with whatever energy you choose."

"How?"

"How is not the important thing to understand right now. What is important to know is that if you focus on any one thing which is important to you, the technology will allow you to attune yourself to that very frequency and see wherever it is in the great expanse of time, at this very moment."

"So if I focus on someone and put these headphones on, I will be able to see whatever it is that is going on with the people I want to see? Wherever they are or whatever they are doing?"

"Exactly. Although there is one caveat; when you become much better acquainted with these abilities, they can be used as a defensive measure as well as an offensive."

"Defensive? Like repelling someone from seeing me? Like how Natalie kept her physical location hidden from the Chinese who were looking for her?"

"Yes. But it's not that specific. Jim and I couldn't find her either, because to put up those defensive measures means to block it from the energy trying to record it, not from a particular person. Think of it as a geometric forcefield causing you to be invisible to space, energy and time."

"And there are others who can do this?"

"Yes. And not only to themselves, but to other people or things they want to remain hidden. But that is far beyond the scope of what we'll be doing now. Today, we focus on a single person. Someone who isn't hiding, so we can help you understand just how powerful this is and what you can do with it if you refine your abilities."

"Ok," I added, taking in a deep breath and letting it out.

"Let's get started."

Jacob reached for the headphones around my neck and began to speak.

"I want you to concentrate on someone, anyone who's important to you, who you have a connection to but isn't anywhere near us at the moment. Picture them in your mind, remember a certain memory that sticks out about them. The more specific you can make that mental image, the better. When I put these headphones on you, you will hear a voice which will give you instructions. The voice will be joined by soothing sounds and a deep vibrational tone. Follow the instructions exactly, and tell us what you saw when you are finished."

As I felt the pressure release around my neck from the large external headphones that Jacob was placing over my ears, I searched my memory banks for a picture of Bulldog.

He and the east coast team were the only ones I hadn't heard from in quite some time, and I didn't know what was going on with them. If this remote viewing really worked, I wanted to see how my Brothers were doing.

I pictured him in my mind, from the first intelligence dump he gave us back in Colorado when we linked up together post-invasion.

How long ago was that?

Time doesn't matter, focus on the memory.

My mind was telling me to focus on the most minute details possible, so I focused on the tenor of his voice, the look of his uniform and the words which he was speaking.

When the picture was locked solidly in my thoughts, I heard the soothing sound of a man's voice, sounding like a highly educated white male aged somewhere in his mid-sixties.

As the man instructed me to clear my thoughts and focus on a particular image and memory, his voice faded into the calming sound of ocean waves crashing against the shore.

My mind became acutely relaxed and the waves were joined by a low vibrational hum, a bassline that followed no music but rather a specific waveform that would have been perfectly symmetrical if I were viewing it on an oscilloscope.

I saw the image of the green lines corresponding to the wave forms had I been looking at the pattern, now slightly opaque and flowing behind the image of Bulldog speaking, which had been held in the center of my mind's eye.

Suddenly those feelings of calm which the sound of waves had brought were replaced with fear.

But it wasn't my fear...it was Bulldog's.

The whiteboard behind Bulldog began to transform as he spoke, from a whiteboard covered in maps and battle plans to a harsh and undulating deep shade of red. I watched as Bulldog giving his speech morphed into another scene, now with him sitting and speaking to someone else.

A group of someone else's.

I focused all of my intent and strained my mind as far as I could push it, while the deep red background began to fade into the colors of his actual surroundings.

But the fear remained.

I could see Bulldog sitting in some sort of cockpit which I had never seen before, his uniform stained with blood and sweat, and a look on his face that told me something was wrong.

Very wrong.

I pulled my mind's eye back and tried to picture what cockpit he was in.

Is it an airplane? Submarine? What in the world is that?

As I focused intently all that I could see was a futuristic interior and white exterior egg shaped cockpit, surrounded by blackness with the occasional white flash screaming past, both above and below him.

Although I couldn't get a clearer view of where he was, there was one thing that was overpowering my emotions. I began to feel my heart tune in to his, which was beating out of his chest. The fear was beginning to overpower us.

I watched as Bulldog sensed something and looked around at his surroundings.

Next I heard another voice...Tony, asking a question from behind him that I couldn't quite understand.

Bulldog closed his eyes and I heard him begin to count to five.

His lips weren't moving, so I assumed that I was hearing his mind and felt my heart slow to a steady pace.

Upon reaching the count of five he opened his eyes, turned to his rear and gave an answer from which I could only make out a small portion."

"...El Toro..."

Bulldog turned to face forward, centering his gaze directly on me. He locked eyes with my field of vision and spoke to me without moving his lips.

"We're going to El Toro. We need you, now."

As the last word echoed in my mind, I began to hear the ocean waves and the deep bass humming in my ears again. I opened my eyes as Jacob removed the headphones.

"How long was that?" I asked.

"About ten minutes," Natalie replied from my side.

"Where did you go, Rob?" he asked.

"Bulldog and the guys are in trouble. I don't know what or why, but they're scared. And they're heading to something called El Toro."

"What is that?" Natalie asked.

"I don't know. All I know is that they're afraid and Bulldog spoke to me, telling me to meet them there. What does that mean?"

"Give me a moment and I'll find out," Jacob answered, standing up from his chair and walking to a phone on the wall.

After a brief conversation, Jacob hung up the phone and returned to his seat across from me.

"Jim says your team on the west coast is about to be ambushed. The men from the east coast are traveling to help them, and Jim's aide is bringing your gear down now so that you can too."

"They were already on the way. And we're a half a country away from them; that's a few hours in a plane much less anything else. How can I get there in time to do anything?"

Jacob grinned and looked at me with a knowing smile.

"You still have doubts, don't you?"

Natalie laughed and tried assuring me by placing her hand on top of mine.

"He's not going to believe it until we show him.'

The men in Bulldog's pod had quickly devolved into their normal fare of making fun of each other and cracking jokes the moment JLo's hand slapped his face upon their initial propulsion.

But as Bulldog felt the pod begin to rapidly decelerate thirty minutes into their journey, he told them to start getting their game faces on.

He didn't know what was going to happen once they stopped, but he knew they'd have to be ready for anything.

When the pod finally slowed to a stop in a terminal which was a mirror image of the one they had set off from, Bulldog looked to their left and saw a young man dressed in an Air Force uniform waving to them.

When the door of their pod opened, he removed his safety restraints and emerged.

Seeing the men also step out from the second pod and fall into a semi-circle around him, the young man finished toying with the controls on his display and stepped out of the doorway to meet the team.

"Welcome to El Toro," the Airman, a Hispanic man in his early thirties began.

"The Consultant called and filled me in when you started on the other side. I'll take you to your friend, then we'll go to the arms room to procure some weapons and I'll fill you in on the SITREP."

"Our friend? What friend?" Corey asked.

"I don't know his name. The Consultant told me he'd be arriving, and he only just showed up as you guys were coming to a stop. We'll go meet him together. He's in another room down the hall."

The men looked at each other confused.

Jim had told them there weren't many friendly forces on the west coast, and the only friends there should be the ones who were about to be attacked.

"I thought most of the bases on the west coast had been decommissioned," Adam commented.

"What are you doing here?"

"They were," the Airman answered.

"So what is this?" Matty continued.

"What lies above us used to be known as Marine Corps Air Station El Toro. It was the home of the Marine Corps aviation for the west coast. Because of its location, long runways and massive infrastructure it was selected as one of our locations when we started building the underground bases. Unfortunately it was decommissioned back in 1999, but we used a private dummy corporation to buy the land that was integral for our use so we could keep this going along with a few buildings up top."

As there wasn't any time to waste on questions, Bulldog ordered the men to stop asking them and follow the Airman.

Not knowing where I had ended up, I was beating frantically on the cold metal door of the sterile white room when the door slid open.

I stood staring at Bulldog, with a look on my face that I'm sure was just as confused as the one I saw on his.

With no need for answers at that moment, I was so happy to see them that I raced forward and embraced him in the biggest hug I could muster, and felt pats on my shoulder from the rest of my team as we stood.

"We don't have much time, guys," the Airman told us as he closed the door.

"Follow me and I'll read you on to our current situation."

The men began to pepper me with questions to which I had no answer as we followed the Airman down a long white corridor, which was eerily reminiscent of the underground base below the temple in Austin.

"All I can tell you is that ten minutes ago I was in Austin," I told the group behind me as we walked.

"Yeah right," JLo said sarcastically as the Airman led us into a meeting room lined with desks and a whiteboard at the front.

"You wouldn't believe me if I went any further," I told him.

"It's been a strange couple of days."

An arm grabbed my shoulder and forcefully turned me 180 degrees. Coming to a stop I was face-to-face with Tony, looking at me half in anger, half in confusion.

"Not so fast Rob," he started.

"I just got out of a freaking egg that took me clear across the country in forty minutes. We were told to come here by a weirdo whose story I don't even want to hear, and as far as we know nobody on the planet knew about our guys getting attacked besides us and the men going to get them. So tell us Rob...how did *you* arrive here before *we* did?"

Having never been a good liar and being the sort who felt dirty saying anything less than the absolute truth, I decided it was worth a shot.

"I used remote viewing to see Bulldog traveling in the pod. When I told Jacob and Natalie, they tuned into your energies and teleported me here, to meet you when you arrived."

"Huh?" Tony asked.

"Exactly," I shrugged.

"I don't really get it either."

"Wait, do you mean OUR Jacob?" Matty asked.

"Dead Jacob? And who is Natalie?"

"Are those really the questions you have after all that?" I asked, astonished.

The Airman cleared his throat with a loud "ahem."

"If we're going to do this, I'm going to need your full attention gentlemen," he directed from the front of the room.

"Please find a seat and we'll begin."

I winked at Tony as I turned and moved to sit at one of the desks.

The Airman pulled a large map of the united states down from a roller at the top of the whiteboard and began to fill us in on the situation.

"NATO reinforcements are inbound as we speak, gentlemen. Your British friends on the east coast are reuniting with their buddies and the German military right about now."

"Wait a minute," Adam asked from the back.

"The Brits and the Germans are fighting a world war on the same side for once? Come on."

"There's a first time for everything, Adam," Bulldog responded.

"Now zip it and listen."

"Thank you, sir," the Airman added and continued.

"The Canadians have been massing on their border along with our Scandinavian friends and will begin pushing south as soon as the troops make landfall on the east coast, which should be momentarily. The Australians, New Zealanders, French and Polish militaries landed in South America and have been making their way through Central America and Mexico. At their current pace they will be engaging the enemy on the Mexican border within the hour."

"What about our west coast team?" Corey asked.

"The Japanese, South Korean and Canadian navies began engaging enemy ships on the west coast about the time you boys got here. They have landing ships full of infantry waiting to make landfall behind the initial attack, and we're hoping that will pull the contingent tasked to ambush your boys back to defend the port. But we're not holding our breath on that one."

"Why not?" I asked.

"We took out their communications satellites before the assault began on the west coast. It was partially eye-for-an-eye, partially to cause chaos and partially to leave their ships and vehicles with no GPS to launch a counterattack."

"But that means they also can't radio the troops going to get our boys and tell them they're under attack," added Bulldog.

"Correct. Unless they sent a call back before the satellites went down, there's no way they could have received word except by courier. And given the amount of fire the navies are laying down over there, it's doubtful."

"How did all of this happen? Who coordinated this?" asked Bulldog.

"As much disdain as we had for the leadership at Bragg, it seemed like they were keeping pretty busy. They went old school and send a few teams directly to the respective leaders of our allied nations to plan this counterattack. Not a single radio or email transmission, all face-to-face. I'm not sure if the dog & pony shows were a decoy or them trying to set up congratulations for what they did behind the scenes, but they saved our butts."

"So what can we do now?" Bulldog asked.

"How do we help our guys?"

"I'm glad you asked," the Airman answered.

"Jacob and Natalie located your friends as soon as they finished sending Rob here," he began as he pulled out satellite imagery of the forest and mountains in which I had first met the west coast team, taping the pictures up along the whiteboard.

"Hold on there hot sauce," Tony demanded from his desk with a look of total confusion on his face.

"Rob was telling the truth about how he got here?"

"We don't have time for that," the Airman responded.

"Let's focus on how we pull your guys out of there before they are annihilated. Rob can answer those questions later."

Looking at the confused look on my face, he walked back his previous comment.

"Ok someone will answer those questions later. For now let's focus on getting your guys."

The Airman pulled a telescopic pointer from the tray in front of the whiteboard and extended it to point at locations on the imagery.

"Since it was the only territory they could gain any advantage in, your team fell back to their original location in the mountains. One of your guys is badly hurt with a head wound sustained last night and the rest are full of either bullet holes, shrapnel or still dazed from losing their men on the mission. Time is of the essence here, men. If the enemy catches up to them, I don't think they're in any shape to put up much of a fight."

"So what are you suggesting?" Corey asked.

"You need to get them out of there. They are currently about ninety-five miles from where we are sitting, which means we can drive there in an hour and a half or fly in a Black Hawk in about thirty minutes. But the second option is pretty dangerous, and you won't have any backup or QRF if the birds go down."

"Why don't we take the hyperloop thing?" Matty asked.

"That's only connected to specific bases around the country, and they're nowhere near any base that has a connection. Sorry, but that's not possible."

"How long do we have until the enemy reaches them?" Bulldog asked.

"Good question. The enemy arrived at the golf course about twenty minutes after your team left. They tried to search it for any leftover intel, but your team placed quite a bit of demolitions inside and the enemy search team snagged a tripwire on their way in. It took out the search team and most of what your guys were using as a headquarters, but they set out tracking teams at the same time they sent the search team into the golf course."

"You're not answering the question," Tony barked.

"One of the search teams has already reached the edge of the wooded area in which they are hiding," the Airman replied in a reluctant tone.

"Do they know exactly where our team is?" Bulldog asked.

"Just like our people who can locate anyone on the planet, the Chinese have people who were tasked to find your guys. So yes, unless someone is hiding their location, the enemy knows where your team is within a three foot radius."

"Hiding their location?" Matty asked.

"Call Jim," I shouted to the Airman.

"Tell him to put Jacob and Natalie on hiding our team from the enemy. Tell him that if it's possible, to mask our travel as well so they don't know that we're going to extract them."

"Wait a minute," Tony began, but I cut him off immediately.

"Tony, we're calling in a hail mary here because it's all we got. Do it now, this is the only chance we have to get there in time."

I thought for a second and added another request.

"You said we had the option of Black Hawks...where are they?"

After The Airman relayed my request to Jim, he led us further down the hallway.

"We have five minutes to be out of here if you want to make it to your guys. Take what you want and meet back here as quickly as you can," the Airman instructed as he opened the door to an expansive room containing lockers full of weapons and gear.

When our group was assembled back at the door, fully loaded down with weapons, ammo and tactical gear, the Airman led us above ground to the parking lot on which there were two Black Hawk helicopters awaiting with rotors spinning and flight crews on board.

"Good luck," the Airman yelled to Bulldog amidst the noise of the spinning rotors.

"Get your men and bring them back here. I'm under orders to send you to Austin as soon as your team is back together."

With a nod and slap on the shoulder, Bulldog gave his affirmation and ran to take his seat on the Black Hawk.

"Set up a defensive perimeter," Chris directed the men as they jumped out of the vehicles and began scrambling to stage their defense.

"Too bad we let Meda's fighters go after the casino raid," Jason said to Chris as he exited the passenger door and moved to the rear bench seats of his truck to continue tending to Klint.

"I think that was a little short sighted."

"Yeah, we'll put it in the AAR, no time for regrets now. I don't think we can spare a man to bag Klint anymore Brother," Chris said to Jason with his eyes on the ground.

Looking up and meeting with their eyes, Chris gave the order that Jason already knew was needed.

"I need you on the line. We're going to have to let God determine what happens to Klint."

"Roger that," Jason replied reluctantly as he pulled his rifle from the seat.

"Where do you want me?"

"Do we still have anyone who can fly the raven?" Chris asked.

"Sure, Ray can."

"We don't have enough men here to stage any kind of real defense, and I'm not going to ask everyone to sit with our thumbs up our butts waiting for the enemy to come to us. Tell Ray to get the raven overhead, pinpoint the enemy location and we'll split up into two sniper teams. You and I will take the eastern perimeter of wherever they are, Ray and Chad can take the west."

"What about Meda and Klint?" he asked.

"If we survive this, which is doubtful, it's going to be ugly. I'll tell her what I need her to do, you tell Ray to put the Raven in the air and take up a defensive posture until I give the word."

"Roger that," Jason complied and started moving towards Ray's hasty position.

"I'm not going to sit here and do nothing," Meda replied in anger when Chris gave her his orders.

"It's not nothing," he replied through clenched teeth.

"Klint is completely defenseless. We don't have enough men to both go on the offensive and watch our back. I need you to keep an eye on our six and, well, if the enemy makes it to your position...make sure that Klint doesn't become a prisoner, at all costs."

"What do you mean?" she asked.

"You know exactly what I mean. If he wakes up in one of their interrogation rooms he'll end up dead anyway. Only they'll bring him back to life just to torture him to death. You'll be doing him a favor."

Chris handed her his loaded pistol as he turned to check in with Ray.

"Please," he pleaded before moving out.

"This is the way he would want it."

Meda closed her eyes and nodded. Chris offered a hand on her shoulder in condolence of the task she would have to undertake if the men couldn't hold the enemy at bay.

"Thank you," he said before jogging off to meet with Ray.

Ray found a clearing several hundred meters behind the trucks from which to launch the Raven.

He had the drone flying for less than a minute when it was knocked off course by something massive moving fast through the air below it.

As he struggled to regain control and keep it flying, he couldn't believe what he was seeing through the camera lens on the now-spinning drone.

"Black Hawks? Who the hell is that?"

The small engine stalled as Ray watched their only hope to safely locate the enemy go into a terminal death spiral towards the earth.

He began to feel a vibration under his feet and heard the loud whooshing of rotors above him.

Instinctively he sprinted for the woodline, took a knee when he was out of view and welled up with tears of joy.

He watched the first Black Hawk set down in the clearing.

Griz, Tony, JLo and Corey jumped out and immediately split into two fire teams running into the woodline with their rifles at the low ready.

Unable to understand what was happening but knowing they may have been saved, Ray ran back into the clearing, shouting and waving his arms just in time to catch Griz's eye before he and Tony disappeared into the trees.

"Ray, where is everyone?" Tony asked as the second Black Hawk, this one with an empty crew cabin, set down and hovered a few feet off the ground.

"This way, I'll take you to them."

The men were sprinting in the direction from which Ray had begun when the woods erupted with small-arms fire, tearing down tree limbs and spitting shards of bark in all directions.

He led them back to the trucks, and as Meda smiled and began running to meet them an RPG tore through the trees and erupted in a giant fireball when it struck Jason's truck.

"Klint!" Ray screamed as he sprinted towards the truck, which had become a violent inferno.

Griz reached for his shoulder to stop him, but Ray slipped through his grasp.

They located the gunfire and saw JLo and Corey along with Chris, Chad and Jason firing into the woodline from behind trees and whatever cover they could find.

The two watched as Ray pulled Klint's motionless body from the burning wreckage, and took a knee themselves to begin providing covering fire.

While the others began leapfrogging back under the covering fire towards Griz and Tony, Ray patted out the fires on Klint's body, picked him up in a fireman's carry and ran toward the clearing with Meda at his back.

When the other five men reached Griz and Tony's position they began to see enemy troops walking through the woodline and firing at them.

"Go!" Tony barked to the others as he moved his grip from the rifle trigger to the M203 grenade launcher affixed under his barrel.

He disengaged the safety and pulled the trigger, shooting a round directly into the middle of the oncoming force.

He was already running behind the others when the explosion went off, and as Chris took a knee to continue returning fire, Tony caught him by the shoulder and yanked him up.

"No time for that. The Black Hawks aren't going to wait forever."

Chris rose to his feet and sprinted behind Tony. By the time they reached the clearing Ray had loaded Klint's body on the helo and the team were jumping in.

As he made the final sprint, Chris heard the minigun erupt from the helo overhead and begin decimating everything that was behind him.

The Black Hawk began to lift off as soon as his torso was in the cabin, and once the other men had pulled him inside he turned to see the chaos they had escaped.

Downed trees, blood and enemy bodies lined the edge of the clearing as the minigun continued to spit furious retribution, now joined with small-arms fire from the team, raining down hot-lead death sentences on everything behind them with their rifles.

Tony and Griz each followed suit with more M203 rounds, adding small explosions in the woodline to further cover their exit.

"Never thought I'd see you again," Chris grinned happily to Tony as the Black Hawk shifted from hovering into a full speed escape back to El Toro.

"Jeez, if I knew you were going to say something like that I would have worn my nice outfit," Tony laughed.

"Besides, you still owe me some money from that poker game a few years back, I'm not letting you go without paying me!"

"Well in that case," Chris smiled, "don't expect any repayment until this thing is all over."

"That might be a lot sooner than you think," Tony replied with a slap on the shoulder.

When the helos set down back in the parking lot at El Toro both the Airman and a man who looked vaguely familiar were waiting to greet us.

I searched my memory banks as our team was unloading, and he walked towards me as I stepped out of the helo.

"Who is that?" I asked Bulldog as the man approached.

"Don't even ask. I think he's a spook but it's anybody's guess at this point."

The man walked directly to Bulldog and I, extending his hand for a shake.

"Where do I know you from?" I asked as I reached for his hand.

"Do you remember me?" The Consultant asked.

"Africa?" I asked, questioningly.

"Right you are," he chuckled.

"Nobody else on your team else seems to remember."

"In their defense they have a little on their mind given, well, the war and all."

"Right again. It doesn't hurt my feelings. It's not my job to have feelings."

I let out a small chuckle and wry smile, unsure of whether he had a really twisted sense of humor or no humor whatsoever.

A half hour later we were once again seated in the classroom, this time being briefed by The Consultant.

He painted a rosy picture of what had transpired in the hours since we set off to extract our team. Our allies had successfully infiltrated the northern border and were making significant progress moving south, already fighting into northern California.

The friendly navies on the west coast had greatly outnumbered and overpowered our enemies there, and had landed their infantry and engineers who were in the process of taking back the coast amidst intense skirmishes.

Our friends to the south had made quick work of the cartel militias, but were engaged at that moment in multiple battles along the border.

Our forces located in Texas, however, had concurrently made a forward push to leave the enemy there fighting on both sides, which wouldn't last long.

The battle for New York city was still underway. The British Navy had decimated the enemy guarding her ports, but the urban warfare inside of the city was, as he put it, intense.

"So where do we go next?" Bulldog asked.

"Are you going to send us back in the hyperloop to get to the east coast?"

"Negative," The Consultant answered dryly.

"Your part of this stage is complete. As soon as we finish here I'll be putting you back in the hyperloop to go to Austin, where you'll be getting a little well-deserved time off with your families."

"Wait a minute," I asked.

"The hyperloop goes to Austin? Why didn't I just take that here instead of doing whatever it was that I did?"

"Jacob and Natalie knew that you needed to experience it to believe it, to which Jim and I agreed."

"Hold the phone," Chris interjected.

"I'm not going to complain about getting some time off with our families, but what do you mean our part is done? There's still a war going on and from what you just told us, it ain't over yet."

The Consultant smiled and responded.

"Finally somebody asking the right questions. I said your part in this stage is done, not your part in the war."

"Pardon me if I missed something, but isn't this war just about over?" asked Matty.

"If the NATO troops are about to wipe out the enemy on both coasts, what's left?"

The Consultant lowered a global map from the ceiling to hang in front of the US map the airman had used during our initial briefing.

"Think of this war as having three main stages," he answered, pointing to various red X's drawn over the capitals of each nation which had attacked us.

"Stage one was the invasion. They got that one. Stage two was both the guerilla warfare and counterattack that is currently underway. But stage three," he said as he turned to face the map, cracking the telescopic pointer loudly against each red x drawn on it.

"For stage three it's your turn to take this fight to their front doorsteps."

CHAPTER 12

OPERATION JEDBURGH

The first round of beers were perfect. The third were just right. And the tenth weren't nearly enough.

Staying true to his word, Jim had not only given us a pass to go out and have fun on the town in Austin but had also chosen to join us for, as he put it, "security reasons." I wasn't sure what that had meant, as he was slugging back more drinks than any of us.

But we were glad to have him.

I was at first worried that the booze-fueled evening would lead to questions which Jim couldn't (or wouldn't) answer, which may have led to anger, resentment and division between the team.

But each man had been so focused on being reunited with their families and having all of our men together again that those questions never came.

After introducing Natalie to the men from the east coast team I received more than a few winks from the guys, which helped our bond grow stronger. She gained their immediate approval, which I had felt would be an integral part of our relationship going any further if it were in the stars.

She had already become a part of our tight knit group, and as we drank numerous toasts to each other and those who hadn't made it, she and I stole glances to each other throughout the evening.

My parents and sister had been awaiting our arrival in Austin, Jim's team having delivered them safely while I was on the extraction mission in California.

My dad, a former military man himself, believed that he was a bit too old for what the night would entail, but my sister had tagged along with us as she knew the men from my team and was in need of a little fun.

Natalie was the first to bring it to my attention, and the big brother inside of me first swelled with a protective anger and jealousy, which subsided when I realized that it was right.

She and Tex had been sitting next to one another during dinner and their puppy dog, love struck eyes hadn't left each other since their initial acquaintance.

"I'd say you've already put him through the most stringent big brother tests anyone could offer," Natalie joked.

"Let them enjoy each other."

The evening turned into night, the night into morning and the morning into day but we still didn't want it to end.

Seated around a table in the dining facility at The Temple the next day, I noted through furtive glances behind the men's puffy and dark circled-eyes that none of us were able to fully relax.

Our building was awash with movement as the final battles for our nation were still being fought. Through bits and pieces of overheard conversations around the building we learned that it would not be much longer.

Yet after less than twenty-four hours to unwind since our last mission, the men were starting to feel antsy.

I could see it in their movements, hear it in their voices and sense it in their energy: they wanted to get started with the last piece of the puzzle and begin the final stage of the war.

We knew better than to bother Jim or his aide while operations were still being run, so we took turns standing at the rear of the TOC to keep everyone abreast of the ongoing actions.

The SCIF was far too small for an extra body to mill about, so the drone feeds and overheard conversations between those manning the computer terminals were the only intelligence we had to go on.

Standing against the rear wall of the TOC watching Jim's tall and lanky frame bark out orders, my eyes were locked on the predator drone feeds of enemy troops being beaten back and bombed into oblivion, street by street throughout New York City.

This was a mission of terrible vengeance by a country who had lost their mothers, brothers, fathers and sisters, and there would be no quarter for any enemy who wished to survive.

No white flags would save them, and unless they jumped into the water and attempted a long swim for their homeland there would be no survivors.

I was watching live video feeds from drones, taken from the sky as platoons of infantry troops walked the streets sweeping up any enemy the bombs hadn't obliterated.

The residents of New York had long ago been moved to concentration camps upstate, which had recently been liberated thanks to the Daemon's on the way back to their home turf in New Hampshire.

A visceral scene of enemy waving white flags being ceremonially slaughtered on Lexington Avenue was playing on the screen at the front of the room when I heard a familiar voice next to me.

"Getting anxious yet?" The Consultant asked.

"They don't have any popcorn around here, and this movie is pretty one-sided. Got any action for us?"

The bright light of a massive explosion caught my attention.

I looked to the screen to see pieces of shrapnel shoot across another when the final enemy armored unit met its end via an array of bombs, falling from a B-52 flying too high above their heads for them to even know it was coming.

"Whatcha got for us?"

"You're no longer a member of the military. And that's a good thing for us, given what we're going to ask you to do. But the next stage of this war is going to be so far off the books that we agreed it's best to offer everyone a choice."

"A choice for what?" I asked.

"This operation will be far different from what you men have been doing since the invasion," The Consultant answered, pausing to look over his shoulders and ensure there were no prying ears within hearing distance of our conversation.

"There will be no coming home between missions to refit and see your families. There will be no downtime, no base to sleep safely in, no respite from the reality of what must be done."

He turned, now facing me directly and continued.

"And there will be no admission, at any cost, by our government of either your existence nor our sanction of your actions. If you're caught, there will be no rescue. If you're killed, there will be no parades in your honor or posthumous awards given. No one can know where you are or what you are doing, and you won't be able to call home lest someone be alerted to either you or your families location."

I mirrored The Consultant 's stance, now standing eye to eye with him.

"Sounds like the mission I've always been waiting for," I smiled.

"Let's get on with it."

Cheers erupted in the TOC as the final enemy line was broken and, to all of those soldiers and the rest of our nation, the war ended.

But for a small handful of us, the real war was only just beginning.

An hour later our team was seated in a planning bay downstairs, having received an overview of what would come next.

As with the OSS in World War II we would be split into small teams, each with a respective country of focus. We would be using a black side air base hidden far in the rural English countryside as our headquarters, base of operations and point of embarkation for our missions.

The Consultant informed us that the intelligence apparatus of the various United States agencies and entities had been cultivating relationships with dissident groups in each of our enemy nations long before the invasion started, waiting on the opportunity to stage a coup or uprising if it presented itself.

As with the original Jedburgh teams of the OSS, each team would be dropped from airplanes in to specific areas within their countries. Those intelligence assets would coordinate a linkup with the local groups whom we would begin to train, arm and fight alongside.

Due to NATO accords and our own fractured government this would not be a sanctioned mission.

Because of those same accords, The Consultant told us, they had been trying but were encountering resistance from our SOF allies in providing a member for each of our teams who would have a better understanding of the local environment than we.

Our resupply missions would come from air drops, pre-coordinated with our headquarters and scheduled in advance for remote regions in our areas of operation.

But in reality, he added, most of our supplies would likely have to either drop in with us or come from battlefield recovery.

If we chose to take part, we would be shipped to Britain for a month of intensive training in the regional dialects of our areas of operation, weapons used by those armies and how to run the intelligence operations which would be required.

"What do you mean if we choose?" Bulldog asked.

"You make it sound as if we have a choice in this."

"You do," The Consultant answered.

"Should you choose to partake in this operation, we will destroy all records of your military service and sever all ties. You will not see your families for quite some time, and will be undertaking operations which are much more dangerous than anything you have been asked to do previously. All, of course, except for you Bulldog."

"Excuse me?" he asked, the insult with which this was taken becoming readily apparent in his agitated tone.

"Your posting at Bragg was not meant to be merely a form of torture. It was a test. We won't be able to pull Jim away for this mission, and your men will need someone at the home base whom they can trust explicitly. We don't want you in the field, Bulldog. We want you running the show."

He was preparing to launch into a fiery tirade telling The Consultant exactly where he could shove it when Chris pre-empted his attack.

"He's right, Sir," Chris spoke from his seat.

"As much as I'd love to have you fighting next to me, we're going to need someone guarding our six from everything else going on. If we're really going to do this, it has to be someone with a level head who we trust to tell us what to do. And I can't think of anyone better."

Looking around the room full of heads nodding up and down in affirmation, the fire inside of Bulldog was quickly subdued.

"I don't think I could trust anyone else in that position, sir," Tony added.

"Me neither," said JLo.

A mumbling of accordance came from the entirety of the group. Although Bulldog didn't want to miss out on the fun stuff, he knew that everyone had their place.

His men had chosen him to be their leader, long after the rank on his chest had dictated so, and he was honored to have earned that title.

"So what's next?" Bulldog asked.

"Where do we start?"

"Well as I said earlier, we can't force any of you to do this. I need everyone who's on board to step up soon..."

Before The Consultant finished his sentence, every man seated in the room raised his hand in unison.

"Questions?" The Consultant asked.

"We're in," Bulldog replied.

"I was going to give you the evening to think about it!" he laughed.

"No need," Tony interjected from his seat.

"I think we're all a little anxious to get it on."

More nodding in affirmation from the seated men.

"So when do we start?" I asked.

"I'll have to get back to you on that," The Consultant answered.

"We already have people in England preparing the base, but I didn't expect an answer so quickly...or unanimously."

"Welcome to 022," Matty said.

The Consultant smiled and took a seat on the desk at the front of the room.

"Rob," he added.

"You have some other training to knock out before you head over there. Are you ready to pick up where you left off?"

"As long as this hangover is gone before then. I don't think it would be very conducive to that type of training."

The Consultant laughed.

"Right you are. Ok, you're on a strict orders for no drinking tonight. That's going to be harder than it sounds given the entire country thinks we've just won the war."

"I've got some things I need to attend to anyway," I grinned.

"That drinking wouldn't be a good idea for, either."

After The Consultant dismissed the men and told them he would provide more information later, he asked me to hang back after the rest were gone.

"Now that you've gotten your feet wet, do you think you have what it takes to be a part of the Gateway project?" he asked.

"Definitely," I answered.

"I couldn't believe how natural the remote viewing came to me. It felt as if I'd done it a thousand times before."

"Well there's a good chance you have," he said, nodding to me.

"What does that mean?"

"Perhaps we should have a seat," The Consultant directed.

As I took my place in one of the chairs, he pulled another from behind the desk at the front of the room, spun it around and sat facing me with his arms folded atop the back of the seat.

"The biggest brains of our time have been studying the idea of using math to explain our universe, Rob. The concept of infinity has been debated since before Archimedes, and our current revelations in string theory, quantum mechanics and the theories of a multiverse have been keeping many a physicist busy and excited to prove those ultimate questions: where do we come from and what are we doing here?"

Raising my eyebrows and scrunching my face, The Consultant could tell I wasn't following how this had anything to do with the briefing he had given.

"Believe me, Rob," he laughed.

"When I started my career in military intelligence, the last place in the world I thought I would spend my days was in laboratories listening to nerds inundate me with math and showing me their hypotheses."

He looked me in the eyes and smiled, hiding a self-assuredness and confidence in his next words.

"But then, one day, those hypotheses started being replaced with proofs, and everything that I thought I knew crumbled into the sea."

I took a deep breath contemplating what, in the greater expanse of meaning, that meant for us.

"If what you're telling me and Jim has told me is true, that these parts of the universe exist and humans can tap into things that we never understood before...then why are we even at war? I mean, you just briefed us to go on what is most likely a suicide mission and now you're saying that string theory is real and other universes exist all around us. We have Jacob, Natalie and I'm sure Meda will be able to help...why don't we use them to end this?"

The Consultant let out a deep sigh of his own and shrugged his shoulders.

"Have you heard the pro-second amendment argument that as long as guns exist, we should all have them to protect ourselves and our families?"

"Sure, because if any bad guy has a gun you should have the right and ability to defend yourself."

"Precisely."

"You also hit on the correct point a moment ago: humans. We can teach some people to harness these energies and do amazing things. But greed, lust and war are probably the most human realities in existence. And like guns, as long as those human desires exist, we need to be able to defend ourselves."

"You're not answering my question. If we have three secret weapons on our side, why don't we use them to win the war from right here, right now, so we can all go home and call it a day."

"Because it's not that easy, Rob. And most importantly, because we're not the only ones who have them."

"Yeah, I think Jim mentioned something about that."

"Additionally, the people who can do this aren't superheroes. They can do some amazing things, but at the end of the day they're only human and have limitations."

"Uh, Jacob is back from the dead. That doesn't sound very limited to me."

"Not back from the dead, Rob. Time isn't linear like we've been taught to believe."

"Yeah, Jim did explain that to me. But I still don't get it."

"Do you understand the true meaning of infinity?" he asked.

"I thought I did," I replied.

"But apparently everything that I know is wrong. So why don't you lay it on me for a refresher."

The Consultant smiled, running his fingers through his jet-black hair and continued.

"First, we take all of these lessons you've learned already and add the multiverse phenomenon which provides an infinite number of universes, each with an infinite number of possibilities and choices being performed every instant and leading to separate paths along those paths in their respective realities. Next, remember that Jacob has been doing this program for about forty years, so a Jacob in any part of the multiverse who has a few decades of experience..."

"Wait," I stopped him.

"So this is Jacob, but from a different, what, universe? I thought he was Jacob from a different point in time."

"Parallel universe, reality, whatever you want to call it. If you can wrap that big brain of yours around this...there is another reality somewhere in which different choices have been made along the wheel of time...and in one of those realities, you never met Jacob."

"Why?"

"Because we found him along the wheel, in that reality, before you met him in Colorado and we brought him here."

The Consultant put the pads of his fingers on his temples, made an explosion sound and emulated his head exploding.

"Woah," I stammered.

"Really? Are you messing with me?"

"Not at all, Rob. Truth is stranger than fiction these days."

"So once I join the Gateway project and learn all of this stuff...I won't be able to die?"

"Not exactly...but maybe. Jacob didn't save himself, we had to find him. And we only found him because his power is so significant and energy so in tune with the intelligence of the universe that we could find him across multiple planes of reality. So no. Remember that he, or the Jacob you met, still died. But if you become that powerful we may be able to find another, well, you."

"So if you plucked me from another reality, would my kids know that it wasn't the same me? And what would happen to the kids from that reality when I disappeared?"

"Now we're getting into philosophy and subjects I'm neither smart enough nor willing to delve into. Let's just focus on you not dying so we don't have to test any of that."

"Roger that," I answered, feeling a massive headache beginning to form at my temples.

"Now go upstairs and enjoy your family. You may want to start planning for the eventuality of your leaving. Jim told me your parents are here...speaking of your kids, someone will have to watch them while you're gone. Do you think they're up to it?"

"There's only one way to find out. You mentioned not being able to call home so the enemy doesn't locate them. Now that the invaders are off our shores, this seems like the safest place in the world and the only one where the bad guys can't get to them. Can they all stay here?"

"If they want to, yes. But from what I understand your dad wasn't too happy to come off the boat...I'm not entirely sure he'd want to live in a barracks room until you return, Rob."

"Yeah good point. But it doesn't hurt to ask. If they say yes, can they?"

"Of course. The other guys' families will have the same choice, but I'm assuming everyone will most likely choose to keep them here. It's going to take some time to rebuild the nation, and it may get nasty outside these walls while we're doing so."

I nodded in accordance, remembering the gruesome news footage of looting and destruction in the wake of recent natural disasters. And those disasters hadn't left military-grade weaponry scattered around the country.

"Let's take this one step at a time," The Consultant continued.

"Go have fun with your family. Jacob will see you downstairs first thing in the morning."

"When?" I asked.

"He'll let you know. Probably while you sleep tonight...he's funny like that."

Shortly after parting with The Consultant I found my way upstairs to start the conversation with my parents.

Being a veteran himself and as patriotic as a man could be, I knew that my dad would understand the mission and my desire to take part. But being a father and understanding the great dangers it would entail would definitely cause him some heartache.

And being a grandfather, now being asked to live in a paramilitary headquarters and look after my kids for an undefined amount of time...possibly forever if I didn't make it back. I didn't know about that one.

"Really Bubs?" was his response when I recounted our briefing from The Consultant.

"And everyone else agreed to do this?"

"Yup, every man from my team volunteered. I can't be the only one to wimp out."

"I don't think it would be fairly classified as wimping out, buddy. I think agreeing to go could be considered borderline insanity, but not going would surely not make you any lesser of a man."

"Dad, I know that you love me and have to say that. But you know me; have you ever known me to flinch? Doesn't this sound like something that would haunt me for the rest of my life if I said no?"

He took a deep breath, looked at the floor for a moment, exhaled and met my eyes.

"I don't know where you get this wild hair up your butt from, son. But you're right. And although I don't want you to go, I won't stop you. Of course I'll watch the kids."

"Here?"

"Of course here. I'm getting a little old and they have too much energy for us to handle alone. We could use the extra help. The families of the other guys on your team are staying here too, right?"

"I think so...that question is being raised in a lot of rooms in this hallway tonight."

"When do you leave?'

"I don't know."

"How long will you be gone?"

"I don't know."

"Where will you be going? Russia, China or back to the Middle East??

"I don't know."

"Well come on, what do you know? You have to give me something."

"All I know is that we'll start with a month of training in England. I don't know when we leave, exactly, but I'm sure it will be soon and we won't be given much time to prepare. I don't think they would have told us yet if we weren't leaving soon, but I don't know *how* soon."

"That sounds about right. Have you told the kids?"

"No, and I'm not sure how I'm going to bring that up."

"Well at least they're used to you being all over the place by this point. And they've made good friends here with the other kids. And they're probably more comfortable in this place now than they were at your home in California."

"Why do you say that?"

"Look, you're the type of person who finds a task or a desired outcome, puts his head down and moves toward the end. You don't do much looking around along the way, but those around you watch while you work. Your schedule back home wasn't very conducive to being a family man. And this one isn't either. At some point, you're going to have to learn to settle down if you want your kids to even remember who you are."

"Sounds kind of familiar, doesn't it, dad?"

"Look, I understand that being the son of a pilot wasn't easy either. But I had to be gone so much to provide you guys with everything you needed...kids aren't cheap, buddy."

"Yeah dad. History repeats itself. Being a doctor was my way of ensuring the kids had a great future. And my doing this mission, well, it's my way of ensuring they have any future at all."

"And what if you don't make it back? What if you never come back from this mission to give your kids a future, leaving them in a future without their father?" he barked angrily.

"Then I ask that you please help them to forget me. I don't want them to carry that baggage around for the rest of their lives."

"Negative. I'll agree to everything else. We'll take care of them while you're gone, we'll make sure they're getting educated, fed and staying safe. But you're a damned fool if you think I'll agree to that last one. Not as long as I breathe. Not a chance."

Tears began forming in his eyes and I decided it wise to change the subject.

"Then let's just focus on me coming back here alive."

"I'll pray for you. It's all that I can do but I know it will help. And I know those guys on your team...you boys have some sort of bond I've never seen in anyone else. You may be a tough nut, but those guys are the toughest nuts I've ever met. Stay close to them, and listen to Bulldog. That's an order."

"Roger that, dad," I chuckled.

"Speaking of the kids, I think I'm going to take them for a walk around the neighborhood. They need some fresh air, and I need to figure out a way to bring this up so they're not caught off guard. Want to come with us?"

"No, son. I think that's something you have to do on your own. But we'll be here when you get back. By the way, have you seen Betsy?"

"I'd bet the farm that she and Tex snuck off somewhere together. Those two have been inseparable since dinner last night."

"Huh," he commented and paused for a moment.

"What about him, is he a good guy?'

"Well he's a Texan, so that's a good start. He's been through a lot with us since Colorado, and as much as I wanted to hate him when I saw him looking at my sister...she's in good hands."

My dad looked at me, squinting and working to formulate his own judgement.

But deep down he understood that I was as adept as it got when judging people's character. If I was ok with Tex dating my sister, he would be alright with him dating his daughter.

The walk with my kids lasted longer than expected but that was by my choice.

It had taken a considerable amount of time for me to broach the subject of daddy being gone again, but as my own dad had said they were used to it by that point.

My son had become fully conversational, and while not yet mature enough to philosophize about the subjects I had been discussing with Jim and The Consultant, he understood the gravity of the situation.

That, in part, made it even more difficult for me to grasp.

It would have been easier had they not been old enough to understand time yet, just seeing me leave one day and come back another.

But there was one question that rocked my soul to its very core and scared me to answer. And I truly hoped that I hadn't lied to them.

"But you're going to be safe daddy, right? I mean, you'll be with your friends, and they'll keep you safe?"

"Of course I will and of course they will, buddy," I responded, praying to everything Holy that it were true.

"They will take good care of me. And I'll miss you two and think of you every day while I'm gone."

"Will you be able to visit us?"

"You know," I said smiling.

"It will be our secret, but I think there may be a way for me to do that..."

To be continued in The Pact, Book III...

OTHER BOOKS BY ROBERT PATRICK LEWIS

ABOUT THE AUTHOR

Robert Patrick Lewis is a Special Forces combat veteran of Iraq and Afghanistan-turned author, entrepreneur, MBA, marketing professional and investor.

Robert served as an 18D (Special Forces Medic) and during his time in 10th Special Forces Group (Airborne) he deployed to Afghanistan, Iraq twice and North Africa as well as multiple other training missions around the globe, with a final deployment to Afghanistan as a military contractor.

He left the Army with a Purple Heart for wounds received in Afghanistan, the Special Forces tab, the Combat Infantry Badge, Bronze Star, Army Commendation Medal, NATO non-article 5, Iraq campaign ribbon with cluster, Afghanistan campaign ribbon and many other awards for his service.

After his time in uniform was over Robert set out to write about his experiences. He has three published books including his non-fiction military memoir *Love Me When I'm Gone: the true story of life, love and loss for a Green Beret in Post-9/11 war* and the first two books of his fictional trilogy, *The Pact* and *The Pact Book II: Battle Hymn of the Republic*.

He has been featured on national programs such as Fox News, The Dennis Miller Show, The Adam Carolla Show, The Herman Cain Show and writes frequent articles for Heroes Media Group.

Robert has two children, two stepchildren and is engaged to the love of his life (and editor) Natalie Pimentel. He writes from his homes in Los Angeles and Dallas.

Made in the USA
Monee, IL
15 December 2020

53553097R00177